MURDER UNDER A TWILIGHT ROOF

TAM MAY

Murder Under a Twilight Roof

Adele Gossling Mysteries: Book 5

Tam May

Published by Dreambook Press.

Click or visit:
https://www.tammayauthor.com

Cover Design © 2023 by Aries/100 Covers

ISBN: 9781734671438 (Print)
ISBN:9781734671421 (ebook)

❀ Created with Vellum

To Aila and Becky for their encouragement and support.

CHAPTER 1

If you're interested in reading more early 20th century mysteries, my free offer at the end of this book is for you! So don't forget to check that out when you get to the end. Happy reading!

*T*he summer of 1905 in the small town of Arrojo opened like any other. Men fanned themselves with their handkerchiefs and women opened their parasols to shield themselves against the harsh sun. Shops kept their doors and windows open to let in what little air there was or shut them so the red dust kicked up by the summer wind wouldn't discourage the tourists from entering. From San Francisco, Sacramento, and even as far as Los Angeles, sightseers strolled through the town's main commercial district to get a glimpse of the small-town life that was slowly beginning to die out.

Early in June, the afternoon train brought an odd sight to the eyes of Arrojo citizens. Five burly men descended the steps of the passenger car, making it bob from side to side. While even Sheriff Hatfield had given in to the latest trend of reducing his mustache to touch the edges of his lips, these men sported long handlebar mustaches curled at the edges with pomade that most people saw only in the films showing at the newly constructed Arrojo Theater.

The men carried posters under their arms as they trudged out of the train depot. They did not speak to one another, though it was clear they all came from the same place. They proceeded to Bridge Street, the business district of town. They gathered near Ada's Millinery in a huddle and later, Ada reported hearing growling and whispers. Then, they dispersed along the street.

By this time, the men had caught the attention of Adele Gossling and her friend Nin Branch. Both women stood in their doorways like the rest of the shopkeepers. The men produced hammers from inside their pockets along with a boxes of nails. Pounding and shaking filled the silent street.

"They're putting them up." Nin stared.

"They'll have a time trying to keep them from being torn down," Adele observed.

Indeed, not far away, Mr. Raleigh was arguing with one of the men whose green checkered suit stood out against the red dust road. The man had gotten one nail into the poster on the board outside Raleigh's General Store before its owner came storming out. Adele was impressed by the man's patience, his voice calm in the face of the irate general store manager. Mr. Raleigh, however, had a reputation for hard-headedness, owing to the constant flow of boys who snuck into his store to steal penny candy, and he wasn't above a little bullying when the occasion called for it.

"I don't think he'll get very far with Raleigh," she observed.

"He will with you," Nin said. Adele knew from the set tone in her voice this was not a guess but one of Nin's predictions.

They watched as the man tipped his hat to Mr. Raleigh and used the back of the hammer to edge out the nail from the poster. Satisfied, Raleigh stalked back into his store. The man stopped in front of Adele's shop.

"Afternoon, ma'am." He tipped his hat.

"Miss," Adele corrected.

"Begging your pardon." His voice was almost as mild as the Arrojo sheriff's. "My name's Ben Clayton. You're the owner of this place?"

"Can't you read?" Nin snarled as she pointed at the swinging sign labeled *Adele's Stationery*.

"My apologies, miss."

"What's your business here, Mr. Clayton?" Adele asked.

"You're welcome to see for yourself, miss." He held up the poster.

Adele studied it with Nin looking over her shoulder. The glaring red letters THE BARRY CIRCUS IS COMING TO YOUR TOWN! sat on a scroll of bright yellow, hurting her eyes. In the corner were illustrations of two women with a man in the middle in a circle frame. The poster boasted of Julius Rowe, "Commander of the Flying Trapeze" and promised "an amazement of daredevil feats, including the triple somersault!" The rest of the poster was illustrated with the man in the picture doing what was presumably the triple somersault, curled up in the air with three circles below him to show the action one would see with one of the women in the picture hanging from another trapeze, ready to catch him and the third standing on the rafters looking on.

"Very impressive," she said.

"Oh, it is, miss, you wait and see." The man grinned. "I'll give you two tickets to the circus if you allow me to put up the poster." He tapped the clapboard that separated her shop and Nin's.

"Why didn't you make Mr. Raleigh the same offer?" Adele asked.

"He never refuses anything for free," Nin added.

Mr. Clayton laughed. "Well, to tell the truth, miss, I didn't like his face. Besides, general stores rarely object to our posters. It brings them good business." He cocked his head. "It will bring *you* good business."

Adele turned to Nin. "Shall we let the gentleman put up his poster?"

Nin shrugged. "If it rattles Raleigh, it's worth the gawking eyes."

Adele laughed. "You're welcome to the space, Mr. Clayton."

"Much obliged." He tipped his hat to both of them.

No sooner had he crossed the street to Dora's Tea Shop, people gathered around and peered at the poster, making remarks. Renee Leighton, one of the prominent citizens in town, turned to Adele. "Did you have a hand in this, Miss Gossling?"

"I beg your pardon?"

"Did you invite them to town?" The woman regarded her with suspicion.

"Why would you think that?" Adele asked.

"It's obvious, isn't it?" The woman sniffed. "You court the police, so it would be no surprise to *us* if you also courted the circus." In the last year, Mrs. Leighton's position with the gossiping brood led by Mrs. Faderman had grown so she referred to them as *us* in her conversation.

"I assure you, Mrs. Leighton, the Barry Circus is as new to me as it is to you," Adele said.

"I'm happy to hear it." The woman hitched up her belt. "I would hate to think you had anything to do with this."

"I don't see anything terrible in the circus," Adele protested. "Perhaps what Arrojo needs is a good dose of harmless entertainment."

"Harmless!" The woman snorted. "You clearly have no experience with such people, and perhaps that's to your advantage."

"You mean the criminals I've consorted with haven't entirely corrupted me?" Adele eyed her. "I'm sure my brother and the sheriff will be glad to hear it."

The woman pulled her veil over her face and clomped down the street.

"If she tells Mrs. Faderman, there'll be a stink," Nin remarked.

"I don't think the Barry Circus is going to let a few clucking hens interfere with their performance," Adele answered.

~~~~~

Adele was dying of curiosity when, the next morning, her brother, Jackson, showed up at the breakfast table with a grim look on his face. He opened the city paper as soon as Tomas brought his oatmeal even though he usually waited until the toast and coffee. She sensed he was in no mood to talk, so she remained quiet for a time. Tomas, who always stood in attendance of their every want during meals, fidgeted and mumbled in Spanish.

When Jackson put the paper down, Adele ventured, "What did Hatfield have to say about the posters?"

"The audacity!" Jackson burst out. "Hammering away without requesting permission from the sheriff's office."

Adele poured the coffee. "They asked permission from the shops, Jack."

"How do you know?" He eyed her.

She held up the two tickets Mr. Clayton had given her.

"Del, you didn't."

"They have a business to run just like anyone else."

"Their business is sensationalism and chaos." He sniffed. "I saw what happened when the circus parade came into town in the east."

"Don't tell me the Anspaches worked for the circus too."

"We were hired to make sure they didn't cause a ruckus," he said.

"And did they?" Adele asked.

"More times than not." He folded the paper. "At least we've enough men at the station to handle them now."

"Three murders have made the position of police officer very popular in Arrojo," Adele agreed. "Every young man wants adventure."

He gave her a wary look. "Hatfield told me he even saw an application from Percy Faderman."

"Heaven forbid!" Adele rolled her eyes, thinking of the homely young man who followed his domineering mother around town like a puppy.

"I suppose you've heard there's to be a town meeting tonight to discuss this circus coming to town?"

Adele thought of the scene with Mrs. Leighton. "I hope you'll have some of the circus people there to defend themselves."

Jackson nodded. "The owner, Paul Barry, and his wife will be there. The mayor was opposed of course, but Hatfield convinced him it was only right."

"The mayor was opposed because Mrs. Faderman was opposed," Adele said simply.

"It's time Mrs. Faderman learned hers isn't the only voice that matters," Jackson said with severity. "The entire town will be there. You're coming, of course."

"Nin and I wouldn't miss it," Adele said.

After the shops had closed that evening, Arrojo citizens crowded the front entrance to the city hall, ready to burst through its doors.

"It looks as if the entire town has turned out," Adele observed.

"They're all here to defend our precious town from the corruption of clowns and bears," Nin snarled.

Missy Grace, the editor of the *Arrojo Courier*, waved and made her way to their side. "I haven't seen a mob like this since the Marsh case."

"The circus coming to town isn't a crime," Adele reminded her.

"Mrs. Faderman will make it one." Nin glanced at the women leaning against the doorframe as if intending to force it open.

A sea of people parted as Mayor Willett made his way through, laughing and pumping a few arms as he did so.

"One would think this was a political rally," Adele snapped.

"He's certainly full of hot air tonight," Nin agreed.

She caught a glimpse of her brother as they settled on the hard benches in the town hall. He and Sheriff Hatfield were seated at a table near the stage where the mayor, Mrs. Faderman, Mr. Raleigh, and a few other board members had taken their places. With them sat a couple in somewhat shabby attire and matching blond heads. On a bench pushed up against the wall were the five burly men, including Mr. Clayton, their hands clenched as if ready to fight at a moment's notice.

Mayor Willett knocked on the table to quiet the room. "Good evening, everyone. We're here to discuss —"

"Get on with it, Hugh," Mrs. Faderman snapped.

"Please, ma'am." He held up his hand. "We're here to discuss a certain group that wishes to enter our town."

"Why doesn't he just say the circus?" Nin whispered.

"Because he has to make a ceremony out of everything," Missy supplied.

"Mr. and Mrs. Barry —" the mayor indicated the couple at the table, "— have applied for a permit to set up their circus tents in the park and, er, several concerns have been brought to my attention that I feel —"

"That *we* feel," Mrs. Faderman interrupted. "We all have concerns, Mayor Willett."

"Quite right, Mrs. Faderman," said the man. "We wish to hear opinions on the matter."

"Disgraceful!" Mrs. Abberton, sitting in the front row with the rest of the hens, burst out. "For these people to come and soil our town with —"

"Oh, fiddle-faddle!" The voice came from the back of the room, deep and majestic. Lady Augusta Hatfield had arrived, wheeled in her movable chair by her companion Rowena, who looked equally stern. Missy vacated her seat in the aisle to them.

"We are indeed honored, Lady Augusta." The mayor gave her a deep bow. Adele imagined the sheriff had tried to persuade his mother to stay home, but she had insisted on venturing out of her sheltered existence to take part in the proceedings.

"I still say it's disgraceful." Mrs. Abberton curled her lip and sat down.

"I couldn't agree more, Hester." Mrs. Faderman rose, her height usurping the mayor's by a few inches, causing him to smear the handkerchief over his face. "I'm surprised you didn't tear down those posters, Sheriff. They're most inappropriate."

"They were putting those posters up on private property, ma'am" Hatfield said.

"Don't blame Horatio," Lady Augusta insisted. "If people on Bridge Street didn't want them, they could have torn them down themselves."

"I don't understand some of you!" Mrs. Cricket burst out. "Don't you realize these people are — well — depraved?" She glared at the Barrys.

Mr. Barry was on his feet, his face red with indignation. "We run a very respectable circus, ma'am."

"Perhaps you'd like to elaborate on that, sir." Mayor Willett pursed his lips.

"We don't allow our performers to misbehave in any way," the man said, "nor do we allow them off circus grounds unless for a very special reason. The moment we hitch our wagons, we put up our own gate which is always locked and watched."

"The ladies don't associate with any of the men about town either," his wife put in.

"Nor do we make any profit outside of ticket sales," Mr. Barry continued.

Mr. Moffett, owner of the jewelry store in town, rose. "What you mean by that, sir?"

"He means," Mrs. Faderman spoke, "thieves!"

"Thieves?" The man was more alert.

"Pickpockets and extortionists," the woman continued. "They work with circuses, you know."

"Not with ours!" Mrs. Barry said in a shrill tone. "Not with any respectable circus, ma'am."

Adele could no longer hold her tongue. "How do you know this, Mrs. Faderman?"

"One gets to know things, Miss Gossling," Mrs. Faderman said. "I fancy, with your criminal experiences, you've heard of such things."

Adele tried not to wince. "If the Barrys say there are no pickpockets and extortionists working with them, I believe it."

"Your trusting nature is a credit to you," Mrs. Faderman said.

Mr. Barry cleared his throat. "Mayor, we've performed all over the West in towns big and small. We come with no other purpose than to give people a little leisure and entertainment."

"You don't deny circuses are breeding grounds for vice and sin?" Mrs. Faderman eyed him.

"They were in the past, ma'am," Mr. Barry said evenly. "Things have changed. The Ringling Brothers follow the same protocols we do and neither Mr. Barnum nor Mr. Bailey tolerate any — well, monkey business, for lack of a better term." There was a chuckle from the crowd.

"But their circuses are on a grand scale, Mr. Barry," Mrs. Faderman pointed out. "They have a reputation to maintain."

"So do we," Mrs. Barry insisted.

"Oh, yes, my how I remember that Mr. Rice was so amusing," Mrs. Lynn lamented.

"We're not talking about clowns, Caroline," Mrs. Faderman insisted. "We're talking about reputation. The Ringling Brothers and Barnum and Bailey are known all over the world. No one has ever heard of the Barry Circus, and, therefore, it can do what it likes."

"A circus need not be grand to make people happy," Mr. Barry said with dignity.

"Hear, hear." Lady Augusta applauded. "I saw many small shows when I was a young lady in London. Even the Queen herself had her favorite lion tamer." She gave Mrs. Faderman a meaningful look.

"And what does your son say, Lady Augusta?" The woman turned to the sheriff.

"Horatio! Tell them your views on the matter," his mother bellowed.

"I was just going to, Ma," he said as he rose. "I met many show people when I was on the Wells Fargo circuit, and I don't recall any of them were particularly shady or immoral. They're people just like the rest of us, ma'am."

"Well said, sir!" This came from Mr. Dunham. "And may I add to Lady Augusta's observation that I, too, spent some time in London and have only met with delight and laughter when the circus came to town."

"We're not in London, Mr. Durham," Mrs. Faderman said stiffly. "We're in America and here, we hold ourselves to a high moral standard."

"I'm sure King Edward would hardly be flattered to hear you think his country is debauched," Nin remarked, earning a cackle from Lady Augusta.

Mayor Willett sighed. "Ladies and gentlemen, we're getting nowhere."

Mr. Barry folded his hands on the table. "Had we known there would be such a hullabaloo over our coming to town, we wouldn't have wasted our time and resources putting up posters."

"You shouldn't have in the first place," Jackson said. "If you would have come to us instead of having your men bulldoze their way into town, we would have told you what to expect."

"We have our way of doing things, Deputy," the man snapped. "Every moment counts for us. You must appreciate we're only in any given town for one day."

"No one forces you to remain only one day in any town, sir," Jackson retorted.

"No, sir, no one does," the man said. "We've many towns who

appreciate the joy and gaiety we bring." He stood up, motioning to his wife. "And they don't subject us to the kind of offensive remarks we've heard in this room."

Adele jumped up. "Please, Mr. Barry! Wait!"

The man put his hands flat on the table. His wife remained in her seat.

"Most of us came here because we felt it was our civic duty. Isn't that right?" There was a murmur of affirmation. "Well, isn't it our civic duty to embrace the leisurely activities of the twentieth century as well?"

"It's also our civic duty to make sure we're not mixing with riff-raff," Mrs. Faderman said.

"Our people aren't riff-raff, ma'am!" Mr. Barry snarled.

"I was speaking in generalities, Mr. Barry," said the woman.

"You were speaking of people like the Cordobas who work for us and Mr. Dunham and Zephyr Brown and people who live down Quarry Lane way," Adele countered.

"Well, yes, as a matter of fact I was," the woman admitted.

"I'm sorry you don't feel they're your social equals, Mrs. Faderman," Adele said,

"I never said —"

"But soon there will be no difference between you and them," she finished.

"We're all aware of your progressive ideas, Miss Gossling," Mrs. Leighton said. "You needn't remind us of them."

"This has nothing to do with progressive politics, ma'am," Adele said. "My point is simply that the circus is for everybody."

"Exactly!" Mrs. Barry piped up. "The circus is for everybody."

Those who had come with poker faces now softened, and some of the younger generation of Arrojo citizens whispered excitedly among themselves, as if anticipating the marvels the Barry Circus posters hinted at. The mayor and other council members sitting on the stage were also whispering among themselves.

Mayor Willett rose. "Mr. Barry, are you willing to allow Sheriff Hatfield and Deputy Sheriff Gossling to inspect your circus and question your people to determine whether your circus is indeed for everyone in this town?"

Adele could see the man's thundering expression, his coarse features gathering, but his wife leaned over and whispered to him. The thunder eased a little and he said in a stiff tone, "If you wish."

"I think in view of Mr. Barry's acceptance, we shall vote to withhold permits until the sheriff and his men have had a chance to complete their interviews. If their findings are satisfactory, then we shall issue a permit. Is that satisfactory to you, Sheriff?" He glanced at Hatfield, who nodded. "All in favor?"

The ayes settled the matter and the meeting broke up. Nin shooed Rowena away from Lady Augusta's chair as she took the handles, and they all waited as the crowd began to filter out. Sheriff Hatfield and Jackson came along with the Barrys.

Mr. Barry approached Adele with a grin. "May I shake your hand, Miss Gossling?"

"Yes, thank you," his wife murmured.

"I'm sorry the permit is delayed, Mr. Barry," the sheriff said.

"I'm glad you don't agree with this balderdash, Sheriff," said the man.

"Agree or not, we shall do our duty, sir." Jackson glared at him.

Ignoring this, Mr. Barry asked, "Why don't you come by tomorrow morning? We'll be at the fairgrounds in Caton."

"We'll do that, sir." Hatfield bowed.

"The hens certainly put up a fight, didn't they?" Adele remarked when the Barrys had left.

"So did you," Jackson said. "I've warned you about spewing forth your progressive ideas, Del."

"Perhaps I got carried away," Adele admitted. "But I trust you and the sheriff will justify my defense."

"You shall be with us to see that I do," Hatfield said cheerfully.

"I will if Jack doesn't complain I'm sticking my nose in police business," she said.

"This isn't a crime," he said simply.

"May I come too?" Nin asked in a timid voice. "I've never been to the circus and I'm curious."

"Then you must satisfy your curiosity. Horatio!" His mother smacked him on the side of his shoe with her cane. "Tell Miss Branch she may go."

"You may go, Miss Branch," he said politely.

*a*dele woke up the next morning feeling as excited as a child. The heat pushed through the window she left open all night, leaving a large rectangular light on the bedsheet. The hills behind the house looked like calm camels resting in the sun, and the sky was just beginning to pitch its blue blanket over the rooftops.

"We might have a circus coming to Arrojo, Ruth," Adele remarked as she helped the woman arrange the plates for breakfast.

"*Sí, senorita.*" The woman nodded.

"Have you and Tomas ever been to the circus?"

"In Mexico, senorita, but not in America."

Adele put her hand on the woman's shoulder. "If it does come, you can take all your children."

"Too much to do —"

"Don't worry about that," Adele insisted.

"Very kind, senorita." The woman smiled. "But Maria, she won't go." The woman gave her a knowing look. "She get married next year."

"Congratulations!" Adele gave her a quick embrace.

"Tomas is happy, but I say she too young," the woman growled.

"She's nearly eighteen," Adele reminded her.

"She wanted to be a nurse. She won't go to school now."

"She can still go." Adele took her seat at the table. "If Maria is in love and wants to marry this young man and he's a good young man —"

"Oh, he is. Tomas say he has his own ranch."

"Then I'm sure Maria will be very happy." Adele smiled. "If she still wants to be a nurse after she's married, she'll find a way."

"Yes, senorita." As Ruth retreated to the kitchen, Adele heard her mumble, "But she be happier if she were a nurse now!"

Jackson, who had been standing in the doorway for some time, burst out laughing. "You've won Ruth over with your progressive views of women, Del."

"Progress means freedom, dear brother," Adele insisted as she poured the coffee. "Freedom for everyone to choose what they like, even if it's a rancher's wife instead of a nurse."

"I'm sure your friend Elsie would have something to say about that," he remarked as Tomas rushed in with his morning oatmeal.

"Elsie and I disagree on a lot of things," Adele said. "Just because I don't choose marriage right now doesn't mean I'm against it."

"I'm pleased to hear it." He opened his paper. "Too bad Bellows doesn't know it."

"John is a good sort, but as straight-laced as they come," she said.

"And as tolerant as they come," he reminded her. "Of your ideas, anyway."

"What John says and what he really thinks are two different things." She stabbed at a tomato slice. "That's how lawyers are."

"Indeed," said her brother, "*all* lawyers."

She glared at him. She knew he was referring to their father.

Otis Gossling had been one of San Francisco's premier criminal lawyers.

"Papa always said what he meant," she snapped.

"But did he mean what he said?" Jackson asked. "That's the question."

"It might be your question but it isn't mine!"

A small whimper came from Tomas standing against the wall, as the man immediately began to fret when he heard their voices rise.

Adele gave him an encouraging smile. "I told Ruth you're all going to the circus when it comes to town, Tomas."

"We don't know if the circus will come, Del," Jackson said.

"Of course it will," she said. "You and Hatfield will find nothing amiss and that will be that."

"If these people aren't who they say they are —"

"Mrs. Faderman and her brood will go after them with pitchforks," Adele finished. Her brother chuckled.

Hatfield came in the new police car, steering with trepidation. The automobile made a distinctive rumble as he pulled up in front of the Gossling house and Mr. Blight, who lived across the street, glared at it as he brought the milk bottle into his house.

"Bothersome thing!" Adele heard the sheriff growl as they came out.

"Maybe you should let me drive, Sheriff," she suggested.

"I must learn sometime, Adele," he insisted. "As you once said, these horseless carriages aren't going away."

"Do you think it's wise to take the police car, sir?" Jackson asked. "That might put them on the defense."

"The mayor insisted on it," he said. "He thinks the more official we look, the better."

"At least you don't have Edison driving," Adele remarked, which made Sheriff Hatfield roar with laughter.

They picked up Nin at her flat above her shop and she seemed as cagey in the automobile as the sheriff. But she soon relaxed as they sped along the dirt road with the summer breeze blowing her unpinned hair, the strands dancing like Medusa's snakes.

Jackson eyed her. "You might have dressed properly for the occasion, Miss Branch."

"I didn't think a hat was necessary for the circus, Mr. Gossling," she snapped. "People take me as I am or they don't take me at all."

"We are on official business," Hatfield ventured.

"You're official," Nin said. "Adele and I are coming along for support. Heaven knows you need it."

Jackson glared at her but the sheriff roared. "Perhaps we do at that."

"I doubt anyone will care," Adele said. "The circus is, well, a world of its own."

Adele knew she was right as they entered the fairgrounds in Caton, where wagons parked haphazardly some distance away from a massive canvas tent. All sorts of people milled around, some of them workmen, some in costume, and some leading animals with ropes around their necks. Nin grabbed her arm when a woman passed with three elephants, one following the other like obedient children. The last lifted its trunk with a roar, and the woman grinned, calling, "Clifford likes the ladies!" Adele laughed and even Nin smiled.

Jackson asked a clown where the owner's wagon was located. The man pointed toward the back corner of the tent, then proceeded to tell Jackson a funny story about a friend of his who almost got arrested one night for being drunk and disorderly, but he only succeeded in making Jackson frown. The man shrugged and retreated inside the tent.

They found the wagon with "Barry Circus, Paul Barry, Owner" painted in lavish gold and green. Mr. Barry was already waiting at the door. There was a red sheen to his face, and his hands moved quickly as he motioned for them to come inside. Mrs. Barry sat at the edge of a chair, her hands resting on her tightly pressed knees. A young man with the same hook nose and pearl eyes as Mr. Barry stood against the wall with his hands in his pockets.

"I didn't expect to see the ladies," Mr. Barry eyed Adele and Nin.

"Isn't it rather peculiar having women accompany the police?" the young man asked. "Miss Gossling is Deputy Sheriff Gossling's sister, Cal," Mr. Barry added. "My son, Calvin." The young man nodded. "I'm afraid I don't know your name, miss." He glanced at Nin.

"Branch," she supplied.

The man's eyes widened. "Estelle and I heard something about you yesterday."

"Paul." His wife's voice was barely audible.

"You're a mesmerizer, aren't you?"

Adele saw her friend's lips grow thin, as she hated the term and associated it with charlatans. Before Adele could jump in, Sheriff Hatfield said, "Miss Branch helps the police on occasion, and we value her gift highly."

Mr. Barry's face reddened. "I'm sure you misunderstood my meaning."

"I'm sure I didn't," Nin growled.

"Paul can be thoughtless sometimes," Mrs. Barry murmured. Her husband glared at her so harshly that she bit her lip.

"The circus, Miss Branch, values mesmerizers as highly as the police," Mr. Barry growled. "I was, in fact, going to offer you a job with us."

"I'm here to satisfy a curiosity," Nin said. "I've never been to the circus."

The man brightened. "Well, then, you're in for a treat tomorrow night. You all get free tickets, of course."

"We can't be bribed with free tickets, sir," Jackson said in a cutting tone, "though I'm well aware many lawmen have been."

"I'm sure Mr. Barry meant nothing of the kind, Deputy," said the sheriff in a biting voice.

This gave Mr. Barry a chance to regain his authority. "Sheriff, we're at your disposal."

"I'd like to see your Caton permit first," said Hatfield. "Mayor Nelson issued it, I imagine?"

"Indeed, sir," said the man.

"A very capable man," Hatfield mumbled. "And a very moral one too."

"That should prove we're all right, then, shouldn't it?" Mr. Barry eyed him.

"I make my own judgments, sir," Hatfield looked over the paper the man gave him. "You realize we have the authority to check with any police in any town for legal violations from your troupe during their stay?"

Mr. Barry leaned back in the chair. "You won't find anything, Sheriff."

"You're terribly confident," Jackson said.

"If any of my workers or performers had broken the law, I would have known about it," the man said in a curt tone. "They know better than to try and hide anything from me."

Adele noticed the expression on his wife's face. Mrs. Barry's Dresden doll eyes grew almost wily.

"You seem very certain of that," Adele murmured.

Mr. Barry leaned forward. "We're not Barnum and we're not Ringling. We're thirty-five people here, not thousands or even hundreds. We're like a family." He sat back. "I can assure you, Sheriff, we've had no accidents and no run-ins with law enforcement."

Just then, a man burst into the wagon and Mrs. Barry jumped. Adele recognized him as the trapeze artist from the poster Mr. Clayton had hung near her shop. She noted the man's mustache was smaller in real life, but he had the same slick black hair and roguish appearance.

"Calvin, this is too much!" The man's voice was a little high-pitched.

"Julius, we're in conference." Mr. Barry glared at him. "And you might think about knocking next time so you don't startle Estelle."

"I wasn't startled," she protested.

Ignoring them, the man continued, "The little puss almost ripped my arm off during the double twist!"

"Julius Rowe, our star performer," Mr. Barry mumbled.

"The Commander of the Flying Trapeze," Adele said.

The man looked at her and his face settled into a smile. His gaze moved to Nin and his smile spread so wide that his eyes narrowed with cunning. "Julius Rowe, at your service." He took Adele's hand and gave it a smacking kiss.

"You've just been introduced," Nin said in her blunt way, hiding her hands behind her back.

"I prefer to introduce myself, Miss — Miss —"

"Branch," Adele supplied as her friend remained silent.

"Miss Gossling defended us at the town hall meeting in Arrojo yesterday," Mr. Barry supplied. "And Miss Branch is a clairvoyant."

The man was clearly taken by Nin's exotic beauty as he leaned toward her. "You must tell me my fortune sometime. Privately in my wagon, of course."

"That is impertinent, sir!" Jackson barked.

Mr. Rowe regarded Nin with a slippery smile. "You won't find me, er, ungrateful."

"I don't tell fortunes," Nin said. "I have auras."

"Indeed?" He took a step closer. "And what aura have you of me?"

"Sickening," she declared.

Hatfield chuckled, and both Mr. Barry and his son smiled. Mrs. Barry looked down.

"You'll feel differently when you see my act tomorrow night," said the man. "We will be in Arrojo, won't we, Paul?" He eyed the manager.

"If the sheriff and his deputy decide we're decent enough," Mr. Barry said. "You bursting in here in that rude manner hasn't exactly given them a good impression of us."

"I apologize if I was rude, Sheriff." Mr. Rowe bowed. "But when one has come near death, one is apt to get a little agitated."

"Aren't you being a little dramatic, Julius?" the younger Mr. Barry eyed him. "Unless you tried the twist without a net."

"Not with Helen catching me!" The trapeze artist looked at him with even eyes. "We must do something about that, Calvin."

The young man didn't answer, only fiddled with the chain on his watch.

"Someone has got to speak to Helen," the man went on.

"Now is hardly the time, Julius," Mr. Barry coughed.

"Isn't it always the time when life or death is at stake?" The man asked in a savage tone. "The sheriff here would think so, I'll wage you."

"We take life and death very seriously," Jackson agreed.

"All right." Mr. Barry rose. "I'll speak to her if it will calm you down."

"I asked Cal, not you!" The man glared at him.

"I'll speak to her if you like, Julius." Mrs. Barry stood up, brushing her hands against her skirt. Adele could see they were red and moist.

"You'll do no such thing," her husband growled.

"Helen likes me," she protested. "If it will help Julius —"

"Well, Cal?" His father looked at him expectedly. Adele almost felt there was a touch of mockery in his voice.

"Let Abby speak to her," Calvin said. "She's her sister, after all."

"Abby!" snorted Mr. Rowe. "You know how blind she is when it comes to Helen. The hen fawning over her chick."

"Then I'll speak to her!" Mr. Barry snatched his hat hanging from the stand. "It's *my* circus, after all."

Hatfield, with his usual tact, said, "I'm sure we've taken up enough of your time, Mr. Barry. My deputy and I would like to look around, if you don't mind."

"What for?" Mr. Rowe eyed him.

"Is that any of your business?" Mr. Barry scowled. "Of course you're welcome to, Sheriff. Let us know if there's anything in particular you'd like to see."

"I have the books prepared —" the younger Mr. Barry began.

"That won't be necessary, sir," said Hatfield.

This eased the young man's expression, and he shook his hand. "I'm sorry if I sounded suspicious, Sheriff. We haven't always been welcome in these smaller towns."

"I wonder why they were so sure you would want to see their accounts," Adele said as they parted ways with the Barrys and Mr. Rowe, all heading toward the big top.

"If we looked at their books, we would know their earnings," Jackson supplied. "Lawmen use that as a way of determining how much the circus can pay them to allow their wagons into town."

"You mean they use it as a bribe?" Nin asked.

"It happens all too often, Miss Branch," Hatfield said.

Adele smiled. "We all know you're an honest man, Sheriff."

Flags appeared on Hatfield's cheeks, unusually smooth and pale in spite of his years as a sea captain.

They went through the circus, peering into open tents and wagons but it was clear to Adele that Hatfield had already made up his mind.

"What do you think of the circus, Nin?" she asked her friend as they rode home.

"I'd think more highly of it if Mr. Rowe hadn't made eyes at me," Nin said. "If he can fly as well as he speaks nonsense, it ought to be quite a show."

Adele laughed. "We'll know tomorrow, won't we?"

"I'm curious to see if Mr. Rowe lives up to his reputation," Jackson said.

"More to the point," the sheriff steered clear of a branch in the road, "will he live up to his own excellent opinion of himself?"

"He certainly was pompous," Nin remarked. "Mr. Barry didn't like it one bit"

"The star performer who thinks he can dictate to the circus owner." Jackson nodded.

"Mrs. Barry, on the other hand, was a different story." Adele drew her coat around her, as the wind coming through the open windows had become chilly.

"She was trying to avoid him without avoiding him," Nin agreed.

Sheriff Hatfield parked the police car on a side road adjacent to the police station. "I agree there was something not quite even about the Barrys. At any rate, it will be interesting to see the performances tomorrow night." He slid a stack of free tickets from his pocket and began handing them out.

CHAPTER 3

*T*he next day was no ordinary day for Arrojo citizens. All shops were closed and later that morning the pavement on Bridge Street became crowded with people in their Sunday best, peering anxiously down the street. Ladies raised their parasols against the hot sun and men pulled their hats forward to shade their eyes. Children darted back and forth, free of their school uniforms for the day, jumpy with anticipation.

"Must they make a show of coming into town?" Nin grumbled.

"It's the circus, my dear," Lady Augusta said with a laugh. "They must play the spectacle from beginning to end."

"Rather hackneyed if you ask me," Rowena remarked.

"Well, nobody asked you, dear," Lady Augusta said promptly. "You'll soon see it's better than those dizzying moving pictures." Her companion ducked her head, as it was common knowledge that she spent most of her days off at the Arrojo Theater since it opened.

An elegant carriage with two plume-feathered horses turned the corner. Roars and applause rose from the crowd as other wagons appeared, equally ornate with scrolls and flags. As the carriage neared them, Adele saw it contained Mr. and Mrs. Barry, sitting a little apart from one another. Mr. Barry caught her eye and gave her a mock salute as they passed.

"Where's the sheriff and your brother?" Nin asked.

"Jack said they're mingling with the crowd," Adele said.

"Horatio was afraid the procession will attract pickpockets," Lady Augusta added.

"If they can't be in cahoots with the circus, they'll work alongside it," Adele agreed. "Very sensible of him to be on the lookout."

A loud roar came from one of the cage wagons and Adele caught a glimpse of an elephant behind the bars with the woman they had seen in Caton standing beside it, her arm raised. Four men dressed as sheiks followed on camels. A group of children rushed to their side, hanging on to the edge of the blanket thrown over the camels' backs.

"That's not safe!" Rowena declared.

"Don't worry, my dear," Lady Augusta assured. "Horatio anticipated that too."

Sure enough, Assistant Deputy Edison and Dooland managed to shoo all the children back to the sidewalk.

"Mr. Barry said he has his own marshals," the elderly woman continued, "but Horatio insisted our men be here too."

"The marshals aren't very effective," Nin remarked as a few men passed on their horses, their silver badges shining in the sunlight. "They're more interested in being on display than maintaining law and order."

More roars came from the wagons but these were, unlike the elephant, much sharper. Adele and Nin clutched each other's arm as a cage passed with two tigers, their bodies weighed down by chains and their faces sullen.

"What if one of them breaks free?" Nin shuddered.

"That's what the chains are for, I expect," Lady Augusta said.

Her voice was drowned out by more roars as another cage passed. Adele stared at the bright sheen on the lion's mane. The animal stared back at her with a lazy gaze. "That golden color," she murmured.

"Like Mr. Sipes' golden cat," Nin said.

The wagon passed as a cloud sheltered the sun, and Adele breathed a sigh of relief. "It's white, not golden!"

"A rare breed," Lady Augusta observed.

Just then, Mrs. Faderman appeared with some of her brood. She leaned over Lady Augusta's chair. "May one make a request of her ladyship?"

"One may," said the woman, taking on the haughty tone of her title.

"Will you please ask your son to make sure his men watch those animals carefully during the performance tonight?"

"Irene, his lads aren't lion tamers," said the woman. "I expect these circus people know what they're doing."

"Parading wild animals in front of children?" Mrs. Cricket screeched.

"It ought not to be allowed," Mrs. Abberton agreed, her coiled curls darting out from under her hat from the heat.

"Don't children have a right to see real lions and elephants?" Nin asked. "I never saw a real camel before today."

"Those cages look very secure, oh, my, yes," Mrs. Lynn said in her twittery voice.

"I will remind you, dear, we already had an incident with a wild beast that scared the daylights out of everyone," Mrs. Faderman said archly.

"You mean Mr. Lionel Sipes?" Lady Augusta asked. "That was months ago, Irene."

"That beast of his is probably long dead," Rowena chimed in.

"He said his cat was tame," Nin said.

"Well, these cats and other beasts are *not* tame," Mrs. Faderman said. "One of them tried to attack me through the cage when it passed just now."

"How discerning of him," Lady Augusta mumbled. In a louder

26

tone, she said, "If it will make you feel any better, Irene, I'll ask Horatio to speak to the manager before the performance tonight."

"It's not about making *me* feel better, Lady Augusta," the woman said with an exaggerated bow. "I'm thinking of the children."

"You might also think of them when you see them holding the sides of the wagons," Nin remarked.

The woman turned her eyes to the procession. The last few wagons were passing, one with an Indian family sitting stoically on top of it in full garb. Children scurried to them. In an instant, Mrs. Faderman and some of her brood were on them, shooing them away.

~~~~~

Adele regarded the day as a holiday, though Jackson, like Hatfield, was busy at the station. That evening, she slipped into a plum-colored dress with a lace collar and brimmed plum hat to match. The dark purple offset her chestnut hair and lively features and when Ruth handed her a pair of gloves and pearled handbag, she smiled with approval.

"You're not going, Ruth?" Adele was disappointed.

"We went early, senorita," said the woman. "They let Ana pet the black and white horse."

"The zebra?" Adele asked.

The woman nodded. "And Marco rode the camel."

Adele smiled. "That must have been quite a thrill for a five-year-old." She eyed her. "They didn't give you any trouble?"

"They say circus is for everybody who pay," said Ruth with a big smile.

"Indeed it is." Adele pressed her hand. "Where's my brother?"

"He say he come home five-thirty," said the woman.

Her brother came precisely at five-thirty, but they spent ten minutes arguing about whether to take the Beaton Roundabout or walk.

"It's absurd to take the car on an evening like this," Jackson insisted. "We can easily walk back when it's over."

"We'll be tired," she insisted.

"I've never known you to be lazy, Del."

"Maybe I want to show off the new paint," she said.

"Violet!" Her brother snorted. "Whoever heard of a purple car?"

"Nobody thought twice about asking Mr. Ford why he made his Model B in red, green, and blue," Adele objected.

He took her arm. "Hatfield wants me to be there at five-forty-five. We need one last word with Mr. Barry about the animals."

"Mrs. Faderman?" Adele asked with a smile.

"She has a legitimate complaint," Jackson insisted as he opened the front gate.

"Jack, how many performances do you think these people have done?" Adele asked. "Don't you think if they had any accident, the papers would have reported it?"

"And how would we know if it happened in Boston or Colorado Springs?" he challenged.

"I thought you were going to give them the benefit of the doubt," she mumbled as they headed toward Bridge Street to fetch Nin.

"Hatfield is giving them the benefit of the doubt," he said with his lip curled. "One of us has to remain skeptical."

They found Nin waiting, dressed in light blue with a veiled hat. Adele could tell her friend was nervous by the way she kept pulling at the fingers of her gloves.

Jackson's sense of chivalry got the better of him, and he held out his arm to her. "You needn't worry, Miss Branch. I'll protect you."

She lost the vulnerable look and glared at him. "I'm perfectly capable of taking care of myself, Mr. Gossling."

"I'm well aware of that," he said, "but sometimes it's prudent to accept an offer of help, especially in unknown territory."

Adele expected a retort but Nin's face softened. "Perhaps you're right, Mr. Gossling. I've been sensing something all day."

"Like what?" Adele took her arm.

"Like when one falls off a bridge," said her friend.

"I can scarcely imagine you falling off a bridge." Jackson chuckled.

"Hush, Jack," Adele snapped. "You mean like your body is separating into pieces?"

"Exactly." Her friend gave her a gracious smile.

"The sheriff will make sure nothing happens tonight," said Jackson. Adele could tell his sincerity touched her friend.

Arrojo Park had been transformed into an exhibition of lights and candles. The evening sky was still bright enough to show the colors of the performers' costumes. Small tents and concession stands stood on either side of a grassy walkway that ended at the big tent which, Adele admitted, looked massive and inviting. Clowns lingered with the crowds, performing tricks for the children and bowing at the pennies they received from the parents in return.

"It's like a madhouse!" Nin declared.

"That's the joy of it, dear," Adele said. "Watching everyone have a good time."

"I wish I could watch everyone have a good time," Jackson said ruefully. "But I have to watch for thieves."

"A deputy's work is never done." Adele smiled. "Will we see you later under the big top?"

"Save us a seat," he said as he made his way to the back of the tent where wagons lined up farther away. His crisp uniform and deputy badge flashing a glare from the pale sun made some people regard him with unease.

She caught sight of Lady Augusta near a peanut vendor. Nin instantly took hold of the handles of the rolling chair, and Adele could see her grip was fierce.

"Don't tell me your son has left you all alone." Adele took her hand.

"I have declared my own liberation for tonight," the woman said in a firm tone. "Rowena's friends from Blue Springs are in town, and I insisted she go with them. Horatio doesn't know of course."

"You shouldn't be left alone," Nin said with compassion, petting the woman's shoulder.

"But, my dear, I'm not alone. Why do you think I was waiting here with these inedible things?" The woman frowned as she held up the bag of peanuts. The vendor glared at her.

Adele smiled. "You were waiting for us?"

"I shouldn't think you would miss an old woman who barely has all her teeth foolish enough to buy peanuts!"

Adele laughed. "We'll find you a cool lemonade, and then we'll take you to the big top."

They found the lemonade stand and Adele offered to brave the lines while Nin wheeled Lady Augusta between a few smaller tents where it was quieter. As she waited, she glanced every so often at the strange pair — Lady Augusta with her regal pose and Nin with her dark hair and alabaster skin showing against the gas lamps.

Just as she left the stand with a cardboard box filled with drinks, she saw two heads darting away between the two tents where her friends were waiting. She couldn't make out the faces but the moon shot a beam against the hatless blond hair she recognized as Mrs. Barry's. The woman was talking to a man and once, when the man turned toward the crowds, she thought it might be Mr. Rowe.

Lady Augusta looked as delighted as a child. "Sakes, I haven't had lemonade for I don't know how long."

"It's too sweet," Nin said, coughing.

"I shall tell Rowena to make us a pitcher the next time you

visit, and you'll see what good lemonade tastes like," Lady Augusta said with a laugh.

Adele hardly heard them. Her attention was on the two figures. She could see a little more now that she was closer. She heard nothing of what they said but violent gestures flickered between them.

"We ought to get going if we want to find a seat, my dears," Lady Augusta said.

At that moment, the two figures disappeared, leaving the space between the tents dark and dusty.

Inside the main tent, Adele felt like a child again. The massive circle in the center barely left room for the benches where the spectators sat. Some had to stand behind them, craning their necks to see. She had not realized the white canvas walls were a disguise for the painted tent roof. It was entirely black with yellow stars. Large velvet curtains hung behind the bandstand, quivering every so often and sometimes a small part opened to show a head staring out to the crowd.

In spite of all the strange faces, there were enough townspeople to recognize them and soon a bench in the back was emptied for the sheriff's mother and the deputy sheriff's sister. Hatfield and Jackson showed up with Edison at their heels just as the gaslights dimmed.

"Where the devil is Rowena?" Hatfield's usually mild voice rose agitated above the crowd.

"Now don't lose your temper, dear," Lady Augusta said. "I insisted she go with her friends."

"She takes too many liberties," her son grumbled.

Lady Augusta took on the stern pose. "I shall decide whether she does or not, Horatio. She's not our servant, and she has a right to be with her friends on this special day."

Hatfield sank on the bench beside her, taking her hand. "I worry about you, Ma."

"My dear, I've had the most delightful time with my own

friends." Lady Augusta winked at them. "Now take these awful peanuts away from me, and mind you don't get the grease on your new trousers." He laughed and obeyed.

The elephants they had seen in the parade came first, a man with a beard coaxing them while three women, one of whom they had seen in the parade, performed their feats. Adele marveled at how the massive beasts obeyed, and one even seemed charmed by the crowd.

Next came Miss Clara Spore, the tightrope walker. She and Nin clutched each other's hand as the woman climbed on a unicycle and held a bar steady while riding to the end of the tightrope and back again.

"Don't worry, dear," Adele whispered. "There's a net under her." The black net stretched tight and lazy below.

A clown act came next, performing silly acrobatics and delighting the children in the front rows. The clown they had seen the day before was dressed in a police uniform, which made Jackson frown, and parodied police business with such precision that he had Edison roaring with laughter and even Hatfield found it amusing. Her brother's frown deepened.

"Don't look so serious, Jack," Adele said between tears of laughter. "When it comes to jokes, lawmen are ripe for the picking, as they say."

"I don't like to think of myself as a ripe plum being plucked and squashed by a silly clown," he snapped.

"But, sir, you must admit, he's not far off the mark," Edison ventured. "I s'pose we do fumble like that sometimes when we're trying to make an arrest."

"Perhaps *you* do, Assistant Deputy, but I should hope my job requires a little more skill than that!"

The police clown suddenly turned in their direction and, taking off his hat, gave them a deep bow and backflipped off the ring.

"Impertinence!" Jackson growled.

The light dimmed in the ring. "Ladies and gentlemen!" barked the ringmaster. "We now bring you the daredevil of the century! The man no one can top! The one, the only, Commander of the Flying Trapeze! Ladies and gentlemen, Mr. Julius Rowe!"

The applause deafened as the velvet curtains parted, and Mr. Rowe came flying out in a silver leotard, his name spelled out in black letters on his cape. Two women dressed in gold leotards followed, both with crinkled dark red hair and globe faces. They looked almost identical except that one was clearly older than the other.

Nin leaned toward her. "The infamous Helen must be the younger one."

"Infamous?" Jackson asked.

"The argument between Mr. Barry and Mr. Rowe yesterday," Adele reminded him.

The performers climbed the ladder as the iron trapeze hung above patiently waiting for them. Adele marveled at the height, for when they reached the top, they looked as if they were part of the big top's starry sky.

The marching band began to play, and Mr. Rowe spent some time waving his arms around, turning all sides to the crowd with a glistening smile.

"Hatfield was right," Adele mumbled. "The man really does think highly of himself."

She was interested in the two women. The younger one sat in the catcher's place, her arms almost wrapped around the ropes. Adele could see even from the ground that her arms were muscular. The older woman stood on the platform alongside Mr. Rowe holding on to the flyer's trapeze.

Mr. Rowe threw out the second trapeze, letting it pick up speed. He did his flying act, earning enthusiastic applause from the crowd as he twisted and turned in the air. The catcher grabbed his arms in perfect timing. The older woman did some tricks as well, though, Adele had to admit, they weren't as impressive as Mr. Rowe's.

The music stopped and the voice of the ringmaster pounded, "Ladies and gentlemen! The Commander will now perform the most astounding trick! In front of your very eyes, he will do the stunt that dazzled millions since Miss Jordan first performed it eight years ago. The triple somersault, ladies and gentlemen!"

A howl rose from the crowd, and the ringmaster continued, "We ask everyone to be absolutely silent, please!"

The entire big top was like a church service. Adele almost felt Mr. Rowe taking a deep breath. Her eyes wandered to the net below. The Commander swung the trapeze again and again, studying its speed and height. The catcher rubbed her hands together, waiting. The older woman held on to the rail with both hands, her shoulders stiff.

Mr. Rowe grabbed the trapeze and was up in the air. Adele, along with the rest of the crowd, counted silently to herself — one, two, three —

Shrieks broke the silence. The velvet curtains twisted every which way and people in front of Adele rose, blocking the view of the stage. She managed to squeeze her way into the aisle. She caught a glimpse of the deflated net and a crumpled figure cradled in the blanket of meshing.

a half hour later, the crowd had disappeared, and the big top was empty except for the circus people, the police, and Adele. Nin had taken Lady Augusta home. In spite of her brother's annoyance, Adele had insisted on staying.

Mr. Barry looked like a wooden statue while Adele comforted his weeping wife. He shouted, "What the blazes happened?"

"Isn't it obvious?" asked Abby Call, the older sister of the infamous Helen. "He fell to his death."

"To his death!" Her sister Helen burst out crying.

She put her arms around the young woman. "Don't cry, dear. It's the risk we take."

"I don't want to take risks!"

"Helen, sweet —"

Calvin Barry's voice rose like a ghost. "That wasn't supposed to happen."

Hatfield glanced at him but the man only gave him an empty look.

"All right, everybody, no use staring at the horror," Mr. Barry said. "We still have a job to do. Steve, Joe, wrap him up in the net and get him out of here."

"I'm afraid that's impossible, sir," Sheriff Hatfield said in a clear voice.

"We'll give him a proper burial outside town limits, if that's what you're worried about," the man promised. Estelle Barry let out a shriek.

"It wasn't what I was worried about," the sheriff said. "There's the matter of official paperwork."

"Please, Sheriff, now is hardly the time."

"Now is exactly the time, sir." Jackson looked a little taller and larger than he had only an hour ago. "Sheriff Hatfield is the county coroner, and he has a right to demand an inquest."

"Inquest!"

"Conducted by me," said the sheriff with a crooked smile. "We do things rather informally in the country."

"I haven't been in this business for eighteen years without knowing that, Sheriff," Mr. Barry said grimly.

"How could this have happened?" Mrs. Barry choked out.

"I told him not to attempt the triple until he was good and ready," Mr. Barry said.

"The Barry Circus has been lucky," Miss Call said, "but luck has to run out sometime."

Mrs. Barry sobbed again and leaned her head against Adele's shoulder. Adele heard her murmur, "Our luck has run out."

"What exactly does this official paperwork entail?" The ringmaster stepped forward.

"Mr. Henley, Sheriff. My manager," Mr. Barry mumbled.

"What exactly does it entail?" the man repeated.

"First, you're under orders to clear the ring of all these people." Sheriff Hatfield nodded at Edison and a few of the assistant deputies he managed to round up in the crowd. "My men will do that. And make sure they don't touch a thing, Edison!"

"Yes, sir," the young man said.

"Well, I've no objections to that," said Mr. Henley.

"It's not your place to have objections!" Mr. Barry growled. "I'm running this circus, or have you forgotten?"

Mr. Henley glared at him, then stalked out of the tent. A woman Adele learned later was Mrs. Henley scurried after him.

"All right, Sheriff," Mr. Barry said warily when the place was quiet. "You've cleared the tent. Now what?"

"Now we wait for the medical examiner to come and examine the body," said Hatfield. "I sent one of my lads so he should be here at any moment."

"What for?" Miss Call asked. "We know how he died."

"We need the official examination, ma'am," Jackson explained. "Once we have that, the sheriff can make his ruling."

"But I still don't understand —"

"In case the death wasn't an accident," Adele supplied.

The woman stared at her while Mrs. Barry gasped, "Not accidental?"

"Sheriff, do you know how many accidents occur in the circus?" Mr. Barry sat down on the stool vacated by Mr. Henley. "Wagons overturning, animals fighting, performers becoming injured during practice. Circus folk are a resilient bunch. We accept accidents like a doctor accepts a patient dying on the operating table. We consider it a matter for a higher power to resolve."

"But we can help that higher power along, can't we?" This came from Martin Sanders, the medical examiner's assistant, who had just entered the tent.

Miss Call glared at him. "I consider such words too blasphemous for a young lady's ears." She patted her sister's shoulder.

The younger Miss Call's head shot up. "I'm not a child, Abby!"

"Abby, I think you'd better take Helen to your wagon," Mr. Barry said. "Unless you have questions for them, Sheriff?" He looked at Hatfield.

"Not at present, sir," said the sheriff. "But I may have questions for everyone later."

"Later?" Mr. Barry echoed as the two trapeze artists left the tent. "We're moving out tonight."

"That remains to be seen, sir," Jackson said.

His face grew red. "What the devil do you mean?"

"It depends on the coroner," said the deputy sheriff, glancing at his superior.

"This is preposterous!" the man bellowed. "You have no authority to hold us. I demand —"

The snap of Martin's bag interrupted his words. "Broken neck."

"Isn't that rather obvious?" Adele asked. "You're beginning to sound like Dr. Rhodes."

"Heaven forbid!" Martin snorted.

"These things aren't always cut and dried, Del," Jackson said. "Mr. Rowe's heart might have given way or the trapeze might have hit him in the head and knocked him out before he hit the ground."

"Such things have happened?" Hatfield eyed Mr. Barry.

The man gave a rueful smile. "Most everything has happened in the circus, Sheriff."

"The trapeze looks intact," Jackson said.

"No heart attack or bruising on the head here," Martin confirmed.

"A broken neck from a fall," Adele said. "All straightforward."

"You can't have a murder every time, Adele," Martin said, not without a little amusement. They had grown to be friends since their first case three years ago.

"The net collapsed," Mr. Barry said. "When I get my hands on Wharton —"

Calvin Barry's voice floated in the air. "This wasn't supposed to happen."

"You're damn right it wasn't supposed to happen!" his father snarled. "We should have fired Wharton last season."

"The net has never given way before?" Jackson asked.

"Of course it hasn't," Mr. Barry said. "And it wouldn't have tonight if Wharton had paid proper attention to it. Wharton!" A man with gray sideburns and clothes smeared with dirt entered the tent. "Why the blazes didn't you check the net?"

"I did check it, like always," the man sniveled. "Weren't nothing wrong with it when I saw it, sir. Not my fault."

"No, and the open lock on the zebra cage last year wasn't your fault either," Mr. Barry snarled.

"That was Gerry's responsibility," the man snapped. "Honest, sir, I checked the net myself right before Miss Spore went on. You saw me!" He looked pointedly at Calvin Barry.

"It's true, Pa," said the young man.

"You should have double-checked it then, Cal," his father said.

"I didn't think —" The young man hunched over.

"You never think!" his father shouted. "You think about the numbers but never the people."

"That's not true and you know it, Paul!" Mrs. Barry shrieked.

The younger Mr. Barry collapsed in a chair. "Oh, it's all so ghastly!"

Hatfield, who had been leaning against the bandstand, now straightened to his full height. "According to you, Mr. Wharton, the net was intact when it was brought out before the trapeze act?" The man nodded.

Mrs. Barry grabbed her husband's arm. "It was fate! It had to be fate!"

"Perhaps it wasn't," Adele said softly.

"Del —" Her brother warned.

"If Mr. Wharton checked the net and saw it was intact, why didn't it catch Mr. Rowe's fall?" she inquired.

"Why indeed?" the sheriff murmured. "I'd like to take a look at that net, if you don't mind."

"Do you need me anymore, Sheriff?" Martin inquired.

"No, lad, go home to bed."

Martin nodded, a look of sympathy appearing in his eyes, and left.

"What possible reason do you need to look at it?" Mr. Barry asked. "A torn net is a torn net."

"I know a little something about nets, you see," said Hatfield. "I was a sea captain of a fishing boat for a number of years." He bent down to inspect the net. His features hardened. "Jackson, come look at this."

Adele peered at it. The fibers of the net were twisted, and a few frayed hairs uncoiled from the bunch. "What does it mean?"

"It could mean any number of things," Jackson said. "It could indeed be the wear and tear from dozens of performances. I've seen nets like that."

"So have I." Hatfield leaned back on his heels. "Did I ever tell you the story of Jumping Jones?"

"I don't believe so, sir," Jackson said.

"He was an ambitious young sailor on the *Augusta*. I made him second mate. One day, we were pulling in a catch of tuna at the peak of the season and the net burst. We lost the entire day's catch."

"It was Jumping Jones' fault," Adele ventured.

"It was his doing," said the sheriff. "So I found out later. The lad was so ambitious, he let the captain of the *Manifest* — he was the rival tuna fisher on the wharf — talk him into making sure the waters were clear for his crew by promising him the first mate."

"You mean he destroyed the net?" Jackson asked. Now he was fully alert.

"It only takes a few cuts in the right places," said Hatfield. "We examined the net more closely after he was arrested. Nets, you see, fray and twist and fibers lose their grip. But these are all on one side."

"I see what you mean," Adele said. "Someone who wants to tamper with a net wouldn't just make some cuts on one side so that a hole would rip through it. They would do it cleverly so people would think the net were naturally falling apart."

"Bravo, Adele." The sheriff gave her an admiring smile, which made her blush.

"It could still be an accident, sir," Jackson pointed out.

Hatfield rose. "I'm not ruling that out, Deputy. But we must take precautions." To Mr. Barry, he said, "I'd like to have an expert examine this."

"Expert?" The man eyed him.

"An old friend of mine, a former seaman and expert on ropes," Hatfield said. "If you would kindly let us take this as evidence —"

"Evidence?" Mrs. Barry looked alarmed.

"Possible evidence," the sheriff corrected.

"Surely, you don't think —"

"I don't think anything, ma'am," said Hatfield. "I only confirm or reject my own suspicions. This net may have torn naturally, as you say, from daily practices and performances. Or it may be something else."

"What else could it have been?" Mr. Barry demanded.

"We don't know yet, sir," the sheriff said calmly. "We'd like a few more minutes to look around, if you don't mind."

"I do mind!" Mr. Barry advanced but his son took hold of his arm.

"Let them do their duty, Pa," he insisted. "If there's something wrong, we need to know about it, don't we?"

"Your son is very sensible, sir," said Jackson.

"The police in this town set the rules and we follow them, is that it?" Mr. Barry growled.

"If you'll just step aside." Hatfield gently led them to a bench.

Adele took a chair one of the clowns had used in his routine and watched as her brother and the sheriff conducted their search. She realized the workers had not yet taken down the trapeze. She studied the swing hanging just above her head. It was still now, and she shuddered, remembering how Mr. Rowe had so expertly handled the bar between his strong hands and elegantly swinging body, back and forth — she held her head in her hands.

"Are you all right, dear?" Mrs. Barry's voice was now calm and sympathetic.

"I felt a little dizzy just now," she admitted.

"It's a great height, isn't it?" Mr. Barry said.

"I don't see how they do it," she admitted.

"Lots of practice," his wife said. "And they start young so they develop agility and skill. Julius started when he was sixteen. He was already doing a double somersault when he was eighteen."

Her husband gave her a sharp look. "How did you know that, Estelle?"

"I know more than you think, Paul," she said in a quiet tone.

"So do I," her husband countered.

His wife blinked, then turned to Adele. "I used to be an aerialist myself."

"She was quite good," Mr. Barry admitted.

"What stopped you?" Adele asked.

"Becoming a wife," she said in a hard voice.

"Becoming *my* wife," Mr. Barry echoed.

Adele felt sudden tension rise between the Barrys as they looked at one another like two sparing partners.

Both policemen were standing next to the bandstand with a perplexed look. "I take it you didn't find anything," Adele said.

"We still haven't looked behind there, sir," Jackson said, glancing at the black curtains.

"When one sees possible foul play, one expects to find *something*," Sheriff Hatfield said.

"As I told you before, Sheriff," Mr. Barry approached them, "nets get frayed and weak. Wharton ought to have paid more attention."

"All the same, sir, I think we'll take a look behind the curtain, if you don't mind."

"Would it matter if I did?" the man snapped.

Adele came with them. It reminded her of being backstage at the theater one night. Pieces of wood and cloth were thrown about everywhere and it looked as if a million feet had trodden the dirt. She saw wide, flat shoes of men and dainty slippers of women and prints of animals, though some she couldn't recognize. A flash of color was flung near the wall of the tent among some flat boards and she picked it up.

"Look at this, Sheriff."

The teal blue scarf spilled all over her hands as she held it. The silk was fine, and a row of delicate jeweled stars were sewn into the edge.

"It probably fell off one of the lady performers," Jackson observed.

"This is imported," Adele said, "probably from Europe. I doubt any woman wouldn't notice it had fallen in the dirt unless she was preoccupied with something else."

"For a New Woman, you have an eye for fine things," Hatfield said.

"One needn't be interested in ornaments to know about them, Sheriff," she said stiffly.

"If it's so precious, what is it doing in the dirt?" Jackson inquired.

"That's what we must find out, Deputy," said his superior.

They went back into the main tent. Mr. Barry was there alone. "I hope you don't mind that I went ahead and asked Cal to take his mother back to our wagon?"

Hatfield held up the scarf. "Have you ever seen this before?"

The man was silent for a moment.

"It's a simple question, sir," Jackson said.

"It could belong to one of the performers here," he said. "Ladies of the circus sometimes spend their money on such things."

"We'll have to inquire amongst your people, then." The sheriff put it in his pocket.

"What the devil for?" the man growled. "Scarves are lost every day, aren't they?"

"This one might belong to someone involved with that net," Adele said.

"Oh, surely this is all nonsense," said the man.

"I assure you, sir, none of this is nonsense," said the sheriff, giving him a hard look. "Including that young man who was just taken away with his neck broken."

"But what does this all mean?" Mr. Barry sounded exasperated now.

"It means," said the sheriff, "we must ask you not to move your wagons for the time being."

"What!" Mr. Barry jumped up, and the chair where he was sitting flew back. "This is ludicrous!"

"Your circus may be a crime scene, sir," Jackson insisted.

"What exactly makes it a crime scene, Deputy?" Mr. Barry scoffed. "An old net and a scarf that probably slipped off the neck of a careless performer?"

"The sheriff of any county has a right to prevent anyone from leaving town," Jackson argued.

"I mean to have my friend check that net," Hatfield said. "As it's too big for us to take, I would appreciate it if you would set it aside in a place where no one can tamper with it."

"Sheriff," Mr. Barry spoke in a slow voice, "you must appreciate we have a job to do. We have bookings in small towns from here to Sacramento. We have engagements to fulfill."

"I can't help that, sir." Hatfield cocked his head. "Have you considered there might be a murderer in your midst?"

"Nonsense!" the man exploded. "It was all — well, it was an accident!"

"Until we can determine that for sure, nobody leaves Arrojo,"

Hatfield said. Adele could see he was losing his patience, his face becoming more like stone.

"And how do you propose to stop us?" Mr. Barry folded his arms.

"I'll have deputies stationed on the road outside of town," said the sheriff in a calm voice.

"Can we at least extend our performances here so we can recoup some of our losses?" Mr. Barry gave Hatfield a pointed look.

"I'm afraid not, sir," said the sheriff. "Until we know if you have a murderer in your midst —"

"We do not have a murderer in our midst!"

"Until we know for sure," Hatfield's good will had worn thin, "everyone in your circus is to remain here and this tent is to be guarded. Is that clear?"

Rather than answer, the man spun around and strolled out of the tent.

CHAPTER 5

The morning after Circus Day was less festive than the day before. Children made their way to school, chattering about the kiddie shows and the animals they had seen. The adults dragged themselves to their shops and businesses, looking subdued. Their conversation was less light-hearted than their children's, as the death of Julius Rowe appeared in the headlines of the morning's *Arrojo Courier* with BIG TOP TRAGEDY! greeting their morning coffee.

As Hatfield had asked her to accompany them to conduct circus interviews the night before, she walked alongside Jackson, whose uniform looked ill-fitting in the summer heat

When they reached the station, she asked, "Did you notice Calvin Barry last night, Jack?"

"What about him?"

"He kept saying, 'That wasn't supposed to happen.'" She sighed.

"I'm sure it wasn't, Del." Her brother stepped back to let her into the station.

"He was more shaken than any of them," she said as she folded her parasol.

"Who was shaken?" Hatfield herded them out the door and into the police wagon.

"We were talking about Calvin Barry," said Jackson. "Del thinks he acted rather strangely yesterday."

"Well, I suppose none of them expect a performer to be killed, even if they're taking risks," Hatfield lamented. "I should think his mother behaved more strangely than he did."

"Mrs. Barry was quite distraught," Adele agreed, "as if she had just lost her best friend."

"Or her paramour?" Hatfield eyed her.

"You said it, I didn't," she mumbled.

"If it's true — and mind you, I don't say it is —" Jackson gave his sister a meaningful look, "— a rejected love can be a dangerous one."

"We don't know yet if we should be thinking in those terms, Deputy," said the sheriff as he opened the circus gate.

"It can't hurt to consider the possibilities," Adele said as she stepped inside.

The chaos they had witnessed the evening before was gone. The candles were burned out and the streamers sagged. Posters were half torn on the ground along with the remains of the concession stands. A few workers hobbled around picking up the refuse.

Paul Barry was at his desk, playing with an elastic band and ignoring the papers in front of him. His wife was curled up on the bed, fully dressed. Her face was sagging and white, and her blond hair fell in strands across her face.

Hatfield eyed the bottle of whiskey sitting on the desk. "I thought you said you didn't allow your people to touch liquor while in town."

"Under the circumstances, Sheriff, I wouldn't forbid my people to do anything," said Mr. Barry. Nevertheless, he put the bottle in a cupboard.

"We're all devastated," Mrs. Barry said in a thick voice.

"My wife means she's devastated." The sour look he gave her made Adele grit her teeth.

"Will you be replacing Mr. Rowe?" Jackson inquired.

Mr. Barry stiffened. "As we're unable to perform, there's no hurry in deciding, is there?"

"I'm sorry about that, sir," Hatfield said. "I'm sure you want to find out what happened as quickly as possible."

"We know what happened," Mr. Barry said. "The net was old and it tore. I told Cal it would happen one of these days but he refused to replace it. He insisted we didn't have the money."

"We don't know if it did tear," Hatfield said. "My friend, Mr. Evans, will be arriving in a few days to confirm or deny that. In the meantime, we must treat this as a — possible suspicious incident."

"You mean as a deliberate attempt to take Julius' life?" Mrs. Barry's voice shook. "Who would want to do such a thing?"

"We were hoping you could tell us." Jackson looked at her steadily. "Was there anyone who had a grudge against Mr. Rowe?"

"I wouldn't say a grudge," said Mr. Barry. "We have our tiffs, to be sure."

"Did you have a tiff with Mr. Rowe, Mr. Barry?" Adele folded her hands on the handle of her parasol.

He shot her a look. "Why do you ask that, Miss Gossling?"

"Mr. Rowe didn't seem to be in a very good mood in Caton."

"Oh, that." The man relaxed. "That was about Helen."

"Mr. Rowe wasn't fond of his partners?" Jackson asked.

"He got along with them all right," Mr. Barry said.

"And yet he wanted Miss Helen Call out of the act," Jackson pointed out.

Mr. Barry leaned back in his chair, his hands intertwined. "I don't know if I can explain the circus to you, Deputy."

"What has that to do with it?" Jackson seemed annoyed.

"Everything," said the man. "You see, Abby and her sister came from circus people."

"Their parents were quite successful," Mrs. Barry echoed.

"Children born into the circus are much like children born in the theater," Mr. Barry continued.

"They're brought into the business from birth." Hatfield nodded.

"Whether they chose to be or not," Adele added. "Their destiny is set."

"You don't approve, I take it." Mr. Barry studied her.

"I don't approve of anybody, man or woman, dictating the life of anybody else," Adele said.

"One must be free to do what one likes," Mrs. Barry lamented.

"I imagine it's much like the sea," Hatfield said. "I've seen veteran sailors push their sons into the way of life regardless of how they felt."

Mr. Barry nodded. "Abby took to the circus like a fish to water. Helen — well, her mind was always in the clouds."

"You're being too harsh, Paul," Mrs. Barry said sharply.

"You know there is no room for carelessness in the circus, Estelle." He glared at her.

"Then why didn't you replace her?" Hatfield asked. "I assume as the owner of the circus, you had that right."

"It's never that easy, Sheriff," said Mr. Barry. "When dealing with an act, one must think of all those involved."

"You mean Abby Call?" Adele guessed.

Mr. Barry nodded. "She would walk out on the act if we replaced Helen. And Julius wouldn't perform without her."

"I see your wife is right," Adele said. "They were devoted to one another."

"Abby is devoted to her sister," Mr. Barry said shortly.

"I find that admirable," Adele said.

"It would be," said Mr. Barry, "if she kept at least one eye open to her faults."

"We all have faults, Paul," Mrs. Barry said softly. "Even you."

"I hope I'm not as blind to mine." He sniffed.

Adele noticed his wife pressed her lips together as if forcing herself to remain silent.

"I see," said the sheriff. "As a matter of routine, sir, I must ask you and your wife your whereabouts before the trapeze act performed last night."

"I was where I always am," said Mr. Barry. "Behind the curtain. There's a lot of work to be done to make sure each act goes on as planned and leaves the ring in time for the next act."

"Wouldn't your manager take care of that?" asked Jackson.

"Lester, as you saw, prefers to be in front of the crowds." There was an almost rueful tone in his voice. "He likes to make a show of himself as the ringmaster."

"And you, Mrs. Barry?" The sheriff turned to her.

The woman dropped her handkerchief. Adele bent down to pick it up and, handing it to her, saw her hands were shaking.

"I was where I always am too," she said. "I was collecting the money from the cashiers and the concession stands and counting it up."

"Wouldn't your son do that?" Jackson asked.

"He has to help Paul behind the curtain."

"There's a lot to coordinate, Deputy," Mr. Barry said. "And the Barry Circus has never once made a mistake."

"Very admirable," Hatfield said. "Did you see the net before it went out into the ring?"

"Of course I saw it," said Mr. Barry. "I didn't check it, you understand. I trusted Wharton to do that. Apparently, that was a mistake." A hard line appeared across his face.

"I don't know as you can blame Mr. Wharton if anything did happen to it," Hatfield said. "With the chaos you must have had backstage —"

"As I said before, Sheriff," Mr. Barry snarled, "there is no room for carelessness in the circus."

"What act comes after the trapeze act?" Jackson asked.

"Dan and his troupe," Mr. Barry supplied. "But they usually remain outside until they're called."

"We shall have a word with them as well," said Hatfield.

"Yes, I think you should," Mr. Barry said. "Dan and Julius had quite a falling out not long ago."

"Paul!" His wife was alarmed.

"The police need to know these things, dear."

"What kind of falling out, sir?" Jackson asked.

"A week or so ago there was a violent row between them in the cookhouse," said Mr. Barry.

"Cookhouse?"

The man smiled. "The tent where we take our meals, Deputy."

"Go on," Hatfield said.

"I wasn't there but my son told me. Dan accused Julius of, well, making eyes at his fiancée, I guess you would call it. When Julius denied it, Dan attacked him."

"Any damage?" the sheriff asked.

The man gave a sly smile. "Julius got a boxed ear and a black eye. Luckily the trapeze was so high up, people didn't notice it."

"That's rather heartless, Paul." Mrs. Barry's eyes filled with tears.

"Did Mr. Patton threaten him?" Jackson asked.

"I really don't know, Deputy," said Mr. Barry. "You'll have to ask Cal about that."

"We intend to see him next, sir," Hatfield said. "But tell us first, who else uses the net other than the trapeze act?"

"Clara, our tight rope walker," said Mr. Barry.

"She was very good last night," Adele complimented.

He smiled. "Clara was at the top of her game, I'll grant you."

"Meaning she isn't always?" Jackson asked.

"I didn't say that!"

"It's what you meant, Paul," said Mrs. Barry. "You're always so critical of her."

The man looked embarrassed. "Clara — well, she's a little dreamy."

"Isn't it rather dangerous to let her go on if she's distracted?" Jackson eyed him.

Mr. Barry stiffened. "Clara is a professional, Deputy, just like every performer here."

"But as you said, sir," Hatfield's tone was even, "in the circus, there is no room for carelessness."

The man was on his feet, his face darkened. "Are you implying I don't know how to take care of my people?"

"You take care of everybody, Paul," said Mrs. Barry in a soft tone, "but in the way that suits you"

"I keep my eye on everybody, especially on opening night," the man continued in a rough tone.

"Did you keep your eye on Mr. Rowe last night?" Jackson asked.

Mr. Barry played with the cap on the ink bottle. "Julius was always capable of looking after himself."

"You sound as if you resented it," the sheriff observed.

"Perhaps I did," the man admitted. "I don't like it when a performer refuses to fall in line."

"Then you didn't get along with him as well as you claim." Adele raised an eyebrow.

"I realize, Miss Gossling, you choose to tag along with the police because of your brother's position, but do the police allow you to be rude as well?"

"I'll thank you to abstain from being rude to my sister, sir."

Jackson's fierce look made the man back down. He rubbed his fingernail against the cap. "As I said before, we all had our tiffs."

"Why don't you tell them the truth, Paul?" Mrs. Barry leaned forward, her expression fierce "You didn't like Julius because he liked women and treated them with respect."

"Respect!"

"He gave them the sort of attention you think is a waste of

time." Her voice broke and she buried her face in her hand-kerchief.

"All right, I didn't like the man!" Mr. Barry snapped. "Julius was altogether — well, too self-assured."

"He did seem to think highly of himself." Jackson glanced at the sheriff.

"He had his own ideas about how the circus should be run."

"And his ideas weren't your ideas?" Adele asked.

"Julius knew what he was doing," Mrs. Barry said. "He could have run his own circus. Oh, a waste, such a waste!"

Something in the definitiveness of her tone made Adele ask, "Then why didn't he?"

"What?" Mrs. Barry looked at her.

"He had good looks and charm and charisma," Adele continued. "I imagine it wouldn't have been a stretch for him to go from performer to circus owner."

Mr. Barry gave her a rueful smile. "That takes money, Miss Gossling."

"If he'd had the money —" Mrs. Barry stopped, clutching her handkerchief.

"But more than money," Mr. Barry continued as if he hadn't heard her, "one must make careful decisions."

"And Mr. Rowe had daring but not caution?" Jackson inquired.

Mr. Barry snorted. "He didn't even have much daring, Deputy. Oh, physical daring, yes. But he was a coward underneath."

"You knew nothing about him, Paul!" his wife screeched.

"And neither did you, my dear," said the man. "Why do you think he always went to Cal when he wanted something? He wasn't man enough to come to me himself."

"Maybe he was more manly than you think," his wife murmured.

"It's the way with many of these star performers, especially the daredevils," Mr. Barry continued. "They put on a show in front of an audience but when there is no audience, they deflate like balloons. And then they have to have their private audience to make them feel like men again."

Adele watched his fingers flick across the rim of the cap. She reached out and moved it aside. "You'll stain your hands, Mr. Barry." She put the cap on the bottle.

"One last question." Sheriff Hatfield pulled out the scarf they had found the night before. "Mrs. Barry, we showed this to your husband yesterday and he said he didn't recognize it? Do you?"

Adele watched their eyes. Mr. Barry blinked. Mrs. Barry barely glanced at it before she said, "I don't wear scarves."

This made something in her husband's eyes flicker, and he said, "It doesn't look familiar to me."

"Perhaps you ought to look at it again, Mrs. Barry," Adele said.

"I have!" The woman rose. "I'd like to go for a walk, if you don't mind."

"You haven't really," Adele said. The sheriff handed her the scarf, and Adele laid it on the bed. "It's a very pretty scarf, don't you think?"

"I don't wear scarves," the woman repeated in a curt tone. "They choke me." Suddenly, she growled, "If you don't believe me, you can search the wagon."

"We never said we didn't believe you," said Jackson in a quiet voice. "But my sister is right. You barely looked at it."

The woman held her forehead in her hand. "Please, I have a headache."

"Who, then, in your troupe wears scarves?" Hatfield asked.

"Many women here do," said Mr. Barry. "I told you that yesterday, Sheriff. I suppose it comes from being in the public eye."

"Public eye," Mrs. Barry lamented. "Living in the public eye and dying in the public eye." Her eyes filled with tears, and she ran out of the wagon.

"I'm sorry if we upset your wife, sir." Hatfield put the scarf back in his pocket. "But we do have a job to do."

Mr. Barry led them to the doorway. "We're all upset about this tragedy and then being told we have to wait around for an investigation — you don't know us, Sheriff, but we're not people who are content to do nothing."

"We're working as fast as we can," Jackson said.

"I know you are, Deputy." The man sighed. "I've let my people know you'll be asking questions, and I expect their full cooperation."

"We're grateful to you, Mr. Barry." Hatfield gave his hand a vigorous shake.

"We go by first names here, Sheriff," said the man. "You may as well too."

When they stepped out of the wagon, Adele caught a glimpse of Mrs. Barry. She was leaning against a wagon, her sobs audible above the clanging and shuffling of the circus people around them. Adele saw the wagon sign read *Julius Rowe, Commander of the Flying Trapeze*.

CHAPTER 6

*O*utside, the sheriff looked thoughtfully at the big tent. "Adele, you know women, don't you?"

"I hope I do," she said with a little smile.

"Don't you think Mrs. Barry's behavior is — odd?"

"I'm not sure I know what you mean, Sheriff." She leaned against her parasol.

"Not the weeping, I grant you," said Hatfield. "That's to be expected. I'm not talking about last night."

"You mean this morning," Jackson suggested. "I noticed it too."

"You mean the fact that she doesn't love her husband anymore?" Adele asked. "That was obvious to me from Caton."

"Indeed?" Her brother eyed her.

"The Barry wagon has one bed, and it's a rather small one," Adele said. "His wife clearly doesn't sleep there."

"Del!" Her brother blushed.

"These wagons are small," the sheriff pointed out. "Perhaps it's not by choice."

"It's by choice," she said confidently. "I have a feeling Mr. Rowe may have been the cause. Or one of the causes, anyway."

"That's pure guesswork," her brother growled.

"We know how much you hate guesswork, Jack," she retorted, "but even the sheriff will tell you the police sometimes have to go on guesses."

"Not guesses," her brother insisted. "Hunches backed up by the possibility of fact."

"I agree with your sister, Jackson," said Hatfield. "Mr. Barry didn't strike me as being very affectionate toward his wife. She might have looked elsewhere for it."

"Wouldn't that make him more a suspect than her?" his deputy questioned.

"At the moment, everyone is a suspect," the sheriff grumbled. "The father, the mother, and the son."

Calvin looked completely different than the night before. His face was as scrubbed and pressed as his clothes and he greeted them with a smile. Unlike his father's wagon, his looked more like an office than a home.

"I see you didn't waste any time, Sheriff," he said.

"A crime may have been committed, sir," said Hatfield, adjusting himself in the small chair.

"*May* have been committed," the man emphasized. "I still maintain it was an accident."

"Why is that, Calvin?" Adele asked. When he gave her a strange look, she added, "Your father said we were to call everyone by their first names."

"As Pa told you last night, accidents aren't unusual in the circus." He picked up a pencil. "They're tragic but a part of our life."

"He also said the Barry Circus has never had such an accident," Jackson said. "How do you explain this one?"

The man kept his eyes on his pencil. "I think that's a question you'd better ask Pa."

"Your father seems like a very forceful man," said Jackson with some delicacy.

Calvin looked at him with steel eyes. "He is indeed, Deputy. I won't lie. I never wanted to be part of the circus. I wanted a sane, steady job."

"So you went to school to study accounting," the deputy sheriff guessed.

The man nodded. "Only my father had different ideas about what I would do with my education. I suppose I ought to have been stronger and refused him."

"Why didn't you?" asked Hatfield.

"My mother, Sheriff. She hasn't had an easy time of it." He grimaced. "I suppose it's natural for a son to want to take care of his mother."

"Indeed it is," said the sheriff in a soft voice. Adele smiled, thinking of how devoted he was to Lady Augusta.

"Is that why you go backstage the first half of opening night instead of her?" Jackson asked. "To protect her?"

"In a way," he said. "There's always chaos, and Mama gets nervous. She would rather sit in my wagon and count the earnings."

"But you weren't behind the curtain the entire night," the sheriff pointed out. "Your father told us."

"Naturally," he said. "After Mother gets through and puts the money in the safe, I put it in the books."

"You're very methodical," Adele remarked.

"We have to be, Miss Gossling." The man's face became stony. "My father doesn't tolerate mistakes."

"Is that what you were doing when the trapeze act went on?" Hatfield asked.

"I went to my wagon just as Clara finished and the clowns went on," he said. "I like to know how much profit we made as soon as possible."

Jackson peered at him. "Is the circus losing money, Mr. Barry?"

The man gave a chuckle. "Most years we barely break even, Deputy, like most small circuses. I have some ideas to expand next year, and if I can get a bank loan, we might make money yet."

"Do your parents know about your plans?" Adele asked.

"Mama knows," he said. "I prefer to tell Pa once I know if I have the loan or not."

"Was Mr. Rowe in on your plans?" she continued.

"I don't know what you mean by 'in on the plans.'" Calvin said.

"It seemed to me like you and he had a secret that day in Caton," Adele remarked.

"You make it sound so clandestine." The man gave a short laugh.

"My sister sometimes has curious ideas." Jackson glared at her.

"I assure you Julius and I had no secret." Calvin shifted positions.

"He asked you if you would do your duty," Adele pointed out. "I only thought he might be referring to something in particular."

There was silence for a moment. Calvin wrote something down in a book in front of him, his eyebrows peaked together.

"Was he referring to something specific, sir?" Hatfield's tone was firm. "It does no good to hide things from the police, you know."

"If he were, it would have nothing to do with his accident."

"It's best to let us be the judge of that," Jackson said.

"My father and Julius — well, they didn't see eye to eye." He put down the pencil and looked at the sheriff. "Papa thinks he knows the circus better than anybody else. He's not very open-minded to other people's ideas."

"Go on." The sheriff leaned back.

"Julius had a lot of ideas, some of them quite good," he continued. "He knew how Pa would react if he heard them, so he came to me."

"And he thought it was your duty to execute them," Hatfield said.

"We have a duty to our performers and the people who work hard for us," said the man firmly.

"Mr. Rowe was trying to send you a message, then," Jackson said.

"You could put it that way," Calvin said.

"It was a strange time to bring it up, though," Adele remarked. "Out of the blue like that."

"I suppose he thought it had something to do with disciplining Helen." Calvin crushed the pencil in his fist. "What does it matter?"

Adele couldn't resist glancing at the pencil, her professional interest perked. She saw it was square-shaped and the wood casing was red.

"If you're thinking Helen was responsible for Julius's accident, you're wrong," he suddenly said. "Helen has been in the circus since she was a child."

"So your parents told us," the sheriff said. "They also told us Miss Abby Call would surely leave if you ever restricted her sister."

"No one was grounding anybody, Sheriff," the man declared. "The act's contract was renewed a few weeks ago."

Jackson raised his eyebrow. "Your father didn't tell us that."

"He doesn't know everything that goes on around here!" Mr. Barry growled. Then, in a calmer tone, he added, "Pa doesn't like to deal with contracts because performers sometimes argue and make demands, so he leaves it to me."

"Did Mr. Rowe make demands?" Hatfield coughed.

The man looked out the small window. "He had some concerns."

"What concerns?" asked Jackson.

"He said Abby told him a young man had been buzzing around Helen lately."

"Oh?"

"One of these studious types that latches on to the circus with wide-eyed fascination. Like the clergyman's son who sneaks into vaudeville shows at night."

Adele noticed her brother could barely hide his smile. "I've known some of those young men."

"Why would that bother Miss Call?" the sheriff asked.

"Abby was afraid he would distract Helen from her work," he said. "His father has money, you see."

"That might impress an impressionable young woman," Jackson agreed.

"Abby wanted it put in the contract that Helen couldn't have any visitors without her permission and the boy run off." He again picked up the pencil.

"And did you agree?" Jackson probed.

"I'm not my father, Deputy," said the young man. "I don't make conditions for the performers. I told him if Helen found the boy troublesome, she should come to me herself."

"And what was Mr. Rowe's reaction to that?" Hatfield asked.

Calvin sneered. "He said as far as he was concerned, since the boy was paying his ticket every night, he had a right to stare at anybody he chose."

"A rather cavalier attitude," Adele grumbled. "One would think he would be more concerned about Helen being distracted since it might cost him his life."

The man sighed. "Daredevils think they're invincible, Miss Gossling."

"Adele," she said kindly.

"Adele." He smiled. "Have I answered all your questions, Sheriff?"

"I have a question," Adele said. "Why did you say 'That wasn't supposed to happen' after Julius fell last night?"

"I don't remember what I said," he murmured. "It was such a

shock to see it happen, I was probably babbling all manner of incoherent things."

"Your father didn't turn a hair," Jackson said.

"My father, Deputy, was probably thinking more of the trouble he'll have replacing his star performer than Julius lying in that net with a broken neck!" Calvin snapped.

"That's rather harsh, isn't it, sir?" Hatfield asked.

The man turned away. "Is that all, Sheriff?"

The sheriff took out the scarf and waved it at him. "Does this look familiar to you?"

"It's a woman's scarf." The man blinked.

"We're aware of that," Jackson said. "It was found behind the curtain."

He studied it. "It looks familiar but I can't place it."

"So you have seen it around here?" Hatfield asked.

"Yes," he said. "That I'm fairly certain of." He rose. "Is there anything else?"

"When was the last time you spoke to Mr. Rowe?" the sheriff asked.

"Just before the parade," said the young man. "I go around and make sure everyone is in their right place before we start out."

"What was his mood?" asked Adele.

"Mood?"

"Was he excited, agitated, relaxed?"

Calvin's grave face broke into a smile. "He was in full performance mode. Julius, unlike most of the troupe, loved appearing before a crowd."

Adele murmured, "He liked being admired."

"Yes," said Mr. Barry, a little distant. "He liked being admired."

CHAPTER 7

*C*alvin invited them to lunch at the cookhouse but, to Adele's surprise, the sheriff declined. "It's best, I think, if we get back to town and return this evening," he said. "You'll lunch with us, of course?"

"Nin and I will," Adele said. "She's likely to skip lunch if we don't take her."

They went to The Soaring Eagle, a new place that had opened only the month before.

As Adele was filling her friend in about the interviews that morning, Nin drew her shawl closer to her shoulders. "There's a chill in the air."

"I find it rather warm here," Hatfield remarked.

"It's the beer," Jackson said.

"Ale, if you please." Adele smiled. She had chatted with the owners, Mr. And Mrs. Eagle, when they had come in to buy some rubber stamps, and they had made a point to say they only sold "the best ales this end of California."

"I don't care, as long as it washes away the bitter taste of the Barrys," he remarked.

"Ah, that it will, sir, that it will," Mr. Eagle said with a jolly note. "A pint of the best pale ale to start, sir?"

"I'm afraid not, Mr. Eagle. We're on duty, you see."

"I see no harm in a little ale, Jackson," said his superior. "I'll have a glass myself."

"And the ladies?" The man peered at them.

Adele was amused at the annoyed look on Jackson's face, for she knew the idea of his sister drinking liquor in public bruised his sense of propriety. "I will. Nin?" Her friend wrinkled her nose.

"And the stew?" he persisted. "Ale goes well with beef stew." They all nodded.

After the man left, Jackson sniffed. "I'm not at all sure this is an appropriate place for ladies, Sheriff."

"It's not as if we've never seen a glass of beer before," Nin snapped.

"Why shouldn't we enjoy ourselves as well as men?" Adele asked.

"I can't disagree there," Hatfield said with a laugh. "If Ma were here, she'd be tucking away her second glass by now." In an almost thoughtful tone, he added, "She always liked pale ale."

The drinks came and Adele took a tentative sip. "It does take away the bitterness of this morning's interviews," she remarked.

"It's all a façade, isn't it?" Nin sighed. "The clowns, the acrobats, the animals."

"It is when there's murder about," Adele said. "It always happens, doesn't it, Sheriff?"

Hatfield nodded. "Crime brings out the cuts and bruises in people."

"It's as if they're bleeding out the uncomfortable truths they keep hidden so well," Nin said.

"Well stated, Miss Branch." Jackson smiled for the first time that day. Nin looked away, as she still had a difficult time accepting compliments.

"There are certainly cuts and bruises with the Barrys," Adele remarked.

"The question is, do those cuts and bruises have to do with Mr. Rowe's death?" Jackson asked.

Adele leaned back a little as Mr. Eagle placed a steaming bowl of stew in front of her. "I think it has everything to do with Mr. Rowe."

Her brother looked amused. "You always did love to build intrigues, Del."

"This is more than building an intrigue," she argued. "I think there was something between Julius and Estelle."

"Lead." The word came like a shot from Nin's lips.

"I beg your pardon?" Hatfield leaned forward.

"Lead," she repeated. "I smell lead."

"From my pencil, perhaps," Jackson said as he put the writing utensil he used for notes in his back pocket. "Anything would smell in this damp place."

Hatfield tore the end of a fresh loaf of bread Mr. Eagle had put on the table. "It doesn't seem as if Mr. Rowe had any dispute with the Barrys. Otherwise, he wouldn't have renewed his contract."

"He might have done that out of necessity," Adele pointed out. "Maybe the Calls were determined to renew so he had no choice."

"Or maybe the Barrys made it worth his while," Jackson added. "The star performer must earn a pretty penny."

"The star performer can also get a pretty penny if he takes his star performance elsewhere," Nin said.

"Not if he believed he had privileges," Jackson countered. "We already know Mr. Rowe considered himself an asset to a circus, maybe even thought he was responsible for its success. If he took a job at another circus, he would be starting all over again."

"I have a feeling privilege was very important to Mr. Rowe," Adele murmured.

"So were the admiring eyes of ladies." Nin shuddered. "I had to bathe with Epsom salt after that visit to Caton."

"I'm sorry about that, Miss Branch." Sheriff Hatfield looked genuinely humbled. "I should have stopped him."

"It was better you didn't, Sheriff," Adele said. "Since he's our murder victim, we need to know the best and the worst about him."

"I gather we'll get plenty of the worst when we go back this evening." Jackson wiped his mouth.

Adele was able to return to her shop for a little while, as Hatfield insisted on going back to the station to wait for the final report from Martin and see if there was any further word from his friend Abe Evans. A flurry of people came in mainly to get the word on the circus death they read about in the morning paper.

She expected to see Mrs. Faderman's triumphant figure march into her shop, and indeed, just as she was closing up, the woman appeared followed by the meeker Mr. Faderman. Her matted hair lay neatly inside her hat, and her entire countenance showed self-satisfaction.

"Mr. Faderman is in need of a new lamp for his study, Miss Gossling."

"I'm sorry, but I'm in a hurry tonight," she said.

The woman looked surprised. "I've never known you to turn down business."

"She's not." Nin appeared at the doorway, her loose hair lying over one shoulder and her dress dusty as usual. "She's postponing it."

"He needs it rather badly," said Mrs. Faderman. "Don't you, dear?" She looked at him expectedly.

"Oh, indeed, indeed!" the man said.

"You wouldn't want him to ruin his eyesight, would you, Miss Gossling?" The woman gave her a sour smile.

Adele sighed. "No, I suppose not." She unlocked the door and ushered them in.

But it soon became clear the lamp was the last thing on Mrs. Faderman's mind. She was, in fact, determined to catch Adele's attention more than her husband who, it seemed, was now taking advantage of the pretense and looking in earnest at the row of desk lamps she had on display.

"I don't like to say 'I told you so,' of course —" the woman began.

"You will anyway," Nin grumbled.

"— but I knew only bad would come of letting those people into our town."

"Is this glass or crystal, Miss Gossling?" Mr. Faderman inquired, pushing his thinned hair over his forehead.

"Oh, what does it matter, Harold?" the woman snapped.

"Well, I was just —"

"The man was intoxicated, no doubt," Mrs. Faderman continued.

"Why do you just assume circus people are evil?" Nin eyed her.

"I really don't see how this is any concern of yours, Miss Branch," the woman said stiffly.

"It's certainly no concern of *yours*," Nin countered.

"Whatever affects this town is my concern!" the woman growled.

"I think I'll take this one," her husband said.

"Yes, yes, Harold, well, look around a bit more. I haven't quite finished."

Adele's nerves grated like sandpaper. "Mr. Rowe was not intoxicated."

"Oh? The police have determined that?" The woman perked up.

"The Barrys assured us they're very particular about their performers' conduct," she said as she wrapped the lamp in tissue paper. "They keep close to their wagons."

"Indeed?" The woman smiled like a cat. "Your innocence has always been endearing, Miss Gossling."

"I assume you don't mean that as a compliment." Adele tried to keep her voice steady.

"I saw several of those people in town last night after this tragedy happened," said Mrs. Faderman. "They were heading toward Quarry Lane. You know what *that* means." Quarry Lane was the unsavory side of town with all the bars and saloons.

"What if they did?" Nin asked.

"What if they did!" The woman wrinkled her nose.

Adele's fingers pounded the cash register. "Their friend had just plunged to his death in a rather gruesome way. Anybody would want a drink or two after that."

"Friend?" Mrs. Faderman snorted. "They don't make friends, Miss Gossling."

"How do you know?" Nin leaned one hand against the doorframe. "Did you run away to the circus when you were a girl, Mrs. Faderman?"

The blunt question had its effect, as the woman turned pale. "One hears things when one keeps one's ear to the ground, as they say, Miss Branch. I'm sure if you would take your nose out of those intoxicating herbs of yours, you would know more about the way the world works."

Adele steeled herself, expecting Nin's temper to get the best of her. But the dark-haired woman's lovely features contorted with sadness. "Perhaps you're right, ma'am. Perhaps I don't know much about how the world works."

This softened the woman. "I'm sure the police are doing all they can to put this matter to rest so we can get these people out of here. That's all we want, really." She strolled out of the shop with her husband trailing at her heels.

"For once she's right, much as I hate to admit it," Nin said as she closed the shutters. "We all want them out of here. There's a black cloud over them." She glanced in the direction of the park.

"Before we do that, there's work to be done, dear." Adele took her friend's arm.

~~~~~

That evening the circus was somber. There were no sparkles, no lamps, and no candles. In fact, as they walked through to the manager's wagon, Adele felt as if she had entered a ghost town.

Thankfully, the Henley wagon was more jovial. Some clowns, including the one who had teased Jackson, were outside playing the marching band's instruments while the Henleys sat on the steps of their wagon. Other performers were standing around dressed in street clothes. A few poodles from the dog act danced around, and a llama from the children's zoo sidled up to Nin, peering at her with liquid eyes. She petted its head, and the animal nuzzled her hip. One of the brothers who ran the zoo led the animal away, mumbling apologies.

The jolliness immediately ceased as the music died down and people dispersed.

"My apologies for spoiling your party, Mr. Henley." Sheriff Hatfield shook the man's hand. "I'm afraid the police have a habit of clearing a place."

The man led them into the wagon, which was decidedly warmer and more inviting than Paul Barry's. "We were just trying to pass the time. We were told we can't move on until this nasty business is settled."

"I'm afraid not, sir," the sheriff said, his voice hardening, "but this is no time for fun and games."

The man stiffened. "We take the circus very seriously, Sheriff, even if it looks like fun and games to you."

"Sheriff Hatfield only meant it would be difficult for us to perform our duties with crowds coming in every evening," Jackson chimed in. "We still don't know if this is a crime or not, but if it is, we need the area to remain as clear as possible."

"Well stated, Deputy." Hatfield shot him a gracious glance.

"And if it was a crime, you wouldn't want anyone else injured, would you?" Adele asked.

Mr. Henley sniffed. "It isn't a crime — Miss Gossling?" She nodded. "Julius was no doubt careless with his timing. Trapeze acts are all about timing."

"How do you know they were careless?" Nin asked.

"I'm only guessing, of course," said the man. "I've watched these act for years, Sheriff. I've seen how many falls they take during practices."

"But this happened during a performance," Jackson pointed out.

"You believe it had something to do with the net?" Mr. Henley eyed him. "It's all over the circus, of course."

"I'm afraid we can't say anything until we have our expert examine it," the sheriff said.

"I've been in the circus twenty-seven years, Sheriff," said Mr. Henley. "Not once have I seen a performer die when it wasn't his own fault."

"I should think you're well acquainted with the performers in your duty as ringmaster," Hatfield said.

"Oh, I know them all right," he said.

"I assume you were also behind the curtain last night in between acts," Jackson began.

"I was on and off the ring like I always am," said Mr. Henley.

"You do your job very well, sir," Hatfield complimented. This seemed to ease the man's peaked eyebrows and he bowed with gratitude.

"Did you see to the trapeze act before it went on?" Jackson continued.

"Well — no." The man paused.

"One of the Tar little ones was ill," Mrs. Henley supplied.

"Tar?"

"The Ohlone family," said Mr. Henley. "They're part of Dan's show."

"I see," said Jackson.

"The boy had some kind of attack," the man continued. "I was in their tent helping to calm him."

"And I was helping to calm the mother," Mrs. Henley added.

"Can a doctor verify that?" asked Hatfield.

"There was no doctor, Sheriff," said the man. "The Ohlone prefer to take care of their own."

"They have knowledge of the healing arts," Nin said knowingly.

"I suppose so, Miss Branch," Mr. Henley said. "I've never seen them fail yet."

"Better than some of the medical men we've called in." Mrs. Henley smiled.

"You were there until you had to announce the trapeze act?" Jackson inquired.

"I was almost late getting back into the ring," said the man. "Paul will verify that. I got reprimanded good and proper for it."

Hatfield nodded. "We understand Mr. Rowe wasn't very well liked here."

"His ego got the best of him," Mr. Henley agreed. "The ladies didn't mind, but the men did."

"Did he try to flirt with you, Mrs. Henley?" Nin asked in her coarse way.

"That's rather indiscreet, Miss Branch," Jackson mumbled.

"I'm only asking what's on your mind, Mr. Gossling," she retorted.

But the Henleys didn't seem put out. They both laughed. "He did when he first came," Mrs. Henley said. "Lester and I had a good chuckle over it."

"Then you weren't concerned for your wife?" Adele asked, enduring a glare from her brother.

The man reached for his wife's hand. "We've been married too long for either of us to have any suspicions of the other."

"Did Mr. Rowe say anything to either of you the night of the performance?" Hatfield asked.

"I was late, of course, so I didn't get a chance to exchange words with him," Mr. Henley said.

"We were behind the curtain just before his act while Lester was in the ring," Mrs. Henley said. "We didn't speak, though."

"What was his mood like?" asked Jackson.

"He was excited," she recalled. "Jumpy, even, I would say."

"More than usual?"

"Oh, yes," she said. "Julius didn't get excited before performances or even nervous."

"And yet he was excited that night?" Adele asked.

"Yes, and I thought it unusual," she admitted. "I don't want to offend any of you, but Arrojo is just a town like any other to us. It's not San Francisco or Sacramento."

"Nothing special and no special guests in the crowd." Hatfield nodded.

"I think he was planning on doing something," Mrs. Henley ventured. "I thought maybe it was the triple somersault he'd been working on all winter."

"He wasn't even close to perfecting that, dear," said her husband. "Paul forbade him to even try until next year."

"I know, but you know how Julius could be strong-willed."

"You mean pig-headed," Nin mumbled. This made the Henleys chuckle.

Hatfield rose. "We appreciate your being candid with us. One last question. Have either of you any ideas on who might have wanted to harm Mr. Rowe?"

"Paul, of course," Mr. Henley said.

"Why 'of course'?" Jackson asked.

"His flirtation with Estelle, naturally," Mr. Henley said.

"It's been a rumor around the circus for months," said Mrs. Henley.

"That may be all it was, though," said her husband. "Just a rumor."

The sheriff studied the woman for a moment. "You look like you're in touch with the fashions, ma'am."

Mrs. Henley was pleased. "Why, thank you, Sheriff. I do try to look my best."

"Would you consider this the latest fashion, then?" He produced the scarf.

The woman drew back a little. "If you're asking me if it's mine, the answer is no. My taste is a little more somber than that." She rose and opened a trunk where clothes in muted colors of brown, red, white, and gray lay.

"Who, then, in your troupe wears colors like these?" he asked.

She studied it. "It looks like it might be Estelle's style. Or Abby's." She reached her hand to touch it. "You know, I believe I might have seen something like it on one or both of them." She chuckled. "Abby and Estelle were once quite close."

Thank you again." Hatfield tipped his hat.

Mr. Henley paused in the doorway as Jackson helped the ladies down the rickety steps. "May I ask who you're going to see next, Sheriff?"

"We'd like to see the Call sisters," he said. "They were the only ones with Mr. Rowe, in a manner of speaking at the time of his death. They may be able to shed some light on all this."

"May I suggest you wait until tomorrow morning?" the man asked. "They've taken this rather hard."

Jackson was clearly put out. "We must gather all the evidence we can as soon as possible, sir."

"I realize that," Mr. Henley grumbled.

"It's only that they've been very upset," Mrs. Henley chimed in. "Helen especially. She isn't strong, Sheriff. Last night —" She bit her lip.

"We found her near the tiger's cage," Mr. Henley said quietly.

"She had her hand on the door. Thank God it was locked, and she had no key She's — she's not quite herself."

Adele felt a tug at her heart. "We all need a good night's sleep, Sheriff."

"She'll have recovered by then," Nin assured.

Hatfield glanced at them, and his own face softened as he nodded.

CHAPTER 8

*T*he sun rose very early the next morning. Adele felt the heat blanketing her as she readied for their excursion to the circus.

They all arrived just as the troupe was having its breakfast. The cookhouse tent was even larger than the big top and more lavish with tables and chairs and trays where warm food sat.

They found the Call sisters in a corner table a little apart from the rest. "We wanted to be alone," Abby explained. "It's not easy for us."

"I imagine so." Hatfield sat down, his bulk filling the small folded chair. "We're sorry for your loss."

"He was smashed, smashed!" Helen uttered, her fork shaking in her hand.

Her sister put her arm around her. "I've told you, darling, it's the chance we take."

"Not my chance!" the girl screeched. "Not mine."

"Helen, I think you ought to go rest," Abby said.

"No." Her countenance calmed. "No, I want to help the police."

"You don't seem as affected by your partner's death, Abby," Adele remarked.

The woman brushed the dirty-blond strands of hair that had fallen into her eyes. "Helen and I have an act to work on. That's where my priorities lie. It's tragic what happened to Julius, but nothing will bring him back."

"The show must go on?" Jackson asked with a little irony.

The woman looked at him with fierce eyes. "We can't disappoint our audience, Deputy."

Hatfield leaned forward. "You got on well with Mr. Rowe?"

"We wouldn't have stayed with Julius for nine years if we hadn't."

"It seems odd, if you'll pardon my saying so, that he would have chosen two women to join his act," Jackson remarked. "I shouldn't think women would have, well, as much courage for it, for lack of a better word." He earned a glare from both his sister and Nin.

Abby gave him a crooked smile. "Many women have taken to the trapeze in the last years, though it has little to do with courage."

"And I'm not a flyer," Helen chimed in. "I'm a catcher."

"You'll be flying soon, dear." Her sister patted her hand. Adele did not miss the shudder that went down the young woman.

"You knew Mr. Rowe for nine years, then?" the sheriff asked.

"Longer than that," she said. "His mother was the one who got me interested in the trapeze."

"Indeed?" Adele asked.

Abby smiled. "She was a lovely woman and very skilled. Our parents were constantly trying to come up with new acts, you see and —" She stopped.

"They didn't have much time for you," Adele finished. "I should think that would make you want to leave the circus."

Abby shook her head. "I got my first taste of the trapeze when I was sixteen, and it was like magic."

"You weren't afraid?" Nin ventured.

The woman looked at her with surprise. "Circus people learn to ignore fear, Miss Branch."

"One can't ignore life or death," Nin retorted.

"She's right, Abby." Helen's voice ripped through the now nearly empty tent. "You can't erase death!"

"Dear," her sister said with patience, "I really think you ought to go to the wagon."

"No!" The girl's voice was determined. "I have a right to stay here unless the police send me away."

"They won't send you away." Adele glanced at Hatfield, who gave her a sign to continue, as he usually did when it was time to interview sensitive ladies. "Was it like magic for you too, Helen?"

She glanced uneasily at her sister.

"Naturally," Abby answered. "We were both born to it."

"You didn't give her much choice, did you?" Nin eyed her.

"We're a sister act, Miss Branch," Abby said with her fierce gaze. "I promised my parents when they died that we would always remain together. Helen understands that."

"Yes," her sister said in a vague tone. "I understand that."

Adele turned to Helen again. "How did you feel about Mr. Rowe?"

The girl blinked. "Feel? I don't think I felt anything." She looked at her sister with wild eyes. "I'm frightened. So frightened!"

"It will pass, darling," said Abby in a soothing tone.

"He never tried to flirt with you?" Nin asked.

"Certainly not!" Helen gave her a horrified look.

"He knows what your sister would have done to him if he had," Nin said, looking at Abby.

"Julius was always a gentleman to both of us," Abby insisted. "People don't think circus performers are ladies and gentlemen, but we are."

"You hated him," Nin declared. The conviction in her voice made even Jackson sit up.

"You've no cause to say such a thing," the woman snapped. "We had a mutual respect for one another."

"Unlike his 'respect' for other women in the circus?" Adele asked.

Abby grimaced. "No man can respect a woman who so easily gives in to his charms, Miss Gossling."

"He was always getting money from them," Helen piped up.

"And you had little respect for those women?" Adele glanced at Abby.

"I'm not a folding flower, Miss Gossling." She regarded her with even eyes. "From what I've heard, neither are you."

"Then we understand one another," Adele challenged.

"Yes, I think we do," the woman said quietly.

Adele turned to Helen. "Were you aware Julius was unsatisfied with your performance?"

Abby's eyes lit up."How dare you!"

"We went to see the Barrys in Caton, and Mr. Rowe was complaining about something your sister did," Adele said.

"I don't always do things well," Helen admitted. "Abby says you have to have an understanding of the circus. Maybe I haven't enough understanding."

"Nonsense!" her sister insisted. "You have as much understanding as I do. You'll see when — well, you'll see."

"I'm sorry if I made you feel uncomfortable." Adele felt genuinely humbled by these two women who were clearly still reeling from the death of their partner.

"I'm sure the police have to know these things," Abby said. "Though what *your* interest is, I can't imagine."

The sheriff intervened, "Miss Gossling helps us with our inquiries."

"A lady detective?" Helen's eyes widened.

"Why not?" Nin growled. "If we can fly in the air, we can dodge bullets, can't we?"

"But you're not dodging bullets, are you, Adele?" Abby eyed her. "You're trying to make an accident into murder."

"I'm not trying to do anything," Adele said in a sharp tone, "except perhaps prevent someone else from being killed."

"Circus people are God-fearing people," Abby said. "We have faith whatever happens to us is God's will and nothing else."

"The net didn't catch him, Abby," Helen piped up. "Do you call that God's will?"

"Nets get old, dear," said her sister in a soothing tone. "I'm sure Paul is taking care that it won't happen again."

"Especially since he just renewed your contract," Nin chimed in. "It wouldn't do to have another flyer fall to her death."

Helen shrieked and her sister put her arms around her.

"That was insensitive, Miss Branch," Jackson hissed.

"But it's true, it's true!" Helen sobbed.

"Helen, darling, nothing is going to happen to us." Her sister's voice was so soothing that even Hatfield looked at her.

"You seem certain of that," Adele said softly.

"We have a whole new act planned," she said. "We'll be taking extra precautions from now on. Believe me, nothing will happen."

"Because the one who may have killed Mr. Rowe won't try to kill you?" Adele eyed her.

"Nobody tried to kill Julius!" Abby fired. "His timing was off and he fell into a faulty net."

"How simple you make it sound," Adele said softly.

For the first time, a flicker of fear crossed the woman's face. But when she spoke, her tone was light. "I hope we've answered all your questions and I can take my sister back to our wagon where she belongs."

"Almost all my questions," Adele said. The sheriff handed her the scarf. "Does this belong to either of you?"

Adele saw a change in Abby's face. Her cheekbones became sharper and her eyes more alert. "Why, where did you get that?"

"We found it behind the curtain," Hatfield answered.

"My but the police are thorough," she remarked. "Did you dig into the sawdust and the refuse too?"

"Please answer the question, Miss Call," Jackson said.

"It looks like a scarf I gave Estelle last summer," she said. "I'm sure she told you that, though."

"Mrs. Barry told us she didn't recognize it," Jackson said.

"How interesting," Abby said. "I gave it to her as a birthday present. Didn't I, dear?" She glanced at her sister.

Helen slowly nodded.

"Why would she lie about it?" Adele asked.

"I'm sure I don't know," said the woman. "I saw her wearing it on opening night when she was talking to Julius."

"Talking to Mr. Rowe?" Jackson asked.

A slow smile spread on her lips. "You must have heard from others here that she and Julius were having an affair."

"Abby!" Helen's cheeks turned red.

"It's true, dear. We all know it," she said.

"Mr. Rowe told you that?" the sheriff asked.

"He didn't have to," said Abby. "She looked like a lovesick cow whenever he passed by."

"She did come to watch us rehearse more lately," Helen admitted.

"Did her husband have any idea of this affair?" Jackson asked.

"Why don't you ask him, Sheriff?" She rose. "I really think I ought to take my sister to the wagon now." She took Helen's arm and the girl rose.

As the sisters made their way to the door, Abby supporting Helen, who seemed to move with trepidation, Abby called out, "Estelle is looking for a savior, you know. Women like her always do."

They left, the wind pushing against the walls of the tent.

"I don't know as I could believe someone like Mrs. Barry could commit murder," Jackson said to his superior.

"I agree it seems unlikely," Hatfield said, "but her husband might if he had found out about the affair."

"Kill his star performer?" Adele asked. "That seems equally unlikely to me."

"A performer is easy to replace," Jackson argued. "A wife isn't."

"I'm glad you think so, Deputy," Hatfield said dryly.

Adele noticed her friend had moved to the edge of the tent, her hands spread out as if resting on an imaginary table. Her face was white as it sometimes became after one of her auras had gone through her.

"It's a tapestry of trouble," Nin said in a low voice.

"What is?" Adele took hold of her shoulders.

"This place," she said. "Not this tent, but this entire place."

"Let's hope it won't unravel in front of us before we can solve it," Adele said.

CHAPTER 9

*A*s breakfast was over, they went to question the Wild West show people next. Mr. Patton was outside near the big tent in a makeshift corral guiding a few men dressed in cowboy gear who were lassoing hogs. He was what Adele expected: a Buffalo Bill type with tall, lanky limbs and a well-worn face. His attitude reminded her of Mr. Abbott, the owner of the Arrojo Finance Company, whom Nin called "the wooden beaver."

"Good morning, Mr. Patton." Hatfield tipped his hat.

The man did not even glance up as he continued to distribute instructions to one of the cowboys.

"The sheriff is speaking to you, sir." Jackson's tone was authoritative. "You best answer."

Mr Patton looked at them over his shoulder, then turned back to the cowboy and finished his instructions before he hung the rope on the gate and approached them. "My apologizes, Sheriff," he said, though he sounded anything but apologetic. "Hogs won't wait, you know."

"I'm afraid I don't know," said Hatfield. "I've been a seaman and a lawman and even a Wells Fargo detective, but never a rancher."

"Wells Fargo!" The man who had been helping him with the hog grinned. "Did you hear that, Dan?"

"You best get on with your work, Ernie," said his superior.

"But, Dan, we got coming in —"

"I know what we've got coming in, Ernie," said Mr. Patton. "Get on with your work, I said."

The man sniveled a little but left.

"I'm glad you find my time with Wells Fargo impressive," Hatfield mumbled.

"He did. I don't," Mr. Patton said. "Paul told me to expect you. We can talk over here." He nodded toward the wooden benches around the ring.

"We'll want to speak with your crew as well," the sheriff said.

The man stopped. "I don't know as I can allow that."

"It's not a request, sir," Jackson said.

The man's lengthy hair blew back in the wind, and Adele saw the muscles on the back of his neck tighten. "Paul instructed us to cooperate with you, so I suppose I have no choice."

Hatfield glanced at Jackson as they settled on the wooden benches. "How well did you know Mr. Rowe?"

"Not very," the man said. "He barely spoke to me or our people. He considered our show a necessarily evil, given the fashion of Wild West shows these days."

"But you considered your show a main attraction?" Adele suggested.

He glared at her. "I don't approve of ladies involving themselves in men's business."

"That's rather hypocritical," Nin snapped, "considering your show features a woman billed as the next Annie Oakley."

A pert young lady appeared dressed in a cowgirl's uniform. "Dan, why didn't you call me?"

"Go back to your practice, Cora," he said.

Adele glanced at her. "Funny we were just talking about you, Miss —"

"Call me Cora," she said.

"It's good you've come." Adele made room for the woman next to her.

"Miss Dodds isn't involved in any of this," Dan insisted. "Why don't you just ask me what you want to ask me, Sheriff?"

"Which is?"

"Where was I when Julius had his accident."

"We're not sure it was an accident, sir," the sheriff said.

Beside her, Adele heard Cora's sharp intake of breath.

"I was here," said the man. "Helping to get the horses ready."

"I should think that would be the responsibility of your crew," Jackson said.

"You mean the head man doesn't do the dirty work?" Dan grimaced. "That might be the way it is with the police, Deputy, but I always look after everyone in my show personally, human and animal."

"Dan cares about his people," Cora said softly.

"We heard there was some kind of problem with the Tars," Hatfield said.

"Little Gabriel was ill." Dan nodded.

"Gabriel?"

The man smiled. "These people, whatever is left of them, live more like the Mexicans than they do like the Indians, Sheriff."

"What was wrong with him?" Adele asked.

"Had a swim in that pond where the swampland is outside of town," he said. "Some sort of parasite, I reckon."

"I'm glad you're telling us." Sheriff Hatfield gave Jackson a meaningful look. "We'll have it seen to."

"Poor boy," Nin murmured.

"He'll be all right in a day or two," Mr. Patton assured her. "The Tars know what they're doing."

Adele turned to the cowgirl. "Were you with them, Cora?"

"I wanted to go, but Dan didn't think it was a good idea." She glanced at him. "He's very protective of me."

"So we see," Nin said.

"We're engaged to be married, you see." Cora smiled and took his hand.

"It wasn't a pretty sight," the man mumbled.

"Where were you, then?" Jackson asked.

The man was on his feet. "Look here —"

"We're asking everyone these question, Mr. Patton," Hatfield said. "I suggest you sit down."

Mr. Patton sank back onto the bench.

"I've nothing to hide," said the young woman. "I was helping Warren and Harriet with the elephants." She smiled. "They get a little touchy after they've been on stage."

"The elephants or Warren and Harriet?" Nin asked.

Her genuine question earned a laugh from Cora and even Dan's caution broke and he chuckled. "The Youngs don't always see eye to eye on how the performance should go. There's always a fight afterward unless someone is there to distract them."

"You spent the entire time with the Youngs?" Jackson asked.

The woman looked uncomfortable, playing with her skirt fringes. "Well, no. I caught the last half of the trapeze act." She turned pale. "Oh, it was horrible to see Julius fall like that!"

Adele covered her hand. "You liked him?"

"He could say things that made you feel as if he saw something in you no one else did," she said in a choking voice.

"Some men have that power," Jackson remarked.

"Fiddlesticks!" Dan growled.

"Oh, Dan!" The woman leapt up and ran out of the tent.

The man looked genuinely distressed. "I shouldn't have said that. I didn't like the man, but I shouldn't have said that."

"I'm afraid to have to ask you this, but we know Mr. Rowe liked the ladies," Sheriff Hatfield said briskly. "Was your fiancée one of them?"

Adele expected the man to get huffy again but, to her surprise, he answered very calmly, "He flattered Cora like the rest, if that's what you mean."

"Is that what made you start the fight with him in the cookhouse?" Jackson inquired.

Dan gave a twisted smile. "I see you heard about that."

"Is it true?" the sheriff asked.

"Yes, but it's not what you think," he said. "I roughed him up a little, I'll admit."

"I'm sure he had it coming to him," Nin said.

"Indeed he did, Miss Branch," said Dan, relaxing a little more. "But there were no hard feelings. In fact, we made up later."

"Made up?" asked Adele.

"Julius — well, he had his faults, but he was also a man to admit when he'd done wrong. He came to me later and admitted he shouldn't have started up with Cora, her being so young and us being in love." Here, he turned a little pink. "He promised he would leave her alone from now on."

"And you believed him?" Jackson asked.

"I haven't run a troupe of fifteen people for twelve years without knowing how to judge a man's character, Deputy."

"Can anyone verify this, sir?" asked the sheriff. "Anyone see you two talking on friendly terms, for example?"

"Cora, of course," he said. "And some of my troupe, I imagine. You can ask them, if you like. It wasn't as if we were hiding it."

"So you parted, so to speak, as friends," Adele concluded.

The man flinched, as if the idea of parting from a friend because the man broke his neck carried some kind of bad omen.

CHAPTER 10

*B*efore they left, the sheriff turned to Dan. "Mr. Patton, it occurs to me you might be able to help us."

The man was surprised. "What can I do, Sheriff?"

"I'm having an expert come and take a look at that net," Hatfield said.

"So you're going on the theory that it wasn't an accident?" Dan stared. "You're barking up the wrong tree, as they say, Sheriff."

"Perhaps we are, sir," he said. "But I imagine you know something about ropes."

"That I do," Dan said.

"Will you come to the big top and take a look at it with us?" he asked. "Give us your opinion?"

"If you wish, Sheriff," he said, though he sounded anything but happy to oblige.

They entered the tent, and Hatfield spread the net where Julius's body had fallen. As Dan inspected it, his ornery countenance eased.

"I see now why you think Julius's death might not have been an accident," he said.

"Then you agree the net doesn't look right?" asked Jackson.

"As much as I know about such things, Deputy," he said. "I'd say these gaps weren't made by wear and tear."

"You think someone cut them?" Adele asked.

"There's no doubt in my mind," he said. "Of course, as I said, I'm not an expert on nets." He laid the net against his hand. "See this gap? The fibers here are smooth. You don't get that from wear and tear."

"They would have been frayed." Hatfield nodded.

"Can you tell us what weapon was used, sir?" Jackson asked.

The man looked at him oddly. "Would that matter?"

"It might," said the deputy.

"Some kind of knife, I think," he said. "Serrated, I would say."

"Serrated?" Nin asked.

"A knife that looks like a saw." The man grinned. "Like this one." He pulled a knife out of his belt. It gleamed under the sunlight penetrating the thin walls of the tent. "Not many of them around, really. Most are skinning knives."

"All of your cowboys carry knives like that?" the sheriff asked.

"No, sir." The man was firm. "Theirs are just for show. I don't allow my people to work with real weapons. Even the guns have blanks in them."

"Very sensible," Jackson said. "So yours is the only one that's real."

It took a moment for the man to realize the suggestive tone in the deputy's voice. He dropped the edge of the net as if it were on fire. "If you think —"

"In spite of what people believe," Hatfield said, "the police don't accuse every person they meet of a crime. Do they, Deputy?" He glared at Jackson.

"No, Sheriff." Jackson sounded almost humble.

Nin gave a half-smile. Adele, feeling sorry to see her brother squirm, said quickly, "I think what Jack was trying to say is if the net was cut with a serrated blade someone could have taken your knife and used it."

The man calmed down. "They could have. We don't lock our wagons when there is no crowd about."

"May I see the knife, Mr. Patton?" Sheriff Hatfield ventured.

"I've nothing to hide." The man handed it to him.

The sheriff examined it closely. "Looks clean."

"I told you, Sheriff, it's only for show," said the man as he slid it back on his belt. "If you don't need me any further, I'd like to check on my fiancée."

"Certainly, sir," said the sheriff. "We appreciate your help."

"Are you willing to testify about the net if we should need you at the trial?" Jackson asked.

"Only if I'm there as a witness and not as the accused," the man said dryly.

"At least now we can justify the expense of bringing Abe in," Hatfield remarked when Dan had gone.

Her brother's face went rigid as he stared behind her. Adele turned around. A man dressed in a shabby suit with familiar hazel eyes had slipped in.

"Why, Mr. Sipes!"

Jackson was as quick as a gazelle and as the man tried to escape, he lunged at him and grabbed him by the shoulders. Adele heard a snap and realized her brother had put the handcuffs on him.

"Do you mind explaining what you're doing, Deputy?" Hatfield spoke in his mild-mannered tone.

"This man has the audacity to return here, sir."

"But he hasn't returned," Nin insisted. "He's here with the circus."

Hatfield looked both annoyed and amused. "I would be much obliged if you would remember we only use handcuffs on people who have actually committed a crime."

"But, sir —"

"I believe Miss Branch is right," the sheriff continued. "Mr. Sipes, I'm sure, can account for his presence here?"

"Indeed I can, Sheriff," Mr. Sipes said in a weak voice.

"Well, sir, what have you to say for yourself?"

"I've been with this circus for the last eight months, on my honor." Mr. Sipes shook his arms as if trying to free himself of the cuffs. "Mr. Barry knows of my unfortunate past. You may ask him if you wish."

"And your cat?" Adele asked. "Still golden and performing for the King of England?"

"Alas, dear lady, the police took Sinbad away from me." The man glanced at her with sorrow. "He tried to escape to get back to me and they shot him down."

"I'm sorry to hear that," said Adele.

"What do you do here, Mr. Sipes?" Hatfield asked.

"My duties here are harmless, Sheriff," said the man. "I help take care of the cats for Mr. Verner's act."

"In other words, you feed and clean up after them," Nin remarked.

"A crude way of putting it, Miss Branch, but I suppose it amounts to that." He winced.

"I'm satisfied with Mr. Sipes' explanation, Jackson," said Hatfield. "We'll check with the Barrys, of course, but I think the man has been cuffed long enough."

Jackson unlocked the manacles and shoved the man away, making him collapse on the ground. Both Adele and Nin helped him up.

"Thank you, dear ladies." He tipped his hat to them. "You're kind to help a poor misfortunate soul like me. As for you, sir," he glared at Jackson, "you may be a lawman, but you're no gentleman."

The stormy look on Jackson's face made the sheriff give him a warning look. Jackson shoved his hands in his pockets. "Who is Mr. Verner?"

"Verner the Great," Mr. Sipes dictated, "the man who turns lions and tigers into pussycats."

"I expect they stay well-hidden until it's their turn to perform," Adele said.

"As a matter of fact, we're backstage most of the time," said Mr. Sipes. "The animals can be, well, a little difficult to call to cue, if you know what I mean. Once we get them preened for the act, it's difficult to keep their attention, and as Mr. Barry is ever so strict about timing —"

"We have more interviews, then, Jackson," said the sheriff. "We'll start with you, Mr. Sipes. What do you think about this business with Mr. Rowe?"

"Ghastly, sir, simply ghastly!"

"Have you any idea who might be responsible?" Adele asked.

"Not a clue, my dear lady," he said. "I didn't know the fellow, you see. Our paths, shall we say, never crossed."

"I can imagine," said Jackson. "He was in the air and you were in the muck with the cats."

"Exactly, Deputy," said the man, grinning. "So you see, I couldn't have had anything to do with it."

The sheriff chuckled. "All right, Mr. Sipes, you may go. But, as they say, keep your nose clean."

The man bowed gratefully and hurried out of the tent.

CHAPTER 11

*A*s they headed toward the animal tent, Jackson said, "I don't think we'll get much out of these people, Sheriff. I expect they were more concerned about their animals than anything else."

"You never can tell what they might have seen," Hatfield insisted.

"You ask one set of questions and we ask another," Adele said. "Between us, we can get to the bottom of Julius Rowe's murder."

"So you've decided it's murder, have you, Del?" Her brother eyed her.

"Haven't you?" she countered. "Mr. Patton confirms what the sheriff believes. That net was cut deliberately so Mr. Rowe would be killed in his fall."

"If it was murder, how could the murderer know Mr. Rowe would fall?" her brother countered.

"That's a question mark we'll need to answer, Deputy," said the sheriff. "First, we need to determine the net was indeed tampered with. We'll know for sure when we get an expert's opinion."

"When will Mr. Evans get here?" Adele asked.

"His telegram said tomorrow morning first thing," Jackson said.

"And Abe is always true to his word," Hatfield said. "In the meantime, we can make a little headway with our inquiries."

"All we've gotten so far is scraps from people who seem capable of ignoring details," Jackson growled.

"Can you blame them, Jack?" Adele asked. "Opening night, dangerous acts and fussy animals to worry about... one wrong move and one could — well, one could lose one's life." She shivered, thinking again of the way Mr. Rowe's body had fallen.

"Chaos is hardly conducive to details, Mr. Gossling," Nin pointed out.

"It's chaos to us, Miss Branch, but not to them," he said. "I should think they would notice if *something* was off."

"Like a cut net?" Hatfield asked with a crooked smile.

"Or a man's odd behavior," Adele said. "We've already heard Mr. Rowe wasn't quite himself that night."

"It might not have anything to do with his death," Nin pointed out.

"We've also heard Calvin Barry wasn't himself," Adele continued. "They were both behaving peculiarly." She eyed the sheriff. "You think there might be a connection, Sheriff?"

"What do *you* think, Adele?" He eyed her back.

"I think you ought to talk to Calvin again," she said.

"He was hiding something." Nin nodded as they entered the animal tent.

Adele caught sight of a man in a Viking uniform, a whip in hand. He had beady eyes and a long handlebar mustache.

"Verner the Great," she said in a low voice.

The man approached a cage where two growling lions sat. They rose and showed their teeth. He called to them, cracking his whip. "Alex! Venus! Come now, we have guests. Bow to the ladies." He uttered a few more cries in what sounded like

German, cracked his whip, and to Adele's amazement, the animals bowed their heads in unison.

"Very impressive, sir," Hatfield remarked.

"It's cruel!" Nin burst out.

"I assure you, Miss —"

"Branch," she said.

"Oh, yes, the mesmerizer in this godforsaken town."

"I am *not* a mesmerizer!" Nin's face grew savage.

"My friend is a clairvoyant with a rare gift," Adele insisted.

The man cleared his throat. "This whip is only for show. I never touch a hair on any of my cats' heads."

"Then why are they looking at you as if they would gladly eat you alive?" Nin asked.

"That, my dear, is because they're still wild animals," he said promptly. "One may train a lion or a tiger, to be sure. But one may never tame them."

"How long has Mr. Sipes been with you?" Jackson inquired.

"Less than a year," Mr. Verner answered. "He's a good mucking out man, but no more."

"He's made his living honestly all that time?"

"Jack, leave the man alone," Adele insisted.

Mr. Verner's mustache spread with a smile. "You're referring to Mr. Sipes' rather shady past, aren't you?"

"You know about it?" Adele asked.

"But of course," he said. "He told me right away. I give the man credit for his honesty."

"And you don't mind?" Jackson ventured.

The man gave him a stern look. "The circus accepts all people if they have something to contribute. I myself came here with no connections and barely a word of English on my lips, and now, as you can see, my act is one of the highlights of the show."

"Indeed it is, sir," Adele said, smiling.

"One cannot judge one's present by one's past," he said with a bow.

"Unless that past includes a violation of the law," said Hatfield in a hard voice. "One must accept the consequences of a shadow following one's dirty deeds."

"Perhaps you're right, Sheriff." The man shrugged. "At any rate, it was the Barrys who hired him, not me."

"While we're speaking of the show," said Hatfield, "did you notice anything unusual the night of your performance here?"

"You mean when Julius fell to his death?" The man sighed. "Ah, a sad thing." He played with the edge of the whip.

"Answer the question please, sir." Adele could tell Jackson had lost patience with the hemming and hawing of circus folk.

"There was one odd thing, I suppose. I almost ran into Mrs. Barry. Literally, that is."

"Oh?"

"She's usually hidden on opening night just before we go on," he said. "She doesn't like the roaring of the cats, you see."

"But she was here?"

"Well, around here," said the man. "I always go around the back to get to the big top to avoid the crowds. It was quite dark, I grant you. But I know it was her I ran into." His brows knitted. "She looked rather disturbed."

"Disturbed?" Adele asked.

"I imagine it was because of the cats," he said. "Oh, they make a fuss before they go on, rather like children being put to bed. But they calm down once they're in the ring."

"I'm glad to hear it," said the sheriff dryly. "Thank you for your time, sir. Sorry to keep you away from your cats."

"No trouble, Sheriff." The man smiled. "As you can see, my cats are quite docile."

When they emerged from the animal tent, a large wheelbarrow piled high with straw pushed at Adele's skirt. "Excuse me!" a voice croaked.

"I beg your pardon." Adele moved aside.

She saw a woman with large muscles pushing the wheelbarrow. Her countenance was plain but womanly even though she was dressed in a man's shirt and trousers.

"You must be as strong as an ox!" Nin said.

The woman looked proud. "You bet I am!"

"Are you the strong woman act?" Adele asked.

"Strong woman!" she growled. "That's nothing but a freak show. It ain't dignified."

"But pushing a wheelbarrow is?" Jackson asked.

"We can't all be lawyers or bankers, Jack," Adele snapped. "Or even detectives." She gave him a satisfied look.

"Oh, you're the police!" The woman rested the wheelbarrow on the ground. "Word's gotten around you're asking questions. Well, I'll save you time. My name's Geraldine Cowell, I help with the animals, and I didn't know Julius!"

"I see you've been well informed," Jackson said.

"As I said, word gets around," sniffed Geraldine, "and we look out for our own here."

"Including shielding one another from police inquiries?" Hatfield asked.

"We're all trying to do our duty, just as you are, Sheriff," she said.

The sheriff glanced at the wheelbarrow. "I suppose you wouldn't have any connection with the trapeze act."

"I know Abby all right," she said. "She's a right nice lady. She knows what I'm about."

"And what are you about, Geraldine?" asked Adele.

"Call me Gerry," the woman said. "I got ideas, let's just say. I won't be shoveling manure all my life."

"Think yourself rather fine, don't you?" Jackson eyed her.

"Why shouldn't I?" She glared at him. "I'm not like the pigs around here. I can't even eat in front of them. I take my meals outside so I don't get sick watching them."

"You're friendly with Miss Call but you weren't with Mr. Rowe?" the sheriff asked.

"*He* never gave me a second look. Not young or pretty enough." There was self-satisfaction in her voice.

"Lucky for you," Nin remarked.

"It sure was!" The woman laughed. "For him too. I would have given him something to regret if he had paid the least bit of attention to me."

"A woman with some definite ideas," Jackson remarked as they watched her trudge into the animal tent.

"I can't see she would have anything to do with this case," Hatfield said as he lowered his hat further over his forehead. "Most of them don't, I should say. It's a shame they weren't more observant."

"You'll find out what happened, Sheriff," Adele said kindly. "You always do."

He bowed. "We're almost through here," he said. "We have only Miss Clara Spore left."

"I doubt that will give us much," Jackson said.

"Nevertheless, no stone unturned, Deputy," said his employer.

Clara's wagon was near the entrance to the park and looked smaller than the others. Adele thought this odd for such an important act, but when they entered, she saw why. Clara was a tiny thing, no bigger than one of the Wrigley girls. But she was beautifully proportioned and slim as a reed.

"Miss Spore, we hope you can help us resolve this case quickly," Hatfield said as he leaned against the wagon wall. He looked like Gulliver entering the land of the Lilliputians.

"I don't see how." The woman sat in front of the mirror and started to put her hair up in pins. "I hardly knew Mr. Rowe."

"But your act went on before the trapeze," said Jackson. "You may have been the last one to see Mr. Rowe alive, other than his partners during the act, of course."

"I'll do what I can, of course," she said.

"Miss Spore, have you any enemies?"

Clara gazed up at the sheriff. "Why do you want to know?"

Adele could tell Hatfield was deliberating whether he should answer her question or not. His brows gathered with troubled indecision. Finally, he said, "We must tell you, Miss Spore, we think Mr. Rowe's death was not entirely accidental."

"Wasn't it?" the woman echoed.

"We think he died because of a faulty net," Jackson said.

"Faulty net?"

"There is evidence the net used during the trapeze act was cut," Adele said softly.

"Someone ruined it," Nin added.

Clara stared wide-eyed into the distance. Adele followed her gaze and saw she was looking at a rosary hanging from the wall on a nail. She gently unhooked it and held it out to her. "Would you like this?"

"Thank you." The woman took it in her hands. "It belonged to my father."

"Mementoes are very comforting," Adele agreed. She fished out the silk handkerchief with *O. G.* on it. "This was my father's." She heard Jackson clear this throat.

The woman smiled. "It's good you have that comfort." She looked at the sheriff again. "The net was cut, you say?"

"We still need to confirm that," the sheriff said quickly.

"You're thinking it might have already been cut when I went on because it was meant for me?"

"We're only exploring possibilities, Miss Spore," Jackson said.

"But it wasn't." She put the rosary on the table. "I know that for a fact."

"How do you know?" asked Hatfield.

"Because I saw Mr. Wharton checking it before I went on," she said. "He's a very kind man, always fretting over me like a father."

"Are you sure about that?" The sheriff leaned forward.

"I saw him." The woman was insistent now. "If there had been anything wrong with it, he never would have let it go into the ring. He's very careful."

"May I ask how long your act is?"

"Oh, ten or fifteen minutes, no more." She gave a little laugh. "I never really counted them!"

"You just pray your way through," Nin said.

The woman looked at her. "Yes. I suppose that's just what I do."

"You're afraid," Adele observed.

Clara ducked her head. "One isn't supposed to be afraid in the circus."

"No wonder Mr. Wharton is so careful with the net," the sheriff said softly.

Jackson, who was more business-like, asked, "How long in between your act and the trapeze?"

"Another ten or fifteen minutes," she said. "The clowns do their routine to calm the crowd. People get rather anxious watching two daredevils acts in a row."

"Very sensible." Hatfield nodded. "Is there anything you can tell us about that night?"

Clara's hand reached for the rosary as she stared into the distance again. "Mr. Barry broke a pencil."

"Do you mean Paul or Calvin Barry?" asked Adele.

"Cal," she said. "He had it right in his hand, and it snapped in two."

"Why is that strange?" asked Jackson.

"He wasn't supposed to be there," she said. "Not then, anyway."

Adele could see her brother was losing patience, so she took Clara's hand. "Be where?"

"Behind the curtain," she answered.

"But he told us he spends part of the time on opening night behind the scenes," the sheriff said.

"The first part," she said, "before the trapeze act. Not the second."

"Oh, I see." Adele nodded.

"He was pacing too," she said. "Like the lions in their cage."

"He was nervous," Nin murmured.

"He's usually so calm," Clara lamented.

"Thank you, Miss Spore." The sheriff held out his hand. Adele couldn't help noticing he looked like a lion himself, taking the hand of a mouse. "You've been a great help to us."

"It's awful to think —" She gazed up at him with worried eyes. "Please find out who did this."

"If anyone did anything," Jackson remarked when they had left the circus and were driving back into town. "The net still could have collapsed accidentally."

"At least now we know it was intact twenty or twenty-five minutes before the trapeze act went on," Hatfield said. "If it was tampered with, it must have been while the clowns were on."

"Curious that Calvin Barry was there," remarked Jackson.

"Question marks, question marks," the sheriff murmured, turning the corner into town.

CHAPTER 12

The next day, Adele convinced her brother to let her accompany him to the police station.

"I thought you had your work to do," he said in an arch tone.

"I rather dread work today," Adele admitted.

"Aren't you the one who's always telling me a businesswoman who turns away business doesn't stay in business for long?"

She pushed her coffee cup aside. "I'm trying to avoid the prying eyes of Mrs. Faderman and her brood."

"You mean their prying questions." Jackson could barely contain a grin. "The woman prefers to get details on our policing from you rather than us."

"That's not fair, Jack!" She put down the fork and knife and Tomas, standing in his usual determined position against the wall, winced. "You know I never tell her anything she can't get from the *Arrojo Courier*."

"Speaking of the *Courier*," he handed her the paper, "I see the circus people weren't exactly close-mouthed about our inquiries yesterday."

Adele glanced at the article. Missy Grace indeed had picked up on several points about their interviews she knew Hatfield would have wanted to keep silent. Her eye caught the following: *Mr. and Mrs. Barry are confident that, while Mr. Rowe's accident is being investigated, they will be allowed to entertain our community. Permission from the police is expected any day now.*

She pointed it out to her brother. "That's rather presumptuous, don't you think?"

"The sheriff won't be pleased," Jackson agreed. "He won't cave in to journalistic insinuations."

"Missy would never do that," Adele insisted. "She was only printing what she was told."

"Then she's misleading her readers." Jackson swept up the crumbs from the table with his napkin.

"It might not be such a bad thing," Adele said.

He stared at her. "You can't be serious, Del."

"They have to earn their living," she defended.

"With a possible killer on the loose?"

"We don't know that, Jack."

"We will today," he said. "Hatfield's friend Mr. Evans arrived last night."

"The rope expert?"

Jackson nodded, straightening his tie. "I'm meeting Hatfield at his house."

Adele rose. "We can pick up Nin on the way."

"We?"

"She won't want to work today either." Adele slipped on her jacket. "We're both curious to see that net again."

"I don't recall Hatfield inviting you," he said.

"I think it's safe to say that by now, Nin and I may invite ourselves," she insisted, clutching her parasol with resolve.

Her brother sighed. "How you got around his better judgment, I'll never know."

She smiled her most charming smile.

They arrived at the Hatfield house and ran into Mr. Dunham,

the sheriff's handyman and gardener, just coming out of the greenhouse, a bunch of petunias in his hands.

"The flowers are looking fine, Mr. Dunham," Adele complimented, glancing at the glass structure.

"Thank you, miss," he said. "I tend to them as if they were my own youngsters."

"I imagine the plants and flowers are much tamer than youngsters," Jackson remarked with a smile.

"Oh, you never can tell, Deputy," the man said. "Some of them are like wild cats."

"We've seen plenty of wild cats lately," Jackson said. "I'm sure the sheriff doesn't need them in his backyard."

Adele laughed and held out her hands. "I'll take those into Lady Augusta, Mr. Dunham."

"Thank you, miss." He handed them to her as if he were handling a delicate newborn.

Lady Augusta was as pleased to see her as she was the flowers. "We've missed you these past few days, my dear. Horatio!" She tapped at her son's shoe with her stick. "Invite Miss Gossling to dinner more often."

"Ma extends her invitation to come to dinner any time you please, Adele." The man bowed.

"I'm sorry," she said. "I've had a lot to do in the shop lately."

"Good!" The woman nodded. "That's the way it ought to be with a woman who runs her own business."

"Should she also come home late for dinner every night?" Jackson mumbled.

Lady Augusta eyed her. "You ought to think about getting some help, my dear."

"That's what I've told her," Jackson said. "She can well afford it."

"It's not the money, is it?" Hatfield asked. "It's giving your duties away to someone else."

She couldn't look at him, feeling her face grow even rosier.

"Even an independent woman mustn't drive herself into an early grave." Lady Augusta took her hand.

"Who's going to their grave?" A man entered the parlor, his voice booming. He swept off his wide-brimmed hat. "Abe Evans, at your service!"

Adele had expected a stringy, wrinkled sort of man like many ex-seamen she had seen trailing the wharf in San Francisco in her settlement house days. But this man looked almost like one of the politicians in the caricatures. He was portly and rosy-cheeked with a wide smile, a bald head, and suspenders.

"My deputy, Abe." Hatfield clasped Jackson on the shoulder. "I had to persuade him to forgo a young man's leisurely life in San Francisco to stay here. And I don't mind saying in front of the ladies that I was damn lucky to get him."

"You don't do me justice, sir," Jackson mumbled, but Adele could see he was pleased.

"On the contrary," said Adele. "I think it's more than justified."

"You're a little one-sided, aren't you, my dear?" Lady Augusta winked.

Adele laughed. "Jackson's my brother, Mr. Evans."

"So you're the sleuthing woman Lady Augusta has been telling me about?" Mr. Evans pumped her hand. "I saw a policewoman in the newspaper once. She looked more frightening than her male counterparts!" He gave a jovial laugh. "But you're so dainty and lovely."

"Thank you, sir." Adele bowed, but inside, she was annoyed the man seemed more taken by her "daintiness and loveliness" than her help with the police.

"Glad you're here, old man." Hatfield pounded his shoulder in an amiable way. "We really need your help."

"I shouldn't wonder." Mr. Evans produced a folded *Arrojo Courier* from the pocket of his coat. "Says here there's been an accident."

"That's what we need you to tell us, sir," Jackson said.

"If anyone knows nets and ropes, it's Abe," Lady Augusta assured him, maneuvering her rolling chair aside so they could pass. "This man once saved Horatio from being shanghaied by undoing a very cleverly tied rope."

"You were shanghaied?" Jackson stared at his superior.

"A long story I shall tell you one day, Deputy," Hatfield said, but Adele could tell he was embarrassed. "Now we have other business to attend to."

They stopped in town to pick up Nin, who, as Adele predicted, was more than happy to accompany them.

Just as Adele and Nin snapped closed the last of the shutters, she caught sight of Mrs. Abberton and Mrs. Cricket coming out of Dora's Tea Shop, waving their parasols.

"Oh, Lord!" she murmured.

Her friend shoved her into the police car. "Drive!"

The three men sitting in the front looked bewildered.

"You heard her, Jack," Adele said.

Her brother hit the gas and the car puttered down the street. Adele glanced out the back window. The two ladies were still waving their parasols.

"I would give anything to hear what Mrs. Abberton is saying now," Adele said with a laugh.

"Probably words not fit for a decent lady's ears," her friend agreed.

"Do you mind telling us what this is all about?" Jackson asked in an irritated voice.

"I believe your sister is trying to dodge some rather emphatic ladies," Mr. Evans said.

Sheriff Hatfield roared with laughter. "They can be rather persistent and, er, demanding."

"As much as I hate to admit it, sir, we have a duty to tell the public what we know," Jackson reminded him.

"When we know, we'll tell them, Deputy," the sheriff said.

"Right now, we still don't know whether Julius Rowe was killed or died in an accident."

"Nasty business." Mr. Evans wrinkled his flat nose. "I imagine these circus people aren't too pleased about the whole thing."

"They insist it was one of those things," Hatfield said. "The net was old, the man miscalculated, he fell, the net ripped and he was killed. Simple as that."

"As I recall, Horatio, you were never satisfied with simple explanations." His friend grinned.

"He still isn't," Adele said with a laugh. "He's always chasing 'question marks.'"

"When a lawman stops asking questions, Miss Gossling, justice is lost," said Mr. Evans.

"And what about the woman who asks questions?" Adele eyed him.

"That, my dear, is one for the gods," the man said.

The circus atmosphere was less forlorn than it had been the day before. Trainers led animals around. Clowns practiced their acrobatics on the grass. Inside some of the smaller tents, people were rehearsing.

"These circus folk certainly bounce back quickly," she remarked.

"Why should they let anything stop them?" her friend inquired.

"I thought, after all that talk about their keeping to their own people, they would still be mourning," she admitted.

"Perhaps if it were someone else who died," Nin said. "No one seemed to like Mr. Rowe much. Except the ladies." The last she said with a sniff.

"And perhaps not even them," Adele said. "It's possible to be infatuated with someone without really liking them."

"Only if you know their real character," her friend said. "When women fall for a charlatan, they don't want to see the real character."

Assistant Deputy Dooland stood just outside the big top when they arrived. He had filled out since the year Hatfield promoted him from a temporary deputy to one of the force. He immediately came to attention at the sight of the sheriff.

"Anyone suspicious around here last night, Dooland?" he asked.

"No, indeed, Sheriff," said the young man. "You said no one was to go in and no one did."

"Did you patrol around just to make sure?" Jackson asked.

"Well — well, no, sir, you see, Assistant Deputy Moran —"

"What about Moran?" Jackson assumed the pose of the aggravated lawman.

"Well, he had some sort of quarrel with his girl and —"

"He came on duty late," Hatfield finished.

"Well, no, sir. The fact is, he didn't come at all." The boy turned red.

"You fool!" Jackson exploded. "Why didn't you get word to the station to send someone else?"

"Well, sir, I didn't hear the whole story until this morning," the young man said. "I thought he would come, and so I kept waiting for him."

"Don't be hard on the boy, Sheriff," Adele said. "How was he to know Moran would be so irresponsible?"

"I think we ought to give Moran a temporary deputy's badge." Jackson turned to the sheriff.

"You know how love guides a young man's folly," Hatfield said in a mild tone. "I'm willing to give him one more chance. Dooland, you may go now, but stop by the station and tell Edison I want Moran here as soon as possible, and he'd better plan on staying here the rest of the day."

"Yes, sir." There was a satisfied look on the man's face. "Ain't no room for a lawman who can't do his duty, eh, Sheriff?"

"Nor one who judges another lawman's duty." Hatfield eyed him. "Now, off you go, lad."

The young man scurried away.

Mr. Evans was shaking with laughter. "Worse than those scarecrows you had working for you on *The Augusta*, eh?"

"They'll learn," said his friend as he stood back to allow the ladies to enter.

The net was just where they had left it. Adele couldn't help but stare at the limp pile of threads, thinking how impossible it seemed they had proven to be so menacing.

It didn't take long before a piercing whistle came from Mr. Evans' lips.

"I was right, wasn't I?" Hatfield watched him.

"You're seldom wrong about these things, Horatio."

"Just this once, I was hoping to be." The sheriff sighed. "These people were so convinced it was an accident."

"No accident here," Mr. Evans said. "Just a cleverly disguised attempt to make people believe it was."

"How so, Mr. Evans?" Jackson asked.

"These are the cuts." He pointed to three places on the left side. "All anybody had to do was make those three small cuts. The weight of the fall would do the rest."

"One of the performers here who knows about ropes told us he thought a serrated knife was used," said the sheriff.

"I would agree," said the man. "I can't be entirely sure, of course, but from the jaggedness of the cuts, it fits."

"Someone knew what they were doing," Adele said.

"Indeed they did, Miss Gossling."

Hatfield sighed. "So now we know what we're dealing with."

"This puts a whole new light on things, doesn't it, Sheriff?" Jackson asked.

Nin had wandered away, as she sometimes did. Adele found her behind the velvet curtain just beyond the musician's platform. Her friend stood with hands pressed together, the wind from the loose tent flowing through her wild hair and billowing her skirt.

"You felt something?" Adele asked.

"Lead," her friend murmured.

"You said that when we were at the pub too." Adele took her arm.

"It's lead," Nin insisted. "I can feel the weight of it."

Adele gently poked around with the edge of her parasol. The ground was covered with the fluffy red dust that permeated the Arrojo streets. Patches of dry grass emerged now and then in her examination.

At the far corner of the tent, she felt a lump under her parasol. Moving away the dirt, she discovered two sticks, one of them with a sharp-edged point. She picked them up carefully with her gloved hands.

"Pencil lead," she breathed.

She slipped them into her purse. They emerged into the sunshine with the clouds making a magnificent roof over the white tents and colorful wagons. Hatfield was talking to Paul Barry.

"Sheriff, I thought you would see it from our point of view," Paul was saying as she and Nin approached.

"We must consider we're dealing now with a crime, not an accident," the sheriff answered.

"That's preposterous!"

"I will swear to it. There is no doubt about that net," Mr. Evans insisted. "It was cut sure as I'm standing here."

"And we know it was intact before the trapeze act went on," Jackson added.

"You only have Clara's word for that!" argued Paul.

"We asked Mr. Wharton to look at the net just now, and he confirmed the holes weren't there when he checked it before Miss Spore went out to the ring," Jackson said.

"I wouldn't entirely trust Wharton now," Paul growled.

"He was damn sure about it, sir." Mr. Evans was clearly impatient. "It's all right under your nose!"

"Steady, Abe." The sheriff gave him a cautious look.

"Be that as it may," the man said, "this is our livelihood. We've already lost two days. It might not seem like much to you, two days, but with the performers and crew to pay and the animals to be fed —"

"What exactly is the problem?" Adele asked.

Sheriff Hatfield moved his hat forward to block the sun. "Mr. Barry wants us to allow his troupe to continue putting on their show while they're here in Arrojo."

"I don't think it's an unreasonable request," Paul insisted.

Jackson stared at the circus owner. "Don't you realize, sir, there's a killer loose amongst your people?"

"If someone killed Julius, and I'm not convinced someone did —" the man gave the sheriff a meaningful look, "it has nothing to do with the rest of us."

"What about your other performers?" Adele questioned.

"Don't you care they might get hurt?" Nin growled.

The man stiffened. "My performers are all professionals, Miss Branch. They know how to handle themselves, and they're anxious to work."

"The idea of going on when there's a murderer running about —" Mr. Evans shook his head. "Why, it's morbid!"

"But very practical." Adele turned to Hatfield. "Sheriff, what if the Barry Circus were allowed to continue with just the safe acts, like the elephants and dogs and clowns?"

"People could still enjoy the circus without fear of watching anyone plunge to their death," Nin added.

Hatfield rubbed his chin, his eyes falling on a pair of plumed horses that an equestrian was leading toward one of the smaller tents.

"Would that help you with your bottom line, sir?" he asked.

Paul was clearly displeased, but he said, "It sure would, Sheriff."

"I'll need my deputies to patrol the crowds," he insisted, "just in case."

"In case of nothing!" Paul growled. "They'll stick out like sore thumbs and make my performers nervous."

"You keep saying they're professionals," Adele said. "I should think professionals are used to all manner of people scrutinizing them."

"They'll be there to keep an eye on things," Hatfield said. "That's all."

"I don't see we have a choice, do we?" the man snarled as he left.

"Sir —" Jackson began, but his superior held up his hand.

"There's no harm in seeing what one night will bring," said the sheriff. "If there's no trouble, I don't see any reason why the Barry Circus shouldn't do what it can to earn its livelihood."

"There'll be no trouble," Nin said in her assured way.

"You know if Nin says so, it's true," Adele said.

"I'm not sure Miss Branch's predictions would surpass a killer's mind," Jackson mumbled.

"I don't make predictions, Mr. Gossling," she snapped. "I deal with certainties."

Adele knew her brother was anything but satisfied, and when they returned to the car, he immediately started in. "I don't think it's wise to let them, Sheriff. With the chaos and the crowds, anything could happen."

"I reckon your sheriff knows what he's doing, son," Mr. Evans said. "Never seen him make a bad decision."

"I wasn't thinking of that, sir," Jackson said carefully. "We just don't know what these people are capable of."

"I think Mr. Barry understands the gravity of the situation," Hatfield said as he started the car. "He'll probably have his people keep watch better than Edison and the lads."

"Of that you can be sure, Sheriff," Adele said with a wink.

CHAPTER 13

*H*atfield dropped Adele and Nin off in town while he and the other men continued on to the police station. But instead of peeling back her shutters, Nin followed Adele into her shop.

"I saw you digging in the dust," she said.

Adele smiled and produced the sharp-pointed sticks from her bag.

"Someone wanted to set the tent on fire?" Nin stared at them.

"Hardly the thing to do if you want only one man dead," said Adele. "You were right."

"I was right about what?" Her friend put the kettle on the burner.

"It *was* lead," said Adele. "Pencil lead."

Nin examined them again. "This isn't like any pencil I've seen."

"That's because it's a square pencil," Adele said. "Like these." She took out a box of Shreve pencils. "Calvin was playing with one when we interviewed him."

"There's no surprise in that, is there?" Nin asked. "Clara told us she saw him with a pencil that night."

"And she said she saw him break the pencil in two," Adele added.

"But what does that prove?" her friend asked.

"It takes a bit of strength to break one of these." Adele gave her a knowing look. "Or quite a lot of of agitation. We're going to find out which applies to Calvin."

"You're not going to show it to the police?" Nin raised her eyebrow.

"Not yet." Adele wrapped the pieces in paper and put them back in her bag. "It might mean nothing at all, and Hatfield has enough to baffle him right now."

The bell above the door rang as four young ladies entered her shop. Beatrice, Mary, and Rachel beamed at her while a girl she didn't recognize stood a little behind them. Their girlish pinafores and hair ribbons were gone, replaced by high-necked shirtwaists and skirts. They carried their adolescence like a badge and Beatrice, whose mother had already consented to let her put her hair up, kept dabbing at the back of her head as if checking to make sure the pins were holding.

"You've heard the news?" Mary thrust out the *Arrojo Courier*.

"I thought Missy would wait until the afternoon paper," Nin said.

"Missy, my dear, is as sharp as a nail." Adele smiled.

"Is it true?" Beatrice demanded. "Mr. Rowe's death was no accident?"

Adele sighed. "Yes, it's true."

"And to think we saw it happen!" The girl looked satisfied. "A murder right under our very noses."

"I don't know if that's anything to brag about," Nin said.

"This is Agnes." Mary nodded to the girl standing a little behind them. "Agnes is joining our little circle this year."

"You have to ask Adele's permission," Rachel said in a high tone. "We can't just allow anybody to help us catch murderers."

"Murderers?" The young woman's face turned white as her eyes slid from one to the other.

"I've never seen you catch a murderer," Nin snapped at Beatrice.

Adele shook the girl's hand. "Don't let their morbid talk frighten you, Agnes. I ask for help sometimes, that's all."

"It's so exciting," Mary said. "Listening in on conversations, finding things out that other people don't know, stealing things."

"Stealing!" Agnes looked even paler.

"Borrowing," Adele corrected.

"It's all for a good cause," Rachel assured her.

"I shouldn't think Mrs. Wrigley would be very pleased to hear you went to the circus," Nin said in a sly tone.

"Bum it, we're practically young ladies," she insisted. "We ought to be able to come and go as we please."

"Young ladies are too old for clowns and poodle acts," Nin remarked.

"We saw you enjoying yourself." The girl gave her a dry look.

Adele laughed. "You don't outgrow candy or the circus."

"We're going again tonight." Mary unrolled a poster from under her arm. It had some clumsily drawn pictures of elephants, bears, and lions with the message CIRCUS RESUMES TONIGHT! COME SEE THE SIGHTS AND DELIGHTS!

"I don't think it's very smart, considering there's a murderer lurking about," Beatrice said with authority. "It might be someone out for blood."

"I don't think we need go that far." Adele examined the poster, her mind turning. "You say you're going tonight?"

"We're taking Agnes," said Rachel. "She's never been to the circus."

"Do they really fly in the air?" The girl looked with wondrous green eyes.

"No one will be flying in the air tonight," Mary said. "He's dead, remember?"

"Nor will they be walking the tightrope or shooting out of a canon," Nin said. "The sheriff forbade it."

"Bum it!" Beatrice snarled.

"Bea, stop saying that!" Rachel blushed. "You sound like a sailor."

"Sailors say worse things," her friend countered.

Adele rolled up the poster and gave it back to Mary. "Suppose I give you the money?"

"What for?" Mary asked.

"For a job, silly." Beatrice was immediately all ears.

"You're letting your imagination run away with you," Nin sniffed.

"I can use some open eyes and ears," Adele admitted. "They know us too well by now."

"We won't have to catch the murderer, will we?" Agnes shuddered.

"No, you bean, Adele just wants us to look and listen," Beatrice snapped.

"We've done it before," Rachel assured her. "Many times when we were children."

Adele exchanged a look with Nin but went on, "Watch the performance and have a good time. Then walk around the concession stands and see if you can get behind the wagons. Keep your eyes and ears open."

"Pretend like we're lost little girls." Rachel nodded.

"Oh, I can do that." Agnes relaxed.

"What are you looking for?" Beatrice eyed her.

"I don't know," Adele said. "But now that the word about the murder is out, there's sure to be talk among the circus people. I want to know what they're saying."

"You think one of them did it?"

"It stands to reason," Rachel said. "Why would anybody in town do it? Nobody knew the man."

"Listen for anything uncommon or interesting," Adele

instructed as she pulled money from the cash register and gave it to Beatrice.

They went off with a gleeful giggle, their sashes flying back from their waists.

"Do you really think they'll find anything?" Nin asked.

Adele shrugged and went back to stacking the ink bottles on the shelf.

~~~~~

Though she and Nin had managed to avoid the town gossips the day before, now the ladies took full revenge, and when the late afternoon settled in, they appeared on the sidewalk with teacups and cakes in hand.

They both stood in the doorway of the shop watching them. "The attack of the buzzing bees is near. I can feel it," Nin remarked.

"I suppose we can't dodge them forever," Adele sighed.

But it was Missy who caught her arm. "Adele, is it true that net was intact when the tightrope walker went on before Mr. Rowe?"

"You ought to know," Nin said sharply. "You sent that bird-brained assistant of yours to spy on us while we were there."

"Carla couldn't spy on a flea and you know it, Anita." The woman had gained the privilege of calling Nin by her first name the year before.

"Then where did you get your information for the paper this morning?" Adele asked.

Missy slipped her pencil behind her frazzled curls. "These are show people. They love a good scandal."

"Even when it's their scandal?" Nin asked.

"Apparently so. They were more than eager to talk to me," Missy said.

"Mrs. Faderman is waving you down," Nin observed.

"You mean waving us down." Adele grabbed both Nin and Missy's arm. "I'm not going into the lion's den alone."

The three women marched into the moveable tea party, a tradition in Arrojo that Adele had thought at first charming but now dreaded.

"It's as I said at the town meeting." Mrs. Faderman held out a teacup to Adele.

"I don't recall you mentioning murder, Mrs. Faderman," she mumbled.

"I'll admit, I didn't think they would go *that* far," said the woman.

"It was rather in the cards, don't you think Irene?" Mrs. Abberton prompted.

"Oh, certainly, certainly."

"They were ripe for scandal, just as I said," Mrs. Cricket chimed in. "That woman was with that flying young man just before it happened, and I can tell you—"

"What woman?" Nin interrupted.

"Why, the owner's wife," she said. "Hiding in a dark corner, they were. Nearly scared the daylights out of me."

"And what were you doing in a dark corner?" Nin eyed her.

Mrs. Cricket gave her a nasty look. "What does it matter what I was doing, Miss Branch? *I* wasn't making eyes at a man not my husband!"

"How do you know she was making eyes?" Adele asked.

"Because one can hardly find much else to do in a dark corner, Miss Gossling." The woman sniffed. "For all your progressive ideas, I should think you would be wise to such things."

"Now, Belinda." Mrs. Faderman, for once, came to Adele's rescue. "You know we have nothing to fault Miss Gossling for on *that* score."

"Thank you for the kind words, ma'am," Adele said. But she was thinking of what she had seen on opening night with the two dark figures in the shadows between the tents.

"I thought that flying young man looked shifty," Mrs. Leighton added.

"They're always that way," Mrs. Abberton insisted, pushing a few of the artificial curls back on place. "It makes them more appealing to the ladies, and don't think for a moment they don't know it!"

"Yes, but one would think with all their experience, they would know enough not to dally with the owner's wife." Mrs. Faderman shuddered.

"That's not true!"

The objection came from two women who had just emerged from the crowd. Adele saw they were Abby Call and her younger sister, both looking far from elegant but simple and modest in their walking suits.

"And you are?" Mrs. Faderman glanced at the young ladies from the top of her pince-nez.

"We were Julius Rowe's partners," the woman declared.

"Oh!" Mrs. Lynn almost dropped her teacup as she fluttered forward. She took Abby's hand with her small one. "So sorry for your loss, my dear."

"Thank you." But Abby seemed more intent on addressing Mrs. Faderman, whom she looked at with hard eyes. "You spoke just now of us as if Julius were something slithering across the grass."

"That's rather an inelegant description." Mrs. Faderman stiffened.

"But accurate for your narrow mind," Nin mumbled.

"We're very aware of our civic duties here, Miss —" Mrs. Faderman glanced at Adele.

"Miss Call," Adele supplied, wondering why the woman thought she would know her name.

"Abby, let's go!" Helen pulled at her sister's sleeve. "They don't like us here."

"Wouldn't it be your civic duty not to spread vicious gossip about people you know nothing about?" Abby sneered.

"I don't spread vicious gossip, Miss Call," Mrs. Faderman protested. "I call it as I see it."

"Did you see Julius and Estelle—"

"I have no idea who Estelle is."

"The owner's wife," Abby said with impatience. "Did you see them together, as this woman said?" Abby glanced at Mrs. Cricket.

"I refuse to attend that farce you call a circus." Mrs. Faderman's chin lifted.

"It's not a farce!" Helen insisted. "We're honest, hard-working entertainers."

"Did you see them together?" Abby demanded, glaring at Mrs. Faderman.

"Of course I didn't," she said. "But if my friend said she did then I believe her."

"I suppose you think Julius deserved what he got?" Abby gave her a fierce look.

"Abby!"

Adele caught Helen's shoulders and Nin put her arm around her. "Abby, I think you'd both better come into my shop."

"Yes, yes!" her sister crowed.

She and Nin pulled Helen into Adele's Stationary while Abby followed. She eased Helen into a chair and shut the door, the bell banging against the wooden frame. "I see Mrs. Faderman is in a particularly nasty mood today," she remarked.

"Isn't she always?" Nin snorted.

"Is it true?" Helen peered at her sister with large, sad eyes. "About Julius and Estelle, I mean."

"I'm afraid so, dear," said her sister, "though it hardly matters now."

"It might matter to the police," Adele said.

Abby glared at her. "I rather doubt the police would be interested in circus gossip."

"You just said it wasn't gossip," Nin pointed out.

"Yes, but nobody knows that except me," the woman insisted. "Julius told me about it. He liked to brag about his conquests."

"He bragged about them," Helen repeated in a shaky tone.

"Now I ask *you*," Abby looked at Adele squarely, "is it true the police are going on the assumption Julius was murdered, just like we read in the paper?"

"The evidence points that way," Adele said.

Abby stared at the floor for a few moments. "Maybe your sheriff isn't seeing the evidence in the right way."

"What do you mean?" Nin asked.

"Helen and I grew up in the circus," she said. "We've seen every sort of mistake, haven't we, pet?" She glanced at her sister.

Helen stared out the window with waxy eyes. "Yes. Oh, yes." She rose and wandered to the front of the shop.

"Ripped nets can look like they were cut," she insisted.

"Mr. Patton agreed with the sheriff," Adele argued. "I should think he's also seen every sort of mistake too."

"I don't care what Dan said!" The woman's voice was icy. "It still could have been an accident."

"The sheriff brought in an expert," Nin said.

"An expert?" The color drained from the woman's face.

"A man who knows about nets and ropes," Adele said. "There's no doubt about it, Abby."

Abby sank into the chair her sister had vacated. Her shoulders heaved forward, and her hands pressed together. "I wonder what Paul will do now."

"Hire a new flyer, I expect," Adele said.

"He won't be hiring anybody if he's in jail for murder," Abby murmured.

"You think he might have killed Julius?"

"I wouldn't blame Paul if he, well, lost his head." Her eyes were on the window. "His wife was having an affair with Julius, and Paul isn't the sort to take such a thing lightly."

"According to you, that's circus gossip." Adele looked doubtful. "I should think he wouldn't take much notice of circus gossip."

"I don't know what Paul would do," Abby said. "I only know he's more unpredictable than people think. Once, a tiger pawed Clara, and Paul got so enraged he went right into the cage with a whip and beat the poor animal until it was nearly dead."

"Verner the Great must not have been thrilled about that," Nin remarked.

"If he could do that to an animal, think of what he could do to a man." Abby rose. "Helen, we must go, love."

Adele looked out the window, relieved to see the tea party had dispersed. She observed Helen loitering on the sidewalk, a young man beside her in tweeds and a bowler hat that looked too big for him. They were talking and suddenly, Helen smiled. It was the first smile she had seen on the young woman's face.

Abby joined her near the window. Her anger at the ladies now turned to rage, and her pleasant features contorted with shrewdness, reminding Adele of the face of a Medusa she had seen in a storybook. Behind her, Nin took in a breath.

"Is that the young man who's been distracting Helen?" Adele asked.

"Nothing will stand in her way now," the woman declared. "Nothing!"

She flew out the door. Adele watched as she clawed her sister's arm and, without even a nod at the young man, who tipped his hat to her, hurried her down the street toward Arrojo Park.

CHAPTER 14

The next morning, Jackson left the house early to take care of some business in Rosa Gris for another case, and Adele took the opportunity to come to Bridge Street while it was still quiet, with nothing open except for the *Arrojo Courier* office and the Rutledge Bakery. The scent of the latter floated out the open doorway, making her head expand like the yeast used in their bread. She dusted the shelves in her shop and mopped the floor. The cleanness made up for the more sordid details she had experienced the past few days since Mr. Rowe's grisly death.

The first to enter her shop were not customers but the flapping girls from the Wrigley School, their arms filled with paper bags from the bakery. As teenagers, their studies were surprisingly less intense than in previous years, and Mrs. Wrigley seemed less concerned about their whereabouts than those of her younger pupils.

"It was divine!" The words came from Agnes as she puttered in first.

"The circus, you mean." Adele smiled. "I remember my first time at the circus. I was frightened of the clowns!"

"Oh, that was just child's play," the girl said with a haughty gaze. "But to see real lions and bears and tigers —" She shuddered.

"And the strong man who ruled them?" Adele suggested with her eyebrows arched. She had not forgotten Verner the Great's impressive figure.

"Never mind about all that." Beatrice gave Adele a meaningful look. "We had work to do and we did it."

"I'm sure you did," Adele said.

"They were all so happy for people who just lost one of their own," Mary said, munching on a cream puff.

"Save that for after lunch, dear," Rachel said. "You don't want to get too sleepy before the first class."

"Everybody falls asleep in Mrs. Fern's class anyway," Mary grumbled. "I don't see that it makes any difference."

Beatrice quieted them, then cleared her throat like a lawyer about to make a speech in court. "We didn't find out anything around the concession stands," she said. "It was so crowded."

"So many out-of-town people," Agnes added. "We barely knew a soul."

"The cotton candy was delicious," Mary chimed in. "And we heard the man say to one of the clowns that he didn't know what he would do if he kept making a jitney every night with this police investigation."

"Jitney?" Adele wrinkled her nose.

"Five cents," said Rachel.

"And how would you know that?" Beatrice eyed her. "Did your fellow down at the drugstore tell you?"

"He doesn't use such vulgar language." Rachel sniffed.

"So you've nothing to report?" Adele asked. She slid the cash register open, fishing out some coins to give them.

"We didn't say that, did we?" Beatrice asked. She was in the plain-faced stage of her adolescence, though her hair was still a magnificent strawberry blond and smooth as silk.

"You haven't said anything so far." Adele was getting annoyed. "I thought you were through with such games, Bea."

"Is it a game to say we wandered away from the crowds to the wagons and snuck around, keeping our eyes and ears open, like you said?" the girl asked archly.

"It was Bea's idea," said Mary. "We were all terrified, but Bea said we could always play the dumb schoolgirls if anyone caught us."

"But no one did," Rachel chimed in. "They were all too busy."

"So you listened in on what people were saying in the wagons?" Adele leaned against the counter. "I'm impressed with your daring, Bea."

The girl grinned. "Bum it, maybe I'll be a lady detective like you someday."

"I'm not a lady detective," Adele protested. "I'm merely helping the police. We all are."

"I don't see why they can't do their own work," Agnes said in a peevish tone.

"Because ladies do it much better," Bea assured her. "We can play dumb and people believe it. We learn much more that way."

"All right, Bea, what did you find out?" Adele asked.

"That man you told us about," she said. "The one with the face like an eagle and the gruff voice."

"Paul Barry?" Adele straightened.

"He and his wife were talking," said Beatrice.

"They were doing more than talking," Rachel said with some indignation. "He was furious with her!"

"They were having an argument?" Adele asked.

"And a big one!" Mary said with a nod. "He actually put his hand on her throat once. We thought he was going to choke her."

"You peeked through the windows?" Adele stared at Beatrice.

"We had to see who it was, didn't we?" Beatrice insisted. "We were in the back of the wagons so we couldn't see the signs."

"What was the argument about?"

"A man!" Mary's eyes widened.

"Not just any man," Agnes said. "*The* man."

"*The* man?" Adele sighed.

"The man who was killed, she means," Beatrice said. "That dashing trapeze flyer."

"They were arguing about Julius Rowe?"

"He said, 'Just how close were you?'" Bea related. "She said, 'That's none of your business.' Then he said, 'You're my wife. Of course it's my business!' She said, 'I did nothing to be ashamed of, Paul.'" With each line, Beatrice assumed the role, once of a towering angry man, then, a shaking woman.

"We could do without the theatrics," Adele said dryly. "Go on."

"He went on and on about how she had made him the laughingstock of the circus because everybody knew of her insane infatuation — that's what he called it — for 'a scalawag of the first degree who's better off dead.'" She eyed Adele. "I think that's very significant, don't you?"

"We'll see," Adele said. "Go on."

"Then he said, 'That scarf the police found — you gave it to him, didn't you?' She said, 'What are you talking about, Paul?' He then sneered at her, 'It would be just like you to get all sentimental about a scalawag!'"

"So romantic." Mary sighed.

"It's sordid, that's what it is," Rachel said. She took out her rosary and began rolling the beads.

"But she said she did nothing to be ashamed of," Agnes said. "I believed her."

"Well, he didn't," Beatrice said. "That was clear."

"Why do you say that?" Adele asked.

"Because he said, 'The police better not find out to whom that scarf belongs, my dear, that's all I can say,'" she said. "Did they really find a scarf?"

Adele avoided answering her question. "What else did they say?"

"She said he was being ridiculous," Beatrice said. "And he said, 'I hope so, for your sake.'"

"What a foul man." Agnes sniffed.

"Then someone came into their wagon, bum it," Beatrice concluded. "They all left."

Adele smiled, patting Beatrice on the back. "You did good work, Bea. But you shouldn't take such chances anymore. You're no longer children who can play innocent."

"I rather like being the goop girl." Beatrice grinned. "I like to show them up by being deliberate about it."

Adele distributed coins and locked up her shop. She walked with them as far as the police station, waving as they toddled along in the direction of the school. Then, she went into the station.

Assistant Deputy Edison immediately fumbled to his feet, knocking over his chair as usual. Assistant Deputy Dooland and two others Adele had only seen a few times followed his lead. They were used to seeing her but they still treated her as if she were a visiting diplomat.

"There's no need for ceremony, gentlemen," she said, leaning her parasol against Jackson's empty desk and arranging herself on his chair. Hatfield had persuaded the council to replace the rickety furnishings with new ones for the permanent deputy sheriff. Adele guessed they had needed little persuading, as many of them saw Jackson's procedural ways of keeping law and order a welcome contrast to the sheriff's more roughshod ways.

"Deputy Sheriff Jackson went to Rosa Gris, miss," Edison began.

"I know that, Assistant Deputy." She said, amused. "We do exchange a word or two at the breakfast table, you know."

"Yes, miss." The young man blushed as his fellow officers sniggered.

"It's the sheriff I've come to see," she said.

Edison nodded toward the closed door in the corner which,

Adele knew, led to a small sink where the sheriff often times shaved in the mornings when his mother made him sit down to a hearty, hot breakfast.

"I'll wait, then," she said.

Edison leaned forward with an eager look. "Have you news about that circus fellow who was killed?"

"What makes you think I do?" Adele asked.

"If you won't be offended, miss —"

She cocked her head. "Assistant Deputy, we've known one another for three years now. It's unlikely you could say anything that would offend me."

"No, miss, you're very thick-skinned. Not like other girls — ladies." He blushed.

"Perhaps you ought to court a different kind of lady, then," she said in a light tone. The two young assistant deputies chuckled again. "What was it you wanted to say that might offend me?"

"Only that you get a certain, well, look on your face when you've learned new facts or found new evidence," he said. "Like it all shines."

Adele considered this. "Is that a good thing?"

"Oh, for us it is!" said the young man. "The sheriff's never been stingy about help."

"No, he hasn't," said Adele in a soft voice. It was one of his most admirable qualities. Hatfield had once told her he had seen enough of territorial jealousies between police in San Francisco to make him feel like he had a "bellyful of lead" at the thought of keeping everything to himself.

"But I think, miss, it ain't — isn't — so good for the rest of the town," he ventured. "I mean — if you'll pardon me — it's not so good for your standing."

"You mean my womanly reputation?" Adele raised her eyebrows. "I should think that went out with the dust from my Beaton when I drove into town three years ago."

"Oh, your Beaton is a fine car!" This outburst came from the slightly pompous Dooland.

Adele turned to him. "You're interested in automobiles, Mr. Dooland?"

"My father is looking into getting a Ford next year," said Dooland in an eager tone. "What with my earnings, we might be able to afford it."

"I'm glad to hear it," Adele said, smiling.

"You ought to get one of the new Fords, Miss Gossling," Dooland continued. "That Beaton of yours, it's a fine car —"

"So you said," Adele said dryly.

"— but, well, it looks like it's about to give way, if you don't mind my saying so."

"I do mind, as a matter of fact," she said with a raised eyebrow.

"Well, miss, I only meant a car's not a thing to keep for years with new models coming out all the time." The young man blushed. "Why, my father knows a dealer who could get you one of the new Fords at a good price."

"Thank you, Assistant Deputy," Adele said, trying to hide her smile. "I'll keep that in mind."

"Dooland!" The familiar roar came from the now-open doorway in the corner. "What are you chattering on about?"

"Miss Gossling is here, Sheriff," said the young man, quickly turning back to his work.

"With some new evidence," Adele added. "Maybe."

"Then get the lady a cup of coffee, lad," said the man as he buttoned his coat and rubbed his chin. "And then get to those forms. Marland asked for them yesterday, and he's not a man to be kept waiting."

"Yes, sir!" Dooland flew to the burner and put the kettle on. Adele noticed Edison grinning over his work at having shirked the sheriff's wrath for once.

"Now, what is this possible new evidence?" Hatfield turned to Adele.

"I had my young ladies do a little work for me last night at the circus."

"Young ladies?" The man looked at her curiously. "Oh, you mean your schoolgirl spies."

"They're young women now, Sheriff," Adele insisted. "One already puts her hair up."

"I can guess which one," he said. "What kind of work?"

"I asked them to keep their eyes and ears open," she said. "They were taking Agnes to the circus for the first time anyway so I thought, why not have them help us in the meantime?"

"You know how your brother feels about that."

"That's why I'm here while he's away," she said with a sly smile.

He grinned. "And what did your young ladies find out?"

"Miss Call may not have steered us wrong," said Adele.

"About?"

"Estelle Barry."

"The owner's wife?" He sat up.

"Her husband accused her of having an affair with Julius Rowe last night," said Adele.

"My, but your young ladies go where angels fear to tread," he remarked.

Adele felt her face grow hot. "I didn't ask them to go that far. But you know Beatrice."

"I know Beatrice," he snorted. "What did Mrs. Barry have to say to her husband?"

"She's done nothing he need be ashamed of," Adele said promptly.

"Well, perhaps she's telling the truth," he said.

"That depends on what you consider shameful behavior, Sheriff," Adele said. "Abby was in my shop today. She confirmed Julius told her of their affair."

"The question is, did her husband know about it?" Hatfield asked.

Adele shrugged. "Abby said it was common gossip among their people."

"That doesn't mean he believed it," Hatfield pointed out. "And even if he did, did he believe it to the point of doing something about it?"

"Abby thinks he did," Adele said, remembering the young woman's words: *He's more unpredictable than people think.*

Edison glanced up from his typewriter but quickly went back to his work after a stern look from his employer. "Anything else your young ladies had to report?"

"The scarf we found may be Mrs. Barry's," Adele said.

"She admitted to having one like it?"

"Not exactly," Adele said. "But the argument the girls overheard made it seem as if she did."

"Why is that?"

Adele fingered a paperweight on Jackson's desk, realizing it was the pair of brass dogs that had sat in her father's study in San Francisco. "Paul thinks she gave it to Mr. Rowe as a gift."

"That would be rather stupid of her," the sheriff said unkindly.

"Perhaps you ought to talk with the Barrys again," Adele suggested. "Let the lady speak for herself."

"She's already lied once," Hatfield pointed out.

"We don't know she lied," Adele said.

He studied her. "You sympathize with that woman, don't you?"

"I think there's more to her than meets the eye," Adele said.

"Then perhaps you ought to come with us tonight when we question them."

She smiled. "I'd like that very much." She picked up her parasol, looking down at it for a moment. "Do you think they're likely to speak more freely now that they know it's a murder investigation?"

"What do *you* think, Adele?" He eyed her.

"I think circus people are used to living by their own rules," she said. "Those rules might not be ones we would live by."

"They're still subject to the law like everyone else." Hatfield picked up a fountain pen.

Adele took the pen out of his hand, examining it. "I think the sheriff of Arrojo County deserves a pen less than five years old."

The man blushed as he fiddled in his desk drawers. "I learned at sea to make do with the simplest things."

"You're too modest, Sheriff." She handed him back the pen.

"That's what Ma says." She could see he was ready to say more but pressed his lips together.

"What else does Lady Augusta say?" Adele prompted.

"She says it's why I haven't — haven't a lady friend." He coughed several times.

Adele strolled to the door. "There are plenty of ladies I know who value modesty in a man. Especially one who could easily abuse his power."

"I've never done that." He looked almost hurt.

She smiled. "You never would, Sheriff."

Later that day, she sent one of the boys who ran errands for shops on Bridge Street to the police station with a shiny new Conklin S3 pen with orders to Hatfield that he was to burn the old pen, lest people think Arrojo County couldn't afford to give its police force the best.

~~~~~

The circus was clearly not as chaotic as it had been on opening night but nevertheless, the band played heartily in the middle of the park, their music vibrating to every corner. Adele observed many strange faces, wondering how far out of Arrojo the circus posters had reached.

"Mr. Barry was right," Jackson said. "They can do quite a good business with neighboring towns."

"I've a feeling they sent advertisements as far as Sacramento."

Hatfield frowned. "I thought I made it clear they were to keep it local."

"You can't blame them, Sheriff," Adele said. "They're not used to being in one place for more than a day or two."

"When the sheriff of any town lays down the law, Del, visitors are expected to follow it," Jackson said severely. "Entertainers don't have special privileges."

"Entertainers, dear brother, have their living to earn," Adele argued. "They bring fun and relaxation to sleepy places like this."

"The Barry Circus didn't bring us much fun and relaxation," Hatfield said. "They brought murder."

"You can hardly prosecute them for that," she said.

"I intend to prosecute one of them," said the sheriff, "if one can call an arrest prosecution."

Mr. Barry was just finishing his dinner in his wagon, hunched over his desk with a schedule in front of him. Mrs. Barry was nowhere to be seen.

"It's rather late for a meal, isn't it?" Sheriff Hatfield remarked, pulling out a chair for Adele.

"A circus owner never has his meals at the proper time," Mr. Barry said. "It's why so many of us have dyspepsia." He leaned back, wiping his lips. "So we're to have a murder investigation after all, are we?"

"Your people seem to be none the worse for it," Jackson remarked. "The crowds outside are bigger than they were on opening night."

"I would appreciate it if you would keep your posters to local towns from now on, Mr. Barry," Hatfield said. "We don't want mobs trampling all over the place, and once the news of the events that took place here reach the city papers —"

"What took place," the man scoffed. "You needn't be so coy, Sheriff. I told you, circus folk have seen tragedies in life you couldn't imagine in your wildest dreams."

"Having been a seaman and a stagecoach detective, I doubt that very much," Hatfield answered.

"We're as anxious to find out who killed your star performer as you are, Mr. Barry," Adele said.

He eyed her. "Am I to understand we're to have ladies asking questions as well?"

"If I see fit to send them," Hatfield said in a steady voice. "We do things differently here, Mr. Barry."

"So I see." The man's tone softened. "I don't mean to sound obstinate but this has been trying for all my people, and I'm concerned it will start to affect their performance."

"I should think the death of one of their own would be enough to affect their performance," Jackson said.

"They understand the show must go on," Mr. Barry said.

"Is it just the show, Mr. Barry? Adele raised her eyebrows. "Or is it that many of them feel no love lost for Mr. Rowe's demise?"

The man did not bat an eye. "Perhaps that too, Miss Gossling. I can hardly blame them."

"Obviously, since you thought him arrogant," Hatfield remarked.

"You misunderstood me, Sheriff," said Mr. Barry. "I meant nothing personal. It's not unusual for the star performer to think rather highly of himself."

"But there was another, more personal, reason for you to dislike the man," Jackson said.

Mr. Barry slid the half-finished plate away from him. "I don't know what you mean, Deputy."

"You were overheard arguing with your wife the other night," Jackson said.

The man laughed. "I never argue with my wife."

"Never?" The sheriff eyed him.

"Oh, we might bicker about small things here and there," he admitted. "We've been married for twenty years. Twenty this November, in fact." He gave a small smile.

"I find it hard to believe after twenty years you would only find small things to bicker about," Jackson said.

The man's smile was condescending. "You're not married, are you, Deputy?"

"I haven't had that pleasure yet," Jackson mumbled.

"When you are, you'll understand," said Mr. Barry.

The door to the wagon opened with some difficulty and Mrs. Barry stepped in. She stopped when she saw the lawmen.

"Don't be alarmed, Estelle," Adele said kindly.

The woman looked even more worn than she had the night of Mr. Rowe's death. It was as if the little vigor she had shown as the circus owner's wife had drained out of her. She sat down on the edge of the bed with her hands balled in her lap, a child waiting to be taken care of.

Adele's heart immediately went out to her, and she sat down beside her. "I promise you the sheriff always makes this the least trying as he possibly can."

"Indeed, ma'am," Hatfield said with respect. "We know how difficult things are for you."

The woman put her head in her hands, nodding.

"The police need to find out who killed Julius, dear," Mr. Barry said.

Mrs. Barry uncovered her face and said in a grated tone, "I realize that. But it's all so sordid!"

"Mrs. Barry." Hatfield slipped out of his large pocket the scarf they had picked up the night of the murder. "We'd like to ask you again if you recognize this."

"Why?" The woman glared at her husband. "Has someone been telling you it's mine?"

"Miss Call told us she gave you one like it," Jackson said.

The woman's shoulders sagged. "She did give me a scarf once."

"Was this the scarf?" asked the sheriff.

Adele noted Paul was watching her carefully, his features frozen.

The woman examined it carefully. "No, I'm sure of it."

"Are you?" Jackson asked quietly.

She glared at him. "I ought to know my own scarf!"

"Then why did your husband accuse you of giving it to Mr. Rowe?" Hatfield asked.

"What the devil are you talking about?" Mr. Barry snarled.

"You did say that, didn't you, Mr. Barry?" Adele asked.

"I said no such thing!" The man's face grew lined. "Who's been telling tales?"

"It's no use, Paul," said his wife. "We did have an argument about it, yes."

Jackson glanced at her husband. "Mr. Barry told us you only bicker."

Mrs. Barry stared at him. Then, she let out a hysterical laugh. "He said that, did he?" A little of her vigor returned.

"Well, wouldn't you, if there was a murder investigation going on in your circus?" the man challenged.

"I would if I had something to hide," Jackson said quietly.

"We have nothing to hide, Deputy," Mrs. Barry sighed. "Abby did give me a scarf and yes, it did look very much like that one. But that isn't *my* scarf."

"How can you be so sure?" Adele asked.

"I threw my scarf away," she insisted. "It got stained with tar during our performance in Los Angeles so I couldn't wear it anymore."

Adele observed the line melting on Mr. Barry's cheek. "Of course! Now I remember."

"Can anyone confirm this?" Jackson asked.

"I just did, Deputy," Mr. Barry snarled. "But I suppose it's your duty to doubt every word anybody says during a murder investigation."

"We understand, Mrs. Barry, you and Mr. Rowe met earlier in the evening," Jackson said.

Estelle stared at him. "What are you talking about?"

"My sister saw you arguing in the shadows between two tents."

"I didn't say they were arguing, Jack," Adele said quickly.

"Mr. Verner said he nearly bumped into you, and you seemed upset," Hatfield added.

Paul gave him a vicious look. "I've heard of the police doing, what do you call it? Inventing evidence to make their case."

"They're not inventing anything," Estelle said in a tired voice. "I did see Julius that night. And I was upset."

"Opening night is always upsetting," her husband lamented. "Don't let them sway you into incriminating yourself, Estelle."

She glared at him.

"Why were you upset, Mrs. Barry?" Jackson asked.

"I can't tell you that, Deputy," she said. "Suffice it to say I had reason to be upset."

"You realize this is a murder investigation, ma'am?" Hatfield gave her a hard look.

"If our argument had anything to do with Julius's murder, I would tell you, Sheriff."

"Maybe it did and maybe it didn't." The sheriff looked at her for a moment, then turned to her husband. "You didn't know about this meeting, Mr. Barry?"

"Of course I knew nothing about it!" Paul snapped.

"Then why did you accuse your wife of giving the scarf to Mr. Rowe as a gift?" Hatfield asked.

"I never made such an accusation," the man insisted. "I simply forgot my wife had gotten rid of it."

"Oh, stop, Paul!" Estelle's voice was shrill. "A man has been killed, for God's sake!"

Her husband grasped the edges of his desk. "I don't deny we had a discussion about Julius."

"A discussion!" his wife snarled.

"All right! An out-and-out fight, is that what you want to hear, Sheriff?"

"I want to hear the truth, sir," Hatfield answered in a quiet voice.

"*I* would like to hear which one of our people told you we had a fight," Mr. Barry said in a steel voice. "I'll have the busybody fired!"

"Paul!"

"They were my people, Mr. Barry, not yours," Adele said.

He gave her a seething look. "What business did 'your people' have eavesdropping on my wife and me?"

Adele sat straight. "The walls of these wagons are very thin."

"Del," her brother warned.

"What did your people say?" the man asked again.

"They overheard you accusing your wife of being involved with Mr. Rowe." It took all of Adele's courage to look Mrs. Barry in the face. "Is it true?"

The woman stared at her but Adele felt her eyes were glassy, as if her consciousness had gone blind.

CHAPTER 15

*P*aul was on his feet. "I realize you're one of those brazen modern ladies who says what she likes —"

"You will speak with respect to my sister, sir." Jackson's fierce protective nature made him look taller and more menacing than he was.

Paul drummed his fingers on the table, making it echo. He turned to the sheriff. "I must say, Sheriff, using a young lady to do your dirty work —"

"Now, just hold it right there!" Hatfield was also on his feet.

"— and make such scandalous accusations against my wife —"

"My sister was making no accusations, sir," Jackson said. "She asked a question. One your wife has yet to answer, I might add."

"She doesn't have to answer!" the man thundered. "I shall get a lawyer, if necessary. And I will certainly call the mayor of this town and tell him —"

"Shut up, Paul!"

All three men stared at the blond-haired woman, her Dresden doll face angled with determination.

"What did you say?" Her husband's voice was almost dangerous.

"I said, shut up." She looked squarely at Adele. "It's true. We were seeing one another." Her voice was calm. "We'd been seeing one another for months."

"I'm sorry, Mrs. Barry." Hatfield looked at her with sad eyes. "We had to know."

"Sorry!" Paul roared. "Sorry for her? She deserves to be whipped!"

"We were in love."

"Estelle!"

Jackson cleared his throat. "I think you'd better calm down, Mr. Barry."

The man deflated. "You're right, of course, Deputy. It wouldn't do to have the entire circus know."

"I think they already do," Adele said in a quiet voice.

"Well, you needn't go around confirming the rumors!" he bellowed.

"I can assure you it will go no further than this wagon if we can avoid it," Hatfield insisted.

"I don't care if it does!" Estelle gave him a wild look. "He was going to take me away from here. We were going to leave when his contract was up."

"Leave?" Paul gave her an incredulous look.

"Yes, Paul," she said. "Leave."

"My God, Estelle, how could you do this to me?" he choked.

"I wanted to be free." Her voice was meeker now.

"To be free to do what you liked," Adele echoed, remembering the conversation they had had opening night.

"Yes, I suppose that's it," she said.

"You say you were waiting until Mr. Rowe's contact ended?" Hatfield inquired. The woman nodded. "But Mrs. Barry —" Adele could see he was struggling to put things delicately. "Your son told us he renewed the contract for the trapeze act."

"That can't be!" The determined look dropped from the woman's face.

"You didn't know about this, Mr. Barry?" Adele looked at the man whose face had gone white.

"Blast the boy!" He shouted. "Blast him!"

"Keep your tone civil, sir," Jackson growled.

"Mrs. Barry, did Mr. Rowe actually say he was going to leave once his contract ended?" the sheriff asked.

"*He* wasn't going to leave, Sheriff," Estelle said. "*We* were going to leave."

"You needn't keep saying it!" her husband barked.

"He didn't actually say so, Sheriff, but I understood —"

"Understood!" Paul smirked. "You were taken, Estelle."

The woman's determination returned. "I told you, we were in love."

"But he did renew his contract, just as the sheriff said," Jackson said quietly.

"I don't believe it." The woman grasped the edge of the bed. "I simply don't believe it."

There was silence for a few moments with only a woman's voice commanding one of the elephants outside. Estelle rose slowly. "I must go to Calvin's wagon. I must see for myself."

"So you can soil him with your sin?" Paul looked at her with bright eyes. "If you want to make a public spectacle of yourself, Estelle, I suppose I can't stop you, but leave my son out of it."

"It's you who's making the public spectacle of yourself, Mr. Barry." Adele glared at him.

Hatfield cleared his throat. "Jackson, please ask Calvin to bring the contract for the trapeze act in here."

Jackson gave his superior a troubled look as he left the wagon.

When he was gone, the sheriff asked in a soft tone, "I gather your son knows nothing about you and Mr. Rowe, Mrs. Barry?"

The woman shook her head. "Don't tell him, Sheriff, please."

"No, don't tell him." Paul turned his wrath on his wife. "A son should never know when his mother is a —" He turned away.

"Leave her alone, Mr. Barry." The sheriff slid his hands in his pockets. "I think she's been through enough, don't you?"

"I don't regret anything," Mrs. Barry voice came out a whisper. Then, in a louder voice, she repeated, "I don't regret anything!"

"I wonder if you really didn't know Julius hadn't signed that contract," her husband sneered.

Estelle turned pale as she stared at him. "What on earth do you mean?"

"You're not much of a woman, my dear, but a woman scorned can be dangerous."

"It works both ways, Mr. Barry," Adele said.

"What are you talking about, Miss Gossling?"

"You had just as much a motive for killing Julius as your wife."

The man looked from one to the other. "He was my star performer."

"Paul would never kill anybody, no more than I would," Estelle insisted.

"Thank you for that vote of confidence, Estelle," her husband said in a acerbic tone.

The door creaked open and Calvin came in followed by Jackson. The young man had the impassive look of someone at a business meeting. Adele couldn't help but feel the irony of his innocence.

"I understand you want to see the contract I drew up for the trapeze act, Sheriff?" he asked. "Though it seems rather useless now."

"I assure you sir, it's very useful to us." Hatfield held out his hand.

Calvin handed him the folded paper. The sheriff glanced at it, then handed it to Mrs. Barry. As he watched his mother read it, Calvin's impassive look started to melt into worried lines. "Mama, anything wrong?"

With his usual taste and discretion, Hatfield said, "We're just trying to verify some things. Your parents informed us they knew nothing about your renewing the contract for the act."

"I take care of the paperwork, Sheriff," said Calvin. "It's always been my job."

In what seemed like a flash, Adele saw Mr. Barry fly at his son and his hand swipe across his face. "You damned idiot!"

"Paul, stop!" Mrs. Barry pulled her son away.

All at once, the man's stormy countenance eased and his breath slowed. "You should have told me, Cal."

The young man glared at his father. "You told me never to bother you with paperwork unless there was a problem."

"Mr. Rowe had concerns about Miss Helen Call," Jackson said. "You didn't consider that a problem?"

"Concerns are not problems, Deputy," Calvin said. "That was between Julius and Helen."

"From now on, I want you to run every contract by me before you get the signatures," Paul said.

The young man studied his father. "Why?"

"Because I said so!" the man shouted.

Silence buzzed like a swarm of bees. Estelle murmured, "April twelfth." She let the paper flutter to the ground. Adele picked it up.

"A little over three weeks ago," Paul lamented. "Just as you said, Sheriff."

"That's right." Calvin looked from one to the other. "Their contract ended at the end of April. I thought it best to make sure they're continuing with us as early as possible."

"Oh, God!" Mrs. Barry collapsed onto the bed.

All at once, Calvin's cool countenance disappeared and he rushed to his mother, his voice as soothing as a little boy's. "It's all right, Mama. No one could have known what was going to happen."

Mrs. Barry looked at him. All at once, the tears stopped and she put her arms around him. "Of course you're right, dear. I shouldn't be so upset that — that Julius renewed and then died."

"You mean was killed," Calvin said with a sigh. "It's murder, isn't it, Sheriff?"

"I'm afraid so, sir," said Hatfield.

Adele's gaze wandered to the paper in her hand. She couldn't help but notice Calvin used the best quality paper for his contracts so the typewriter ink didn't even smear. The letters stood out clearly.

"You ought to get that 'S' key fixed on your typewriter," she remarked in a hollow tone. "It looks like an eight."

"Del," Jackson groaned.

"I'm sorry," she said, handing the contract to the sheriff. "Occupational hazard, I suppose."

"Yes, it's a very old typewriter," Calvin admitted. "Julius told me the same thing." He glanced at her. "You don't happen to sell typewriters, do you, Miss Gossling?"

Adele smiled. "Next year, perhaps."

"Next year." The man looked down at the desk. Adele knew he was thinking about what might become of next year.

~~~~~

Adele reached her shop at lunchtime and skipped the midday meal to attend to customers coming in during their lunch hour. There were enough to keep her busy, as the new stationery, which she had advertised in her window, attracted a fair amount of people. But even as she did her job, her mind was on the Barrys.

Later that evening, she and Jackson had a quiet dinner and retired to the parlor for their usual evening coffee. She had abandoned the embroidery she had been trying to complete since she moved to Arrojo in an effort to live the town's idea of domestic bliss and now sat on the couch with the latest Edith Wharton novel in her lap. Jackson had been contemplative for some time and now sat with his pipe between his lips.

She played with the fringes on the pillow she had taken to her lap. "I suppose you and the sheriff are now looking at the Barrys as suspects."

"You can't deny Mrs. Barry had a motive for killing her paramour," Jackson said, "unless she was telling the truth about not knowing he had no intention of leaving the Barry Circus."

"Her husband has a motive too," Adele pointed out. "Don't forget that."

"He knew nothing about the affair," her brother argued.

"Assuming *he's* telling the truth." She gazed into the unlit fireplace.

Her brother frowned. "I'm inclined to believe him."

"And I'm inclined to believe *her*!" She looked squarely at him.

"That man was as shocked as we were when his wife told her story."

"Perhaps a little too shocked," she said.

"I don't think he was shamming, Del."

"But you think Estelle was?"

"I didn't say that!" He put the paper down.

"Because she 'sinned'?" Adele demanded. "Is that it?"

"We only have her word that she knew nothing about Mr. Rowe renewing his contract," Jackson said slowly. "We know they had a clandestine meeting on opening night and that she was upset."

"And you think she was lying when she said Julius didn't tell her he renewed his contract that night," Adele guessed. "I think this is a case of you putting two and two together, but two and two don't always make four, Jack."

"They might in this case," he insisted.

"What makes you think so?"

Jackson scooped tobacco from the pouch and filled his pipe. "We went back to the circus this afternoon with a search warrant. Hatfield wanted to look in her wagon, just to make sure."

"Make sure of what?"

"The scarf, Del," he said. "Her story about the tar stain was a little too pat. We didn't find the scarf, but we found something else. Something rather odd."

She looked at him carefully. "But you think it might be important."

He smiled. "You were always too shrewd, Del. Father used to say, 'if you break something of your sister's, you'd better own up to it because she'll find out anyway.'"

"You broke my favorite china doll," Adele pointed out. "I didn't notice that until Elsie told me."

"Only because you hated that doll and were glad." He laughed. Then, in a more serious tone, he said, "We found a box without a key."

Adele groaned. "And you accuse me of talking in circles!"

He put out the pipe and laid it on the table. A little of the ash spilled out and Tomas, always the diligent one, shot from the corner of the room and, fretting, wiped it clean with the dust rag he always seemed to have on him.

"What kind of box?" she asked.

"A rather elaborate wooden box with a red velvet lining," he said. "The lining had an imprint of a key."

"What did Mrs. Barry have to say about it?"

"It belonged to an old jewelry box of hers," he said. "We asked to see the box but she said it broke during their European tour a few years ago and she threw it away."

"My, but she throws away so many things," Adele remarked.

"And from what Calvin told us, she can't exactly afford to," Jackson added. "The circus isn't making so much that she can carelessly toss things like that."

"I gather, then, you didn't believe her."

He chewed on the end of his pipe. "When we opened the box her face blanched like she expected the key to be there and it wasn't."

"That is interesting," she observed.

"Her story was so elaborate I got the feeling she was making it up on the spot," he continued. "The imprint inside the box showed a key that was far too large for a jewelry box."

"Maybe a trunk?" Adele suggested.

"It wasn't that large, Del."

"Then what do you think it was for?" she asked.

He shrugged. "We don't know right now." He cocked his head. "And the more surprising thing is we think Mr. Barry doesn't know either."

"Oh?" She raised her eyebrows, interested.

"He backed her up, of course," he said. "Just as he did when we asked her about the scarf. But it was clear he was seeing the box for the first time."

"A woman hiding a key," Adele sighed. "So many secrets hidden behind the chills and thrills of his circus."

Her brother stared ahead with a distant look.

CHAPTER 16

*T*he next morning, a string of wagons arrived in town with a group of sightseers who decided to make the trek to "the country" to take advantage of the mild summer day and stay in Arrojo to see the circus in the evening. They brought a tidal wave of business to Bridge Street, filling the street with the kind of shouting and laughter Adele had not seen even when the circus procession had come into town only a few days before.

She tried to convince Nin to stay in her shop, as the strange curiosos and scents always attracted people. But Nin, who had moments of misanthropy, took one look at the buoyant faces and brightly colored hats and immediately locked her door, hiding out in Adele's place. She consented to help Adele at the counter, which pleased Adele, as her friend proved herself to be an unyielding businesswoman, taking no promises of later payment and coaxing people to buy more than they planned.

The steady flow of customers petered out at lunchtime, though with promises of bringing others in later. Adele brought a basket of food Ruth made that morning and insisted Nin share it with her.

"The papers this morning seemed to point the finger at the

Barrys," Nin said, unwrapping a sandwich. "Considering what you found out yesterday, that isn't far from the truth, is it?"

"We don't know," Adele said. "Jack thinks Paul wasn't lying about knowing nothing of his wife's affair, and I think she wasn't lying about knowing nothing about Julius signing a new contract."

"Somebody's lying." Nin leaned back on her elbows. They had taken a place on the floor with a blanket laid out as if they were having a picnic.

"Your hunch or the Generous Ones?" Adele asked.

"The Generous Ones have been agitating me since this all began," she admitted. "I feel like that lion we saw pacing in his cage. I'm in a cage in my mind, pacing, waiting for the door to be opened."

After they ate, Adele opened the door to her shop all the way. On the sidewalk in front of her appeared a large bouquet of blooming roses attached to the figure of a man. She backed into her shop, feeling startled.

Mr. Lionel Sipes had changed little, though the shabby clothes were more presentable and the clean-shaven face dignified with a brushed mustache.

"Dear lady," he said in a more subdued tone than the showman enthusiasm he had had when he came into town the first time.

Adele folded her arms. "Well, Mr. Sipes?"

"It was destiny!" he declared as he took her hand and kissed it.

"A rather unfortunate destiny," Nin said dryly.

"Ah! How well I remember the lady who bewitched my Sinbad." He reached for her hand to kiss it, but she slid away from him behind the safety of the counter.

"Are you surprised to see me here, dear lady?" he asked Adele with a smile.

"Surprised isn't the word," Nin said. "We're wondering how you dared show your face again."

"As I told the sheriff, I've turned over a new leaf," he insisted. "Won't you take my posies as a sign of forgiveness?" He thrust the bouquet at Adele.

The wrinkle of his eyebrows and corners of his mouth showed a real anxiousness to please, and Adele felt her sympathy rise. "That wasn't necessary." She took the flowers. They had a clean scent that always signaled the Powlett Florist's best bouquets freshly cut that morning.

"A man who's turned over a new leaf must make amends for past behavior." He took her hands in both of his. "Especially toward a lady he admires."

Adele felt a shiver go down her spine, remembering the last time she met the man and the trouble he caused in town. Nin was watching her closely.

"That isn't necessary either," she mumbled.

"Now that you've delivered your apology, you can leave," Nin said in a brisk tone.

He leaned against the counter. "I know I did some unforgivable things the last time we met —"

"I wouldn't call them unforgivable," Adele said. "You didn't kill anyone, after all."

"And neither did your cat," Nin added.

"Nevertheless," he said. "They were criminal acts."

"You paid for them, as you told my brother," Adele said.

"You realize he would tie you up and throw you in Tanner Swamp if he found you here?" Nin didn't bother to hide her satisfied smile.

"He was only doing his job," Mr. Sipes said in a humble tone. "So was the sheriff. After all, they're at the mercy of those greedy, mangy dogs too."

"Good of you to forgive them," Adele said dryly.

"You must believe I'm not the sort of man who goes around doing such things," he said, the anxious gaze returning in her eyes.

"You don't have to explain, Mr. Sipes," Adele said.

"You're so understanding." Before she could say a word, he took her hand again and kissed it several times.

"You've been with the circus for eight months, Mr. Sipes?" she asked as she wiggled her hand away.

"And as sober as a judge the entire time," he vowed. "Nothing more expensive than a lion's leather collar has touched my hands."

"I doubt that," Nin mumbled.

"I wasn't implying anything, Mr. Sipes," Adele said as she went back to arranging the ink bottles on the shelf. "Do you like your work with Mr. Verner?"

The man groaned. "A boorish man, but good with the cats."

"Perhaps you'll replace him one day." Adele looked over her shoulder with a smile. Her prediction that he would rise to the bait proved true.

"Well, I don't want to take anybody's livelihood, of course," he said with false modesty, "but I assure you the cats like me better than him."

"Why is there a scar on your arm, then?" Nin asked in her plain way, pointing to a well-worn mark that extended from his wrist to his elbow.

"That, my dear lady, was Sinbad's doing," he said. "I made the mistake of trying to use the whip on him in our early days together. He didn't like that."

"I shouldn't think so," Adele said dryly.

"It was then I realized I would have a much better chance with him if we were friends rather than adversaries," continued the man. "I was right, of course. You saw how he behaved with me."

"Yes, well, would you like a cup of tea?" Adele moved swiftly to the burner where the kettle had boiled some time ago.

"I'd be delighted."

Adele was slow to make the tea, contemplating her next move.

"This nasty business with Mr. Rowe must have upset

everyone terribly," she went on, picking up her dust rag again and moving to another shelf.

"Oh, it has!" He took this up eagerly. "But I've told everyone what a solid man your sheriff is, and he shall find the culprit soon."

"That was good of you," Adele said.

"Did you also tell them you knew this from personal experience?" Nin raised her eyebrow.

"There was no need," he said. "The Barrys know about me, of course, and so does that wretch Verner."

"Is that why you're only his assistant?" Adele asked.

"Ah, you're a shrewd lady, Miss Gossling," he said with a smile. "Yes, I'm afraid so. He said he'd be hanged — I beg your pardon, but it's his word, not mine — if he would allow, well, someone with my reputation, into the cage with his precious cats." He snorted. "I can't imagine what he thinks I will do to them."

"The same thing you did to Sinbad," Nin said.

The man ignored this. "The Barrys are good, honest people, Miss Gossling. Perhaps if you would tell the police that —"

"What makes you think they don't consider them good, honest people?" Adele asked.

"Why, it's been all over the circus how they interrogated poor Mrs. Barry yesterday." He sighed. "A woman with a delicate disposition."

"I'm surprised you know about it," Adele remarked.

"The circus is a crucible, Miss Gossling," he said, sipping his tea. "We know all there is to know about one another, whether we want to know it or not."

"An interesting way of putting it, Mr. Sipes," Adele said, thinking of the shock she felt when she discovered how easily tongues like Mrs. Faderman's wagged at the slightest provocation.

"Of course, we all knew Estelle was — well, rather taken by Julius."

"Including her husband?" Nin asked.

The man grunted. "Paul sees only what he wishes to see. I shouldn't imagine a philandering wife would be within his range of vision."

Adele smiled. "That's very helpful for us to know, Mr. Sipes."

The man looked genuinely mortified. "I didn't mean —"

"I know you didn't," she said.

"We were rather surprised to hear she had acted on her infatuation," he continued.

"Caesar's wife is above suspicion?" Nin inquired.

He laughed. "Not because of her morals, dear lady. Because of her lack of cash." He rubbed his hands together. "Julius was known to live off women whenever he could. And Estelle hasn't a cent to her name."

"So Mr. Rowe chose his ladies by their purse rather than their charm," Adele mused.

"I suppose he thought he had all the charm so all he needed was the purse." The man grimaced.

"I found him rather charming," Adele said lightly.

"You met him?"

"Only briefly."

"And you really thought he was charming?" The incredulous tone made Nin, who had been watching the exchange, give an almost evil grin.

"Only in passing," Adele assured him. "There are some men who have that kind of charm."

"Personally, dear lady, but I always thought he had the charm of a billy goat," Mr. Sipes said.

Adele laughed. "You may be right, Mr. Sipes." Then, more seriously, she said, "I'm surprised his own partners didn't fall for him."

"Oh, Helen was much too young for his taste," he said. "Not to mention her sister hardly lets anyone near her."

"But Abby?" Nin suggested.

The man shuddered. "Miss Call has a sensible head on her shoulders." He swerved toward Adele. "Rather like you, dear lady."

"Yes, we got along well when we spoke," she said quickly as she veered between the envelope display and the wall, out of reach of his grasp. "Perhaps Julius wouldn't fall for Helen, but I could see her falling for him. She seems — well, vulnerable."

"Helen has eyes for a much younger man." His own glistened. "Estelle was really more his type anyway."

"She struck me as rather, well, soppy," Adele ventured.

"Don't underestimate Estelle," he said. "She has more gumption than meets the eye, I assure you."

"Still, you don't approve of her relationship with Julius?" Adele eyed him.

"Again, shrewd as a cat," he said. "Yes, when one sees a seasoned woman falling for a swine like that — well, it makes a man lose faith in the fair sex." He turned his gaze on her again. "That is, until one finds a fine lady like you to restore it."

Adele cleared her throat. "You're a very observant man, Mr. Sipes."

He grinned. "I like to think so."

"Was there anything you saw on opening night that might help us find Julius's killer?"

He rubbed his chin with his hand. From the corner of her eye, Adele saw Sibyl Pringle marching down the street toward her shop and groaned inwardly. Sibyl was getting married in a few months and had taken it upon herself to accost Adele with the most exhausting questions about wedding stationery, though she had yet to buy any. Nin, alert as always, darted outside, and after a few moments of exchanging words, the young woman took her rather slope-shaped chin and dippy eyes further down the street to Dora's Tea Shop.

Nin returned and snapped at Mr. Sipes. "Well? She hasn't got all day."

He pressed his lips together. "I remember I was bringing the tigers their dinner, and I saw Julius go into Calvin's wagon."

"Well, that wouldn't be so strange, would it?" Adele asked. "Calvin helps his parents run the circus, doesn't he?"

"Oh, he might see Calvin for a few moments," he said. "But not an hour."

"An hour!" Adele raised her eyebrow. "How do you know this?"

"Because, dear lady, it takes me about that long to feed the tigers — they're a rather persnickety bunch — and when I left to return to my wagon, I passed by Calvin's again and ran into Julius coming out."

"Did he say anything?" Adele asked.

Mr. Sipes shrugged. "He would hardly have said a word to *me*. Star performers think themselves rather superior."

"Did you notice anything peculiar about him?" Adele persisted.

"I certainly did," said the man. "He was smiling."

"Smiling?" Nin wrinkled her nose. "Smug, I'll bet."

"Precisely, dear lady," said the man. "He had a smile on his face that was well above him."

"Charmingly put, Mr. Sipes." Adele saw Sibyl emerge from Dora's Tea Shop. "And now, if you'll excuse me, I believe I have a customer." She darted to the doorway and motioned for Sibyl to cross the street.

"I should be delighted if you would join me for dinner tonight, and we could continue this conversation," he said, looking hopeful.

"I'm afraid that's impossible," Adele said. "You see, if my brother saw me anywhere near you, he would tan your hide. I don't want that to happen, Mr. Sipes. Do you?"

The man turned pale and, making his excuses, scurried out of the shop. Nin burst out laughing.

~~~~~

Adele couldn't resist bringing up Mr. Sipes that night after dinner when she and her brother took their places in the parlor with the new lamps illuminating the room and the new lace project in her lap, a tablecloth Ruth promised her even the least nimble fingers could complete.

She began, "I know you take an interest in my personal relationships, Jack."

"You make me sound like a barbarian rather than a concerned brother." He shook out one of his evening city newspapers.

"You might turn into one when you hear about this," she said slyly.

His attention was still on his paper. "Well?"

"I have a new admirer."

"Oh?" He folded half the paper back. "I thought after Percy Faderman bumbled his invitation to the dance last month you would be finished with the provincial boys in this town."

"Boys is right," she murmured. "Not an angular chin among them. All round and flabby."

He laughed. "Well, then, I needn't worry."

"Oh, but this admirer is someone entirely different," she said.

"Indeed?" He raised an eyebrow.

"Someone I don't think you would appreciate."

He put down the paper. "Stop talking in circles, Del. Who is it?"

"Lionel Sipes." She said the name matter-of-factly.

He growled, "Really, Del. I don't find this amusing."

"It isn't a joke, Jack," she retorted. "He was making eyes at me in my shop this afternoon."

"He was probably making eyes at your inventory," he sneered.

"Exactly," she said. "My personal inventory."

"Don't be vulgar, Del."

"He also wanted me to have dinner with him."

She had at last garnished his full attention as the paper fell into his lap and he stared at her. "The gall of the man!"

"Ask Nin," she challenged. "She was there."

He relaxed a bit. "Well, if your man-loathing friend was there, I can assume he didn't get very far."

"He wouldn't have gotten very far even if she hadn't been there," she declared. "I'm no innocent, Jack."

"I realize that." He looked annoyed, tapping his pipe on the arm of his chair. "I told Hatfield we should have run him out of town."

"I'm glad you didn't," she said. "He has some illuminating insights into his co-performers."

"He's no performer," Jackson grunted. "He's a charlatan."

"But a very useful and observant one," she said.

He eyed her. "I'm assuming you got information out of him that might help our investigation."

"Mr. Sipes had some interesting observations about opening night."

"Oh?"

"Julius visited Calvin's wagon," Adele said.

Jackson filled his pipe with tobacco. "I'm certain many performers visit the man on opening night. He does take care of their salary, after all."

"I highly doubt Julius would slip into Calvin's wagon for an hour just to get his pay," Adele said.

Jackson heaved a sigh and put his paper down. "All right. And why, according to the amenable Mr. Sipes, did he spend an hour in Calvin's wagon?"

"He couldn't tell me that." Adele jumped as she pricked herself with the lace needle, "But he did say the man emerged with a big grin on his face."

"Perhaps they were talking about salary after all," Jackson

said. "If Calvin agreed to a substantial raise, that would cause Julius to come out grinning."

"Julius had just renewed his contract a few weeks before," Adele pointed out. "One would think they would have discussed salary then."

"Del, what are you really getting at?" Jackson chewed on the edge of his pipe.

"'A smile well above him,' according to Mr. Sipes," Adele added.

Jackson's eyes narrowed. "It would seem Mr. Sipes is well versed on the idea of thinking well above oneself."

"Calvin must be hiding something," Adele insisted, "something about Julius that night." She rose, going over to the desk in the corner. "I found these behind the curtain." She handed him the two halves of the broken pencil.

"You think they belong to Calvin?"

"I know they do," she insisted. "It's his brand. And Cora told us he broke a pencil that night, remember?"

"What would this smug smile on Julius's face have to do with a broken pencil? It makes no sense, Del."

"I think you ought to talk to Calvin again," Adele said. "You remember his words when he saw the body, Jack? 'That wasn't supposed to happen.' Find out from him why it wasn't supposed to happen."

He raised his eyebrow. "Is that your professional opinion, lady detective?"

"I'm no detective," she retorted. "But I have eyes for some things you regard as inconsequential. It can't hurt, can it, Jack? You're at a dead end."

"I wouldn't say that," Jackson said quickly.

"I say it," she said, fluffing up one of the cushions and putting it behind his back. "And you know I'm right."

He wrinkled his nose at her, his way of agreeing without actually agreeing.

CHAPTER 17

The following morning Adele was in her shop for barely an hour when Hatfield and her brother sauntered in. The sheriff's heavy steps upset a tiered display of pencils she had just set up in a beautifully colored fan.

"You ought to be more careful, Sheriff!" Adele said, feeling her irritation rise as she bent down to the scattered pencils.

Always the gentleman, Hatfield helped her gather them up and lay them back in the fan pattern. "Jackson told me about the broken pencil."

"You ought to have given it to us earlier, Del," her brother chided.

"I forgot about it earlier." She sniffed.

"So you want us to see Calvin again, eh?" the sheriff continued.

"If he spoke to Julius that night for that length of time, it must have been serious and possibly relevant to his death."

"I agree." The sheriff nodded. "Like to come with us?"

She wiped the dusty lead from the pencils off her hands with a damp cloth, studying him. "Is this official or unofficial?"

"I haven't seen you wearing a badge yet, Del," her brother said with some annoyance. "Don't get ideas above yourself."

"It was the sheriff's idea, remember?" She eyed him. "Last year he offered to speak with the mayor on my behalf to hire me as a police consultant."

"Police consultant!" Jackson stared at his superior. "You didn't tell me, sir."

Hatfield's voice dropped its mild manner and became almost bull-like. "I didn't think I needed your permission, Deputy, even if it is your sister."

"Not my permission, no," Jackson said softly. "But I would have liked to know about it."

The sheriff's good will overrode his defensive tone. "You're right, Jackson. I should have said something."

"It was my fault," Adele said quickly. "I'm sure you assumed I would tell Jack and I didn't."

"Yes, you conveniently left out that small detail in your conversations," her brother growled.

"Your obvious dislike of it was exactly why I didn't mention it," she retorted. "I know how you feel about women working. You nearly hung me up by my ankles for opening this shop."

Her brother chuckled. "I wouldn't go so far as to say that, but I still don't see the need for you to work at all."

"And what would you have your sister do, stay home and tend her lacework?" Hatfield inquired.

"More like rip through it," Jackson snorted. "I don't think Del has a domestic bone in her body."

"You never know, Jackson," said his superior. "One day, Adele might — well, she might decide to settle down."

"That day has not yet come, thankfully," Adele said.

"I'm afraid your police consultant day hasn't come yet either," said the sheriff, clearly embarrassed. "I've put in the proposal to the council and Mayor Willett's office, but I've heard nothing so far."

"That doesn't surprise me in the least," Adele said. "They still have the same antiquated ideas about my place here as they did when I came into town three years ago."

"I wouldn't say that, Del," Jackson objected. "You're doing a nice little business here."

"Only because I charge less than the Rosa Gris shops," she said. "And my merchandise is of better quality than anything Raleigh is likely to bring into his general store, the tightwad."

Hatfield laughed and put on his hat. "I promise you I will not relent until I get an answer."

"And I won't hold my breath for one," she said as she picked up the key to the door.

Calvin was in the cookhouse bent over a ledger with a man who wore a chef's uniform and had a curling mustache. When the latter saw Sheriff Hatfield, he immediately rushed out and came back with a cup of coffee and a large piece of pie.

"People remember lawmen have good appetites," Hatfield said jovially.

"You're welcome to our hospitality anytime," said Calvin, though he seemed a little finicky about it.

"It looks like you've recovered from the tragic events," Jackson remarked. "At least, in terms of your business."

"Don't be fooled, Deputy." Calvin glanced at the ledger. "We've lost a lot of money these past few days." He turned to the sheriff. "How much longer must we remain here before we can move on? I'm trying to see if we can get something going at the amphitheater in San Francisco."

"You're sure to see big crowds there," Adele remarked.

"I hope so," he said. "We have to recoup our losses somehow."

Sheriff Hatfield nodded. "I can understand that."

"Then you'll finish with this business soon and let us go?"

"We're not keeping you here out of fun, Mr. Barry," Jackson said. "We're trying to solve a crime."

"Then solve it!" The man's roar surprised even the cook, who glanced at him. "I'm sorry." He rubbed his forehead.

Hatfield leaned back. "You might be able to help us, sir."

"I know nothing more than what I've already told you."

"You didn't tell us what Julius was doing in your wagon the night of his death," Hatfield said.

The man blinked. "I assume you're trying to get at something?"

"We were informed you spent quite a lot of time speaking with Julius a few hours before the performance," Hatfield said. "Someone saw him enter your wagon and leave an hour later."

"Someone?" Calvin eyed him. "One of the workers, you mean."

"You could say that," Adele said.

"He also described Julius as having looked very satisfied about something."

The man leaned back. Adele could see he was squeezing his hands in his lap by the way his shoulders tensed.

"There's no use denying it when there's a witness," Jackson said.

"Witness?" The man gave a short laugh. "Am I on trial?"

"No, sir," the sheriff said. "We're merely asking questions."

"And we expect answers," Jackson added.

Calvin reached for the salt and pepper shaker on the table and started playing with them. "I suppose it's useless to keep it from you, and it doesn't really matter now anyway." He said the last with some distaste. "Julius did visit my wagon that night and stayed for quite a while."

"Why?" Hatfield asked.

"We had things to discuss about his contract."

"You said he'd signed that a few weeks before," Adele said.

"They all signed it," said Calvin. "But there was a certain part of the contract Julius was interested in."

"A certain part?" Jackson eyed him.

He shuffled through some papers and came up with a folder, which he handed to the sheriff. "You'll find the complete contract in there."

"You mean what you showed us before was a bogus?" Jackson glanced at his superior.

"It was a real contract," the man growled. "You saw the signatures. But what I didn't show you was the addendum."

"Addendum?" Sheriff Hatfield ruffled the pages. As he read it, his face grew puzzled. "It looks to me as if this is about Helen Call."

Calvin nodded. "If you remember, we can't fire Helen without Abby leaving too. I would never risk that."

"Then it was about finding another place for her," Adele said.

"In a way," said Calvin. "It was all Julius's idea. Helen was beginning to make some costly mistakes."

"So the talk about grounding her wasn't just talk after all," Adele said.

He bent his head a little. "Not for Julius."

"I shouldn't think Miss Abby Call would be amenable to signing such an addendum, let alone her sister," Jackson said. "Yet, the signatures are there."

The man rose and walked around the table, his hands in his pockets. "They didn't know they signed it."

"I think I'm beginning to see." The sheriff's tone was icy. "Very cleverly done."

"It was all Julius's idea," he repeated. "He thought if we put the addendum amongst the pages, they wouldn't notice."

"And so, in one swoop of the pen, a young girl's career is ruined," Hatfield snarled.

"A career she didn't want," Adele said softly.

"That was the only reason I agreed," Calvin said. "Well, one of the reasons. I thought when Helen found out, well, she would be relieved."

"And the other reason?"

He let the glare of the sun narrow his eyes. "A couple doing a trapeze act is more appealing than a threesome, especially if we can generate some hint of romance."

"Which you would have done admirably in your publicity, no doubt." The sheriff slapped his thick leather gloves against his knee. "I can't say I'm impressed by your scruples, sir."

The man glared at him. "You don't need to rub it in, Sheriff. I see now that —" He swallowed.

"That what?" Adele asked.

"There was a human element involved," he said softly. "I didn't — I wasn't thinking of that when we discussed the addendum."

"What was the plan?" Jackson asked. "Miss Call would be restricted in what she could do, while Mr. Rowe and her sister were to go on as a couple?"

"Julius had the idea of exchanging roles mid-act," Calvin said. "It's never been done before. Part of the time he would be the flyer and Abby would catch and the other part, Abby would fly and he would catch."

"Very interesting," Adele said.

"He had every intention of seeing that Helen was taken care of," Calvin defended. "He even said he would give up part of his salary if necessary."

"A noble gesture," Jackson said, "if it was sincere."

"It was," Calvin said. "He genuinely liked Helen. Oh, he thought her scatterbrained, too much to ever succeed as a trapeze artist. But he felt sorry for her."

"Pity is a poor substitute for respect," Adele snapped.

"How were you going to get around your parents?" Jackson asked.

"Julius was going to tell my father it was his and Abby's choice," he said. "He was going to tell him Helen wanted to experience other things in the circus. He was sure Pa would get her training with another act by the time the next season opened." His voice trailed off. "We've never had a sword throwing act and Pa's always wanted one. Helen would have been perfect for that."

"You had it all arranged." Jackson eyed him.

"All this doesn't explain what he was doing in your wagon for an hour on opening night," said Hatfield.

"He came to see if I had spoken to our lawyers," Calvin said, sitting down. "There was a legal side to all this, you know."

"Naturally," said the sheriff.

"Oh, I checked on it, of course," said Calvin. "I'm very thorough about those things."

"I'm sure," Adele mumbled.

"I wanted to make sure our lawyers saw the signed addendum and kept it in their files," he said. "What I showed you was a copy, of course. The original is with them."

"And what did your lawyers say?" Hatfield asked. "I'm guessing it wasn't good news, if you spoke to Mr. Rowe for an hour."

"There was a problem," Calvin admitted. "Oh, the paper was legal with Helen's signature. But they said if she or Abby claim they didn't know what they were signing —"

"— and they could prove it wasn't true," Hatfield finished.

"That's precisely it," said Calvin.

"How could they prove it?" Jackson asked.

Calvin gave a grim smile. "By getting their lawyer to get witnesses who had seen our show. A hundred people who attest they saw a flawless performance with Helen catching Julius every time could easily sway a jury."

"I shouldn't think Mr. Rowe would have let that stop him," said Hatfield. "He struck me as a very determined man."

"He was," said Calvin. He rolled a pencil between his palms. Adele saw it was the same type of pencil she had found in the tent. "He was pacing back and forth in my wagon, throwing out ideas. That's why he was there for so long."

"And what idea did he finally decide on?" Jackson asked.

The man's look became distant. "Do to her what she could do to him."

"Eh?" Sheriff Hatfield cocked one eye.

"If Helen and Abby could try to prove Helen's competence with witnesses to the performance, Julius was going to prove her incompetence the same way."

All at once, Adele's memory lit up to the opening night. She saw the dusty ring, the trapeze swinging and bobbing, Julius's uncertain figure, and the reaching arms... reaching and twitching...

She jumped up. "He fell on purpose!"

"Don't be ridiculous, Del," Jackson snapped.

"She's right, Deputy," said Calvin. "At least, that's what he intended to do."

"I don't follow," Hatfield said.

"Julius was going to do his triple somersault that night," he said. "Only he was going to deliberately miss the catcher's hands."

"You mean he was going to endanger his life?" Jackson stared.

"Hardly that," Calvin said with a small smile. "He's fallen dozens of times in that net during practices, and he's never been injured or even bruised. Circus nets are very sturdy, Deputy."

"Except that this one wasn't," the sheriff said.

"But it was supposed to be," Adele said softly.

"Is that why you were so shocked when we found the net had been tampered with?" Jackson asked.

"Mr. Rowe would hardly have undermined his own act in that way," Hatfield agreed. "Unless he was planning on suicide."

"Hardly, for a man of his type," Jackson said.

Adele leaned forward and put her hand on Calvin's arm. "You're a man with a sense of — well, the way things are done. Even your desk is organized to perfection." He gave a rueful smile. "I find it hard to believe you agreed to all this."

The man's balanced features wilted and he broke into a sob, laying his head in his arms. They all remained silent for a few moments. When Calvin had calmed himself, he said, "I was a fool, Miss Gossling. A blinded fool."

"Mr. Rowe was a very persuasive man," said Jackson in a quiet voice.

"He was also manipulative," Adele said in a hard voice.

"He threatened to leave if I didn't agree to his plan," Calvin said. "He knew the circus wouldn't survive if he took his act elsewhere."

"So he appealed to your desire to protect your parents," Adele said softly.

"You could say that, Miss Gossling," he said.

"Nevertheless, you weren't entirely blind to the possibility of something serious happening," Adele said. "That's why you were so agitated that night and why you broke your pencil."

"My pencil?"

Hatfield produced the two sticks from his pocket. "We found these behind the curtain."

"Miss Spore told us she had seen you break it," added Jackson.

Calvin leaned back, his hand on his forehead. He began to laugh, a sort of gasping laughter that made Adele uncomfortable. "Well, it's true what they say, isn't it? A criminal always leaves something behind at the scene of the crime."

"But you're not a criminal, sir," the sheriff said.

"I may as well be!" The man banged his fists against the table. "I agreed to the plot. I killed Julius!"

"This isn't a melodrama, sir," Jackson said. "One does not cause murder by agreeing to a deception."

"But I could have stopped Julius from doing such a dastardly thing!" the man insisted.

"I doubt anyone could have stopped Mr. Rowe from doing anything he set his mind to," Sheriff Hatfield said. "He had obviously set his mind to falsifying this accident. No one could know someone else would hear of it and have different ideas."

"You really think someone else heard of it?" Calvin stared at him.

"It's clear someone else knew about Mr. Rowe's scheme to fake a fall," Jackson said, "and decided to use that as an excuse for murder."

"My God!" Calvin nearly dropped to the floor but Hatfield jumped up and caught the man's arm, leading him into a chair.

"Since the idea came up only that night in your wagon, someone could have been outside and overheard," the sheriff said, handing the man his handkerchief, which had fallen to the floor. "Did you see or hear anyone that night around the time Mr. Rowe was with you?"

"It could have been anybody," Calvin lamented. "People pass through there all the time, especially on opening night. That's why my parents and I make sure our wagons are at the very back. The crowds make the performers self-conscious so they prefer to go out of their way to pass through the back rather than the front."

Hatfield rose. "We thank you for telling us what you did, sir. We know it was difficult for you."

"You're an honest man with high integrity," Adele said kindly.

"Integrity!" the man sniffed. "If my parents knew, they would have drowned me at birth."

The sheriff chuckled. "I think that rather unlikely."

"Do they have to know?" Calvin looked at him with pleading eyes.

"That depends on how much that addendum had to do with the murder," Hatfield said. "The Call sisters will have to know."

Calvin nodded slowly. "You'll find them rehearsing in the big top."

They left the wagon, Adele glancing back to see Calvin bent over the table with his head in his hands.

"The Barrys *will* have to know, won't they?" she asked softly.

The sheriff nodded. "That's their right."

"Even though the addendum is null and void now?" Jackson asked.

"We can't abide by deception, Jackson," Hatfield said. "What Calvin Barry and Julius Rowe did amounts to an illegal act. At least, that's how lawyers will frame it. The Call sisters might even sue Mr. Barry."

"Even with Mr. Rowe dead?" Jackson inquired.

"I agree it's highly unlikely, but they would be within their rights." Hatfield adjusted his hat on his head. "We've a different direction to go on now, Deputy."

"We need to send Edison and the assistant deputies on a wild goose chase," Jackson remarked, "questioning everybody in the circus to see if they were passing through here on opening night and whether they heard anything or saw anyone outside Calvin's wagon."

"If you can find anyone that observant," Adele said dryly.

CHAPTER 18

"*W*hat now, Sheriff?" Jackson asked, buttoning his coat.

"First, we do a little of our own searching," he said. "I want to take a look around before we send Edison and the lads to interrogate people."

"And interrogate they will," Jackson mumbled.

"Edison can be more subtle than you think, Jack," Adele objected.

The sheriff laughed. "I'll instruct them with care, don't you worry."

"And then on to the Call sisters?" Adele asked.

He nodded. "Hardly a task I relish."

"Suppose I make it easier for you." Adele leaned on her parasol. "I'll go back to town and fetch Nin, and we'll meet you at the Call wagon."

"How is that going to help, Del?"

"They like us, Jack," she said. "It might soften things."

Hatfield agreed and they parted ways.

She found Nin just closing her shop. The woman's exotic eyes were wide with worry and Adele realized for the first time her friend had taken the yellowish pallor of one who had been in a struggle.

"What is it, dear?" she asked gently.

"I've a bad feeling."

"About what?"

"Everything," her friend said vaguely. "The Generous Ones are calling but I can't hear what they're saying."

Adele shivered. She had every respect for Nin's clairvoyant gifts but they sometimes frightened her.

The trapeze was set up in the center of the ring with a new and larger black net underneath. People were rehearsing in different corners, such as the woman with the four poodles whom they had seen on opening night and a juggler they had not had a chance to see. A few clowns milled around dressed in trousers and sleeved shirts but with their faces painted. Three of them were rehearsing a night court act, including the police clown. Adele also couldn't fail to see a few gray figures in the back benches of the ring and she saw the woman named Gerry lingering near the walls with a broom.

Abby was perched up on the trapeze her sister had used on opening night. Helen was on the bar, her hand grasping the flying trapeze, her face elongated with fear.

"All you have to do is swing and twist," Abby said in her commanding tone. "You've watched me do it a hundred times."

"I can't, Abby."

"Of course you can." Her sister's tone was more soothing. "The net's right there if you fall, but you won't."

"Suppose it rips like the other one?" Helen shrieked. "Oh, I can't!"

"Just once, dear," her sister pleaded. "Once and you'll see how easy it is."

There was silence as everyone in the ring stopped what they were doing. Even the poodles who had been whimpering for a treat were silent, their wagging tails still.

Helen threw the trapeze out several times, and when it gained height and speed, she swung and twisted into her sister's waiting arms. When she was safely back on the platform, there was a small smile on her face, and Adele had to admit she looked more relaxed. A loud applause sounded from below, and the clowns jumped up and down. She and Nin joined in.

Abby said, "How about a glass of water, honey?"

"I could use it," Helen said breathlessly.

They both climbed down the ladder. Close up, Helen's expression was less relaxed and Abby's face was shining, her prickly eyes determined.

"It was cruel to force her to do that under the circumstances," Nin hissed. "Couldn't you have waited?"

"Waited for what, Miss Branch?" Abby glared at her. "For the circus to fire us because we had no act?"

"You have one now," Adele said.

"Not yet, but we will," Abby said. "I ought to thank your sheriff for forbidding any daredevil acts from performing. It gives us time to practice."

"She doesn't want to be a flyer," Nin said in her far-away voice. "She doesn't want to be anywhere near here."

"I know what my sister wants," Abby snapped. "I would appreciate it if you kept your comments to yourself, Miss Branch." Nin sniffed and turned away.

"It's quite a change for her," Adele remarked. "To be a flyer instead of a catcher."

The woman put a few loose curls that had come out of the pins in place. "We've been preparing for this since we joined the Barry Circus."

"I don't doubt it," Adele said easily. "But do you really think now is the time to train your sister as a flyer?"

"What do you mean?" The woman blinked.

"I mean in the shadow of your partner's tragedy." Adele tried to sound delicate. "You saw how it's still on Helen's mind."

"It's on everybody's mind." Her hand swept around the big top where most of the others had gone back to practicing. "Your sheriff and your brother haven't exactly let us lay Julius to rest. Oh, physically, perhaps. We found a nice burial place for him in your cemetery."

"The soul of the dead isn't buried so quickly," Nin said in a mysterious tone.

Abby gave a half-smile. "You really ought to think about joining us, Miss Branch. You'd be an international sensation."

Nin shrank back with horror at the thought. Adele knew there was nothing that would make her talents shrivel up more than to be exposed to the world more than she had to.

"I'm amazed at how you can concentrate with all these people about," Adele said.

"Nobody pays attention to anything except what they're doing."

"But teaching a poodle to jump through a hoop is very different than practicing a twist twenty feet above ground," Adele remarked.

"Twenty-five feet." The woman smiled triumphantly. "We've raised it since Julius died."

"Raised it!"

"You're insane!" Nin snarled.

"Raising the platform five feet is hardly insanity," Abby insisted. "I've seen them raised thirty-five feet."

"No wonder Helen is so frightened," Adele murmured.

The young woman approached them, looking thin and sickly. "Abby, I'm tired. Can't this be all for today?"

"Not yet, love," said her sister warmly. "You did the somersault yesterday. Let's show Adele and Miss Branch you can do it today."

"Oh, no!" The girl paled.

"You did it beautifully yesterday." Her sister put her arms

around her shoulders. "We have to do it every day until you could do it with your eyes closed."

"I can't!"

"Helen, don't be childish." Abby's voice turned edgy. "You know our situation. We don't have an act yet, and we can't make a living without one."

"Then we won't work for a while!" Helen's shriek caused silence in the tent. "We have some money. We can go away to some little place that won't cost much."

"It's not about the money and you know it," her sister said. "Even a week away would weaken your muscles and we have to keep them in condition for the triple."

"The triple!" Helen dropped the glass of water she had been holding in her hand. It made no sound as it hit the soft ground, but the water splattered all about.

"Stop it!" The cry came from a young man with a broken voice. He rushed into the ring, his tall figure towering over the three police clowns as he passed. "Stop pushing her!"

Adele recognized the young man she had seen on the street with Helen.

"I'll thank you to stay out of our affairs, Mr. Spears!" Abby shouted.

"I've every right," the young man insisted. "Helen has no one to defend her against your tyranny. No one but me, that is." He shyly took her hand.

"It's all right, Stephen," Helen said in a soft voice.

"You were told to stay away, Mr. Spears," Abby said. "I'll be obliged to call the police if you don't leave now." She turned to Adele. "The police are here, aren't they?"

Adele nodded. "They want to see you and Helen. We've come to take you back to your wagon."

"Splendid," Abby said in a brisk tone. "Then they can escort Mr. Spears out at the same time." She took her sister's arm and pulled her away from Mr. Spears's grasp. "We'll just do one somersault, then."

"No, she won't!" the young man declared.

"You have no say in anything we do, Mr. Spears," Abby said with a narrow gaze. "Don't think for one minute you ever will have."

"We'll see about that, won't we?" He eyed her back.

"Sheriff Hatfield is probably waiting for us right now at your wagon," Adele said gently.

"It won't take long." Abby led her sister, who couldn't stop staring at the young man, to the ladder.

"You don't have to do anything, Helen," the young man said, looking at her with gentle eyes magnified behind the glasses.

"Helen, is it?" Abby shot a look at her sister. "I think you'd better go, Mr. Spears, or I'll call Mr. Verner here with his whip and have him run you out!"

"Wait!" Helen gave the young man a helpless glance, then turned to her sister with more calmness. "All right, Abby. I'll do the somersault but only once."

"Good girl." Her sister pressed a kiss on her cheek. "Now you'll really see something, ladies."

"Good luck." Adele pressed Helen's hand with a kind smile.

"She won't need it," Abby said before her sister could answer.

As they climbed the ladder, Adele stepped back, saying to Nin in a low voice, "I hope she makes it."

"She won't," Nin said in the voice of her visions. "But she won't be harmed either." She turned to Mr. Spears and said in a kind tone, "She'll be all right."

"Thank you," the young man murmured.

Sometimes Adele regretted the accuracy of her friend's predictions. Again, the ring fell silent and people watched with their breath held as the trapeze swung back and forth, a little jerky at first, then smoother. Adele could tell even from that distance that Helen's eyes were watching it with both determination and hesitation. Mr. Spears held his hands together as if praying.

Helen grabbed the bar and rolled in the air, almost reminding Adele of the pill bugs she had played with as a child. Her posture was perfect, but when she unfolded and grabbed for her sister's arms, she was already too low and plummeted into the net. A scream sounded as the net bounced and rolled and the circus folk rushed toward it.

Nin's words were true, and the young woman crawled out of the net, clearly shaken but not hurt. "I'm only feeling a little dizzy," she assured them.

Mr. Spears pushed everyone away and took hold of Helen's shoulders. Adele saw the young man was not able to hold back tears.

She marveled even more at Abby's calm descent from the ladder and the way she sauntered into the crowd, taking hold of her sister. "Everyone relax. No harm done, right, honey?" She peered at her sister.

"I'm all right," Helen said. "It was just — as I was falling, it was like a flash."

"What happened before," Nin said softly.

"Yes, yes!" The young woman buried her face in her hands.

"It's just as well we're taking a rest now," said Abby.

Gerry slid up to them. "I'm glad you're all right, Helen."

"Thank you," Helen said in a short voice.

As the woman ambled away, the broom knocking against the ground, Nin leaned toward Adele and whispered, "That woman wants eyes."

"What do you mean?" Adele asked. But her friend only shrugged.

"You mustn't let the police see you out of sorts." Abby gently took the pins that had gone askew out of her sister's hair and arranged the bun again. Adele felt a tug in her heart as she watched the warm gestures, the care Abby took in putting up the thick hair so they wouldn't pinch, making sure they weren't too tight or close. Her nurture was genuine.

"You used to do that when she was a child, didn't you?" Adele asked softly.

Abby smiled. "I had to. Mama and Papa were always busy practicing so I had to take care of her."

Helen stared at her sister then suddenly threw her arms around her. "I'm sorry, Abby!"

"Nonsense," her sister said tenderly. "Don't give it another thought, darling. It takes practice to get the timing right, and you will. We've plenty of time."

"You're not going anywhere," Nin assured her. "Calvin made that clear."

"Yes, he's been most generous," Abby said as they left the big top. Once in the sun, Adele noticed Helen's face brightened, and the tight rings on her forehead disappeared. She also noticed Mr. Spears offer his arm to her.

"He doesn't want to lose a good act," Adele said, smiling.

"He'll get one better than he realizes," Abby said with determination. "A sister act is much more interesting than a man and woman act."

"Unless they're man and wife," Nin remarked.

"Even that has little novelty anymore, Miss Branch," Abby insisted. "But two is scant for an act like ours."

"You're taking on another person?" Adele asked.

"We might." She pulled the jacket over her shoulders. "You sound surprised, Adele."

"I should think it would be too soon to start considering a third person," Adele said.

"Too soon?"

"After Julius's death."

"I'm sure you've heard the show must go on," the woman insisted.

Adele eyed her. "But your show, so to speak, has been delayed. So it's not going on at all."

"It will pick up again when we leave here," said the woman.

"And when it does, you intend to start performing again right away?" Adele asked.

"I have a responsibility to my sister to clothe and feed my sister and keep her out of trouble," Abby said. "That takes money."

"But Helen just said you had some money saved up," Nin pointed out.

Abby gave her a condescending smile. "My sister doesn't keep our accounts. Helen — well, Helen's always been delicate." She glanced back where Helen and Mr. Spears had fallen a little behind. They walked slowly, Mr. Spears grasping both her hands.

"Maybe Helen can take care of herself more than you think," Adele said gently. "She seems to like that boy very much."

"That parasite!" the woman spit out. "He's been following the circus for six weeks now. Paul won't ward him off because he's the son of some big man in the Middle West."

"It would get her out of the circus," Nin said. "She wants to get out."

The woman's tone was as fiery as her red hair. "You don't understand, either of you. Helen's been waiting for this since she was fifteen."

"You mean she wanted to be a flyer?" Adele asked.

"It was Julius who insisted she be a catcher," said Abby. "He thought she was a third wheel anyway, and he said, with her strong arms — she really does have strong arms in spite of her delicate nature — she would be ideal. And, in truth, I'm not very physically adept to be a catcher." She glanced down at her own arms buried underneath the puffed sleeves. "He should have been the catcher — the man always is — but he wanted to be the star and Paul agreed. And Estelle certainly didn't object." The last came with a snort.

"His death has opened some doors for you," Adele remarked.

The woman stared at her. "What a horrible thing to say!"

Adele took her arm. "I'm sorry. Sometimes my thoughts just slip out without any consideration for others. Jack is always reprimanding me for it."

"You say what's on your mind," Nin defended.

"Sometimes that isn't in the best of taste, dear," Adele admitted with a smile.

The door to the Call wagon was open with Hatfield leaning against the opposite wall. He greeted the ladies with the tip of his hat.

Abby was clearly annoyed. "Just because we don't keep our wagons locked is no reason for you to barge in, Sheriff."

"It's not as if they would steal anything," Nin mumbled.

"Adele told us you'd like to talk to us." Abby peeled the jacket from her shoulders. "But I've a favor to ask first."

"Oh?"

"As law and order in this town, and since we are in your town —"

"Yes?"

"Get that man out of here!" This came in a roar and Helen, holding Mr. Spears' hand, jumped. The young man looked like a startled owl behind the large glasses.

"I'd be obliged if you would tell me first who he is," Sheriff Hatfield said with some amusement.

"He's a menace!" Abby snarled.

"Mr. Spears is a gentleman, Abby," Helen insisted.

"Spears?" Jackson eyed him.

"My father is Warren Spears of Cincinnati, Sheriff," said the young man.

"The administrator of the Good Samaritan," Jackson supplied.

Hatfield glanced at him. "How do you know that, Deputy?"

"I heard of him when I was in the Middle West, sir," he said with a quick cough.

"Yes, he's quite well known," Mr. Spears said. "In the Middle West, anyway."

"And you, sir?" Hatfield asked.

"I'm a medical student, Sheriff," he said.

Abby sneered, "A medical student is in medical school, not following a circus around like a dog looking for its tail."

"Is that true?" the sheriff asked. "Have you been trailing this circus?"

"Only for the season, sir," said the young man, looking a little sheepish.

"You must get him away from here, Sheriff," Abby persevered. "He's distracting Helen from her work."

Hatfield turned to the young woman. "Is that true, miss?"

"I don't think so." She looked at her sister.

"You fell into the net just now, didn't you?" Abby asked. "After an argument with him."

"Helen, dear, you know that isn't true!" The young man's face darkened. "Don't let her make you believe lies."

"All the same, sir, I'd be obliged if you would leave," the sheriff said.

The young man looked surprisingly defiant under the glasses. "Is that a threat of arrest, Sheriff?"

"Naturally not," said Hatfield. "Let's just say it's a request."

"I want him to stay." Helen's voice was firm.

"Helen, honey —"

"I want him to stay!"

The young man looked so humble with his head a little bowed and his eyes half closed that Adele could tell even her brother was sympathetic.

The sheriff turned to Abby. "Miss Call, it's my duty to inform you — well, I suppose it's best you see for yourself." He slid the addendum out of his coat pocket and handed it to her.

Abby's eyes grew wide as she read.

"Let me see it too, Abby!" Helen said as she watched her sister. "I signed it too."

"It's too upsetting, darling." She handed it to the sheriff. "What does this mean?"

"Julius didn't want Helen in the act anymore," Nin said.

"Please, Miss Branch!" Jackson hissed.

"That's what it amounts to, doesn't it?" she countered.

Abby threw the paper on the floor. "Even I didn't think Julius would stoop that low!"

"Let me see it!" Helen shrieked. Hatfield handed it to her and both she and Mr. Spears read it. "It calls me 'incompetent'!" She let the page flutter to the ground.

"Of course you're not, dear." Abby put her arms around her shoulders. "That was just something he said to get Calvin to go along with this horrendous trick."

"I don't remember signing anything like that." The woman stared at her sister.

"Mr. Barry hid the signature pages underneath the standard contract so you would sign them," Hatfield said in a low voice.

"Fiend!" Abby burst out. "To think we trusted him!"

"It would have been prudent for you to have read the contract," Jackson said mildly.

Abby glared at him. "That's not how we do things here, Deputy."

"She shouldn't have to read the contract if the manager is an honest man," Nin declared.

"Thank you for understanding, Miss Branch." Abby bowed. "If it makes you feel any better, Deputy, we'll be reading contracts very carefully in the future."

"There won't be a future," Mr. Spears declared. "Not for Helen."

Abby regarded him with narrow eyes. "I'd like to know what you mean by that remark, Mr. Spears."

He took Helen's hand. "I mean to marry her and take her away from all this."

"And when will that be?" the woman scoffed. "When your father dies and leaves you his fortune?"

"Abby!" her sister shrieked.

"You've done your slumming, Mr. Spears, now get out!" The fierceness in her face resembled one of Mr. Verner's lions. "I mean it. Get out!"

The sheriff cleared his throat. "Perhaps you'd better go, Mr. Spears."

The young man gave Helen a determined look as he cocked his hat over his forehead and stormed out of the wagon.

"That wasn't decent of you, Abby," said her sister in a soft tone.

"That man is the one whose indecent!" she fired out. "All men are indecent!"

Both Hatfield and Jackson shifted position.

"I'm sorry." Abby collapsed on the edge of the bed. "That was a childish thing to say."

"Yes, it was," Hatfield said, his tone mild. "But understandable, given what you've just learned."

"Helen's no more incompetent than I am." Abby perked up. "We could have proven that."

"It would have been hard to prove in the face of a man falling into a net," Jackson said.

She looked at him. "I don't understand."

"Calvin told us Julius had a plan for opening night," said Hatfield. "He didn't just fall into the net, Miss Call."

"You mean — my God!"

"It wasn't an accident at all, then." Helen's voice was shaky. "He meant to do it. He meant it!" Adele was surprised to hear relief in her voice.

"Nothing about Julius would shock me," Abby said briskly.

"He intended to fall and make it look like Helen was at fault. Is that right?"

"That's exactly right," the sheriff said.

She gave a small smile. "It's common in our business, Sheriff. One partner gets annoyed or enraged at the other, tempers rise, and one makes an accident look like the other's fault so the other will get fired."

"How awful!" Nin gasped.

"We are artists after all, Miss Branch," Abby said. "We're capable of anything when we're riled up."

"And someone was capable of murder," Adele said softly.

"Yes, so I understand now." Abby leaned back.

"Then you no longer insist it was an accident?" Jackson eyed her.

"How can I?" Abby sighed. "I will say one thing, Sheriff. You certainly know your job."

Hatfield could not hide his pride. "I'm sorry it had to involve you and your sister, Miss Call."

"I can't believe Paul would have allowed such a thing," Abby insisted. "He understood wherever I go, Helen goes."

"According to his son, neither his father nor his mother knew," the sheriff said.

The woman's eyebrows arched. "Oh, well, perhaps they didn't. Paul knows Helen's potential to be a flyer."

"Potential." Helen was grasping the edge of the mattress. "Have I potential?"

"Of course you do, darling." Abby gave her an affectionate look. "Everybody knows that."

"Julius didn't think so," she said in a quiet voice. "He wanted to throw me out."

"He did *not* want to throw you out." Abby's voice was firm. "He wanted to ground you. That was only because he was afraid of your appeal to the crowds. They love seeing a delicate, feminine woman flying through the air."

Helen looked toward the door. "I wish Julius had succeeded!"

"Helen!"

"I wish he had managed to make his fall look like my fault." Helen's voice was growing shrill. "Perhaps it was after all."

"Don't you ever say such a thing!" Her sister jumped up and grabbed her hands. "You're strong, dearest. You could catch that giant Gerry if you had to."

"Yes." Helen looked at her wide, strong hands. "Hands good enough for catching, but not for a wedding ring."

"Don't talk such nonsense," Abby insisted.

"It's no nonsense," Nin said slowly. "It's a wish."

"I'll thank you to stay out of it, Miss Branch!"

"When one voices a wish, one gets it," Adele said softly.

"They're right, Abby," said her sister. "If I had been taken off the trapeze, I could have married Mr. Spears and gone away."

"Married!" Her sister's indignation quickly turned to rage. "To that parasite?"

"He seemed like a nice young man," Hatfield said in a quiet voice. "I'm good at judging young men, Miss Call."

"Everybody thinks money makes a nice young man," she said in a mocking tone. "Would a nice young man abandon his studies to follow a circus for six months?"

A sob rose from Helen's throat. She threw open the door and ran out.

"Would you like my sister to go after her and calm her down, Miss Call?" Jackson asked kindly. "It's one of her talents." Adele gave him an affectionate look.

Abby rose. "I'll go after her. You needn't worry about Helen. She's upset now, but she knows her place."

"Perhaps she's right, sir," Jackson remarked as they left the wagon. "I've met circus people in my travels, and they're very devoted to their way of life."

"Like a seaman is devoted," Hatfield agreed. "When one gets

an opportunity to see the world, it's difficult for one to keep one's feet on the ground."

"It's like a sickness," Nin murmured.

"I don't know as I would say that, Miss Branch," Hatfield said, holding the gate to the park open so the ladies could go through without smearing their dresses with mud and dirt.

"Perhaps that's why she wasn't worried about Helen's fear of the somersault," Adele said. "She thinks Helen will be begging to throw herself up in the air for crowds in a year's time."

"What's this about a somersault?" Jackson asked.

"We watched Helen perform one," Adele said.

"She fell," Nin reported. "Right into the net."

"A safety net that was intact, I gather," the sheriff said in a dry tone.

"And while we were doing that," Adele asked, "did you have any luck with your search?"

The sheriff produced a shiny object from his pocket. "A button off someone's costume."

"Julius's costume," Adele murmured.

"We won't know that until we check it against his clothes," Hatfield said.

"Why didn't you just ask Abby?" Nin asked.

"Because the police can't think of everything, Miss Branch," Jackson said in an annoyed tone.

"When it comes to murder, Mr. Gossling, the police should think of everything," she snapped.

"I would rather rely on our evidence than on the talk of circus folk," the sheriff said slowly.

"You think they would lie?" Adele asked.

"They're beginning to close ranks, Del," Jackson said. "It often happens when we investigate crimes in a close-knit community. They think first of protecting their own rather than helping the police."

"Well, it proves one thing, anyway," Adele said. "Julius was in the vicinity at some time."

"It had to have been the opening night," Jackson argued. "Their wagons didn't arrive at the park until after the parade, and Mr. Barry said they don't get into their costumes until just a few hours before the performances begin."

"Calvin was telling the truth when he said Julius came to see him that night," Nin chimed in.

The sheriff was silent as he shoved his hands into his pockets, but Adele could almost see the question marks jumbling in his head.

CHAPTER 19

*T*hat afternoon was hotter than usual. In spite of Tomas' cautious clucking, Adele had Ruth open all the windows before she retired to the Cordoba cottage for the night, including the ones downstairs. She had no fear of burglars or thieves because everyone in town knew the deputy sheriff lived with his sister. Jackson often slept with his holster hanging on a chair so he could grab it quickly in case of an emergency.

But the only emergency that night was Adele's inability to sleep. The heat kept her awake and even the electric fan did nothing to soothe her fierce nerves. She kept seeing the trapeze flying and Helen rolling in the air. She saw Julius standing with his roguish smile on the platform, shaking his head, and the black net bouncing even though there was nothing in it.

She and Jackson hardly exchanged a word in the morning and as she walked alone to Bridge Street, her thoughts were jumbled. She passed the offices of the *Arrojo Courier* and an idea came to her. She gathered Nin and together they entered Missy's office.

The place was even more chaotic than usual. When Missy had hired an assistant the year before, the girl Carla, though lacking much intelligence, had the iron hand it took to orga-

186

nize and clean the small office. She got rid of moth-eaten furniture Missy's brothers had left behind, had the floor professionally cleaned of all ink stains, and arranged the desks in an orderly fashion. She had even started to organize the archived newspapers in the basement into filing cabinets arranged by date, for which Adele was grateful, since she sometimes found herself digging into the town news of years before on a case.

But walking into the office now, it was as if it had reverted back to the first day Adele came for some archived information about the Blackstone family. Papers flew all over the room, the desks were pushed against the wall, and Missy herself looked as if she had just been through a wind storm.

The young lady greeted them with tired eyes.

"Cleanliness is next to Godliness," Nin said, not very tactfully.

"I leave that to Carla," she said. "Damn the girl for leaving me with all this."

"Her grandmother was very sick," Adele reminded her.

The woman sighed and sank into a wooden chair. "With the flower show in Rosa Gris and the fair in Finn's Creek and the circus still in town, I really need her help just now. I've been up all night writing stories."

"You look it," Nin observed.

She gave her a seething smile. "One cannot be fresh as a daisy every day, Miss Branch, even if women are supposed to be."

"Working women aren't supposed to be," Adele said. "We're supposed to look like working women."

"Well, I carry the torch admirably, don't I?" Missy looked down at the stained apron she wore over her dress.

Adele laughed and helped her untie the apron. "I'll see if I can talk some of the Wrigley School girls into coming by this afternoon and giving you some help."

"They'll do anything for a few pennies," Nin agreed.

"Bless you," Missy breathed.

"Now, for a few hours, you're going to be a lady of leisure because we're taking you to breakfast at Pringles," Adele said.

"I'm told the new breakfast menu is quite extravagant," Missy said. "I've been meaning to write my review of it."

"For today, you just eat," Nin insisted, taking her arm. "You're allowed to just eat sometimes."

"I am starving," the woman admitted.

Adele was surprised to see a young man standing with Mr. Pringle at the platform as the waiter led them to a table. "Don't tell me Mr. Pringle decided to break his authoritative air and hire an assistant manager," she remarked.

"That's Sybil's intended," said Missy.

"I had heard he looked like a horse," Nin said, and the women laughed. Even the waiter grinned as he handed them menus.

"He's teaching him to take over when the time comes," Adele guessed.

Missy glanced at her. "You obviously haven't been reading my paper. I reported that a week ago."

"Jackson hoards all the newspapers at our house," said Adele. "He's getting rather fond of the local press."

"He still has the city papers delivered, doesn't he?" Nin said. "He can't be that fond of them."

Adele laughed. "I suppose a paper is as much about what it doesn't print as what it does."

Missy blinked. "That's a strange remark."

"But a true one, especially in this day and age."

"You mean the yellow journalists." Missy sipped at the orange juice the waiter had just set down in front of them. "I hope you think more of me than that."

"But it's true you sometimes leave things out?"

Missy cocked her head. "You ought to know, Adele. You've asked me yourself not to print things."

"That's different," Nin declared. "She's working with the police."

"There are things I have to hold back," Adele insisted.

"Is this going anywhere?" Adele could sense the annoyance in Missy's voice. "I feel as if you're fishing. Out with it, Adele."

Adele smeared the sauce from her eggs Benedict around the plate. "I'm sorry, Missy. We've known one another too long to fish around."

"Out with it," Missy repeated.

"Is it true Paul Barry asked you not to print that the police found a scarf at the scene of the crime?" she shot out.

She could tell the newspaper woman was weighing her answer. Missy slowly buttered a slice of toast and spread marmalade on it as if it were an exact science before she answered. "Is that important?"

"Maybe it is and maybe it isn't," Nin said shrewdly, spearing a cube of pineapple. Mr Pringle shot her a look, as if he resented her rather brutal handling of the delicate fruit.

"Is it, Adele?" Missy eyed her.

"Right now, let's say it might be an interesting fact," Adele said with caution.

"Not as interesting as the fact that it may have belonged to his wife," Missy said.

"Is that what he told you?"

The woman grimaced. "I'm a reporter, Adele. I can draw my own conclusions just as well as you can. If a man is asking to suppress the mention of a woman's garment —"

"Then he did ask you to suppress it," Adele said.

"— chances are that garment belonged to his wife."

"You don't know that," Nin said quickly.

"At the very least, he suspects it might," Missy said. "Or he suspects the police might think it is." She leaned back. "You want to tell me why he was so anxious for me not to mention it?"

Adele picked up her coffee. "What makes you think I know anything about it?"

"Come, dear." Missy pressed her hand. "As you said, we've known each other too long to play games. So let's make a deal."

"That usually means something suspicious is involved," Nin snarled. The waiter, who had come to put another basket of rolls on their table, glanced at her but when she glared back, he slipped away.

"What sort of deal?"

"A very simple one," said the newspaper woman. "You tell me what you know, and I'll tell you what I know."

"What makes you think you know more than we do?" Nin inquired.

"Because I've learned to sniff around too," Missy said. "I find it rather amusing to carry my camera around and take pictures of people. Their tongues loosen under the influence of publicity."

Adele smiled. "You're beginning to think like a reporter, Missy."

"My reports of the Marsh case were reprinted in newspapers all over the country," said Missy. "Perhaps I've been bitten by the ambition bug." She looked at Adele. "Well, what about it?"

"Don't do it, Adele," Nin said in a low voice. "She doesn't know anything."

Missy put her hand on her arm. "Look, we're on the same side, remember?"

Adele pushed away the eggs Benedict. Suddenly the rich flavor was too much for her stomach. "What is it you want to know?"

"Was Mr. Barry concerned about the scarf being tied to his wife because his wife was involved with Mr. Rowe?" she asked.

Adele poured more coffee into the elegant china cup. "Yes."

"Adele!" Nin dropped her spoon.

"I can't say I'm surprised." Missy arched her eyebrow. "I spoke to Mr. Rowe the day before opening night. He was very happy to give me an interview and flirt with me besides."

"Yes, he had that nasty habit," Nin snarled, and Adele couldn't help but smile, thinking of how he had made eyes at Nin.

"How did you know Estelle was romantically involved with Julius?" Adele inquired.

"Who says I knew?" Missy asked. "I told you, I drew my own conclusions."

"You didn't ask the question as if you wanted to know," Adele said. "You asked as if you were confirming something you already knew."

"You are shrewd, Adele." Missy laughed. "All right. I had heard it, but I wasn't going to print it unless I had it confirmed by a more reliable source."

"From whom did you hear it, may I ask?" Adele leaned forward.

"A newspaper woman never reveals her sources," Missy said stoically.

"I think we can guess," Nin snarled. "A certain former cat tamer, by chance?"

"I can't confirm or deny that." Missy reached for another slice of toast.

"That rascal!" Nin growled. "Talking to the newspapers while he was talking to us."

"I told you, a camera loosens people's tongues," Missy said slyly.

"So Mr. Sipes told you the circus manager's wife was having an affair with Julius," Adele concluded. "My, his tongue has been loose indeed."

"But he told the truth, according to you," Missy pointed out.

"Don't print it, Missy." Adele grabbed her hand.

"Is it confirmed?" The woman eyed her.

"Well — yes, the lady told us so herself, but don't print it."

"Anything else she told you that you can tell me?"

Adele thought about the conversation with Estelle, but she said, "Nothing that would interest you."

"I'd like to be the judge of that."

"If Adele says it wouldn't interest you, it wouldn't interest your readers," Nin said harshly. "You'll turn into a yellow journalist yet."

This cut Missy to the core, as she had vowed never to be like her brothers, who, when they had control over the *Arrojo Courier*, treated it worse than the reporters for the big city papers. "I never said I didn't believe Adele."

"Now it's your turn, Missy," Adele said. "What else did you hear from Mr. Sipes' obliging tongue?"

"You may know it already," said the newspaper woman. "Miss Branch said he came to see you too."

"Did Mr. Sipes tell you how he came upon his information?" Adele asked. "It must have been more than circus gossip if he told the papers."

"He didn't tell the papers." Missy sniffed. "He told a paper. Mine."

"Well, what did he say?" Nin asked impatiently.

"He saw Mr. Rowe going into Mr. Barry's wagon a few nights before the performance."

"Which Mr. Barry?" Adele asked.

"The owner," said Missy. "I forgot there are two Mr. Barrys."

Adele was struck with anger. "He didn't tell us about that, the sly devil."

"So Julius saw both Calvin and Paul before the performance," Nin mumbled.

Missy was alert. "What's this about Calvin Barry?"

"Nothing important," Adele said quickly. "What about Julius going into Paul's wagon?"

"They had heated words," Missy said.

"Mr. Sipes told you that?" Adele was beginning to think Jackson might not be far off the mark in his suspicions of the man. "I'm assuming Mr. Sipes obliged you by relating the heated words he heard?"

"Well, no, he didn't," Missy admitted. "He wasn't close enough to hear them. He could hear the raised voices and made out a few things for himself."

"I'll bet he did," Nin said.

"More coffee, ladies?" Mr. Pringle approached their table with his future son-in-law in tow, who, Adele thought, looked like one of those men who was perpetually nursing a cold.

"We were just getting ready to leave," Adele said cheerfully. The other two ladies took their cue and rose.

"Excellent marmalade, Mr. Pringle," Missy said.

"I told you!" breathed the son-in-law, not without a little triumph.

"I'm glad you thought so, Miss Grace." The pompous man ignored his assistant-manager-to-be. "We've just contracted with a lady who makes them homemade. Give some of these working families a little business, if you know what I mean."

"And save money in the bargain," Nin said in a low voice. "I'll bet the poor woman charges half as much as the wholesaler."

"Why, Miss Branch, what a thing to say!" Mr. Pringle's indignation was more directed at the son-in-law rather than Nin.

"Thank you for a lovely breakfast, Mr. Pringle," Adele said as she took both her friends by the arm. "We don't want to take up the table when you have other guests."

When they reached the newspaper office, Missy was more at ease. "Mr. Sipes gathered Mrs. Barry's involvement with Mr. Rowe was rather serious."

"How serious?"

"Enough to want to run away with him." Missy watched Adele carefully.

"That was rather presumptuous of Mr. Sipes," Adele said, very much aware of Missy's gaze. "A woman like Estelle doesn't leave a husband that easily."

"But it's not unheard of."

"Is anything unheard of?" Nin asked. "People can do nasty things."

"Indeed they can, Miss Branch," Missy said. "They can even threaten murder."

Adele, who had been washing her hands in the washbasin, stared at her. "Is that what Mr. Sipes said?"

"Not exactly." The newspaper woman sat down at her desk.

Adele picked up her parasol from the corner. "I didn't think Mr. Sipes is one to commit himself to such accusations."

"He wasn't accusing anybody of anything," Missy insisted. "He was merely relating what he heard. According to Mr. Sipes, at one point, Mr. Barry said to Mr. Rowe, 'You'll never get past the circus gates.'"

~~~~~

"'You'll never get past the circus gates,'" Adele repeated as she and Nin stepped out to the street.

"You must admit that does sound like a threat," Nin said. "Unless Mr. Sipes was making it up to get some show in the papers."

"In which case, he failed." Adele put up her parasol, as the sun was eating at her skin. "Missy won't print a word of it."

"I'm not so sure of that, Adele," Nin said, taking her arm. "She's become altogether too impressed with the new readership she's acquired since your involvement with police matters made for good headlines."

Adele felt the sting of her words, though Nin, as always, was only voicing what was in plain sight and not insinuating she had done something wrong. Nevertheless, Jackson was forever warning her that her involvement in police business could prove detrimental not only to the police and to herself but to others as well.

"Missy won't print it," she repeated. "I saw the look on her face. I think she understand there's more at stake here than circus gossip."

"There's murder at stake," Nin pointed out. "That's why she might print it."

"Not unless she gets it confirmed," said Adele. "And I doubt Paul would admit to it."

"I'm sure he wouldn't." Nin peered at her. "Are we going to the police with what we know?"

"I think we'd better," Adele said. "It might be important."

"At least we'll have the satisfaction of seeing your brother give Mr. Sipes a good verbal whipping," Nin said.

Nin was right. When they went to the police station and repeated their conversation with Missy to Hatfield and Jackson, the deputy sheriff was glowering.

"I told you that man wasn't to be trusted!"

"I think it's time we had Mr. Sipes in," the sheriff said, his face wrinkled with agitation. "Maybe the sight of a jail cell will persuade him to be more forthcoming with what he knows. Edison!"

The assistant deputy, as usual, dropped everything and stood at attention.

"Take Dooland and go down to the park. Get Mr. Sipes here." He eyed him. "You remember him, don't you?"

"I do indeed, sir," said the young man grimly.

"Let me accompany them, Sheriff," Jackson said with a note of meanness. "It would be my pleasure to haul the scalawag in."

"That's what I'm afraid of," Hatfield said with some amusement.

"Your Anspach intimidation tactics would hardly do much good getting the information the sheriff is looking for, Mr. Gossling," Nin said shrewdly.

"I don't intimidate, Miss Branch," he snapped. "I follow the letter of the law, but sometimes one must be exacting."

"Perhaps we'll need your exactness, Deputy, and perhaps we won't," Sheriff Hatfield said in an authoritative voice. "I prefer to see the man here first."

Mr. Sipes, once settled in the police station, however, was more than willing to speak. "I ought to have told you about the conversation between Paul and Julius." He glanced sheepishly at Adele.

"You should have told *us*, Mr. Sipes," said the sheriff in a severe tone.

"Oh, but you were only asking us about the night of the tragedy," the man insisted. "This happened several nights before."

"You knew we wanted to know about any suspicious activity involving Mr. Rowe." Jackson leaned with one foot on the bars underneath the chair in which Mr. Sipes sat, making the man wince and cup his hands together as if in protection. "Why didn't you, Mr. Sipes?"

The man gave a small laugh. "You know how it is, Deputy. When one is trying to reform, one must keep one's job."

"You were afraid you would lose this one if you implicated your employer in a murder," Nin declared. She had taken a place on the floor, sitting with her legs and hands folded.

"I suppose that's one way of putting it." He glanced at her.

"Of all the lowest forms of life —"

"That will be enough, Deputy." Hatfield's voice was commanding. "Mr. Sipes, tell us what you told Miss Grace."

"Only a bit of circus gossip, Sheriff," the man said easily.

"It wasn't gossip, Mr. Sipes," Adele said. "Missy told us you overheard Paul talking to Julius. A little fact you left out when you came to me with what you knew about Calvin and Julius."

"Dear lady —"

"I don't like to be misled, Mr. Sipes." She gave him a savage look.

"I would never —"

"You'd do better to be straight with us," Jackson said in a fierce tone.

The man played with the edge of his coat. "Julius told Paul that Estelle planned on running away with him."

Even Hatfield looked surprised. "Those were his words?"

"Bold as brass, wasn't he?" Mr. Sipes said in a mischievous

voice. "Julius always thought he could get anything he wanted, especially when it came to women."

"And was that when Paul told him they'd never get past the front gates?" Adele asked.

"Well, yes, something like that." The man turned to her, wrinkles forming around his eyes. "Oh, but surely you don't believe —"

"Believe what, Mr. Sipes?" Hatfield asked.

"Paul would never —"

"Never what?" the sheriff persisted.

The man rose. "Sir, you're trying to make me say something damaging about my employer."

"The thought came to your mind just as it came to everybody else's," Nin said. "He was threatening to kill him."

"Indeed he wasn't, Miss Branch!" The man looked indignant. "Why, he couldn't. His star performer?"

"His star performer who was going to run away with his wife," Adele said. "I should hope the latter trumps the former."

"But murder?" Mr. Sipes asked. "Paul is strict, I grant you, but he's an honorable man." He reached for her gloved hand, but one vicious look from Jackson made him snap it back.

"Thank you, Mr. Sipes," said the sheriff, plucking his hat from the rack. "We needn't trouble you any further."

"I can get back to my work?" the man asked eagerly.

"Better cherish it as long as you have it," Jackson said in an ominous tone. Adele glared at him.

"Work is my life, sir." The man fussed over his shabby suit in the small mirror hanging above the file cabinet. "Why, I was telling your sister the other day —"

"I would be obliged if you wouldn't tell Miss Gossling anything." Sheriff Hatfield stood up with his bull-like figure. "Anything else you have to say you come to the station, or I might consider it withholding evidence."

"Surely —"

"Edison, take Mr. Sipes back to where you found him." The sheriff sounded almost disgusted.

When they had gone, Adele turned to him. "If he does know anything more, he's more likely to come to me than to you. You realize that, Sheriff."

"I realize that and a great deal more about Mr. Sipes," said Hatfield in a rough tone. "If he bothers you again, Adele, send him to me."

"I never said he bothered me," Adele said softly.

"If you weren't so sweet on her, you'd see that yourself," Nin murmured.

There was an uncomfortable silence in the station for a moment with only Dooland clanking at the typewriter. Dooland's hand was much heavier than Edison's, and Adele felt her bones shudder at each key.

"Dooland!" Hatfield rose. "Give that confounded thing a rest."

"Yes, Sheriff." The young man lifted his hands away from the keys. "But these letters —"

"We can only stand so much of that noise at one time," Hatfield growled.

"Are you going to arrest Paul?" Nin asked.

"That depends on what he has to say for himself," said the sheriff, swinging the door open. "You don't think I would take that man's word for everything, do you?"

"He won't admit to murder." Jackson grabbed his hat.

"Paul lied to us, Jack." Adele took Nin's hand as they walked. "He told us he had no idea Estelle's relationship with Julius was so serious."

"There's no surprise in that," her brother insisted. "No man likes to admit he's been duped."

"I would hardly call it being duped," Nin snapped. "He thought more of the circus than he did of her. It would have been more fitting for him to get a divorce and leave her without a penny."

"Divorce is a very unpleasant thing," Hatfield said. "Some men think getting rid of the competition is a better solution."

"Isn't that a little dramatic, Sheriff?" Adele asked.

"I knew a man once," said the sheriff, "several men, in fact. They were convinced if only the 'other man' were out of the picture, their wives would see reason."

"Reason!" Adele snarled. "If a woman wants to leave her husband for another man, she has reason enough to know why."

Paul was alone in his wagon going over a stack of papers. "I asked Cal to get me the contract for every performer," he explained. "I've let him handle that side of things on his own for too long."

"I wouldn't necessarily question his judgment," Hatfield said.

"I didn't say I was questioning it, Sheriff," Paul said. "Some people think I've too much initiative, perhaps, but one has to in order to run a successful circus."

Hatfield leaned against the wall of the wagon. "One takes initiative when one decides to leave out the truth."

The man glared at him. "I've told you all I know."

"Not all, sir," said Jackson. "We've just heard you had a rather volatile conversation with Mr. Rowe a few days before his death."

Paul grasped the contract in front of him. "I had no conversation with Julius, volatile or otherwise."

"But you did, sir," Adele said, "when Julius came into your wagon and told you about his affair with Estelle."

The man's shoulders stiffened. "I really do wish you'd tell me which of my staff is your stool pigeon, Sheriff!"

"Why did you tell us you knew nothing about your wife's involvement with Mr. Rowe?" Jackson asked.

"I didn't want to embarrass her, naturally," he said.

"Embarrass *her*?" Nin sneered. "You didn't want to embarrass yourself!"

The man sighed. "It's all so sordid."

"When a wife intends to leave her husband, it's always sordid,"

Hatfield remarked. "Now we know you knew about that too."

"And you lied about it," Jackson added in a severe tone. "The police don't take lies lightly, sir."

The man glared at him. "What would you have thought if I would have told you I knew my wife was going to run off with him?"

"What we're thinking now, I gather," the sheriff said.

Paul went back to the papers on his desk. "I should think even you would know there is a great deal of difference between being told your wife is going to leave you and her actually leaving."

"You didn't think she would go, Mr. Barry?" Adele asked.

The man gave her a steely look. "I knew she wouldn't, Miss Gossling."

"Is that why you threatened Julius that they would never get past the circus gates?" Jackson asked.

The man's mouth flew open as he remained silent for some time.

"Is your silence a denial, Mr. Barry?" Hatfield studied him.

Paul seemed to come alive. "It wasn't a threat, Deputy. It was an assurance."

"To whom?" Adele asked. "You or Mr. Rowe?"

"Both of us, perhaps." The man sank in the chair. "Oh, it looks bad, I know. I do sometimes say mindless things when I lose my temper and him standing there, looking so smug and so pleased with himself —"

"You wanted to take the wind out of his sails," Nin said.

"Something like that, Miss Branch," said the man.

"It was a rather ominous thing to say," Adele said. "One might say, 'I'll never let you take her away' or 'You'll never run away with her.' But 'You'll never get past the gates' is well, it implies physical constraint."

"In other words, you meant he would never get past the gates because he'd be dead," Nin said.

"Miss Branch, you might confine yourself to facts and not

accusations," Paul snapped. "I said I never made any threats to Julius and I meant it. What I said was in anger without thinking. I'm not a man of words like — well, like that Sipes fellow. I don't think about each one before I say it."

"But anger can make us say things that are more truthful than we'd like to admit," Jackson said. "My sister asked you a question, sir."

"I just answered it." The man rose. "Now, if you'll kindly leave, I have to make my wagon checks."

"Your answers are unsatisfactory." Hatfield was firm.

"To you, I can imagine they aren't satisfactory," said the man. "But I didn't kill Julius. Of that I can assure you."

"They always assure us," Jackson snorted when they were outside. "They think we'll take their word for it."

"He's hiding something," Nin agreed. "The Generous Ones were shaking me to the core while he spoke."

"A shame they weren't generous enough to tell you if he's guilty or innocent," Jackson remarked.

"You may mock them, Mr. Gossling, but for those of us who believe, it's no laughing matter!" Her countenance looked so savage that Adele took a firm grip of her arm in fear she would attack her brother.

"Generous Ones or not, I agree with Miss Branch," said Hatfield. "I think the district attorney will agree too."

"You're going to arrest him?" Adele stared.

"Sometimes an arrest is the only way to get the truth, Del," her brother said. "Mr. Barry's lied to us once already, and he's probably lying to us now. How much he's lying is what we need to know."

"Arrogance is suppressed by those close to him," Nin murmured, her eyes almost glassy.

"Are you all right, dear?" Adele asked.

Her friend looked at her as if she had just woken from a deep sleep.

CHAPTER 20

*T*hat night after dinner, when they were set up in the parlor with the coffee, Jackson told her they received the arrest warrant from Mr. Marland, the district attorney, and had taken Paul to the station.

"Did you question him?" Adele inquired.

"It was too late by then," said Jackson. "Hatfield thought it better the man get a good night's sleep first."

Adele leaned back on the sofa, feeling the prickly fabric in the small of her back. "Mr. Marland certainly didn't waste any time, did he?"

"He never does," her brother observed. "The man is too ambitious for my taste. He has judges and county authorities sewed up in his back pocket. I wouldn't be surprised if he replaces Mayor Willett in the next election."

Adele chuckled. "Who can say if that would be a bad thing or not? Willett is such a mackerel."

Jackson laughed and reached for his new pipe, a horn-shaped thing imported from Hungary.

"How did he take it, Jack?" she asked, playing with her lace work.

Her brother shrugged. "Hard to say. I've a feeling the man has been arrested before. I told Hatfield so."

Adele nodded. "I should imagine circus people are vulnerable to the police even when they've done nothing wrong."

"Someone at the Barry Circus has done something wrong, Del," said Jackson. "We have to find out who it is."

"Too bad that someone didn't wait one day," she observed. "The circus would have moved on, and it would have been the problem of another county."

"That county police probably would have concluded it was business as usual with disreputable people like circus folk and marked the case unsolved," Jackson snarled. "I despise that sort of shirking of responsibility. Hatfield won't rest until he finds out who killed Mr. Rowe."

"He wasn't a citizen of Arrojo," Adele pointed out.

"He was a citizen of the world," her brother said with dignity. "Even the lowest criminal deserves justice." He eyed her. "I thought you and your friend were on the side of justice."

"Justice for women," Adele corrected.

Jackson put the evening paper down. "I suppose the men can go to rot for all you care?"

"I didn't say that."

"Lucky for you, Hatfield believes in justice for all, women and men."

"So do I!" She jumped a little as she pricked her finger with the needle. "Curse the thing!"

"I thought you were going to give up being domestic," Jackson said, unable to hide his smile.

"And disappoint Mrs. Faderman and the rest?" she declared. "Not on your life!"

He burst out laughing.

The next morning, Adele walked with Jackson to the station. The place was more livable since she had first encountered it three years ago, as she had convinced Hatfield to hire Consuela, the

Cordobas' second oldest daughter, to sweep and clean a few times a week. The young woman was there now, discreetly moving her broom in between the desks. She smiled at them as they came in, and Adele marveled at the beautiful young lady she had grown into. Already at fifteen, she was as striking as Nin and the assistant deputies had a difficult time keeping their eyes on their work.

Hatfield, keen on this state of affairs, shouted out orders, his retired manner gone. "Edison! You were supposed to get those files to Dr. Rhodes last week."

"I haven't had a chance at the typewriter, sir." The young man pulled his gaze away from Consuela who had just begun sweeping around his desk. "Assistant Deputy Dooland has been using it."

"What about the other one?"

"That's broken, sir."

"Is that why it's been so blissfully quiet in your corner the past few days?" Hatfield gave a tight smile. "Well, get it fixed, lad."

"It wouldn't be worth your while, Sheriff," Adele said as she sat at the edge of his large desk. "Ward typewriters weren't meant to last for long."

"Why didn't you check that before you bought it, Edison?" Hatfield glared at him.

"Well, sir —"

"You should have come to me, Assistant Deputy," Adele said with a smile. "I would have advised you."

"I wasn't sure —"

"You're never sure about anything, lad!" The sheriff's face was red. "Three years and I expected you to be head assistant deputy by now."

The young man's lips turned into a thin line. Then, he said in a meek tone, "I'll get those files out today, sir."

Adele felt sorry for Edison and placed her gloved hand on his shoulder. "Stop by my shop sometime today, Assistant Deputy, and I'll give you a list of good typewriters." She eyed the sheriff. "Does that meet with your approval?"

Hatfield's face relaxed. "I didn't mean to shout. This is a trying time for all of us."

"Yes, sir," Edison mumbled.

The sound of flat heels pounded on the wooden floor. Abby Call stood in front of the sheriff's desk like a schoolgirl. "Sheriff, I'd like to talk to you."

"Good morning, Miss Call." Hatfield greeted her with a nod. "May we offer you coffee or tea?"

"I'm not here for niceties," she snapped. "You've arrested the wrong person and I'm here to clear him."

"Indeed?" Hatfield offered her a chair.

"Paul is no more a murderer than Albertine's poodles!"

"I hear even poodles can get vicious when they're provoked," Jackson said dryly. Edison and some of the other assistant deputies snickered.

"They've never been provoked and neither has Paul," she declared. "Can't you see he isn't the type?"

"Didn't you tell me he loses his temper, and one never knows what to expect?" Adele eyed her.

"Losing one's temper is one thing," Abby said. "Murder is quite another."

"That doesn't mean he couldn't have killed his wife's paramour," Adele pointed out.

"Julius was not her paramour!"

Her shriek echoed through the station and only Consuela, who had the same good sense as her mother, went on with her work. Edison sat with the typewriter half taken apart, his hands smeared with grease and his eyes wide. Assistant Deputy Dooland was at the file cabinet, his mouth hanging like a fish, and Assistant Deputy Moran, who was polishing the silver handcuffs, dropped them on the ground with a clang.

"Dooland! Moran!" The sheriff came alive. "Didn't I tell you to go and get that dead goat out of the river?"

Their nervous "yes, sir" peppered the station as they hastily left.

Adele sat down beside her. "Assistant Deputy Edison, I think you can bring us a cup of tea now." The young man glanced at the sheriff, whose jerking nod sent him to the small stove.

Abby's words were measured, "I have reason to believe Julius ended their affair the night he was killed."

"Mrs. Barry didn't tell us that." Jackson glanced at his superior.

"No, she wouldn't." Abby's face was set. "Women like that have too much pride."

"Mr. Rowe told you this?"

"Not exactly," she admitted.

"Go on," the sheriff said.

"Before he — before he died, Julius told me he was fed up with Estelle. She expected him to save her from a bad marriage, and he was no savior."

"A savior," Adele repeated. "Yes, that's what Estelle was looking for."

"She thought he was going to go away with her," said Abby.

"We know about that," Jackson said.

"You think he never intended to do any such thing?" Adele asked.

"Certainly not," Abby said. "The first circus where we performed — there was a woman there too. A widow whose husband left her a packet." Abby shifted her bag from one knee to the other. "She made promises to him about 'living in the lap of luxury all his life.' He refused point-blank."

"Because he wanted to be the star of the circus?" Jackson asked.

"Because she was overbearing!"

"He liked the women until they became overbearing," Adele murmured.

"Did you think Mrs. Barry threatened to make trouble for him?" asked the sheriff.

The woman was quiet for a moment, rolling the strap of her bag between her hands. "It's the sort of thing Estelle would do. She was desperate, you see."

"But he didn't say so," Jackson prompted.

The woman looked at Adele with her intense eyes. "Adele, convince them they have the wrong man!"

"I can hardly convince lawmen who know their profession," Adele said quietly.

The woman's mouth was set. "I heard stories about how you convinced the police they had the wrong man when they arrested the son of a prominent woman who was poisoned in her own bed."

Adele shuddered, thinking of the Marsh family. "That was the evidence, not me, Abby."

"I'll give you evidence," she snapped.

"You have evidence there's another man we should arrest?" Jackson eyed her.

"Not a man," she said shortly. "A woman."

Hatfield leaned back, folding his hands in his lap. "You're referring to Mrs. Barry, I take it."

"It all fits, don't you see?"

"What fits, Miss Call?" Jackson asked. A nod from his superior made him take up a pad and pencil.

"I'm glad to see you're taking this seriously, Sheriff," Adele said.

"You know we always take what witnesses have to say seriously, Adele." Sheriff Hatfield sounded almost offended.

"Of course you do," she said, smiling.

"That scarf you found, for one," Abby said, looking from one to the other.

"What about the scarf?" Hatfield asked evenly.

"Paul tried to conceal it."

"Conceal it!" The sheriff was all attention.

"We were so taken up with Mr. Sipes yesterday I forgot to mention it," Adele said in a sheepish tone. "Missy said Paul asked her not to say anything about finding the scarf."

"Well, well." Jackson looked at the sheriff.

"He did that because he knows it's Estelle's," Abby insisted.

"You gave her the scarf, didn't you, Miss Call?" Hatfield asked.

She nodded. "There were two. They belonged to my mother."

"That was very generous of you," Adele said.

"I thought — well, Estelle and I were good friends then, and I wanted to show my appreciation for —"

"For?" Adele prompted.

"For being kind to us when we first came," Abby said. "So I gave her the scarf."

"Mrs. Barry told us she did have a scarf but she threw it away because it got dirty," Jackson said.

"She was lying!" The woman's eyes looked wild.

"Why would her scarf be found behind the curtain?" Jackson asked.

"She must have given it to Julius right before we went into the ring," said Abby. "It could have fallen when he took the jacket off."

"If Mr. Rowe accepted the scarf, that would indicate they were still, erm, involved," Hatfield pointed out.

"It must have been a parting gift, then," Abby said in a shrill voice. "He had no intention of leaving the Barry Circus."

"He did sign a contract, sir," Jackson said, glancing at Hatfield.

"Only a week before he died, we discussed some new routines for next season," Abby said.

"So he had some new ideas for next year," the sheriff mused.

"Don't you see? If he had intended to run off with Estelle, he wouldn't have spent his time and energy going over new routines with me," she said. "Julius never wasted his time on anything or anyone."

"Perhaps he was planning on continuing his act elsewhere with Mrs. Barry," Adele suggested.

"Would he have shown them to me if that were the case?" Abby countered. "They required both of us."

Hatfield rested his feet on the little stool under his desk. "You want us to believe Mr. Barry is innocent because Mrs. Barry had more of a reason to kill your partner than him?"

"You've heard about the wrath of a woman scorned, Sheriff," Abby said.

"Heaven knows I've experienced it enough." Jackson gave his sister a meaningful look, and she wrinkled her nose back at him.

"But is the woman scorned in this case capable of killing a man?" Hatfield pondered. "Question marks, question marks."

"If you knew Estelle, there wouldn't be any question marks," Abby declared. "She's always been looking for a savior. The truth is, she doesn't know what she wants. She gives someone all her love and attention one day, but turns away the next, as if —" She stopped, her face frozen and her eyes wolf-like.

"As if what?" Adele prompted.

"As if you weren't good enough for her," she said quietly.

Hatfield rose. "I appreciate you coming in to speak to us, Miss Call."

She looked at him, her eyes determined. "You know Estelle used to be a flyer on the trapeze?"

The sheriff sat down again. "No. We didn't know."

"You must be very close for her to have told you that," Adele said.

"We were." The woman's eyes dipped for a moment. Then, the shrill tone came back. "My point is she knows how to handle a net, Sheriff. She would know just how to make murder look like an accident."

"So you think she could have damaged it," Hatfield said.

"She's been very secretive lately," Abby continued. "She's been hiding things."

"Such as?" The sheriff leaned forward, folding his hands on his desk.

"I walked into her wagon one day," said the woman. "She was in the corner where that trunk of hers is."

"The large black one with the silver buckle?" Jackson asked.

"No, the other one," she said. "The one against the wall."

"Go on," said Hatfield.

"As I came in, she was putting something inside one of the panels. She turned around, slamming it shut just as I closed the door. She had a guilty look on her face."

"Like she was hiding something?" Adele asked.

"Exactly," said the woman. "And she was. She pulled me out of the room with some excuse to check on the elephants but I saw what she put there."

"What was it?" Jackson asked.

"A box," she said. "I suppose I shouldn't have done this —" She looked down at her hands.

"Yes?"

"I went in later and looked. There was a key in it."

The two lawmen exchanged a look. "What sort of a key, Miss Call?" Hatfield asked.

"A very odd-shaped one," she said. "It looked like a pointed finger." She blushed. "I'm sorry if that sounds silly, but I don't know how else to describe it." She quickly looked up. "Something was engraved on the back, but I couldn't read it."

"Thank you, Miss Call." The sheriff rose again. "I'll get one of my deputies to escort you back to your wagon."

Abby was a little wobbly as she got to her feet. "You see how Estelle is a more likely person than Paul?"

"You've certainly given us something to think about," Jackson remarked as he motioned toward Assistant Deputy Moran.

"Then you'll let Paul go?" She looked at Adele with pleading eyes. "Adele, make them let Paul go!"

"The police will do their duty, Abby." She gently delivered the woman into Moran's care, who, for all his fish-gaping stares, had the delicacy of a mother handling a baby when it came to distressed witnesses.

"Oh, I'm sure of it," said the woman as she allowed the assistant deputy to lead her out of the station.

There was a general noise while everyone seemed to get their bearings. Adele was the first to speak. "She certainly changed her tune."

"Eh?" Hatfield strolled to the sink and washed his hands.

"When we first spoke to her, she seemed certain Paul was to blame for Julius' death," she pointed out.

"Actually, she believed it was an accident," her brother reminded her.

"After that," said Adele, swatting him away. "She insinuated to me Paul has a temper that was unpredictable, and he could have done Julius in."

"And now she's changed her mind and thinks the wife and not the husband did it," the sheriff remarked as he took his chair.

"It happens all the time, Del," Jackson said. "Witnesses believe one person guilty, then when that person actually gets arrested, they point the finger at another."

"What about the key?" Adele asked.

"What about it?" Hatfield countered. "Miss Call confirmed what we saw ourselves. Now we know a little more about it, though I can't see where that gets us."

"The engraving on it might be the manufacturer's name," Jackson suggested.

The sheriff studied his deputy. "You have a theory, Jackson?"

"I came across keys like Miss Call described when I worked for the Anspaches," his deputy said. "They were all keys to some sort of locked box."

"Indeed?" Hatfield showed more interest. "Why would Mrs. Barry need a locked box?"

"Why would any woman need a locked box?" Adele echoed. "To hide her jewelry or her money."

"I didn't see much jewelry in her wagon when we searched it," Jackson said.

"Money, then," Adele said. "An unhappy woman often hoards money."

"I agree with Adele," Hatfield said. "If it is indeed a key to a locked box, it's likely hidden somewhere away from the circus, or it's a box in a bank in another city."

"I think the more interesting question is not what it's for but why is it gone?" Adele glanced at the sheriff. "Another question mark, Sheriff."

"Another to add to my long list," he sighed.

CHAPTER 21

*B*efore Adele left the station, she caught a glimpse of Paul Barry. What she saw touched her heart. The man looked clearly broken, his features sagging as low as the too-large suit he wore. His face was scratched with stubble (Edison confided in her that the man refused to shave), and his eyes had dark circles around them. As she passed by the jail cell, she had heard him mumbling, "Estelle, where's Estelle?"

She walked with heavy steps to her shop and almost bumped into Nin, who was on the sidewalk, seeing off an elderly woman client. As the woman drove off, her friend took her arm and led her into Adele's Stationery, unlocking the door with a resolute click.

When she could finally find the tongue to speak, all she could say was, "Poor Paul!"

"I thought you didn't like him," Nin remarked.

"I don't approve of his commanding ways," Adele admitted. "But it's clear the arrest has broken his will."

"Then you don't think he's guilty?" Nin asked.

Adele looked at her. "Do you?"

"If you mean have I gotten some sign or feeling, I haven't." Her friend said.

Adele pressed her hand. "I'm sorry. I know you don't call upon the auras."

"They come when the Generous Ones dictate," said her friend in a mystical tone.

"All he wants now is his wife," Adele sighed.

Nin filled a glass with water and handed it to her. "He ought to have treated her better, then."

"I don't believe she's untouched by this," Adele said. "Her husband is accused of killing her paramour. It's a nasty business."

"Loyalty is a sign of love," said Nin firmly. "If I'm loyal to someone, I don't care two cents what they've done. They could have killed a dozen people."

Adele smiled. "I'm glad to know I can rely on you if I ever take to crime."

The woman blushed and snatched the ribbon that had fallen from her dress on the floor even though it was coated with dust. "Do you intend to prove Paul is innocent?"

"I'm not sure I can," said Adele. "There's some damning evidence."

"He knew about his wife's affair." Nin nodded. "That would make most men lose their reason, whatever little reason they have in the first place." She said the last with satisfaction.

"That doesn't mean he killed Julius," Adele pointed out.

"If not Paul, then who?" Nin inquired.

"Estelle has been hiding things," Adele said as she opened a box of ink wells. "A key, for one."

"Why should that be important?"

"The key might not be important," Adele said. "The fact that she's hid it is. And it's gone."

"Keys open many things," her friend muttered. "But it won't open the heart of one who no longer loves."

The bell above the doorway shook and Rowena Danvers, Lady Augusta's companion, came in.

"Why, Rowena, what a pleasant surprise!" Adele hardly saw the woman in her shop, though she often ran around Bridge Street doing errands for Hatfield's strong-minded mother. "Has Lady Augusta begun her fall correspondences yet?"

"No, miss," said the woman. "I didn't come for that."

"I've some new stationery with a cornflower pattern." Adele reached on the shelf. "I can give you a few sheets to try and if you like them, I can order more."

The woman's square frame, always immaculate in her dark suits, slackened and her face lightened. "You're always very kind, Miss Gossling. But I'm here on Lady Augusta's behalf."

"Then why don't you come out with it?" Nin asked in a snappish tone.

"I was just going to," answered Rowena, equally snappish. "Lady Augusta requests your presence at tea this afternoon." She cast a critical eye on Nin. "You're invited also, Miss Branch."

"Tea?" Adele glanced at her friend. "A formal tea?"

"Oh, nothing grand," Rowena assured her. "She anticipates Mrs. Faderman and the ladies will be having theirs because of — erm — what's happened —"

Adele frowned. "Missy printed a story in this morning's paper."

"Indeed she did, Miss Gossling," said the woman, clearing her throat. "As I was saying, Lady Augusta anticipates the ladies will be wanting their tea, and she wants to be there. Since she has limited mobility and can't attend one of those ridiculous strolls of theirs —"

"Their movable tea party," Nin supplied.

"Since she can't attend their movable tea party," the woman corrected, "she's decided to hold one at her house."

"And she wants us there?" Adele inquired.

"She insists upon it." Rowena gave her a knowing look. "You know how she is, Miss Gossling."

Adele smiled. "Yes, I know how she is."

"I'm assuming you accept?"

"Naturally we do," said Nin. Though Nin was known for her cagey feelings toward the townspeople and preferring to keep to a select group of those who understood her, she had taken to Lady Augusta like a child to a mother from the moment she met her. "We'd be delighted."

"I'll tell Lady Augusta." The woman slid out of the shop as noiselessly as she had come in.

Adele watched her walking in the direction of the Hatfield house. "I wonder what the real reason for this tea is."

"Lady Augusta has something up her sleeve," Nin agreed.

Adele smiled. "I think she's becoming as interested in crime detection as we are."

"I wouldn't say I'm interested." Nin shrugged. "You're the one who wants justice for every woman, alive or dead."

"Julius was a man," Adele reminded her.

"A pompous ass, you mean," Nin snorted, "who, from everything we know, deserved what he got."

"That's not true!" Adele was surprised at her own passion. "He was immoral, it's true, and arrogant. But he didn't deserve to die."

"You are sentimental," her friend mumbled, ambling back to her place next door.

~~~~~

When Adele went to Nin's shop that afternoon to take her to Lady Augusta's, she was surprised to see her friend looking so refined she could have been one of the ladies at Mrs. Stanford's or Mrs. Crocker's tea parties. Though Nin came from high-mannered stock, her mother defied her wealthy upbringing by becoming an herbalist and clairvoyant well known throughout the county, passing on her gifts to her daughter. Nin roamed around in flowing dresses and long hair, but when the occasion called for it, she could look as elegant as any high-society lady.

"You certainly have gone all out," Adele remarked, suddenly feeling dowdy in her own shirtwaist and linen skirt.

"I thought if I looked formal, the ladies might be more amenable," Nin said, smoothing out a fold in her silk skirt. "They like to be reminded my ancestors were equal to theirs, even if I don't."

"Perhaps they will be more likely to talk if they see we intend to behave in what they consider a proper ladylike manner," Adele agreed.

To that end, she convinced Nin to let her stop off at Caliber Lane so she could change into something more suitable for tea. As she slipped out of her working clothes and into a pale pink dress with lace panels, she couldn't help but feel a little nostalgic, thinking of the events she had attended in San Francisco, when her father had been revered by San Francisco society as the best criminal lawyer in the city. Then the teas and picnics and parties had been an ordeal to her, a mildly interesting way of observing people carrying on conversations they didn't want aired in public. But now, as she let Ruth help with the clasp on the high lace collar, she realized she was doing more than curiously listening. She was searching for killers and thieves and other unsavory people.

With a renewed sense of purpose, she and Nin walked arm in arm the few blocks to the Hatfield house. They were a little late, so when Rowena led them into the parlor, it was already filled with women. Lady Augusta had decked herself out for the occasion and even wore a string of pearls. The tea set was as grand as anything Mrs. Faderman had, and as Rowena handed Adele a cup of tea, she saw the china painted with a shield and a hawk, and the coat of arms read *"iustitia et pudicitia."*

"You know what that is, dear?" The elderly woman wheeled beside her, watching her.

"I assume it's the Hatfield insignia," Adele said.

The woman nodded. "'Justice and modesty.' Rather fitting, don't you think, Irene?" The woman threw a razor gaze that sent the woman flying to her side.

"I don't believe I've ever seen it, ma'am."

"You've been drinking from it," Nin said, pushing the teacup in her face.

"'*iustitia et pudicitia*,'" Lady Augusta repeated with loftiness.

"Justice and — I can't seem to recall my Latin," mused the woman.

"Modesty," Lady Augusta said. "The lord took those words seriously. So do I and so does my son." She eyed Mrs. Faderman. "One can't say he didn't choose the right profession to exercise his birthright."

Adele was surprised to hear the tone of pride in the woman's voice. She felt as if it were coming from another place. It was not the tone of a mother proud of her son's determination to do good, but a self-righteousness that meant something else.

"Indeed he did, Lady Augusta," Mrs. Faderman said in a complacent tone.

"And he's doing it admirably in this case, I must say," added Mrs. Fourier.

"Granted, it wasn't very difficult this time," Mrs. Abberton said, picking up her teacup in an exaggerated delicate way. "Not like some of his other cases."

"No, indeed," Mrs. Faderman agreed. "Not with what he had to start with."

"I find that a curious statement, ma'am," Adele said.

"She means because the circus is corrupt," Nin supplied. She elected to sit on the couch next to Adele instead of her usual position on the rug.

"I wouldn't have put it quite so brutally, Miss Branch," the woman said, "but essentially, yes, that's what I mean."

"You must think they're a band of criminals to have killed Mr. Rowe," Adele said dryly.

"You said it, Miss Gossling. I didn't." The woman took a sip of tea.

"Horatio arrested only one," said Lady Augusta. "The question is, is it the right one?"

Adele could feel the woman's pale blue eyes on her.

"I don't doubt for a moment, ma'am," Mrs. Faderman said. "I understand the evidence is clear."

"How do you know what the evidence is?" Nin shot out.

"Because, Miss Branch, Miss Grace provided everyone with the list in this morning's paper," Mrs. Cricket said.

"How obliging of her to have done so," Adele mumbled.

"I think we all know where she got it from." The woman's seedy-looking eyes slid toward Adele.

"I assure you, Mrs. Cricket, I'm more discreet than that." Adele put her teacup down on the coffee table.

"What a sordid story it is," Mrs. Lynn lamented as she picked up a sugar cookie with a shaking hand.

"Don't waddle so, Carolyn," Mrs. Faderman snapped.

"Here, ma'am, I'll get it for you," Adele said kindly as she placed the cookie and a cucumber sandwich in a plate and put it securely in the woman's hands.

"Thank you, dear," said Mrs. Lynn.

"I agree it is a sordid story," Mrs. Faderman said. "A man killing another man because his wife —" Here, she left the circumstances unspoken. "Well, quite the thing you would expect from such people."

"Even high society ladies have paramours, Irene," Lady Augusta said in her bold way. "I knew a duchess once who was carrying on with a waiter at the Savoy."

The woman flinched. "Yes, well, that sort of thing is very rare among refined people."

"Leaving her scarf lying around like that for the police to find!" Mrs. Fournier growled. "Shameful!"

Adele glanced at Nin. "That was in the paper too?"

"I'm surprised at you, Miss Gossling." Mrs. Faderman put her teacup down and glanced at her from the top of her pince-nez. "I expected you to be an avid reader of the *Arrojo Courier* since Miss Grace is such a good friend of yours."

"She said she wouldn't print it," Nin said. "Paul asked her not to."

Adele gave her friend a light kick in the ankle, though it was too late. She could feel Mrs. Faderman's eyes narrow with self-righteousness.

"A husband asking a newspaper to hush up evidence can only mean one thing," Mrs. Abberton remarked.

"He's guilty!" Mrs. Cricket snarled.

"I don't know that he is," Adele found herself saying.

"Miss Gossling," Mrs. Faderman's voice was forbidding, "you've had these ideas before."

"I beg your pardon, ma'am?" Adele blinked.

"Be plain, Irene," Lady Augusta said. "I thought you didn't approve of shilly-shallying."

"I don't think I'm shilly-shallying." The woman looked hurt. "I'm trying to be kind to the young lady, as a matter of fact."

"Since when?" Nin snorted.

"It seems every time there's some kind of criminal activity and the police have their man, so to speak, Miss Gossling always finds a reason to doubt their dexterity." She eyed her host. "I don't think that's very complimentary toward our very competent sheriff, do you, Lady Augusta?"

Adele felt her face redden, but the elderly woman came to the rescue. "Horatio isn't one of these lawmen who thinks above himself, Irene. He's told me many times how Adele and Miss Branch have helped his investigations far more than his team of assistant deputies."

"That's no surprise," Nin mumbled.

"What makes you think the man is innocent, Miss Gossling?" Mrs. Abberton tossed back her curls. "According to the papers, their evidence is rather conclusive."

"He's not the type," Adele mumbled.

"Oh, really!" Mrs. Faderman snorted. "That's rather flimsy, don't you think?"

"Money always causes trouble," Mrs. Lynn lamented.

"We're not talking about money, Carolyn," said the woman. "We're talking about love, if one may call a relationship between a middle-aged married woman and a young scoundrel love."

"They could have been in love," Mrs. Lynn pointed out.

"They weren't," Nin said. "He had no intention of running away with her."

"Miss Branch!" Mrs. Cricket flinched and grabbed a large sweet bun for comfort.

"Why not?" Lady Augusta said with a chuckle. "I hardly think whatever Miss Branch has to say could soil the conversation more than it already is."

"Well, all I have to say is, thank goodness our town won't be soiled by the likes of *those* people much longer," Mrs. Faderman declared.

"I'm afraid you're too optimistic, ma'am," Adele said with a little smile. "They'll have to be here at least a while longer if Mr. Barry is indicted."

"Oh, he will be," said the woman. "But they won't be here for that."

Adele put her cup down, struggling to get the saucer in a space on the crowded table. "What do you mean?"

"If you read the morning paper, Miss Gossling, you would know what I mean," she said.

"They're leaving town, according to what the son says," said Mrs. Fourier. "About time!"

"Leaving?" Adele glanced at Nin.

"In a day or two," Mrs. Abberton supplied. "They don't want to associate themselves with a criminal, no doubt."

"Abandoning the captain of their ship, it seems," Mrs. Cricket added.

"As a former seaman's mother, I can say any good captain sinks with his ship," Lady Augusta said in a mild tone.

"But the sheriff —"

"He can't do much about it," said Mrs. Faderman. "They went to the mayor and he's signed the release."

"With your encouragement, no doubt," Nin snarled.

"We certainly don't want the likes of them around Arrojo now, do we?" the woman asked. "It's no longer necessary for them to be here anyway now that the police have the guilty man."

Adele looked hard at Lady Augusta. The woman patted her hand. "I'm afraid it's true, dear. So if there's any doubt about Mr. Barry's guilt, one must find evidence of it sooner rather than later." The last was said with such a pointed tone that Adele suddenly understood why Lady Augusta had invited her and Nin to tea.

"No one will, Lady Augusta," Mrs. Faderman said. "That would delay those people which would be intolerable."

"There are some things you can't dictate, Mrs. Faderman," Adele said sharply.

"Such corruption when one makes merry," Mrs. Lynn murmured. "Why, I remember with the Soulry brothers it happened just that way."

"Please, Carolyn." Mrs. Faderman shook out her handkerchief with impatience and rubbed at the spoon she had taken, earning a snivel from Rowena.

"When I was a child," the woman began, as if she hadn't heard, "we had a little circus come here. Just a little one, mind you."

"I remember the little ones," Lady Augusta said with warmth. "Only a few acts, a few animals, but they were delightful."

"The Soulry brothers ran it," the woman continued. "Such nice young men."

"If they ran a circus, I doubt they could have been very nice," Mrs. Cricket remarked.

"Oh, but they were!" The woman looked at her with wide yes. "Jim Soulry used to hand out candy, and Peter Soulry let us pet the monkey."

"How nice," said Mrs. Faderman, but the sour look on her face made it clear the idea disgusted her.

Adele, who knew Mrs. Lynn's babbling stories usually amounted to some unexplored thought, took her hand and said kindly, "Go on, Mrs. Lynn. You were saying something about corruption?"

The woman looked cautiously at Mrs. Faderman, from whom she had taken her cues for years. "Well, go on, Carolyn," the woman prompted. "If you're going to tell your story, you may as well tell it."

"Oh, well, I was just going to say — Oh, it isn't anything bad!"

"Well, corruption isn't good, is it?" Mrs. Fourier raised her eyebrow.

"I was just going to say they were very popular in these small towns," said the woman. "Quite like the Barry Circus, I imagine. They made a lot of money. And one day, we heard about how one brother shot the other in cold blood."

"Over a woman?" Nin inquired.

"Oh, no, nothing like that, Miss Branch. They were both happily married." She gave a vague smile.

"Yes, well, what was the story, Carolyn?" Mrs. Faderman asked with impatience, looking at the clock on the wall. "I really must be getting back home to start the dinner."

"You talk as if you cook it yourself," Nin remarked with a sharp eye.

"I'm sure you want to hear the rest of Carolyn's story, Irene," Lady Augusta said in her regal voice. "And you haven't tried the ginger cake." She motioned to Rowena, who lurched forward, pushing the plate toward Mrs. Faderman.

"It was money, of course," said Mrs. Lynn. "Peter stole from the circus profits. He was most ingenious about it."

"How was he ingenious?" Adele leaned forward.

"He hid it," said the woman. "The cashier was a school chum of his. You know how school chums will do anything for one another."

"Yes, yes, go on," Mrs. Faderman prompted.

"The school chum would take a small amount every night and go to the post office the next morning," Mrs. Lynn said. "He would mail the money to the train station in San Francisco, in care of a friend of *his* who worked there. Then, this man would put the money in one of those train station safe boxes for safe keeping."

"Out of sight, out of mind." Nin nodded. "That is clever."

"Peter had a key, of course," said the woman. "After he shot his brother — it was awful — he took him into the woods so no one would hear, and shot him and hid the body amongst the brush so they wouldn't find him for days —"

"What did he do then, dear?" Lady Augusta asked.

"He wrote his wife a note and took the train, calm as you please, to San Francisco and got that money out of the safe box. Then he took a boat to Africa or somewhere."

"Coward!" Mrs. Cricket sneered.

"Did they ever find him?" asked Adele.

"Oh, yes," she said. "He told his wife where he was going. But by that time, it was too late. The local tribe didn't like him so they —" She swallowed.

"We get the picture, Carolyn," said Mrs. Faderman. "I maintain those brothers must have been sinister in the first place for this Peter Soulry to even conceive of such a thing."

"They say people can get such ideas from books and those moving pictures now," Mrs. Abberton said with a shudder.

"Yes, *now* they can," Mrs. Faderman said. "But back then, they couldn't. One would need to have a corrupted soul to go through with such a thing."

"I don't know as I agree, Irene," said Lady Augusta. "Horatio told me many stories of men with innocent beginnings who did bad things for one reason or another." She looked at Adele. "I'm sure your brother told you stories, Adele."

Adele only half heard her. Her mind was buzzing as if a nest of bees had gotten into it. "What? Oh, yes, Jack told me stories about his days with the Anspaches."

"Well, that's different." Mrs. Faderman rose, putting on her gloves. "Vigilantes encounter more evil than the police."

"They're out to do good, not evil," Nin insisted.

"Why, Miss Branch, I hardly would have expected you to defend Mr. Gossling," said the woman. "Don't tell me your heart is softening for our local deputy sheriff."

Nin's face was a furious white and Rowena rushed to get her a glass of water.

Adele thanked Lady Augusta for the invitation to tea and motioned for her friend to follow her.

"It was my pleasure to have the both of you." The woman pressed both their hands as she followed them to the door. "Rowena always puts out a lavish spread for tea. Horatio is forever chiding her about the waste. I wanted to make sure you got what you needed." She gave Adele a steady look.

Adele looked the elderly woman straight in the eye. "You needn't worry, ma'am. Nin and I got what we needed."

Lady Augusta returned the knowing look and waved them away.

CHAPTER 22

The moment they were outside, Adele held Nin's arm so the ladies fluttered down the street ahead of them. Once they disappeared around the corner, she absent-mindedly headed toward the business district of Arrojo.

"Something's bothering you." Her friend watched her carefully.

"That key," Adele admitted.

"The missing key?"

Adele nodded. "I know I said before that it might not be important, but I've changed my mind. I think I know what it's for and why it's missing."

"Don't tell me that ridiculous story made you solve the murder." Nin chuckled.

"Not solve it, but perhaps answer a few of the sheriff's question marks," she said with a smile.

"Where to now?" Nin asked.

"The police station."

"To tell Hatfield about Mrs. Lynn's Soulry brothers?"

"He's not even there now." A sly look appeared on Adele's face. "Neither is Jack."

"Oh?" Her friend eyed her.

"We're going to get a look at some evidence from our dear friend Edison."

"Adele, maybe you shouldn't." Her friend looked genuinely worried. "It always sets things aflame."

"Elsie and her ladies call it unbalancing the patriarchy." Adele gave her a knowing look. "I should think you would approve of that."

Nin grinned. "When you put it that way, how can I object?"

"Anyway, I might be a police consultant soon." Adele straightened her shoulders. "Then I can go in and look at evidence any time I like."

"But you still can't remove it," her friend pointed out. "After what happened with the Marsh case, I'm sure the mayor, even if he does approve you as a consultant, would insist on that."

"I don't plan on removing anything this time," Adele said. "I just want to see something."

"And after that?"

"We pay Calvin a visit," said Adele.

"What for?"

"To see if the rumors about the circus leaving are true," Adele answered. "If anyone would know for sure, he would."

They reached the police station in the calm early evening. Edison was there with only one other assistant deputy, a new man whose name Adele didn't even know.

"Good evening, Assistant Deputy," Adele said with a smile. She found calling him by his title always softened him.

"Oh, good evening, miss." Edison's fingers slipped over the keys. She couldn't help but be amused at how he still became flustered when she visited the station. "The sheriff ain't — isn't here, miss."

"We know that," Nin said.

"You're holding the fort, as they say?" Adele asked, sitting at the edge of her brother's empty desk.

He looked a little silly. "They all went to Rosa Gris, miss."

"Except for you and —" She nodded toward the back of the station.

"Oh, he's an errand boy, miss." Edison's voice lowered. "The sheriff just hired him. His name's Riley. Going to the academy to study police procedure and all that."

The young man's sniffy tone did not escape Adele. "You don't approve, Assistant Deputy?"

"It's not that, miss," he said. "But, well, being a by-the-book lawman isn't much good, is it? One has to go out and experience it." His chest puffed up. "Be in the line of fire, you know."

"You've done plenty of that," Adele remarked. "And you keep a good eye on the evidence."

"We need some of that evidence now," Nin said.

"Oh, but I have strict orders —"

"From Sheriff Hatfield?" Adele asked quickly.

"No, not from the sheriff," the young man admitted. "Mrs. Faderman."

Adele's anger rose at the thought of the silver-haired woman marching into the station, probably when the sheriff was out, and giving Edison orders.

Echoing her annoyance, Nin growled, "Mrs. Faderman isn't running this station!"

"No indeed, miss." Edison shuddered.

"Assistant Deputy Edison." Adele leaned closer to him. "You've heard, I'm sure, the sheriff put in a request for me to be a police consultant?"

"So the rumors are true!" the young man burst out.

"They are indeed," said Adele. "The sheriff is certain the mayor will approve it. It's only a matter of time before I can have access to anything I like in this office."

"So you'd better give us the key to the evidence room," Nin said gruffly, "or you'll be denying a police consultant information she has a right to see."

Adele saw the young man was still reluctant. She was struck with an idea. "I'll make a deal with you, Mr. Edison. You give me a piece of paper, and I'll write a note telling the sheriff I asked you for the key and I'll sign it. That way, if he comes in roaring, you can show him the note and he'll know it was my doing."

"Oh, but I wouldn't want you to get in trouble, miss!"

"Would *you* rather get in trouble?" Nin asked archly.

The young man chuckled. "I'm used to that, miss."

Adele noticed Riley, the young man in the corner, glancing over his shoulder, his thick glasses slipping down his nose.

"There's something very important I have to see," Adele insisted.

"Something about the circus murder?" Edison's eyes lit up. "But that's all finished."

"A murder case is never finished until someone is hanged," Nin said.

The young man shivered.

"You've helped me so much in the past, Assistant Deputy." Adele gave him a sweet smile. "I hope you won't refuse to help me now."

"Certainly not, miss." He took out the key to the evidence room from the sheriff's desk drawer, handing it to her. "But please, don't take anything out!"

"I won't," she promised.

In light of the number of cases they had had in the past few years along with the governor rearranging positions so Hatfield was now sheriff over more towns in the area, the sheriff had designated a small room next to the files as the evidence room. It was a dark, dry space with no windows and a swinging electric light that beaconed a strong glare. Nin had to shield her eyes from it and, owing to her anxiety over small, closed spaces, stood just inside the open doorway.

Adele found the evidence marked ROWE MURDER CASE and produced the wooden box Hatfield had taken from Estelle's wagon. Opening it, the luscious light blue velvet greeted her. She examined it with her magnifying glass.

"What are you looking for, Adele?" her friend inquired.

"Some sign of what was here other than just a key," Adele said in a vague tone.

"Like trappers look for animal tracks in the snow?" Nin asked.

"Exactly," said Adele, jumping up. "And I think I found the tracks." She gave Nin the box and magnifying glass. "That lining isn't as empty as Hatfield thinks."

Nin scrutinized it. "Why, there's writing!"

"Not only writing," Adele said. "An imprint."

"How clever!" Her friend gave her an admiring look.

"It didn't occur to me until Abby described it. I only saw the box for a moment when we found it but I remembered the lining had that same pointed finger shape as Abby described."

"It certainly looks like what you said about the key," Nin agreed.

"And the imprint is even better up close." Adele felt her excitement grow. "Estelle must have hidden the box under some heavy linens for the key left a distinct mark."

"I see writing." Nin narrowed her eyes. "Mosler"

"Mosler," said Adele. "It's like what Jack said. The name of the maker."

"What else did your brother say?" Nin inquired.

"He suggested the key might be to a locked box."

"A safe deposit box." A slow smile spread across Nin's face. "Just like in Mrs. Lynn's story."

Adele grasped her arm. "That's what gave me the idea. If Peter Soulry could send money to a friend to keep in a locker, why couldn't Estelle do the same?"

"I didn't think she had a penny to her name," Nin said.

"We don't know that," said Adele. "Maybe her family left her some money even her husband doesn't know about."

"So you think this key was to a safe deposit box where she was keeping money to run away?" Nin suggested.

"I'm sure of it." She peered inside the box with the magnifying glass. "There's also a number here, Nin."

"I saw that," her friend said.

"Keys have numbers so the maker can identify them," Adele said. "Perhaps even locate the box to which they belong."

"But the key is gone," Nin insisted.

"Estelle sent it to someone, or someone took it," Adele predicted. "I'm guessing the latter."

"Why?" Her friend stared at her.

"Jack told me Estelle's face was like a ghost when they opened the box, as if she expected to find something there and was frightened to see it was gone."

Nin closed the box. "I think I see now. Paul stole the key!"

"I've a feeling once we find out why, it will clear him," Adele insisted.

She held the box between her hands. It was small enough to fit between her palms. With determination, she slipped it into her bag.

"Adele!"

"I know I said I wouldn't take evidence, but now we need it, dear." She pulled Nin out of the room and shut the door, earning a sigh of relief from her friend. "We've another call to make before we go to the circus."

"What do you intend to do?"

Adele grinned. "Use the imprint to our advantage."

They said a flurried goodbye to Edison as they threw the key to the evidence room on the desk. The young man watched after them, bewildered.

They strolled down Bridge Street past people getting their late afternoon shopping done before dinner. Adele turned into the wooden barn that had no sign but belonged to Elton Good-fellow, the owner of the town's blacksmith shop.

"Good afternoon, Mr. Goodfellow!" Adele sang out.

"What're you wanting?" he growled.

"Some decent behavior, for one," Nin snapped. "You act like a street dog. Is that how you treat customers?"

Adele pressed her friend's wrist. "We're in desperate need of your skills, Mr. Goodfellow."

"Eh?"

"I've lost the key to my father's safe deposit box." She feigned embarrassment. "I'm going into the city tomorrow, and I'd like to visit the bank."

"Lady ain't got no business in a bank," he growled.

"If she makes her own living, she has," Nin said.

"I'm getting some bonds out of the safe for my brother," Adele lied, trying to keep her temper. "He just can't get away from his work to do it."

"That's all right then, I guess," he mumbled.

"So glad you approve." Nin smirked.

"But I can't get in without a key."

"Ain't your brother got a key?"

Adele bit her lip to give herself time to think. "We only had one key."

"And he lets you keep it?" The man raised a bushy eyebrow. "Not very bright of him."

She took a deep breath. "I was hoping, Mr. Goodfellow, you could make a duplicate out of this." She handed him the box she had taken from the station.

He examined it. "Reckon I could, miss. Maybe I ought to make two of 'em so your brother can have his own key."

"He'd only lose it," Nin said, getting into the spirit of the fibs. "He's always losing things. That's why he gave it to her to keep."

To Adele's surprise, the man's face broke into a grin. "Always that way with money gents. They ain't got sense enough to hold on to what they've got."

"I promise I'll hold on to this key as if my life depended on it,"

Adele said with a little fluttering of her eyelashes. "Can you make it without ruining the box?"

"I suppose so," he grumbled. "Cost you extra."

"You bloodsucker!" Nin snarled. "She'll pay for the key just like any other person."

"It's all right, dear." Adele gave her a sharp look. "I value your time, Mr. Goodfellow. Just put it on my account and I'll pay you when I pick it up. Tomorrow?"

"Cost you extra for the rush order too, miss."

"I'll pay whatever you say," Adele said meekly.

"Suit yourself, miss." He gave Nin a triumphant look.

"That man's a leech!" Nin complained when the were on the street.

"He's one of those men who resents the world and takes it out on women," Adele agreed, shaking out her jacket as if she were shaking out his unpleasantness. "But he's the only one who can do what we need."

"What's the good of getting a key?" Nin inquired.

"We might need to confront someone with it," Adele said. "Or we might find the box and see for ourselves what's in it."

"But that's against the law!" Nin eyed her. "Adele, your brother would have a fit if you did anything like that."

Adele smiled, taking her arm. "Only with permission, dear. Even I wouldn't stoop that low."

"I know you wouldn't!" her friend declared.

CHAPTER 23

*T*heir walk to the circus wagons was accompanied by a pleasant breeze. Already, circus people were preparing themselves for the evening's performance. Some workers swept between concession stands while others set up the platform where Mr. Henley would soon take his place, barking out the delights to come in the evening and herding people inside.

Adele expected to find Calvin's caravan bursting with activity, especially with Paul gone, but it was deathly quiet. It was so quiet she doubted at first if he could even be there. No one answered her tentative knock. One of the clowns dressed in a sailor suit passed by and said in a throaty voice, "Just go right in, miss."

"Aren't you the clown that dresses like a policeman?" Nin asked.

The man bowed his head. "Considering recent events, miss, Calvin asked us to take that out of the show." He scurried away in his big shoes.

"It does seem in bad taste," Nin agreed.

Adele and Nin crept in. Calvin was sitting at his desk tapping the edge of one of his square pencils against a pile of papers. His gaze seemed far away but when the light from the open doorway filled the wagon, he returned to the present. He glanced down at the pencil and, as if remembering something, threw it aside.

"Would you like me to send over a new box of pencils?" Adele asked softly. "No charge, of course."

The young man gave a wry smile. "A peace offering?"

"Why should she have to make a peace offering?" Nin asked sharply.

"It was her brother who arrested my father, wasn't it?" he said.

"Jack was doing his duty," Adele said.

"It's also his and the sheriff's duty to see he goes to trial," said Calvin, his voice bitter. "And it's their duty to see he hangs!"

"Only if he's guilty," Nin insisted.

The young man looked at them with steady eyes. "I may not always get along with my father, but he's no killer."

"How's your mother taking it?" Adele sat on a stool. Nin took a place on the floor. "What's the phrase, as well as can be expected?" He gave a short laugh. "Mama's very good at hiding things."

Adele realized he was talking about the story in the newspaper but she kept silent.

"I wish we'd never come to this blasted town!" he growled.

"It would have happened in the next town if you hadn't," Nin pointed out. "Murderers don't wait."

Something about her words seemed to shake him. He picked up the pencil he had thrown aside. "I assume you're here for a reason, Miss Gossling?"

The door swung open, and Estelle came in. She stopped when she saw the ladies. "Oh, you're here again."

"We came to offer our regrets, Mrs. Barry," said Adele, holding out her hand.

The woman took it woodenly. "The police are only doing their job."

"Then you don't believe your husband is innocent?" Nin eyed her.

"Of course he's innocent!" The woman flounced past them.

"Cal, have you some letter paper and a pen? I can't seem to find anything nowadays."

"Take a look for yourself," said her son, his tone almost blasé. "You know where everything is."

Adele watched as the woman went straight to the drawer of a small cabinet behind the desk and extracted paper and pen. As if she noticed Adele watching, Estelle lamented, "I might pay your shop a visit before we leave Adele. I write to my sister in San Francisco often, you see, and it won't do to keep stealing paper and pen from Cal." She smiled and rubbed his shoulder.

"I don't mind, Mama," he said in a warm tone.

"I'll send over some things myself," Adele promised. "I'm sending a box of pencils to your son anyway."

"I don't know —" The woman hesitated, glancing at him.

"She won't charge for it, if that's what you're worried about," Nin said.

The woman stiffened. "We're not mercenaries, Miss Branch. We've done quite a good deal of business in this area, as a matter of fact. Haven't we, Cal?" She glanced at him.

"Enough for now," he muttered.

"Please let me," Adele pleaded. "I feel it would end things on a better note."

"I think Miss Gossling is feeling guilty, Mama." Cal gave her a shrewd look.

"You needn't," said the woman in an aloof tone. "This will all be cleared soon." She left the wagon.

"I imagine you'll be leaving when it does." Adele grasped the folded parasol in her lap with both hands.

He scribbled on the ledger for a few minutes and then dropped the pencil. "The sheriff has released us so we're taking the circus elsewhere."

Adele's stomach tightened. So the gossips had, for once, gotten the facts straight. "May I ask where?"

"The manager of the amphitheater in San Francisco agreed to

let us move our circus there for the remainder of the summer," he said. "I have to take the train out to see him in a few days to sign the contract."

"You're leaving before the trial?" Adele asked. "If there is one, that is."

"We'll leave as soon as we can." His voice was firm. "You don't seem to understand, Miss Gossling, this is business for us."

"And you don't seem to understand your father is in jail!" Nin snarled.

"My father did not kill Julius Rowe." The man was so indignant that Adele felt her heart soften.

"How soon do you plan on leaving?"

He raised an eyebrow. "The police sent you to ask me that?"

"I ask for a good reason," she said. "I also believe your father is innocent."

He studied her. "I had a feeling you didn't like my father, Miss Gossling."

"Whether I like or dislike anybody has nothing to do with whether I believe they are guilty of a crime," she said simply. "I think I can prove he didn't do it but I need time."

He sank back into the chair, staring at her. "Why do you think he didn't do it? After all, Julius and Mama were —" To her surprised gaze, he added, "Oh, yes, Mama broke down and told me. I know she intended to leave with him."

"Your father told us he had no idea she was going to run away," Adele continued. "We know he was lying. He knew what your mother was planning."

He gave a small chuckle. "Papa always finds things out."

"If I can prove he executed a plan to stop them that didn't involve killing Julius then the police would have nothing to hold him on."

He stared at her. "What sort of plan?"

"Money," she said. "Or, rather, lack of it."

"I don't understand." The man put his hand to his head.

"Call it an underdeveloped idea," she said. "But will you try and hold off on leaving town until I can get more information?"

"I don't know if I can," he admitted. "This doesn't only involve me, Miss Gossling. I have performers and workers to think of."

"How have you been paying them now?" Nin asked.

He stiffened. "That's none of your business, Miss Branch."

"But you have been paying them?" Adele eyed him.

"There are the earnings from the circus, of course," he said.

"But they aren't enough," she guessed.

He looked down at the ledger smeared with ink on his desk. "I have money of my own left to me by my grandmother."

Adele pressed his hand. "You're very generous, Mr. Barry. And perhaps more dedicated to the circus than your father realizes."

He gave a small grunt. "I can't let it go to ruin because the police made a mistake, can I?"

Adele rose and began to walk around the small wagon. "If you really believe they made a mistake, then you'll help us correct it."

"How?" He leaned forward.

"We need some information," she said. "The police found a box in your mother's wagon."

"Yes, I know," he said.

"The box was empty but it used to contain a key," she continued. "Your mother told the police it was to a jewelry box but they don't believe it."

"Really, this business of the police hounding everyone about every slight thing —"

"They can't catch a killer otherwise," Nin said.

"They won't catch one in my mother's wagon!" he growled.

"We think that key may belong to a safe deposit box of some kind," Adele said.

"Safe deposit box?" He looked puzzled. "It's probably for Aunt Charlotte."

"Aunt Charlotte?"

"My mother has been sending my aunt money from the household budget I give her." He looked uncomfortable.

"May I ask why?" Adele said gently. "Perhaps I can help."

"I didn't say she needed help," he said quickly.

"I'm guessing your uncle doesn't know about her receiving money," she said. "When a woman receives money in that way, it's usually because she's in trouble or expects to be."

He gave a rueful smile. "I suppose you may as well know, since you know the rest of our secrets. Aunt Charlotte and Uncle David haven't been getting along for years, and Aunt Charlotte is afraid for my two young cousins. He can get rather nasty when he's had too much to drink."

"She wants to leave him," Nin said. "Smart woman."

"But she can't do it without money," Adele finished.

"She can't work, of course, what with two young children in the house," he said. "So Mama opened a safe deposit box in the city in her name, and she's been sending the money there."

Adele gave her friend a meaningful look. "That's what she told you?"

He glanced at her. "I should think you, of all people, would approve, Miss Gossling."

"Oh, I do," she said. "Does your father know about this?"

His face became grim. "He thinks divorced women are no better than harlots."

"He would," Nin grumbled.

"You see now why Mama couldn't tell the police about the key."

Adele nodded, remembering how she used to plan such schemes when she worked in the settlement houses. "I'd like to help your aunt too, Mr. Barry."

"You?" He stared at her.

"I have connections with women's groups in the city," she said. "I would need to meet your aunt and get more details on her situation and her plans, of course."

"It's very kind of you," he murmured.

"We'll be in the city tomorrow," she continued, catching her friend's sharp look. "If you give us her address, we'll stop by to speak to her."

"She's in Oakland, Miss Gossling, not in San Francisco."

"All the better," she said, smiling. "A friend of mine knows places in Oakland that help women like your aunt."

He told her the address as she wrote it down in a small notepad she always kept in her purse. "We'll do all we can for her, and for your father too," she promised.

"I'm beginning to believe all those rumors about you helping innocent people are true, Miss Gossling." He rose, his face more cheerful.

Adele's eyes fell on a covered thing sitting on top of the cabinet where Estelle had retrieved the paper and pen. "Is that a typewriter, Mr. Barry?"

"An Underwood." He uncovered it. "I bought it before we left. If I'd known we would be needing the money for other things —" He gave the gadget a menacing look. "But it makes letter-writing much faster."

"One must always have one's tools for business," Adele said kindly. "I imagine you're the only one who uses it?"

He nodded. "Mama told you she wasn't one for gadgets and she isn't."

"And your father?" Adele asked.

"He's surprisingly modern when it comes to gadgets," he said with a laugh as he led them outside. "He types better than I do!"

"Sometimes you can teach an old dog new tricks," Nin remarked.

Just then, a woman dressed in a ballerina costume walked by, balancing leashes to five poodles in each hand. As if the dogs heard Nin, they started barking all at once, making Calvin's face break into a smile.

When they had left, Nin burst out, "Why are we going to the city tomorrow?"

"Because we want to help Mrs. Long, naturally," Adele said.

Her friend eyed her. "Is that the only reason?"

Adele laughed. "You know my ways too well, dear. If Estelle gave that key to her sister, she might be able to tell us more about it."

"And if she can't?"

"Then no harm done, is there?" She was almost merry as she took her friend's arm.

CHAPTER 24

*E*arly the next morning, Adele left a note for her brother that she had been invited to lunch with Elsie and some of her suffragist friends in the city and would be in San Francisco most of the day. Something inside her creaked like the front gate she shut behind her at having told a fib, along with a mild anger toward Jackson who had assumed the role of her protector since their father died and made such fibs necessary.

She gathered Nin, dressed in her traveling clothes, from her flat above her shop and they stopped first at the blacksmith. Mr. Goodfellow tried in his fiendish way to hold back giving her the box by insisting his early wake-up required more money. Nin lost her temper and grabbed a sledge hammer, holding it over her head with such a menacing look that Mr. Goodfellow's ornery countenance turned frightened as a rabbit. He handed Adele the box without further comment.

"You shouldn't have done that, dear," Adele said as they climbed onto the train to Oakland. "He might go to the police and say you threatened him."

"They all think I'm threatening anyway," Nin said. "They still believe Mama was a witch and I can cast harmful spells on them."

"Let them," Adele said in a savage tone as she arranged the extra bag where she put the box with the key in her lap. "There are plenty of us who love and respect you for your rare gifts."

"He won't go to the sheriff," Nin said. "He wouldn't dare admit he let a woman intimidate him with one of his own tools."

Adele laughed and sat back, enjoying the rolling scenery outside the windows. Nin, too, had gotten over her fear of closed train carriages and touched the glass as if she were a part of the trees and grass and mountains in the distance.

Adele had only been to Oakland a few times in her life. The city gave the impression of a sleepier version of San Francisco. Its streets were cleaner but narrower, so as she and Nin bustled down the road, they were shoulder-to-shoulder with other people. She was surprised to see there were more women on the street than she expected to see at that hour. Their cordiality was more enlightened as well. She and Nin received several smiles and apologies for skirts brushing against theirs in the crowd.

They found the house where Charlotte Long lived on a quiet street off the main commercial areas. Adele glanced at a carriage drawn by two horses that stood waiting on the corner. "I hope her husband isn't in."

"The barbarian!" Nin agreed. "I shall take a poker to his mealy face if he is."

"Only if he's intoxicated," Adele chimed in as she rang the bell.

A maid let them in with hardly a glance. "Mr. Calvin told us to expect you, miss. Will you wait in the parlor please?"

Adele looked around with curiosity. She had pictured a house with a cold and perhaps even bare countenance, like many she had seen from disengaged couples. But the place was decorated in warm colors and laden with pictures, odds and ends, and lace curtains.

"It certainly looks respectable," Nin admitted.

"Pain and suffering gleam through even the most respectable houses," Adele whispered.

When Mrs. Long appeared, she looked like anything but a suffering woman. Her brown hair was neatly made up and her dress was pressed and clean. Her brown eyes were calm, though Adele could see some premature wrinkles on her face.

"I'm very glad you could come," she said. "Calvin says you're trying to exonerate Paul. Such sad business!" She sighed.

"We try to help those in need." Adele watched her. "I've many connections in the area with women's leagues and settlement houses that help women get out of — well, unpleasant situations."

"Like yours," Nin said with her usual bluntness.

The woman blinked. "Oh, but it's not me who needs help, Miss Gossling. It's my sister."

Nin wandered to the fireplace. Her hand reached toward the poker stand. "Is he here?" she asked.

"He?"

"Your swine husband."

"Nin —" Adele felt her face turn red.

"We came for that too, didn't we?" Her friend glanced at her. "I thought you were going to tell her about Vanya and your friends."

"There must be some mistake." Mrs. Long looked troubled.

"If he's passed out in a dead drunk, we can get you and your children out of here in no time," Nin continued.

The woman gasped. "Good heavens, you think my husband is drunk?"

"We saw the carriage outside," Adele ventured. "And from what Calvin told us —"

"He told you my husband is a drunk and that I need help?" The woman's pallor turned gray and then an indignant pink. "I don't believe it!"

"We were led to believe you were in trouble, Mrs. Long." Adele was beginning to feel as if she wanted to crawl under the daisy-patterned rug.

"But I told you, my sister is in trouble, not me!" The woman pressed her hands together. "Perhaps you'd better tell me what Cal said."

Feeling humbled, Adele related what Calvin had told them. When she finished, the stunned look on the woman's face made it clear she and Nin had made a grave error.

"I can't believe Estelle would tell Calvin such lies." Mrs. Long's voice was shaking.

"Then your husband isn't a drunk?" Nin quickly returned to the couch.

"Nothing of the kind." She rang the bell and the maid appeared. "Judy, bring us some tea please. Ask Mrs. Butler to make it strong. I think we need it." She glanced at the two women.

"And he doesn't — beat you?" For the first time since Adele had known her, Nin sounded genuinely embarrassed.

"Good heavens, no!" She rose and extracted a book from the shelf which Adele saw was a photo album. "See for yourselves."

Adele could hardly look at the pictures, as she felt so ashamed. There was no doubt the family in the photographs was a happy one, and the man in the pictures looked anything but a cad who beat women and children.

"Please forgive us." She gave the album back to the woman.

"Given the circumstances, I understand," the woman said kindly.

"Cal shouldn't have lied to us," Nin said.

"He didn't lie," Adele insisted. "He was only relating what his mother told him."

"Then she's the liar!"

"If my sister told Cal she was giving me money so I could leave my husband, she must have been desperate," Mrs. Long said.

"Can you think of a reason why she would make up such a story?" Adele asked.

The woman considered this. "Perhaps — as they say — the shoe was on the other foot."

"You mean it's your sister who wants to leave her husband," Nin said.

The woman gave her a silencing look as the maid entered with the tea tray. When she had left, she said, "I knew she and Paul had been having troubles for a long time. And when she asked me to keep money for her —"

"Keep money for her?"

"You don't know Estelle." Mrs. Long smiled. "She was like our mother. She thought money made the world go around. She once said she'd rather put a bullet through her head than not have money."

"So she sent you money, just as Calvin said," Adele murmured.

"Yes, that part is true," said Mrs. Long.

"And she asked you to put it in a safe deposit box in the city," Adele said.

"How did you know?" The woman stared.

Adele produced the box from her purse and held up the key Mr. Goodfellow had made.

The woman stared. "How in the world did you get hold of it?"

"Then it is the key to the box your sister asked you to keep for her?"

"It looks like it." She glanced behind her as a shadow of male voices rose in the hallway. "My husband doesn't know anything about this."

Adele quickly put the box back in her bag. They were quiet for a moment as the voices died down and a door shut in the distance.

"He's gone back to his office now," said Mrs. Long. "Not that he wouldn't understand if he knew. But Tony thinks Estelle's head is too much in the clouds." She grimaced. "Maybe that's why she made him the villain in her story to cover up her deed."

"Did she tell you where the money was coming from?"

Mrs. Long looked uncomfortable. She picked up the poker and started rearranging the coals in the fire.

"The fire isn't lit," Nin piped up.

She put the poker down. "I'm guessing it came from her household money."

"But you're not sure?" Adele studied her.

"Where else would it come from?" she asked sharply. "Our parents left us very little and Paul — well, he's not very generous."

"How long has she been sending you money?" Adele asked.

"Six or seven months, I should think."

"It's hard to save from the household money for that long," Adele said gently. "I know. I handled the household when I came of age. My mother passed away when I was a child."

"I'm sorry to hear that, Miss Gossling, but I don't see how any of this is going to help Paul." She picked up her teacup a little unsteadily.

"You think she was stealing the money," Nin blurted out.

The woman shook her head. "Estelle can be fanciful, but she would never do anything like that."

"It wouldn't be wrong for a woman to take money from a business she partly owns," Adele said quietly.

"What in the world do you mean?" The woman stared at her.

"She was in love with another man," Adele explained. "He promised to run away with her. From everything we know, this man was the sort to live off women. She would have been desperate for money, and much more than she could save from the household."

The woman swayed and Nin, with her quick compassion, was at her side with her arm around the woman's shoulders. She took out a bag of herbs she carried with her and slipped some in the teacup. "It will steady you." To the woman's frightened eyes, she explained, "It's a Chinese herb good for dizziness."

"My friend knows about such things," Adele assured her. "Her advice is as good as any doctor's."

"Better," her friend insisted.

The woman gave a wan smile and sipped from the cup. "I do feel better. Thank you, Miss Branch."

"I think you know, or you suspect, where she might have gotten the money." Adele watched her.

Mrs. Long fanned herself with her handkerchief. "You're very perceptive, Miss Gossling. Yes, I think I know how she got it." She leaned forward. "Estelle, you know, counts the cashier money once the show begins."

"She told us," said Nin.

"She once joked how she ought to take some of those bills since she works just as hard as Paul," she said.

"You think that's what she's been doing?" Adele asked.

"I wouldn't be surprised." Her sister sighed. "Estelle is like a child. It would be just like her to think they wouldn't be missed."

"You knew nothing about her and this man, Julius Rowe?" Adele asked.

"Is he a flyer?"

Adele sat up straight. "Then you did know about it."

"Only since last week when I received her letter."

"Your sister sent you a letter?"

The woman nodded. "She wrote me she had fallen in love with the trapeze artist, and they were going to buy a circus in Europe. She wanted me to take out all the money from the safe deposit box and take it to Al Carroll."

"A past flirtation?" Nin inquired.

Mrs. Long grimaced. "Perhaps, though I don't know for sure. I do know he was once a friend of Paul and Estelle's."

"Why do you think she asked you to give the money to Mr. Carroll?"

The woman shrugged. "I imagine she and this trapeze artist planned on going to him to get it."

"But she didn't say that was her plan?" Adele asked.

"Well, no." The woman blinked. "I just guessed." Her face brightened. "You think I'm wrong and this was all a joke?"

Adele refrained from answering, not wanting to dash the woman's hopes. "Did you, by chance, keep the letter?"

"I did." Her eyes fell on the fireplace. "I was going to burn it the first chance I got, but it's been mild weather this past week so we haven't had to light one."

"It's lucky for us you didn't," Nin said.

"You want to see it?" Mrs. Long glanced at Adele.

"Yes, if you please," she said.

"But how can all this help Paul?"

"I'm not sure yet," Adele admitted.

The woman hesitated. "Estelle's letters to me are — well, we've always been close."

"She believes her husband is innocent," Adele said gently. "No matter what trouble they've had, I'm sure she wouldn't want to see him hang for something he didn't do."

Mrs. Long shuddered. "Yes, that's true. Estelle may be careless and even selfish at times but she's not cruel." She excused herself and left the room.

Nin sat back. "A fine nest of vultures."

"They're all victims of circumstance, Nin," Adele argued. "Even Mrs. Long had no idea what role she was playing in this intrigue."

"It's all over now," Nin remarked. "One is dead, the other in jail."

"And the third?" Adele sighed. "I wonder what Estelle will do now."

"She won't run off with anyone," Nin said in her assured way.

"No, she's not the type," Adele agreed. "She may have convinced herself she needs men in her life in the past, but I'm willing to bet gold this tragedy has changed her."

Mrs. Long returned. "I brought the envelope too. I wasn't sure if you would need it."

"You're very obliging, ma'am." Adele gave her a gracious smile.

"I have a confession to make, Miss Gossling." The woman's face turned a little red. "I know about you."

"Know about me?"

"I know about your interest in police work and how you help the sheriff in that small town of yours," said the woman.

Adele stared. "But how —"

"Mr. Augustus Rand is a friend of my husband's," she said. "You know him?"

"Russell, Rand & Bellows," Adele said in a flat tone. "Yes, I know Mr. Rand."

"And I'm told you know Mr. John Bellows quite well too." The woman smiled.

Adele tried to keep her temper in check. "Mr. Bellows told Mr. Rand all about me and Mrs. Rand told you."

"Well, yes, in a way," said the woman. "They find it all rather astonishing and — if you'll pardon — rather amusing."

"I'm sure they do," Adele said dryly. She could feel Nin's annoyed gaze, though her friend kept silent. "Mrs. Long, may I trouble you for one more thing?"

"Anything you like," said the woman with a cordial smile. "Both my nephew and I appreciate your efforts."

"Now that you know all about her efforts from the obliging Mr. Bellows," Nin growled.

Adele pressed her hand. "Has your sister written you any other letters?"

"Yes, of course, though I only have a few on hand." The woman looked down at her immaculate skirt. "I'm afraid I don't keep many of her letters."

"Because your husband doesn't like her," Nin guessed.

Mrs. Long relaxed. "No, he doesn't. I suppose it shows."

"My friend has gifts that go beyond what most people feel," Adele explained.

"He won't chase her away," Nin assured the woman. "He knows when he's gone, she'll be a great comfort to you."

The woman flinched. "That's rather morbid, isn't it?" She rang the bell, which the maid answered promptly and gave her orders. When the girl came back with the letters, Adele cleared the small table and laid them out one next to the other.

"What are you hoping to find?" Mrs. Long looked interested.

"Inconsistencies," Adele said. "I see Estelle's letters to you were written longhand but this last one was typed. I assume she wasn't in the habit of typing her letters?"

The woman shook her head. "I thought it odd when I got that letter. She was always shy about trying new things. She refused to use the telephone for a long time. She thought it was haunted."

"I have a man working for me who feels the same way." Adele smiled at the thought of Tomas' frightened face when she and Jackson had first installed the phone. "She signed it in her own hand." Adele took out her magnifying glass. "The signature is quite smudged."

The woman shrugged. "Estelle probably couldn't find a good pen and took what was there. She's that sort of person."

"I wonder." Adele tapped the magnifying glass against her palm. "I'd like to take these with me as well. I promise I'll send them back to you without a scratch."

"Keep them if you like," said Mrs. Long. "With all that's happened, I'd feel safer if they weren't here." In an almost apologetic voice, she added, "My husband is rather particular about rumors, and he's already been badgered at his club for having a sister-in-law who used to be an aerialist."

After they left the house, Nin declared, "That Mr. Bellows and his loose tongue!"

"You mean about me?" Adele couldn't help but smile.

"He had no right to speak of your noble effort to gain justice as if it were a joke," Nin said. "I'll slap his face the next time I see him."

TAM MAY

"If I don't slap it first, dear," Adele said in a light tone. "Right now, we've more important things to worry about than the indiscreet words of a man who's proposed once too often to me."

"Sour grapes," her friend grumbled.

"This letter," Adele indicated her bag, "it interests me."

"I don't see why," Nin said. "Though it does confirm what Estelle told the sheriff about her plans."

"Not the contents, Nin, the form."

"Your epistolary expertise at work." Her friend smiled.

"Remember what Estelle told us?" Adele asked. "She hates new gadgets."

"I remember you telling me that," Nin said as she took her friend's arm.

"Then why would she type a letter to her sister?" Adele asked. "And a very businesslike one at that?"

"Was it so businesslike?" Nin asked.

Adele stopped at a little grassy area with a bench and sat down. She took out the letter. "See for yourself."

Dearest Charlotte,

I know I will shock you in what I'm about to say, but your sister has found her bliss at last. I'm in love! He's a trapeze flyer and wants me to run away with him and start our own circus in Europe!

But I need money. I'm sending you the key to that safe deposit box I have at the bank. I want you to take out everything that's in there and bring it to Al at 3600 Bay Street in San Francisco. I'll let you know what boat we'll be taking and where we're going once everything is settled.

It won't be long now until I'm free!

Don't breathe a word of this to Tony. You know he would tell Paul everything. My going away will give you some peace where he's concerned, at least.

Love, your dear sister

"It hardly reads like a letter a woman in love would write her sister, does it?" Adele put the envelope back in her bag. "And typed, no less, by a woman who abhors modern gadgets."

"Not to mention the illegible signature," Nin added.

Adele smiled. "So you noticed that."

"I take it our next stop is the ferry into San Francisco to see Dr. Blessings?" her friend asked.

Adele smiled. "Am I that obvious?"

"You suspect the signature isn't hers," Nin concluded. "So you asked Mrs. Long to give you other letters Estelle wrote her so you could bring them to him to compare." Her friend's eyes sparkled. "I remember other cases, Adele."

"We might be wrong." Adele rose.

"Do we have to see Elsie too?" Her friend stiffened. Dr. Blessing's daughter, one of Adele's suffragist friends, was not a favorite of hers.

"I expect he's at the university," said Adele. "It might be best if we go there first."

Dr. Blessings' laboratory was in a side building off the university. Adele coughed from the dampness as they descended the stairs to the basement. "It's shameful to put a man of his years in such a place," she grumbled.

"And him with bad health," Nin added.

Indeed, when they entered the laboratory, they saw the elderly man with the kind face sitting in a chair looking as if he were trying to catch his breath. They rushed toward him, and Nin found a glass and filled it with water.

"I'm all right," he insisted as he rose, leaning on a walking stick. "Just breathed a little too much ink and it made me dizzy for a moment."

"Maybe you ought to think about retiring, sir," Adele said softly. She knew from Elsie's letters the woman had been trying to convince her father to give up his work for a year now, and had even promised to partake in only the most inoffensive activities of her radical suffragist group if he did so.

The man placed a hand on her shoulder. "I won't be booted out like a lost dog."

"Not a lost dog," Adele insisted, "a dog that has served its master faithfully and deserves his rest."

Dr. Blessings chuckled. "What would I do with my 'rest' if I had it? I shudder to think. I might even join Elsie in her banner-making!"

Adele couldn't help but laugh, thinking of Elsie's less-than-subtle way of phrasing things when she was in one of her reformer moods.

"You'll be all right for at least a little while longer," Nin said.

He eyed her. "I have your assurance on that?" Nin nodded. "Then I've nothing to worry about, have I?"

"It's getting lunchtime, and you ought to go home," Adele scolded.

"Not until I find out why you're here," he said. "I assume you didn't come all the way from the country just to order me to lunch?"

"As a matter of fact, we need your expertise." She took out the letters. "It's rather like what you did for us for the Blackstone case."

"I'm not a handwriting expert for nothing," he said cheerfully. "What is it you're looking for?"

"A woman wrote these letters to her sister," she said. "I believe one of them wasn't written by her, though." Adele tapped her finger on the typed letter. "This one."

The man nodded. "It does seem rather odd that all the others would be handwritten."

Adele glanced at her friend with a knowing look. "That's what we thought."

"But the letter is signed," he pointed out.

"By the same hand that signed these?" Adele glanced at the others. "That's what I want you to tell me."

"You know I cannot commit myself —"

"Do we ever ask for a commitment?" Nin rolled her eyes.

He examined the letters with a few of his tools. "It's hard to tell," he admitted. "The letters on this one are rather dull."

"I think they're dull on purpose," Adele said.

"They very well might be," he agreed.

"Why do you think that?" Nin asked.

"The smears are even," he said, "as if someone rubbed a handkerchief over the letters."

"When a pen smudges, it does so in different places," Adele agreed.

"It's your job to notice such things," he said with a smile. "You've become as much of an expert on all things written as I am, Adele."

She blushed, knowing such a compliment from someone as distinguished as Dr. Blessings, who was known all over the West as the leading document expert, was an honor.

"Anything else you can tell us about it?" she asked.

"There are some differences," he said. "The signatures here —" he pointed to one of the written letters, "— and here —" he motioned toward the typed, "— aren't in and of themselves special. In fact, I would say they contain enough of the same strokes but in different variations to make me believe they *might* have come from the same hand."

"I see." Adele's heart sank.

"The writing in the letters themselves, that's a different story," he said. "You see here the 'y' curls in a way that is a variant from the signature on the same letter but here, on the typed letter, it's different." He illustrated what he meant for each letter he mentioned.

"So you think the signature on the typed letter is forged?" Adele asked.

"Without committing yourself," Nin added quickly.

"Without committing myself, I would say there is a strong

possibility," he said. "Tell me, have these been stolen from police evidence files like the others?" He eyed her.

"I never steal, Dr. Blessings," Adele said in an innocent tone. "I borrow for the good of the investigation."

He laughed. "Well, are these 'borrowed,' then?"

"As a matter of fact, they aren't," she said.

"They're not police evidence," Nin said.

"The woman's sister gave them to us with her blessing," Adele said. "We're trying to prove her brother-in-law is innocent of a crime, you see."

"It doesn't surprise me." The man grinned. "You've taken quite a shine to this criminal business."

"Would you rather she take a shine to radical politics, like your daughter?" Nin asked a little harshly. Adele gave her a warning look.

But Dr. Blessings only laughed. "I couldn't say at this point which is the lesser of two evils!" He folded the letters. "Naturally, if you leave them with me, I could do further tests."

"I don't think that will be necessary," Adele said. Nin glanced at her with surprise.

He raised his eyebrows. "I thought the police required conclusive evidence."

"I think I know who typed the letter and forged the signature," Adele said. "And I think he'll admit it once we confront him."

"So we won't need the evidence," Nin said.

"Just as you say, my dear." He pressed her hand. "As long as I'm being sent home for lunch, why not join us? Elsie would love to see you both."

Seeing Nin's wrinkled brow, Adele said kindly, "Not this time, I'm afraid. We must be getting back to Arrojo."

"You'll be coming to the city later this year?" he inquired. "I seem to recall Elsie telling me something of that sort."

"Jack and I will be seeing our aunt in Santa Barbara," she said as she held on to his arm, steering him out of the building, even though he was a little unsteady. "We planned on spending a few days in the city to see our friends."

"I hope that includes the Blessings family," he said in a cheerful tone as they walked out into the sunshine. "Ah, this lovely air! I always appreciate how the bay brings us a constant wind."

"Some of it blowing our hats off," Nin remarked.

He chuckled. "Yes, that's San Francisco, my dear. Sturdy and calm one moment, harsh and exploding the next."

"I think I prefer my lazy country existence," Adele said, smiling.

He stopped and looked at her with intense blue eyes. "It's been five years, my dear. No father wants his daughter mourning for him after five years."

Adele's throat tightened. "I'm not mourning anymore, Dr. Blessings. But I can't deny there isn't a day I don't think of him."

"Don't waste your thoughts on the dead," Nin advised in her wise way. "Not on men of such —" She suddenly stopped and held on to the edge of the street lamp, her hands clasping like two claws on it. She closed her eyes.

"Is she all right?" Dr. Blessings whispered.

"An aura," Adele murmured. "An aura about my father." She suddenly grabbed her friend's hand. "What is it, dear? Men of such what?" Panic rose in her chest.

Nin swallowed and looked at her, her face calm. "Nothing."

"There was something!" Adele insisted.

"No, nothing."

They rode in the taxi after dropping Dr. Blessings off at the train station, both silent. The questions were on the tip of Adele's tongue but she was afraid to ask them. She was afraid of the answers.

257

The train pulled into the Arrojo station in the early evening. The sky was still blue, though its brilliant, blustery shade had calmed.

"Tired, dear?" Adele eased the strap of the bag over her shoulder.

Her friend nodded. "Tired and hungry."

"You go rest," she said. "I can see Hatfield alone."

"Nothing of the kind." Nin planted her hand firmly in the crook of Adele's arm. "We made the discovery together and we tell the police together."

Adele pressed her cheek against her friend's shoulder. "We'll have some convincing to do with the sheriff."

"I think he'll listen to us," Nin assured her. "It's your brother who might make trouble."

"Jack can be a little too tied to police procedure," Adele agreed, "and heaven knows this case is hardly one to go by the book."

"A man who was the owner's paramour is killed and not by the owner," Nin said slyly. "That's what you believe, isn't it?"

"It's what I think I know," said Adele. "Of course we can't

know anything until we talk to Paul. It might end up being his word against —"

"Against what?"

"Well, the sheriff's evidence, I suppose." Adele sighed.

The station was filled with lawmen when they arrived. Hatfield was talking to Mr. Moffitt, the jewelry store owner. She and Nin took a place on the new wooden bench Jackson found for a song and brought as a gift to the station.

Edison sidled up to her. "That really wasn't fair, miss," he whispered.

"What wasn't?"

"You said you only wanted to see that box," he said. "You promised you wouldn't take out evidence."

"We don't work by a timetable," Nin hissed. "We needed it."

"The sheriff is hopping mad," The young man said.

"Why should he be?" Nin asked. "We're practically working for the police."

Adele gave Edison a sympathetic look. "Don't worry, Assistant Deputy, I'll take full responsibility."

"Did you find anything?" His eyes brightened.

"I might have," she said with a sly smile. "I just might have."

Hatfield glanced at them, then held out his hand to Mr. Moffitt. "We'll look into it, sir, I promise you."

"I won't have anything taken from my shop again, Sheriff." The man was. indignant. "Not after what happened on Labor Day."

"I'm sure it's nothing like that, Mr. Moffitt," the sheriff promised. "We've had no reports of any thieves in the area."

"I assume you would let the merchants know about it this time?" The man raised his eyebrow. Adele winced, thinking of the fiasco that had occurred earlier that year.

"The moment we find out anything," Hatfield said, his voice stern. "Good evening, sir."

"Good evening," the man mumbled, putting on his hat.

When he was gone, Jackson leaned into his desk. "I don't like to remind you, sir, but Mr. Sipes is still in town."

"And?" Hatfield prompted.

"He could have broken into Moffitt's shop."

"Mr. Sipes wouldn't do that, Jack," Adele insisted. "He said he's honest now, and I believe him."

"Well, I don't," her brother retorted. "I've seen it too many times."

"Once a thief, always a thief?" the sheriff asked dryly.

"You've seen it too, I'm sure," Jackson said.

"According to Mr. Moffitt, nothing was taken," Hatfield pointed out.

"He might not have had time," Jackson argued.

"No one broke into that store," Nin declared.

Jackson stiffened. "Are you seeing visions now, Miss Branch?"

"The Generous Ones don't give me visions, Mr. Gossling," she snapped. "They know things and pass them on to me."

"And they passed on to you that Mr. Moffitt was lying?"

"Nothing was taken because no one broke in," she insisted.

Hatfield leaned back in his chair. "I agree with Miss Branch."

"And why is that?" Jackson asked.

"Because he's complained about this once before, and when Edison and I went to inspect the back door, there was no evidence of a break-in," Hatfield said. "There was, however, evidence the bolt had been left unlocked all night and the wind storm that same evening blew the door open." He glanced at the desk beside his. "Edison! Isn't that right, lad?"

"Yes, Sheriff," the young man said in an obedient voice. "Wind was making the door bang against the wall when we got there."

"Get the ladies some coffee," his superior ordered. "They look all done in."

"We've just come back from the city," Adele said.

"Did Elsie put out a call for stone-throwers?" Jackson asked in a cutting voice.

"She won't be doing that for a while," Nin said, her voice thin. "Not with her father being so ill."

Jackson looked alarmed. "I'm sorry to hear that."

"You saw him, then?" the sheriff asked. Adele nodded. "Personally or professionally?"

Adele looked at him squarely. "What do you think?"

"I think," said the man slowly, "it has to do with that box you took from the station." He held out his hand. "May we have it back now?"

"She didn't plan on doing it," Nin insisted. "An idea suddenly came to her."

"Del and her ideas," Jackson grunted.

Adele put the box on the sheriff's desk. "Edison knew nothing about it, Sheriff. Don't go scolding him."

The man gave a hearty laugh. "I try not to scold him about missing evidence anymore, Adele. I only ask that it go no further than this station house." He cast a threatening eye around the small desks where some of the assistant deputies sat hunched over their papers. They glanced up, then went back to what they were doing.

"Mrs. Faderman would have a field day if she knew," Adele agreed. "She would probably run me out of town for being 'dangerously progressive.'"

"You know I don't turn down help when I can get it," Hatfield said.

"No, you've never been arrogant or territorial." Adele gave him a kind look. "It's one of the many reasons I admire you, Sheriff."

The man's face reddened. As Edison put the coffee cups in front of them, he said in a gruff voice, "Edison, put the box back with the Julius Rowe case file."

"Yes, sir."

"Before you do, Sheriff," Adele said, "I think you ought to look inside. There's something there you might find interesting."

Hatfield flung the lid open. "Well, well."

"The key!" Jackson stared at it. "Is this your doing, Miss Branch? Did you conjure it up from one of your auras?"

"You know better than that, Mr. Gossling," Nin said. "I'm no charlatan!"

"The key is courtesy of Mr. Goodfellow," Adele said, feeling triumphant. "The man may grunt like a pig but he knows his business."

"I don't understand," her brother said.

"Simple, Jack." Adele smiled. "I gave the box to Mr. Goodfellow, and he made the key according to the imprint."

"It even has the writing on it," Nin chimed in.

"Writing?" The sheriff examined it.

"What Miss Call couldn't read," Adele said. "The serial number, I imagine."

"That wouldn't do us much good," Jackson said. "It would only lead us to the model of safe deposit box, but I'm sure the manufacturer makes dozens of them."

"Suppose we let one of the lads find out for us?" The sheriff glanced at the bent heads. "Dooland!"

"Sheriff?" The young man stood up.

"Call the exchange and ask for the Mosley Company," Hatfield instructed. "Give them the number on this key and see if they have any record of where it belongs."

"Be glad to, sir." The young man was almost licking his lips, as he, unlike some of his colleagues, relished using the telephone.

"I don't think they would tell us that information, sir," Jackson pointed out.

"They may not, but Paul might," Adele said.

"What has he to do with it?" the sheriff asked. "The key belongs to his wife, as far as we know."

"That doesn't mean he didn't know about it," Nin said.

Jackson gave his sister a suspicious look. "Why were you in San Francisco with the key, Del?"

"We took the key to Oakland, not San Francisco," Nin said.

"Well, then, what were you doing with it in Oakland?"

"We had some questions for Mrs. Long," Adele answered.

"And who is Mrs. Long?" her brother prompted.

"Mrs. Long is the quite prominent and very happily married sister of Mrs. Barry."

"I thought her name was familiar," Hatfield said.

"We found no evidence she was involved in any of this," Jackson said.

Adele leaned forward, laying her closed parasol across her knees. "What if I told you she almost helped her sister and her sister's paramour escape?"

"You mean her sister and Mr. Rowe?" the sheriff asked. "I hardly think the woman would do that if she's as respectable as you say."

"She didn't know she was being used as a go-between," Nin said.

"A go-between for what?" Hatfield eyed Adele. "Letters?"

Adele shook her head. "Money."

"Money!" Jackson stared at her.

"Mrs. Long suggested Estelle was taking from the circus proceeds and putting it aside for her and Julius," Adele said impatiently. "She had to put it somewhere where her husband and son wouldn't find it. Keeping it in her wagon was out of the question."

"All right, Del." Her brother folded his arms. "You're dying to tell us what she did with it."

"It was like Mrs. Lynn said," Nin insisted.

"What has Mrs. Lynn to do with it?" Jackson sighed. "Now we have two circle-talkers, Sheriff."

"We're speaking plainly if you'd only listen, Mr. Gossling," Nin snapped.

"At Lady Augusta's tea, Mrs. Lynn told the story of two brothers who owned a circus," Adele explained. "One swindled the other and hid the money by sending it to a friend to put in a locker at the train station. This friend had the key." She leaned back, looking expectedly at the sheriff.

"So Mrs. Barry sent money to her sister to put in a locked box?" Hatfield slowly nodded. "I'm beginning to understand."

"Naturally, she told her nothing about what she planned on doing with it," Adele said.

"She thought it was because Estelle wanted to leave her husband," Nin added.

"Well, she did, didn't she?" Jackson inquired.

"But Mrs. Long had no idea she was leaving with another man," Adele insisted. "Nor did she know where the money was coming from. She thought it came from the household account."

"But you think it didn't?" Hatfield asked.

"I think Mrs. Long is right," Adele said. "I think Estelle took that money from the circus profits."

"You mean she stole it!" Jackson looked disapproving.

"It was partly hers," Nin insisted.

"I realize you don't think Mr. Barry killed Mr. Rowe, Adele," said the sheriff. "But I fail to see how all this relates to him."

"I think I can prove he didn't do it," Adele said.

"Here we go again, Sheriff." Jackson rolled his eyes.

The sheriff gave him a sharp look. "I'm willing to listen to any theory as long as it's backed up by evidence."

"Mrs. Long gave us a letter Estelle sent her asking her to take all the money out and give it to a friend in the city," Adele said.

"I still don't see —"

She looked squarely at him. "What if I told you I don't think Estelle wrote that letter?"

"Who did?" Jackson crossed his arms. "Her husband?"

"Exactly!" Adele leaned back with a smile.

"Talk about far-fetched ideas," he snorted.

"I think I can prove he wrote the letter in his wife's name,"

Adele insisted. "And why the letter would make it unnecessary for him to kill Julius."

"You're giving me a headache, Del." Her brother sighed.

"It wouldn't be the first time," she snapped. "Let us talk to Paul and you'll see what I mean."

"I don't think that's fair, sir," her brother said. "We're not even letting anyone from the circus speak with him."

"Correction, Deputy," said his superior officer, "Mr. Barry isn't letting anyone from the circus speak to him."

"He doesn't even want to see his wife and son?" Adele asked.

"I think the man is afraid of the publicity," said Hatfield. "He thinks the more he separates himself from them, the easier it will be on them."

"He's a sensible man," Jackson said with a nod.

"Hardly a man to kill out of passion," Nin pointed out.

The sheriff rubbed his chin, now speckled with the beginnings of an evening beard. "I have no objection to you talking to him, Adele. If he wants to talk."

"But in our presence," Jackson added.

She pinched his cheek playfully. "As long as you don't come at the poor man like a bulldog."

"He's not exactly strong enough to withstand that," the sheriff said. "He's taken all this very hard."

Adele saw what the sheriff meant when Edison brought Mr. Barry in. The man who had seemed robust and commanding on opening night was hardly more than a shadow now. He looked thinner, and his skin had the gray pallor of someone who had been inside a darkened room for more hours than he cared to count. His voice, too, was wary when he spoke.

"You look like a man who's already been convicted," she remarked.

"Well, haven't I?" He looked sharply at the sheriff. "According to you, I killed my wife's paramour because she was going to run away with him and leave me. I even threatened him in the presence of witnesses."

"Eavesdropping witnesses," Nin corrected.

He gave an ironic laugh. "They're willing to swear to what they heard, aren't they? I never denied I had an argument with Julius right before he was killed."

"But you didn't do it," Adele said quietly.

"Of course I didn't!"

Adele produced the letters from her bag and laid them on the table of the interview room. She remained silent as the man's guarded eyes looked them over. "I don't understand."

"I think you do, sir," she said. "You knew your wife wanted to run away with Julius all the time. You also knew how she was going to do it."

"I don't —"

"You knew she was stealing money and hiding it," Nin said.

"Miss Branch, please." Jackson flinched.

"It's the truth," she grumbled. "Why hide the truth anymore?"

"This is all absurd!" the man shouted.

"Is it, Mr. Barry?" She studied him. "Are you really willing to go to jail for a crime you didn't commit?"

Paul pulled at the edge of his jacket, which was less than immaculate after several nights in jail. "Perhaps Miss Branch is right. Why hide the truth anymore, since you've taken it upon yourself to go snooping around my sister-in-law's door?"

"Then it's the truth?" Sheriff Hatfield glanced at him.

"Estelle thinks she's very clever." His eyes looked like dark jewels. "But I've been too many years in the circus not to keep a close watch on who touches the cash box."

"Even your own wife?" Nin glared at him.

"Especially my own wife," he said evenly. "Wives sometimes think they're entitled to things they aren't."

"Like love and money?" Adele asked dryly.

"How did you know it was her who took the money from the cash box?" Jackson asked.

"I followed her to Cal's wagon one night and saw how she made adjustments to the ledger before she left it in the safe."

"Why didn't you stop her?" Hatfield asked.

The man flinched. "I didn't want to make a scene."

"How did you know she was sending the money to her sister?" Jackson asked.

"I found the box with the key," he said. "I knew she was sending letters to Charlotte from nearly every town we stopped. It didn't take much to put the pieces together."

"You don't miss a thing, do you, Mr. Barry?" Adele eyed him.

"No, I don't, Miss Gossling," he said.

"Including an opportunity to keep your wife from leaving you."

"What are you talking about, Del?" Her brother glanced at her.

Paul tapped the typewritten note with his finger. "I believe your sister is talking about this letter I wrote to Charlotte."

"Why did you write it, sir?"

"You don't know my wife," he murmured. "Estelle — well, she's been taken care of all her life. First by her father, who doted on her, then by me. She isn't like Miss Gossling or Miss Branch." He glanced at the two ladies. "She doesn't have the gumption to go it alone."

"She wants a man to do everything for her," Nin said.

"That's unkind, Miss Branch," Jackson snapped.

"But true," said Paul. "She saw herself as a damsel in distress looking for a knight in shining armor." He snickered.

"She thought that someone was Julius," Adele said.

Paul gave her a grisly smile. "Don't women always think they can reform a rogue?"

"But he had no intention of leaving your circus," Nin pointed out.

"I didn't know that at the time, did I?" Paul snapped. "I had no idea Cal signed the act on for another season. And neither did Estelle."

"You knew when she had enough money, she would try to get Julius to run away with her," Adele said.

"That's exactly it, Miss Gossling." A shadow of deviousness came to his face "All I had to do was make it impossible for her to do that."

"And money was the answer," the sheriff said. "I'm beginning to see."

"I wrote that letter to Charlotte in Estelle's name asking her to get the money out of the safe deposit box and send it to Al," he said. "I knew she wouldn't ask questions."

"She thought Estelle had plans to leave you," Nin said in her blunt way. "By herself."

"She should have known better, then!" the man growled.

"What were your plans for the money, sir?" Hatfield asked.

This seemed to confuse Paul again. "I really don't know, Sheriff. I only had an idea of keeping it from Estelle."

"You feel no remorse about that?" Hatfield was now studying the man.

"I was saving my wife from a scoundrel!"

"And keeping her chained to you at the same time," Adele said.

"And avoiding a scandal," Nin added.

"In spite of the Cinderella stories my wife may have told you, she has a good life with me," he said.

"Mr. Barry," Adele glared at him, "I find your type of man loathsome to the core."

"Del!" Jackson growled.

"But loathsome as you are, you didn't kill Julius," she said, "because you had no reason to. A man who thinks he can keep his wife from leaving him by taking her money —"

"It was my money!" the man shouted.

"— by taking *her* money has no need to kill," she finished with determination. "We know what you meant now too."

"What I meant?"

"'You'll never get past the circus gates,'" she echoed. "You didn't mean it as a violent threat. You meant it as a certainty."

"You knew Julius wouldn't venture past the gates without money," Nin agreed. "He'd received handouts from women for so long, he wasn't likely to run away with a woman who had nothing."

Paul wiped his face with his handkerchief. "That was my thinking, yes." He gave Adele a menacing look. "I'm sorry if you think that makes me loathsome, Miss Gossling, but even you admit it doesn't make me a killer."

Adele turned to Hatfield. "You see he's right, don't you, Sheriff?"

"Perhaps," the lawman said with caution.

"Why would he kill Julius if he knew he wasn't going to lose his wife to him?" Nin pointed out.

"We don't know any of this is true," Jackson insisted.

"The typewriter used for this letter was Calvin's," Adele said. "I remember the smudging on the left side on the contract he showed us. There's smudging here too."

"And Dr. Blessings says it isn't Estelle's signature," Nin chimed in.

"So that's why you went to see him," the sheriff said.

"That's why I took the other letters," Adele explained. "I wanted him to compare the signatures. He says they don't look the same."

"Not that he would commit himself, as usual," Nin said.

"But it isn't Estelle's," Paul insisted. He suddenly grabbed a pencil protruding from Jackson's coat pocket and, turning over the typed letter, scribbled his wife's name. "There. That's what I did!"

Adele took out her magnifying glass and examined both signatures. "He's right, Sheriff. It's almost an exact duplicate."

Hatfield took the magnifying glass from her. "I'll admit they look the same."

"I'm sure Dr. Blessings will confirm this."

"And my friend Al will confirm he has the money," Paul said.

Hatfield nodded. "I'll call the San Francisco police department and have them check on it."

"I told him all about the scheme," Paul said. "I also told him about my argument with Julius, so he can confirm what I meant when I told him he would never get past the circus gates."

"He had no motive," Nin concluded. "Can't you see that, Sheriff?"

Hatfield tapped the edge of Jackson's pencil against his chin. Then, as if remembering what it was, he slid it back into his deputy's pocket. "I'll have a word with the district attorney. I can't make promises, though."

"I don't need promises, Sheriff." The man's face relaxed. "I have confidence you'll find I'm innocent. You're a sensible man. And not the loathsome type either." He gave Adele a meaningful look.

"Edison!" The young man appeared at the door. "Take Mr. Barry back to his cell."

"Yes, sir."

"And see that his handkerchief and anything else he'd like be sent to Porter's Laundry," he ordered. "Can't have it be said the sheriff of Arrojo doesn't keep a clean jail."

Paul smiled for the first time as Edison led him away.

Hatfield turned to Adele, leaning against the table. "What suddenly gave you the idea to see Charlotte Long?"

"Calvin told us he thought the key might belong to a box her sister owns," Adele said.

"I don't recall Mr. Barry mentioning anything about his aunt," Sheriff Hatfield said.

"Not to you," Adele said. "He did when we spoke to him."

"When you spoke to him?" Jackson asked.

"Nin and I went to speak to him alone," Adele said.

"Well, if that —" Her brother bit his lip. "Just because the sheriff lets you interview suspects —"

"When I feel she can be of great service, Deputy," the sheriff interrupted.

"I'm not questioning your decisions, sir," he said quickly. "But I feel it my duty to warn my sister not to go too far."

"Maybe it was wrong of us not to tell you beforehand," Adele admitted.

"We only went to see how he was doing after his father's arrest," Nin said.

"And you thought you'd ask him some leading questions in the bargain." Jackson put his hands on his hips. "You realize, Del, if you got him to say anything as a result of your leading questions, that evidence would be disregarded and you and Miss Branch might get yourselves into trouble?"

"We weren't asking leading questions," Adele snapped. "We were there to help prove his father was innocent."

"Both he and his mother believe that," Nin chimed in. "They told us."

"You spoke to Mrs. Barry as well?" Hatfield asked.

"She came into Calvin's wagon while we were there." She sat on the edge of the table, her eyes far away for a moment. "She certainly knows where everything is."

"Eh?" The sheriff glanced at her.

"She knew her way around Calvin's office," Adele said.

"If that's true, sir, she may have been lying to us about not knowing Mr. Rowe signed a new contract." Jackson eyed his superior.

"I see your point, Deputy," said Hatfield. "If she saw it, she could have acted by slipping backstage and cutting the net."

"And you thought my theory of Paul typing that letter was far-fetched," Adele snorted.

"But you may be right," Jackson challenged. "We might be right in this. She may have had motive and opportunity."

Adele strolled around the small office. "A paramour who had betrayed her — provided she knew he betrayed her — her motive. But opportunity?"

"As the owner's wife, she could have easily gotten to the net during the clown act," her brother pointed out.

Hatfield grabbed his hat. "I think it would be worth our while to pay Mrs. Barry another visit and tell her about her husband."

"I agree, sir," said Jackson.

"You'll allow us to come, Sheriff?" Adele asked.

"Yes, I think it might be best," he said. "It's your theory, after all."

CHAPTER 26

When they arrived at Estelle's wagon, they found bureau drawers wide open and clothes thrown all over the narrow bed. The contents of the chest in the corner were scattered between several suitcases on the floor.

"Taking a trip, I see," the sheriff said dryly.

Estelle, whose face was pinched with anxiety, glared at him. "Don't condescend to me, Sheriff."

"We understood your son is still uncertain of your final plans," Jackson said.

"He's unsure about the circus' final plans," she said in a rough tone. "I'm not continuing with the circus."

"Abandoning ship?" Hatfield's tone was even drier than before.

"Your sailing metaphors won't work on me," she insisted. "Not you or anybody else is ever going to make me feel guilty again."

"That's the spirit," Nin said.

"I've felt nothing but guilt and shame since all this happened." The woman began folding linens with heavy hands and throwing them in the suitcase. "Guilty of my feelings for Julius, and for attempting to plan a life without my husband. Guilty for Julius's death and my husband's arrest."

"But Calvin said you didn't believe he was guilty," Adele said in a quiet voice.

"Of course he's not guilty!" The woman took a deep breath. "He's far too careful about his reputation to risk murder."

"He's out now, you know," Nin said.

Estelle collapsed on the bed, her eyes filling with tears. "Everything has fallen apart."

Adele sat next to the woman and put her arm around her shoulders. Hatfield signaled Jackson, and they both exited the wagon.

"I've met women in the settlement houses who were like you," she said. "They thought everything had fallen apart. Their husbands turned on them, their families betrayed them, and their children died of fever. They wanted to run away too." She gave a small sigh. "Some even asked me to stake them a ticket to China."

Estelle's face softened. "Why China?"

"Because it's the other side of the world," Adele said with a small smile.

"Running away to the other side of the world isn't the answer," Nin said. "The two ends eventually meet."

Estelle looked far away. "I suppose there's something to that." She looked at Adele. "What did you advise them to do?"

"Wait," Adele said. "It's the most difficult thing in the world when one feels trapped, but one needs time to think. And seeking help from other women." This last she emphasized. "One can't get anywhere, whether it's China or the next street, without kindness and help."

"Are you proposing to help me?" Estelle eyed her.

"I will if you ask me to." Adele squeezed her shoulders.

The woman peered at her. "Is Paul really free now?"

"He will be," Adele said. "In the meantime, I'm afraid the police have to ask you some questions."

The woman stared at her. "I thought they asked all their questions."

"New evidence has come up," Nin said.

She sighed. "All right. Ask them to come back inside."

The two men stepped cautiously into the wagon but once settled, Hatfield was direct. "Mrs. Barry, up until now, you've been evading our questions about what your argument with Mr. Rowe the night of the murder was about. I'm afraid we must insist you tell us."

She blinked from the bright sunlight coming through the open doorway and Jackson, with his usual discretion, closed it. "I suppose you could call it a quarrel, Sheriff, though it was nothing serious."

"Let us be the judge of that, ma'am," Jackson said.

"Julius — well, he was stalling, I suppose you'd call it. I didn't see it then but I see it now."

"You mean about your plans to run away?" asked the sheriff.

She nodded, reaching for a handkerchief.

"So you did know he didn't want to go with you." Jackson eyed her.

"It was nothing like that," she insisted. "He said we needed money, and he insisted he hadn't saved nearly enough yet."

"Perhaps you should have told him about the money you saved," Jackson said.

She stared at him, then let out a sob. "Oh, God, you know!"

Hatfield slipped his large handkerchief from his pocket and handed it to Adele who gave to Estelle. "Frankly, Mrs. Barry, I'm impressed by your foresight."

The woman burst into hysterical laughter. "Paul always accuses me of being careless about the future. I'm not as flighty as he thinks."

"Where did you get the money, ma'am?" the sheriff asked.

"Does it matter?"

"It does if you stole it from the circus profits," Jackson said. Adele gave him a warning look.

She glared at him. "I've worked eighteen years alongside my husband, helping him to build this circus, Deputy. Paul never gave me so much as a few pennies for a new bonnet!"

"It was yours just as much as his," Nin said with a satisfied nod.

"But you took it without permission," he insisted. "According to the law, that's theft, Mrs. Barry."

"You don't understand, Deputy," she said. "Paul didn't marry me. He acquired me for his circus, like a wagon or a clown."

"That doesn't make it right —"

"I suggest you keep quiet, Mr. Gossling." Nin's voice was almost threatening. "You've already put both feet and an elbow in your mouth."

Jackson retreated to the corner, his lips a thin line.

"Do you know what he said the day we were married?" she continued. "'Now I have a partner who understands the circus.'"

"If you're his partner, you should be paid like one," Adele agreed.

"Your purpose for taking the money and putting it in a safe deposit box was to allow you and Mr. Rowe to leave," Hatfield concluded.

"One needs money to start a new life, Sheriff," she said. "I won't give it back!"

Jackson cleared his throat. "That depends on your husband, Mrs. Barry."

"The hell it does!" Nin burst out.

For the first time, Mrs. Barry smiled. It was a confident smile, one that relaxed her face. "When we got married, Deputy, Paul had me sign papers giving half the circus to me. It was more an insurance, really, in case he was injured and there was no one else to run it."

"He trusted you," Adele said softly. "Like a major trusts his sergeant."

Hatfield crossed one ankle over the other. "I'm afraid we have some unpleasant news for you, Mrs. Barry. You're not going to find the money in the safe deposit box."

"Not going to find it?" She blinked.

"Your husband knew what you were doing," Jackson said.

Her face turned pale. "He never said a word!"

"It wasn't his intention to say anything," said the sheriff. "It was his intention to do something about it."

"I don't understand." She dabbed her face with the handkerchief.

"He wrote a letter to your sister on your son's typewriter and signed your name," Adele said.

"What letter?"

"A letter telling her to take the money out of the safe deposit box and send it to a Mr. Alfred Carroll," said Hatfield. "You know him, don't you?"

She nodded. "He's a friend of Paul's from childhood. He's runs errands for Paul when we're not in San Francisco."

"He was your friend too?" Jackson asked.

Estelle gave him a rueful smile. "Hardly, Deputy. He tried to convince Paul not to marry me."

"That's probably why he sent him the money," Jackson remarked.

She looked out the window with heavy eyes. "So Paul got the best of me again."

"Not necessarily," Hatfield said. "If you can get hold of a copy of those papers you signed, you can prove you are part owner of the circus and have a right to the earnings. I would advise you to get a lawyer."

Adele could see from the expression on her brother's face he hardly approved of this advice.

Estelle gave him a wan smile. "You're very kind, Sheriff."

"Mrs. Barry," the sheriff propped his foot up on a stool, leaning against his knee, "you realize your actions put you in an awkward position regarding Mr. Rowe's death?"

Adele expected the woman to protest her innocence, but she now seemed to acquire a new resolve. Her face dry of tears, she crossed her arms. "You mean if I am capable of theft, as your deputy seems to think, I'm also capable of murder?"

"Were you being truthful when you said you had no idea Mr. Rowe renewed his contract?"

She glared. "What makes you think I wasn't?"

Adele intervened, "When my friend and I were in Calvin's wagon the other day, you knew exactly where everything was."

"What of it?"

"I noticed your son has a habit of leaving paperwork scattered all over his desk." Adele eyed her. "Including contracts."

The woman turned pale again. "All right. Perhaps I didn't tell you the whole story."

"You'd better tell us the whole story now," Jackson said.

"I did go into Calvin's wagon one day to get a stamp, and I saw some contracts on his desk," she admitted. "And, yes, one was for the trapeze act and it piqued my curiosity so I glanced at it. But I didn't get further than the first few pages before Cal came in."

"But it worried you all the same."

"Well, yes, frankly, it did," she said in a meek tone.

"You cornered Julius that night to ask him about it," Nin concluded.

"I wouldn't say 'cornered.'" She flinched. "We met between the concession stands all the time."

Hatfield's face was grim. "What did he say when you confronted him about the contract?"

"I told you, he put me off," she insisted. "He said it was just Calvin doing his job and it didn't mean anything."

"You wanted to believe Mr. Rowe was going to refuse to renew," Jackson said.

"I wanted to believe what Julius told me." Her face crumbled. "I must be the greatest fool living!"

The sheriff rose. "I'd like you to come down to the station with us and sign some statements."

"Am I under arrest?" She glanced at him.

"The district attorney will have to decide based on your statements."

She buried her face in her hands. "How could I have allowed myself to be so taken?"

"You're not even angry at him, are you?" Adele asked quietly.

She removed her hands. Her face was clear. "I feel too defeated to be angry."

"You're not defeated, Estelle," Adele said kindly. "This is only a setback."

The woman nodded, slipping on her coat, her eyes glossy for a moment. "I read in the papers the net was cut by a serrated knife. Is that right?"

"That's right, ma'am," said Hatfield.

"Did you know Dan owns several serrated knives?"

"He showed us one of them," said Jackson.

"No one else here likes them," she mused. "We had a performer once who cut off two of his fingers with such a knife. Paul ordered all of them to be thrown out, but Dan insisted on keeping his."

"What are you implying, Mrs. Barry?" The sheriff leaned against the door.

She glared at him. "If you think I'm trying to save my own skin by accusing Dan, you're mistaken."

"There's no skin to save, ma'am," Hatfield insisted. "You're not under arrest unless the district attorney orders it."

"If you have something you think is important to this investigation, you're obliged to tell us," Jackson said in a firm tone.

"A week or so ago, not long after Julius —" she swallowed, "I saw Dan bury one of his knives."

"Perhaps it had lost its usefulness, and he didn't want one of the Tar children getting it," Adele suggested.

"He was very proud of that particular knife," she said. "It had a handle made out of redwood, and he told me his father had made it himself."

"A man would hardly be likely to give up an object of sentimental value, sir." Jackson glanced at the sheriff.

"I'm not saying he killed Julius," she insisted. "But perhaps he knows who did and he was — well, trying to shield that person by burying the knife."

"Do you remember where he buried it?" asked Hatfield.

She shook her head. "I only got a glimpse as I was hurrying away. It was somewhere on the other side of the park."

"Thank you, Mrs. Barry." Hatfield opened the wagon door. "Naturally, we'll follow it up."

Estelle looked down at the half-packed suitcase.

Adele followed her gaze. "You're staying?"

"If I'm to be arrested, I'll have to, won't I?" She shrugged. "May I ask a favor, Sheriff?"

"Certainly." Hatfield tipped his hat.

"Paul's still there and I don't want to see him." Her face was stiff. "Is there anywhere you can put me where I won't have to see him?"

"It's a most unusual request, ma'am," Jackson mumbled.

"Even you must have compassion for a troubled lady, Mr. Gossling," Nin snapped.

"I didn't say I didn't, Miss Branch," he retorted. He turned to his superior. "Sir, if I may make a suggestion."

"I'm listening, Deputy," said the sheriff.

"The station in Blue Springs might be a good place," he said. "I know they keep an assistant deputy there all night and he's very accommodating."

"I don't think Sheriff Summers would object to that," Hatfield agreed.

"It's only five miles away besides," Adele added.

"Oh, thank you, Sheriff." Mrs. Barry's face melted with gratitude. "You're a good man."

"Always happy to help a damsel in distress," he mumbled. "I trust you'll stay here while the deputy sheriff and I make the arrangements. Then we can drive you to the Blue Springs station."

"I won't run away," she said in a firm tone. "Adele was right. That was a mistake."

After the men had left, Adele took out of her reticule Vanya's card and handed it to Estelle. "When this is all over, if you decide to leave the circus after all, you can contact my friend. She's helped many women and she'll help you."

"I haven't asked for help, remember," Estelle murmured but she fingered the card.

Adele looked at the woman one more time before she closed the door. She was relieved to see she looked less defeated.

~

"*W*ell, sir," Jackson said, shaking out the dust that had collected on his vest from the bumpy ride to Blue Springs. "Are we going to follow up on what Mrs. Barry told us or do you think it's a blind?"

"I doubt it, Deputy," said his superior in a severe tone. "The lady was clearly much affected."

"Poor woman," Adele sighed.

"A defeated woman doesn't kill," Nin declared.

"She's defeated now, Miss Branch," Jackson said. "But she wasn't that night."

"If we find the knife, that might tell us something," Hatfield said.

"All you have to do is turn up every stone and tree in the park," Adele said dryly.

"Why not?" her brother countered. "It's city property and we don't need a warrant for that."

"Shall we go and get our shovels then?" his sister asked cheerfully.

The sheriff glanced out the car window. "I think it can wait until tomorrow."

"And you're not getting any shovel, Del," her brother said firmly. "This is a man's job."

"We can get Edison and the lads to help us," the sheriff agreed.

"I thought you said it was a man's job," Nin said dryly. Adele laughed.

CHAPTER 27

*I*n the morning, the heat pressed against the windows, and Adele was thankful for the cool breeze on the porch in back of the house. She and Jackson sat at breakfast, Adele lost in thought over eggs, bacon, and toast, Jackson with his nose buried in the *Arrojo Courier*, the bowl of noxious oatmeal cooling in front of him.

Adele's thoughts had been entirely on Estelle and the woman's defeated look the day before. She had been sitting with her chin in her hand for some time. The paper across from her, blocking her brother's face, blurred. She blinked away a few specks of dust brought on by the wind, and her vision cleared. Jackson held the paper like a book so she could read the print clearly: PAUL BARRY LET GO FOR MURDER OF WIFE'S PARAMOUR!

"Jack!" She grabbed it from him. "You didn't tell me!"

"I would appreciate it if you would give me back my paper," he grumbled.

She tapped the headline. "So that's why you and Hatfield went back to the station after we took Estelle to Blue Springs."

"Hatfield contacted Marland when we got back," said her

brother. "Interrupted his dinner, but Marland isn't like Dr. Rhodes." He gave her a meaningful look.

"He doesn't grouse about a spoiled meal when the interest of justice is at stake," Adele agreed. "Good man."

Her brother nodded. "As it happens, Mr. Marland's ambitions worked to our advantage."

"You mean with Paul?"

"With Mr. Barry and our digging expedition in the park this morning."

"You said you don't need a warrant to search the park," she said. "Public property and all that."

"City property," he corrected. "We don't need permission, but Hatfield is thinking we might need to search the wagons, and he doubts Mr. Barry or any of his people will be very hospitable about that."

"I shouldn't imagine Paul would be very happy about his wife being held for questioning," Adele remarked. "I hope Hatfield didn't tell him where she was."

Jackson shook his head. "I'm certain Paul's seen the morning paper by now."

She walked with him to the police station. Adele was astonished by what she saw. It seemed as if Hatfield had summoned every assistant deputy working for him, plus several young men who had been recruited to do search work on past cases. Each was dressed in work clothes and held a shovel in his hand.

"Didn't think there was any sense in spoiling their uniforms," Hatfield remarked. "Edison!" The young man saluted. "The lads all here?"

"All except Assistant Deputy Curd, sir." The young man grimaced.

"Late as always." The sheriff sighed.

"The second time this week," Jackson remarked as he picked up the shovel lying on his desk. "You ought to leave him here, Sheriff."

"We need all the men we can get," Hatfield said. "I'm sure I'll find an appropriate punishment — ah, Curd! We were just talking about you." The young man in question scurried in, his nearly white-blond hair ruffled from the wind and his clothes looking just as wrinkled. "I said working clothes, Curd, not hobo clothes."

The young man blushed. "These were the only clothes I could find at the last minute, Sheriff."

"Well, we'll let it go for now." Hatfield waved him away.

Adele's heart softened at the eyes still bulging with fear. "Don't worry, Assistant Deputy," she whispered. "He really has quite an affection for the men working under him."

"Yes, miss," mumbled Curd, though he sounded far from convinced.

"Sheriff, may I tag along?" She turned to Hatfield.

"Gee willikers, a woman digging for clues!" said one of the extra men under his breath, causing a sniggering among his colleagues.

"Quiet!" Hatfield's tone was more arduous than Adele thought necessary. "You will all treat Miss Gossling with respect. Remember, she's the deputy's sister."

"Not to mention she'll make sure you regret it if you don't," Jackson added. "And if she doesn't, I will." His face turned granite.

"I'm capable of kicking any young man too bold for my taste in the shins better than you are, Jack," she said in such a good-natured tone that it made the assistant deputies laugh and blush at the same time. More seriously, she added, "I'll leave the digging in your capable hands, Sheriff. I was thinking of looking in on Abby. She and her sister have had quite an ordeal. After all, it was their partner who was killed."

"You're welcome to come if you like," Hatfield said. "Who knows, we might ask you to work your wiles on Mr. Patton. If he isn't forthcoming with his information, that is."

It was Paul who was waiting for them at the front gates, his face ready for battle. "Where is my wife, Sheriff?"

"In a very safe place, sir," said Hatfield, his face equally ready for battle.

"The newspaper said you're holding her for questioning," the man continued.

"Your wife told us about some important evidence buried in the park," he said.

"And what would she know about it?" the man sneered.

"She knows more than you think, Paul," Adele said.

He glared at her. "May I ask what you're looking for or is it as much a secret as my wife's whereabouts?"

Dan Patton came from behind the tent with Cora. "It's all right, Paul. I know what they're looking for." He looked at Hatfield. "I told you before that I have nothing to hide, and I meant it."

"It was a mistake," Cora added.

"Let them in, Paul."

But the manager refused to unlock the gate. "I suppose I have a right to demand a warrant?"

"We're searching the park, Mr. Barry, not your circus," Sheriff Hatfield said. Adele admired how firm and unflappable he stood.

"You mean turn this place into a swamp!" Paul glared at the assistant deputies with their shovels.

"They won't have to dig up the entire park, Paul," Dan said. "I'll tell them where to find what they're looking for."

"And what are they looking for?" Paul demanded. "I hope I have a right to know since this involves my circus."

"One of my serrated knives," Dan said. "Probably the one that was used to cut the net."

"My God!" The manager stared at him.

"I suppose it's a waste of time to say I'm not the one who used it?" Dan eyed the sheriff.

"You'll have ample opportunity to tell your story when we find it, sir," Jackson said.

"And if I made a phone call to the mayor's office?" Paul eyed the sheriff.

Hatfield took out a piece of paper of his pocket and handed it to him. "That won't be necessary. Mayor Willett was kind enough to sign a letter."

As Paul read the letter, Adele glanced around. She noted several circus people gathered near the gate, some in costume and some in street clothes. None looked very kindly upon the sheriff or his assistant deputies. Near the platform Abby and Helen stood huddled together, still in their dressing gowns.

Paul folded the paper and handed it back to the sheriff. "We've no choice — again."

"Open the gate then, Paul," said Dan.

This seemed to put things back into perspective, and the hostile looks ceased. Many of the performers went back to their wagons or the practice tents.

Adele joined Abby and her sister as the police followed Dan. "I'm sure you're glad to see Paul back," she said, trying to smile.

"I knew he would be," said Abby. "He couldn't have killed anybody."

"He's strict but a good person," Helen ventured. She looked the same shaken bird as the last time Adele had seen her.

"I'm glad he's being more cooperative," Adele remarked.

"He knows Dan didn't do anything," said Abby. "He's loyal to his people." There was a sharp edge to her voice. Her sister flinched.

"You sound like you mean something by that." She eyed Abby.

The woman shielded her eyes from the sun. "We all know the police now think Estelle killed Julius."

"Isn't that what you've been saying all along?" Adele asked.

"Abby, how could you?" Helen stared at her.

"You're mistaken, Adele," said the woman in a firm voice. "I was only trying to answer the police's questions."

Adele cleared her throat. "Where's Mr. Spears?"

"The attentive Mr. Spears," Abby answered in a dry tone, "has gone back to his people."

"Temporarily," Helen added.

"Permanently, if I have anything to say about it," her sister snapped. Then, in a more cheerful tone, she said, "You ought to see Helen fly now. She almost has the somersault down pat."

Again, the young woman flinched. Her sister put her arm around her shoulders. "One has to fall many times before one can fly, dearest."

"Yes," the girl whispered.

"I admire you for what you're doing." Adele felt this sincerely. "I can only imagine how many daredevils would shrink from the idea after one of their performers — well, died like that."

"I've told you, Adele, it's the nature of the business," said Abby in a firm tone. "Some fall and some soar."

"I won't fall," Helen said in a throaty voice.

"Of course you won't, darling," said her sister in a soothing tone. "You're taking your chance now."

Something about the way the woman said this made Adele feel uncomfortable. She played with the magnifying glass hung around her neck. "Do you still intend to make it an all-woman act?"

"It already is," Abby said.

"But will it be when you find a new catcher?" Adele asked.

Abby smiled. "I've a few things up my sleeve, if that's what you mean. I'm not prepared to reveal them yet."

"Calvin said that too," Adele murmured. "Something up your sleeve."

"You must come one night to see us when we perform," Abby said kindly. "I feel we owe it to you."

"More like I owe you," Adele said. "I sometimes feel guilty having a brother with a badge."

"Is it true they're looking for the murder weapon?" Helen peered at her with large eyes.

"What a thing to say, dearest." Abby laughed.

"Well, isn't that what you would call it?" the young woman demanded.

"If it's the knife that cut the net, it is," Adele said.

"They really think Dan buried it?" Abby asked.

"That's what Estelle told us."

"Oh, Estelle!" The woman scoffed. "How would she know where someone might hide a knife?"

"She was very clear about it," Adele insisted.

"Circus people are good at hiding things," Abby said. "It could be anywhere. We leave our wagons unlocked, and we're coming and going all the time."

"But we respect one another's privacy," Helen chimed in. "We don't go barging in anytime we please."

"Hatfield has already thought of the wagons," Adele admitted.

"You mean he brought a warrant with him, didn't he?" Abby looked at her.

"It's as if we're all criminals now!" Helen shrieked.

Abby took her sister's hand. "I must get her back to the tent. We'll be leaving soon, you know?"

"Oh?"

"Cal is in San Francisco right now inspecting the amphitheater. He always does that before we move on."

"Will you and Helen be performing your new act there?" Adele asked.

Abby gave a small laugh. "Hardly. I think we'll have to wait until we get to the Middle West for that. Paul says it's time for us to get out of this territory."

"I can't blame him," Adele said. "It hasn't been very pleasant for any of you."

Abby pressed her shoulder. "You've been kind to us, Adele. So has Miss Branch. Will you join Helen and me for lunch this afternoon?"

"I'd be delighted." Adele smiled. "I'm sure Nin will like it too."

Just then, the sheriff and her brother appeared.

"You look disappointed, Sheriff," she observed.

"You would be too if you found nothing but an empty hole," he said.

"You didn't find the knife?"

Jackson shook his head. "Mr. Patton is as flabbergasted as we are."

"He swears he hid it there," Hatfield said.

"Do you think he's lying, Sheriff?" Adele asked.

"We saw groves in the dirt," Jackson said. "It's clear *something* was there and from the imprint, it looks like some kind of a knife."

"Why would someone dig up a knife?" Adele murmured.

"Isn't it obvious, Del?" Jackson asked. "We found some evidence of fibers in the hole. They could have come from the net."

"Someone wanted to remove it to keep Mr. Patton from being incriminated," Hatfield surmised.

"Cora?" Adele suggested.

"She would never do that!" Helen shrieked. "Cora's as gentle as a lamb."

"She doesn't have that kind of gumption," Abby agreed.

"It's clear someone removed it," Hatfield said. "It could be at the bottom of Tanner's Swamp by now."

"It looks like you'll need to use your warrant, Sheriff," Abby said.

"Eh?" He glanced at her.

"Adele told us you brought it to search circus property," the woman continued.

"If the knife is gone, sir, I'm not so sure it would still be on the premises," Jackson pointed out.

"We've no alternative, Deputy," said the sheriff, motioning to his assistant deputies lingering close by. "All right, lads. Put down those shovels. We're going to search every inch of this circus. Tents, wagons, and concession stands. You all know what we're looking for."

It took a full hour, with Paul storming about, threatening to call the governor, before Assistant Deputy Dooland fell against a chair propped in the corner of Estelle's wagon and a loose board in the wall slid back. A knife fell to the floor.

Hatfield was more ecstatic than Adele had ever seen him. "Good work, Dooland!" He gave the young man a hard pat on the back. "I'll see you get your reward." Assistant Deputy Dooland beamed and, Adele noticed, cast a self-righteous look toward Edison, who seethed.

"A hidden panel?" Adele asked.

Her brother inspected it. "More like a double wall."

"How odd!" she lamented.

"Not so odd," Jackson said. "Circus wagons need to be well protected to survive all kinds of weather."

"Someone was very clever." The sheriff nodded.

"But you don't think that someone was Estelle?" Adele asked.

"It's a little too obvious, sir," Jackson pointed out.

"A foolish misdirection," Hatfield agreed.

"And yet, if we're dealing with a clever killer, why hide it within the confines of the circus at all?" Jackson asked. "She, or whoever used it, could have easily thrown it in Tanner Swamp or even the brush near the old Blackstone house. It would have been found days, perhaps even weeks, after the circus had gone."

"Question marks," Hatfield lamented.

Adele stared at the knife. "It was just where she said it would be." The sunlight from the window cast a beam on the silver blade. Although part of it was brushed with dirt, the tip was clean enough for the light to shine back on her like a winking eye.

"May I see it?" she asked. "I'm rather curious about it."

Jackson growled as Hatfield willingly handed it to her, draped in a handkerchief. "We still need Dr. Rhodes to check for fingerprints, of course, now that we have the lab equipment for it." His puffed chest showed how proud he was of having convinced the mayor to allow the funds for the new lab.

"Fingerprints are still regarded as unreliable evidence, Sheriff," Jackson reminded him.

"One day they won't be, Deputy," his superior assured him.

Adele carefully took the knife in both hands. It was nine or ten inches and had, in spite of its homemade appearance, a smooth handle that showed off the warm red shade and wide grooves of the tree from which it had been carved. The blade itself had small, precise teeth.

"Someone made this with care," she remarked.

"It's very sharp," Jackson said. "Be careful of it, Del."

She glared at him. "I think I'm capable of handling a knife, Jack." The sheriff laughed.

She turned it over to the other side. Sand-colored strings bled from some of the teeth. She took out her magnifying glass and held the blade close to her eye. The strings were ragged little fibers going every which way like the beard of a woodsman who hadn't shaved for years.

Without thinking, she reached out to the edge, but miscalculated and felt the sharp sting of the blade on her palm.

Jackson grabbed the knife with one hand, while clasping his handkerchief on her palm with the other.

"It's only a small cut, Jack," she insisted. And, indeed, there was hardly any blood.

"Edison!" Hatfield shouted. "Run and get Dr. Rhodes and hurry!"

"No, no, Sheriff." Mrs. Tar appeared with a basket. "I heal."

The woman dressed the wound with sage and wrapped it with cloth. Within a few minutes, Adele felt the sting ease and the throbbing of her hand cease.

"Thank you." she murmured. The woman bowed and left.

Hatfield inspected the strings. "They match those we found in the hiding place."

"What do you think they are, sir?" Jackson asked.

Adele saw the sheriff squinting. "Take my magnifying glass, Sheriff," she insisted.

He obliged. "Hemp, I think."

"If we can match those fibers with the ones in the torn net, that would prove for certain this is the murder weapon," Jackson said.

Hatfield nodded. "I think our Mr. Lom Brethren is the man to do it."

"Won't Dr. Rhodes have a fit?" Adele inquired.

"I imagine he'll be only too glad to hand the dirty work over to someone else," the sheriff remarked, earning a guffaw from his assistant deputies. "All right, lads! Go home and clean up and then back to the station with you." As they dispersed, Hatfield took Edison by the scruff of his neck. "Not you, Edison. We might need you."

The young man grinned and shot the same self-righteous look at Dooland he had received earlier. The young man went away sulking.

"It still won't tell us who cut the net," Adele said.

"We should question Mr. Patton again, sir," Jackson suggested.

Hatfield brushed mud off his sleeves. "Edison! Go and get Mr. Patton."

"Who, sir?"

"Mr. Patton." His superior sighed. "The Wild West man. He's probably rehearsing somewhere."

The young man scurried away.

"Sheriff, he told us he made amends with Julius before opening night," Adele reminded him. "Cora was a witness."

"I realize that," he said. "Nevertheless, we need him to verify this is his knife."

Edison returned with Mr. Patton carrying a whip in his gloved hands.

"I believe you recognize this, sir?" Hatfield held up the knife.

Dan swung the whip a few times in the air. Edison, who was still standing behind him, backed away. "I didn't use it to cut the net that killed Julius, if that's what you're thinking."

"I didn't say I was thinking anything, sir," the sheriff said. "But we would like to know why you hid this knife."

"I'll tell you the truth, bizarre as it is."

"Much obliged," the sheriff mumbled.

"The knife is one of mine," he confirmed. "For what it's worth, I don't use it for performances. I keep it as a good luck charm." Here, his tone softened. "My father made it and gave it to me on our first hunting trip."

"An heirloom." Adele fingered the magnifying glass around her neck.

"If you could call it that," said the man. "Of course, it's worth very little to anyone but me."

"Go on," said Hatfield.

"I kept it stashed away in my wagon," he said. "But everyone here knows about it. I confess I take it out now and then and boast about it." He gave a small smile. "I'm quite proud of it."

"As you should be, sir," said Jackson. "It's a fine piece of work."

"Thank you, Deputy," he said. "I would expect a man of your reputation to recognize good craftsmanship when you see it." Hatfield sniffed at this. "The day after Julius's death, I went into Cora's wagon to fetch her a shawl. I came upon the knife hidden underneath a pile of linens. I noticed the fibers in the blade right away."

"So you knew what they were." The sheriff eyed him.

"It was right after you asked me to look at the net," he said. "I had it on my mind."

"And you realized that knife might have been used to cut the net." Hatfield crossed his arms. "You also realized we might suspect your fiancée if we knew it was in her wagon."

The man nodded slowly. "I know it was a foolish thing to do."

"Very foolish, sir." Jackson's stoic face hardly looked kind.

"He did it to protect Cora, Jack," Adele protested. "I think it was very gallant, Dan."

"Thank you, Miss Gossling." He bowed his head.

"But what reason did you think she might have to kill Julius?" Jackson questioned.

The man glared at him. "I didn't say I thought she had any reason."

"But you must have to go to all this trouble, sir," Hatfield pointed out.

Dan grasped the whip with both hands. "I thought maybe Julius had broken his promise to remain only friends and — well, one never knows about a man."

"So you thought she might have committed the crime?" Jackson asked.

"Of course not!" The man looked horrified. "But I knew *you* would think she did."

"And have you any explanation as to why it was in her wagon?"

"All I can say is what I've said before. Everyone knew I had it."

"But they didn't know where," Jackson pointed out.

The man looked almost amused. "There aren't many hiding places in these wagons, Deputy."

"Do all the wagons have this double wall?" Adele asked.

"I believe so," he said. "Paul would know more about that than I do."

"Someone could have easily slipped in and taken the knife,"

Adele agreed. "And then put it in Cora's wagon because it was well hidden from the crowds. It's a possibility, Jack."

"I didn't say it wasn't," Jackson mumbled.

"I think the real question here is how did it end up in Estelle's wagon?" Hatfield asked as he wrapped the knife in a cloth lying on the dresser.

"If you don't mind, Sheriff, I'd like to get back to rehearsing our show," Dan said. "We need it."

"I'm sure you do, since you'll be leaving soon," he said.

"Thank God for that!" The man strolled out of the wagon.

All the way back to town, Adele couldn't get the winking eye from the knife out of her mind. She felt as if it were trying to tell her something.

CHAPTER 28

*A*dele had a time convincing her friend to accept Abby's invitation to lunch the next day.

"I don't like those people," Nin said as she propped a rickety ladder against another shelf. For once, Adele had closed her shop and was helping her with inventory instead of the other way around. Adele had been working on Nin to treat her strange little shop of curios and herbs more as a business, including knowing what she was selling and how much of it.

"It's not a question of like," Adele argued. "They're involved in a case. If we want to catch the person who killed Julius, we have to see them."

"Ever since that night," Nin held on to the sides of the ladder, "the auras come to me like little tornadoes. It's all I can do to keep from leaping up in the air."

"But they tell you nothing?" Adele asked.

"Only that all is not as it appears," said Nin.

Adele marked the page in front of her with her pencil. "That's exactly why we have to go to this lunch, dear."

"You think Abby has the answer?" Nin asked, fingering the bottles of rhubarb on the shelf.

"She might," Adele murmured.

"Why do you say that?" Nin asked. "Twelve ounces of rhubarb powder."

Adele wrote it down. "She knew about the scarf and the knife."

"She doesn't like Estelle, you know." Nin climbed down the ladder.

"But is that enough of a reason for her to incriminate Estelle or are there other reasons?" Adele asked. "That's what we want to find out."

Nin rubbed the harsh wooden shelf for a moment. "I'll come with you. If only to keep you out of trouble."

Adele laughed. "You sound like Jack."

"Heaven forbid!" Her friend rolled her eyes.

"We'll drive into Blue Springs first and see Estelle," Adele said. "I want to talk to her again."

She tended Nin's shop while her friend went up to dress for lunch, though no one came in. A few travelers strolling down Bridge Street to pass the time between trains did peer into the window with some interest but didn't step inside. Adele was relieved, as she had none of her friend's expertise about herbs. She didn't even know what some of them were.

Sheriff Summers was cordial and allowed them to see Estelle in his office. She pulled a chair near the window and peered out, her hands in her lap. "Does Paul know where I am?"

Adele shook her head. The woman looked relieved.

"Did you think he would storm in here with a revolver pointed at Sheriff Summers' belly?" Nin asked.

"Frankly, yes." She laughed. "Now I see how terribly melodramatic that is. And Paul is certainly not the melodramatic kind."

"Have the police told you about the knife?" Adele asked.

"They were here this morning," she said.

"For what it's worth, I don't think Hatfield believes you hid it in your wagon." Adele sat on the edge of the desk.

"It would be rather a stupid thing to do, even for me," she agreed.

"You're far from stupid," Nin said firmly.

"You're very kind, Miss Branch." She smiled. "They need to speak with the district attorney, but they don't think I'll have to stay here much longer."

Adele studied the woman. Her face had lost the Dresden doll look and her hair was stringy. "Did you have breakfast?"

"Breakfast?" she echoed.

"Never mind, I can see you haven't." Adele rose. "I'll tell the deputy sheriff to send out for something. There's a lovely cafe just across the street."

Estelle gave a wan smile. "I suppose there's no harm in it."

"On the contrary," Adele said. "You need to keep up your strength for whatever comes." She grasped the woman's shoulder. "And good things will come, Estelle. I'm sure of it."

"Good things will come," Nin echoed in an assured way.

The woman rose, nodding. "Well, if you put it that way, I suppose I can't refuse."

They coaxed Sheriff Summers into letting Estelle wash her face at the station sink and helped her tidy up her dress. Adele noticed she wore a string of beads with three different shades of blue. These small gestures lifted the woman's mood as she accepted the comb Adele offered her and combed her hair back singing a little tune.

"That's an attractive necklace," Adele observed.

"Abby gave it to me."

"She gave you the scarf as well, didn't she?"

"We were once very close," Estelle said. "Almost like mother and daughter. She used to come to me with everything that troubled her. Then she just stopped coming." She shrugged. "I must have said or done something to offend her, though I've no idea what."

The woman's solemn tone lingered in Adele's mind as they rode back to Arrojo and she parked her Beaton near the park.

Adele noticed the appearance of the Call wagon had changed. The dry brown tones were gone, now covered with pink and gray paint. The pink was rather glaring, and Adele noticed Nin turning her eyes away from it. There was a scrolled wooden sign on top of the door that read "The Lightning Calls" with carved lightening rods on either side.

Nin stepped in front of her and pushed the door open. Adele caught a glimpse of a man's back.

"Good afternoon, Mr. Spears." She tipped her head a little as she rested her closed parasol down.

"G-good afternoon." The young man bowed, his shoulders still shaking.

Helen's face twisted with fear, then relaxed. "We thought you were Abby!"

"I was told you had gone back home." Adele looked at him as she took off her gloves.

"You weren't scared off by her, were you?" Nin eyed him with sympathy.

"No, indeed, miss." Some of the young man's apprehension left. "I meant what I said. I intend to marry Helen when I can."

"A very noble thing," Adele said kindly. "But perhaps you shouldn't be here just now."

"Abby is with Cora," said Helen. "The poor girl had night-mares all night about the police arresting Dan."

"Too bad she didn't wait," Adele said. "We could have told her the police don't suspect Dan in the least."

"It's an awful mess, isn't it?" Mr. Spears declared.

"Murder always is," said Nin.

"Oh, I didn't mean — of course the police are doing all they can."

"Adele's right, Mr. Spears," said Helen. "It's best you go now."

She regained a little of her dignity. "You may tell the cook you're a friend of mine and he'll give you lunch."

"Oh, he knows me well enough by now," said the young man with a little laugh. Then his face reddened. "Your sister won't be there?"

"Abby and I are dining here with Miss Gossling and Miss Branch," she said.

"I'll be back," the young man promised. His eyes lingered on her for a few minutes as he stood in the doorway. His moony look made Nin roll her eyes.

"You didn't have to do that," Adele said, glancing at the small table and four chairs in the corner of the wagon. "We would have been glad to dine in the cookhouse with everyone else."

"Abby thought it would be more fitting for us to dine here," she said. "With you being our guests and all."

"And she always makes the decisions, doesn't she?" Nin asked.

"That's how it's always been." Helen took the plates sitting on the bed wrapped in linen and began setting the table. "She promised Ma and Pa, you see."

"Sometimes parents make unreasonable demands of older siblings," Adele said softly.

"They made her promise to see I was always taken care of," Helen said, her voice growing a little shrill. "To Abby, that meant making me the star."

"Misguided ambition," Nin murmured.

The young woman put down the plate. "Why, whatever do you mean, Miss Branch?"

Adele studied her. "You don't like the circus, do you, Helen?"

The young woman didn't answer at first but Adele saw she was thinking about it in the way she took up the silverware as if each one was a finger, carefully cradling it in her hand. "Abby says one can't avoid one's destiny."

"It might be hers but it need not be yours," Adele said gently.

"No one has to bear what they were born to if they don't want to," Nin added. Adele knew she was thinking of how her own mother defied the constraints of her aristocratic upbringing.

"But one must have courage to do that." Helen looked at them. "I'm talking nonsense, aren't I?"

"Not in the least," Adele said kindly. "It sounds like maybe your sister needed to have a mother, not be one." She leaned against her parasol. "Estelle told us she and Abby used to be like mother and daughter. What happened, Helen?"

The young woman laid glasses above the plates. "It's hard to explain how Abby is with people. She expects so much of them. When they let her down, she isn't very understanding some-times." The table set, the girl sat down on one of the chairs.

"You mean she expected Estelle to be a mother and she wasn't?" Nin asked.

"Not exactly," said Helen. "Mind you, I don't know everything. This is just from my observation."

"Your observations are more accurate than you think," Adele said with a smile.

This gave the young woman more confidence. "When we first joined the Barry Circus, Abby was like a puppy who found the perfect master with Estelle. She spent all her free time with her. Julius would get annoyed when he had to go looking for her before practices and found her in a corner somewhere with Estelle, telling her funny stories."

"I can well imagine how that would grate on his nerves," Adele said.

"He was that sort of self-centered dolt," Nin agreed.

"Yes, he did rather like all the attention on himself," Helen said, smiling for the first time. "I remember Abby telling me, 'Don't worry, we'll soon show him he's not the only one the crowds want to see.'"

"What about Estelle?" Adele put her chin in her hand.

"Abby came in one night after a visit with Estelle and said, 'I'd like to take Estelle's morals and put them in a sack like so many rats and throw them in the river!' I thought that was odd."

"I wonder what she meant," Adele murmured.

"Abby can sometimes see the smallest thing as a big infraction," said her sister. "When we were children, she had one friend, the daughter of an equestrian. She was like that too — very attached to her. And then, one day, the girl told her she couldn't sit in the stands with her because she promised to sit with someone else. From then on, Abby avoided her. She said she smelled like horses all the time anyway."

"That does seem rather harsh," Adele said. "I wonder what infraction Estelle committed for her to stop giving her gifts."

"She did give Estelle a lot of gifts," Helen agreed. "Some of them belonged to my mother."

"Like that scarf we found?" Nin asked.

Helen's smile was vague. "They all belonged to my mother."

"All?"

"Ma often bought more than one of the same scarf. She loved them, you see, said they gave the crowds something to remember her by. And since we were always traveling, well, sometimes it wasn't easy to wash things as often as we wanted to." Her face flushed. "She had two, sometimes three of the same scarf. That way, she could always wear one even if the others were dirty."

"Very sensible," Adele complimented. "I love scarves myself, only I use them mostly to cover my head when I drive."

"With your Beaton, you need it," Nin said, a little unkindly.

"Would it be too much trouble to see them?" Adele inquired.

"I'd like to see them too," Nin said with surprising sincerity.

The young woman pulled a suitcase from under the bed and opened it. Inside, two thin wooden rods held silk scarves. Some were patterned and some plain, but all had the signs of loving wear.

"I see you're right." Adele examined them carefully. "Most of these are in twos or threes."

"Except this one." Nin pulled out a scarf which, Adele saw right away, contained the pattern of the one they had found. "But if your sister gave Estelle the other one, it would be."

"There were three of those." Helen lovingly took the edge of it. "It was one of Ma's favorites. She only wore them on opening night in a big town."

"For good luck?" Adele suggested.

Helen shook her head. "She wasn't superstitious. She was really quite vain. I think she wanted the biggest crowds to see them. And there was always a chance we would appear in the local paper the next day, so she wanted to look her best." The young woman chuckled. "Terrible to think one's own mother was so proud!"

"It is a beautiful scarf." Nin fingered the smooth tassels.

"One is here and one is with the police." Adele felt her breath quicken. "And the third?"

"I really haven't any idea," Helen said. "We may have lost it during our travels. We've lost several of the scarves, I'm afraid. The clasps aren't very tight." She showed them the clasps of the suitcase. "They sometimes fall open when we're moving between towns or fall onto the road without our knowing it until it's too late."

"This one didn't fall out," Nin declared.

"No, I don't think it did," Adele said softly.

"What are you doing?" A violent screech made them all jump.

"Abby, dear." Helen rose. "You were gone so long." She quickly closed the suitcase, snapping the clasps, and shoved it under the cot.

"It was our fault," Adele said. "Helen told us about your mother's scarves and they sounded so lovely that Nin and I had to see them."

"They aren't a secret, are they?" Nin eyed her.

The woman's face softened. "No, Miss Branch. But they are precious. To me, anyway."

"We didn't soil them," Nin insisted.

The woman smiled. "Of course you didn't. I'm glad Helen showed them to you." She took off her shawl and smoothed her hair.

"How is Cora?" Adele asked.

"Calmer." Abby unfolded some linens on the bed. "I'm afraid a cold lunch is all we can manage here. We didn't want to ask for something hot and have it be served cold."

"You were gone such a long time," Helen lamented.

"One doesn't leave a sobbing woman, does one?"

"I thought you said she was calmer," her sister said.

"You know Cora, dearest," said Abby as they all sat down. "Things come and go with her. She's sobbing one minute, cheerful the next."

"She's lying!" Nin hissed in Adele's ear.

Adele watched as the woman served the salad and sandwiches. Her eyes were concentrated on the food and her hands moved slowly from the serving dishes to the plates as if she were a mime. Adele knew her friend was right.

"It was very kind of you to reassure her," she said.

Abby gave her a sharp look. "We're like a family here."

"You don't consider Estelle family," Nin remarked.

The woman laughed. "What does Estelle have to do with it?"

"I would rather think it was her job to comfort Cora," Adele said. "If she were here, that is."

A wary look appeared on Abby's face. "Estelle couldn't comfort a cat."

"That's not true, Abby!" Helen stared at her. "You found her very comforting once."

"Sometimes people aren't who you think they are, sweet," said her sister.

Helen fiddled with her sandwich. "Why don't you like Estelle anymore, Abby?"

Her sister laughed again. "What a silly question!"

"Helen was telling us how close you were to her," Adele said.

"That was when I was young and naive."

"It's not naive to try and find another mother to replace the one you lost," Nin said softly.

"Did you, Miss Branch?" Abby regarded her with her intense gaze.

But unlike Adele, who flinched at the personal question, Nin met it with her own cat-like gaze. "I don't trust many people."

"Because they mock your gifts?" Abby nodded. "Yes, we understand here."

Nin's shoulders sagged a little as she took another sandwich from the platter.

"I wish I had been like you," Abby said with a sigh. "That was my mistake. I trusted her too much."

"What exactly did she do, if I may ask?" Adele peered at her.

"It wasn't really anything she *did*," Abby said. "She was just not the person I thought she was."

"Or the person you wanted her to be," Nin mumbled.

To Adele's surprise, Abby agreed. "Perhaps that too, Miss Branch."

"Who did you want her to be?" Helen asked, her voice filled with curiosity. "Not Ma, surely."

Abby pressed her sister's hand. "No one could take Ma's place."

"No one can take any mother's place," Adele agreed.

Abby looked at her, amused. "Yours, no doubt, was in Seneca Falls with Miss Anthony and Miss Mott?"

"I never really knew my mother," Adele said. "She died when I was five years old." She leaned back against the hard chair. "My brother was close to her, though."

"But you know enough about her to know she wouldn't have approved of your progressive ideals," Abby said.

"I never said that."

The woman gave her a shifty smile. "You didn't have to."

Adele stared at the pink wall opposite her. "She was very womanly. I mean Victorian womanly. I do remember her always shushing me at the dinner table, telling me 'Ladies do not speak unless they are spoken to.'"

"Posh!" Nin growled.

"It is now." Adele picked up her fork. "I threw a tantrum because Jack could talk his head off and she never shushed him."

Abby laughed, but Helen's eyes were grave. "That wasn't fair."

"Life is hardly ever fair, love," said her sister. "We must be grateful Ma never gave a thought to what women should and shouldn't do. She worked alongside Pa until the day she died."

"That was indeed fortunate," Adele said.

"I suppose I did try to find another mother in Estelle," Abby admitted.

"You thought enough about her to give her a string of beads and your mother's scarf," Nin pointed out.

"Yes, that was rather impetuous of me." Abby laughed.

"Weren't there three of those scarves, Abby?" her sister asked, buttering a slice of bread.

A clang echoed in the wagon, and Abby bent down to pick up the serving spoon that had fallen from the salad bowl. "Aren't there three?"

"Not now," Adele said. "The police have one and there's only one in the suitcase."

"I suppose it got lost." She shrugged, putting the spoon aside. "Wagon wheels break and things get tossed out before we realize it. Helen, remember that time in the Sierra Nevada?"

Her sister nodded. "Our suitcases and cabinets kept falling open and the wind was so strong, it burst the door open and things flew right out over our heads and down the mountain." She shuddered. "I lost my favorite brooch."

"It was a terrible sight," her sister agreed. "I wouldn't be surprised if we lost the scarf then and perhaps several others. But we expect such things when we're on the road."

"You're very calm about it," Adele remarked.

"Considering the scarves are so precious to you," Nin added.

"I still have some, Miss Branch," Abby said. "They're precious enough for me."

Adele rose. "Thank you for the lovely lunch, Abby." Nin nodded her gratitude.

"I'm glad you came," she said. "I met Cal on my way back and he says we'll be leaving the day after tomorrow. Everything is all set."

"We can get away from this horrible place?" Helen asked. Then, blushing, she said, "I'm sorry. I didn't mean —"

Adele laughed. "I can see how you would find Arrojo horrible, Helen. But come back to us one day when all this is behind you and I think you'll find it pleasant enough."

"It won't ever be behind us," she murmured.

Nin, her sympathy roused, put both her hands on the girl's shoulders. "Your aura is dark moving into light. It will be dark again soon, but the light is there." Abby gave her a sharp look.

Adele closed the buttons of her jacket. "Abby, you offered to give your scarf to the sheriff when Paul was arrested."

"Scarf?"

"The one that matches what we found after the crime," Adele said. "I think it might be a good idea to give it to us now so we can give it to him."

Abby looked annoyed. "But he said he didn't need it!"

"I think he'll want to see it now," Adele insisted.

"Because there was a third one that was lost?" Abby jumped up. "Oh, that's ridiculous!"

"He'll want everything accounted for," Adele said.

"He'll probably give it back to you right away," Nin said.

"I don't see why —"

"Oh, give it to them, Abby!" Helen shrieked. "It frightens me now."

"You're being fanciful," her sister snapped.

"I don't want to see it again ever." Helen buried her face in her hands. "The sheriff can keep it for all I care!"

Abby sighed. "All right, darling. If it upsets you so much, I'll let Adele take it."

Adele watched as she opened the lid and lovingly slid the scarf from the wooden bar. She spread it out on the bed and folded it into a small square. She found a small box and, lining the inside with some of the clean linens left over from lunch, packed the scarf before she handed it to Adele. "You'll take special care of it and return it to me as soon as you can?"

"Of course," Adele promised.

As she and Nin left the wagon, Helen was crouched on the cot, her face buried in her hands with her sister comforting her.

CHAPTER 29

The moment they were out of the wagon, Nin said, "She was lying about being with Cora the whole time."

"I gathered that," Adele said. "The question is, why?"

She had no time to contemplate, as she was nearly swept away by Mr. Sipes' leaping figure.

"Dear ladies!" He spread out his arms.

"Gad, what do you want?" Nin glared at him as if he were a roach.

"You never did get to see my cat do tricks, did you?" he asked.

"Considering his tricks on Labor Day, I don't think we missed much," Adele said dryly.

"I've given all that up, Miss Gossling." The man looked hurt. "I promised you, and I am true to my word." He leaned closer, his hands behind his back. "Shall I tell you about my latest idea?"

"If it's something criminal, we'll tell the police," Nin warned.

"Nothing of the sort," he insisted. "But perhaps I shall get one up on that beast Verner."

"How will you do that, Mr. Sipes?" In spite of her hurry, her curiosity was aroused.

His voice dropped to a whisper. "I've been secretly training Griselda."

"And who is Griselda?"

"A startling she-devil with green eyes and coal-black fur," he said. "I won't be painting her gold or any other color. She's magnificent as she is."

"I thought you said you were staying loyal to Sinbad," Adele said.

"Oh, but he would have wanted me to go on with our act," said the man.

"If you'll pardon me, Mr. Sipes, you weren't exactly an act when we met you," Adele said.

"You were performing tricks on the street for pennies," Nin said.

"Indeed, and that's about to change." He took Adele's arm. "Come, let me show you."

Picturing the way Sinbad had roamed her shop, Adele felt sick to her stomach. "We really must be going," She grabbed her friend's hand.

"You misunderstand, dear lady," said the man with a bow. "I won't let Griselda take one step out of her cage. The door will be closed the entire time."

"It's sickening to watch a man go at a cat with a whip," Nin snarled.

The man looked horrified. "I'm not a barbarian like that Verner."

"Please, Mr. Sipes," Adele said.

"But you're my inspiration," he insisted, pulling her arm. "You must come and see."

Adele gave Nin a look, but suddenly she remembered how Mr. Sipes' earlier observations had led to clues and said in a calm voice, "If you promise to keep the cat inside the cage and the cage door locked at all times, we'll come."

"Adele!"

"It will be all right, dear," she assured her friend, taking first grasp of her hand. "I have a few questions for Mr. Sipes."

"About this ghastly business with Dan's knife, no doubt?" He said as he led them to the animal tent. "And in Estelle's wagon too."

"Then you think she's innocent?" Adele asked.

"My dear lady, I *know* she's innocent."

They followed silently in the walkway between the cages. Most of the animals were, thankfully, sleeping with the calmness of having just been fed. In the back of the tent was Griselda. Adele had to admit she did look magnificent with her shining black coat and green eyes.

"It's a cub," Nin said with a sigh of relief.

"Quite a novelty, don't you think?" The man smiled as he stepped into the cage. Griselda rose, reaching the edge of the bars and sticking her nose out as if to sniff at the ladies. Nin, no longer afraid, petted her head and even Adele reached out a hand to her.

"Until she grows up," Nin remarked.

"Mr. Sipes, why are you so sure Estelle didn't kill Julius?" Adele asked. "The knife that was used to cut the net was found in her wagon, after all."

"Isn't that what your police call circumstantial evidence?" Mr. Sipes managed to get Griselda to do a few rolls on the straw ground.

"It's not circumstantial anymore," said Nin. "Mr. Brethren tested and confirmed it."

"Another policeman?"

"A lab man who works with organic substances," Adele supplied.

"But nobody can prove Estelle was the one who put it there," Mr. Sipes insisted. "It's still circumstantial, dear lady."

"Men have been hanged on less," Nin said.

Mr. Sipes flinched. "Please. I abhor violence."

"Odd remark from a man who plays with lions and panthers," Nin said.

"We're training, not playing, Miss Branch," he insisted. "Come Griselda, show the ladies how you can jump over the stool so prettily."

"You may keep this confidential, Mr. Sipes, but Estelle admitted to us she knew Julius had no intention of running away with her," Adele said. "She may have been enraged and acted."

"Estelle isn't the type," he insisted. "Griselda liked her."

"What does that prove?" Nin asked.

"A great deal." He gave up trying to get Griselda over the stool and sat on it. The panther promptly toddled to the corner of the cage and lay down to sleep. "Cats have a natural instinct for people like no other animal. Their sensitivity to repulsive people is remarkable."

"So because Griselda took to Estelle, you think she's not a murderer," Adele said.

"It isn't as silly as it sounds," he insisted.

"I don't think it's silly in the least," she promised. "But the police are going to need more evidence than that."

He sniffed. "Why can't they simply look at a man and know he's not a criminal by nature?"

"Such as yourself?" Nin eyed him.

"Such as myself," he said. "I don't say I didn't deserve what I got. But if your sheriff had been able to see into my soul, he would have known —"

"He did see," Adele said. "But the law is the law, Mr. Sipes."

"Yes, unfortunately," he grumbled.

"Who else did Griselda take to?" she asked.

"She adores the elephant girls," he said.

"Elephant girls?"

"Agnes, Birdy, and Clementine," he explained. "That's what we call them. The ladies who take care of the elephants."

"The elephant act." Adele nodded.

313

"And she played with Helen like a kitten." He smiled. "She was a great comfort to Helen after Julius's fall."

"Was she a great comfort to Abby as well?" Nin asked.

Griselda raised her head and gave a baby version of a roar.

"I'm afraid Abby was rather unkind to her," he said.

"Oh?"

"Not that she wasn't provoked," he said quickly. "Griselda was certainly a bad girl."

"What happened?" Nin asked.

"She scratched Abby's shoulder," he said. "Nothing serious."

"But rather unpleasant, I imagine," Adele said.

"Abby started it," he defended. "She went after her with a piece of pipe." His eyes were set.

"Was this before or after Julius died?" Adele asked.

"Oh, after," he said. "A lucky thing your sheriff forbids dare-devil performances so she didn't have to perform. Those scratches on her arm wouldn't have looked pretty in her costume."

"I can't blame Griselda for biting her if she went after her with a pipe," Adele admitted.

"No, that was afterward," he said. "Griselda scratched her because she knows what sort of person she is."

"And what sort of person is Abby?" Nin asked.

He looked distant for a moment. Griselda knelt beside him and he petted her absently. "Suffice it to say I never trusted her."

"Why is that?"

"She's highly inconsistent, for one," he said. "Looking down on us animal people as if we were trash. And then getting chummy with Gerry." Rising, he gave her a grand smile. "Come, Griselda, shall we try to jump over the stool again?"

"The woman who helps clean the cages?" Adele asked.

"I told you that woman wants eyes," Nin mumbled.

"For another, she breaks the rules," Mr. Sipes continued, trying to coax Griselda over the stool.

"What do you mean by breaking the rules, Mr. Sipes?" Adele asked, nearing the cage.

"The circus rules, of course," he said.

"You mean the rules Paul makes?" Nin asked.

"Precisely, dear lady." He smiled. "Look, she almost made it that time."

"What rule did she break?" asked Adele.

"I saw her a few times at that bar in town."

"The Bright Lights Saloon?" Adele glanced at Nin.

"Why, yes, not that I would expect fine ladies like you to know it." He glanced at them.

"We met a cowboy there once," Nin said.

"I assure you Abby wasn't meeting any cowboy." He chuckled.

"Who did she meet?" Adele asked.

"Gerry, of course," he said. "They were bending their heads together like two canaries in a cage."

"When was this?" Adele asked.

"Three or four nights ago," he said. "She's been there nearly every night since we came to town."

"Isn't that risky?" she asked. "If Paul were to find out —"

"Paul has been preoccupied with this murder business," he reminded her. "Come, Griselda, let's try again."

"How do you know she's been there every night?" Adele inquired. "You saw her go out?"

"Certainly not." He sniffed. "I'm no sneak-thief —" He flinched as if remembering Labor Day and corrected, "I mean, I'm not the sort of person who goes creeping around spying on other folks. The bartender told me."

"How obliging he was to offer the information," Nin said.

"Well, I admit, I intended to report her, but there was no one to report her to." He shrugged. "I expect now that Paul is back, she'll get reprimanded as she should."

"She's still going out, then?" Adele asked.

"I imagine so," he said. "I don't see Gerry in the cookhouse at dinnertime, and I can't imagine her missing a meal. She's rather timely about throwing down her work when the meal bell rings."

"Maybe she thinks she's too good to eat with the rest of you," Nin suggested.

He laughed and Griselda gave another baby roar. "I'm sure she does, dear woman."

Adele tapped the parasol on the straw ground, hearing it crunch underneath. "Mr. Sipes will you take us there tonight?"

"Where?"

"The Bright Lights Saloon, of course."

He stared at her. "Fine ladies in a place like that?"

"I told you we've been there before," Nin said.

"We'll take *you* to dinner," Adele said. "Let's put it that way, shall we?"

"Oh, but —"

"We would be most obliged, Mr. Sipes." Adele's face dropped with modesty, a tactic she found often worked with men when they got on their high horse about woman's place. "If we went with you, it would be respectable."

"But why do you want to go?"

"I'd like to see if Abby meets with Gerry tonight," she said. "Call it curiosity."

"You mustn't mention curiosity in front of Griselda." He flinched. "You know what happens to cats because of it."

"We're not cats, Mr. Sipes, we're women," Nin said.

Griselda gave a roaring yawn and rested her head on the straw to go back to sleep.

"It would be against the rules," he said softly.

"You'll be with us," Adele said. "We work for the police, remember?"

"This is for the police?" he questioned.

"You could say that," she said. "It might be important to the investigation."

"What about your brother?" he asked. "He's made it clear he doesn't like me."

"Jack won't know anything about it," she promised.

"Well, in that case," he bowed, "I shall be delighted to accompany such lovely ladies to dinner tonight."

"Without the cat," Nin added.

"Oh, naturally, naturally."

Griselda opened her eyes, sniffed, and went back to sleep.

When they left the animal tent, Adele felt Nin watching her as she stopped to put on her gloves. "You have ideas."

"Nin, I think we were all wrong."

"Were we?"

"I think Abby is the key to this entire crime," Adele continued. "Her ambitions led her too far."

"So she killed for them?" Nin stared at her.

"Perhaps yes, perhaps no, but there's more to this murder than we thought," said Adele. "More than animal motives, shall we say."

"Animals like Griselda?" Nin chuckled.

"They say the female is much deadlier than the male," Adele reminded her.

"Not to me," Nin snorted. "The male is not only deadly, but just plain stupid."

Adele laughed and took her arm. "We must make one more stop before we leave here."

Nin shrugged. "I should think you were tired by now of the circus."

"Perhaps I am," said Adele. "It's no longer fun and games."

"I knew that the first night we were here," said Nin as they started walking.

Adele turned to her. "It's all illusion. The roaring tigers, the daredevils, even the clowns."

"One must peel the mask off to see behind the illusion," Nin said.

"That's just what we're going to do, dear," said her friend.

She led them to the Henley wagon. Mildred answered their knock, her eyes widened with surprise as she let them in.

"We wanted to ask a favor of you, Mildred," said Adele.

"Regarding the investigation?" She looked suspicious.

"No, regarding the circus," Adele said. "As the manager's wife, you would be the perfect person to help us."

The woman looked pleased. "I'll be happy to do what I can."

"You've heard of the Wrigley School for Girls in town?"

"I believe I passed by it when I went for a walk some days ago." The woman nodded. "I heard rumors the proprietor wasn't very keen on our being here."

"She's rather prim and proper," Nin agreed.

"Those girls are dying to see the circus," Adele said. "If I could convince Mrs. Wrigley to allow it, would you see to them personally?"

"You mean supervise their visit?" Mildred smiled.

"If they were accompanied by the manager's wife, I think Mrs. Wrigley would be all right with it," she said. "Performers would hardly behave badly in front of you."

"They wouldn't behave badly even if I weren't there," Mildred insisted.

"We know that, and you know that," Adele said, "but Mrs. Wrigley has other ideas. If she could see how moral the circus really is, it would get back to some of the town council members —"

"And redeem us in their eyes," the woman finished.

"You would have no trouble coming back this way in the future if you chose," Adele said.

"I suppose it would be good for the circus," she agreed. She added in an official tone, "When can we expect the girls?"

"Tomorrow you'll have a Saturday matinee, I gather?" Adele asked.

Mildred nodded. "Our last. We leave for San Francisco on Monday."

"They shall be here in the afternoon," Adele promised.

When they left the circus, Nin asked, "The Wrigley School now?"

Adele glanced at the watch hanging from her lapel. "The girls ought to have retired to their studies by now. It's always the time Mrs. Wrigley is at her calmest."

And, indeed, Mrs. Wrigley looked subdued when they entered her office. She had gained a few gray hairs in the last year, but it only added to her felicitous countenance.

"I'm just making tea," she said, offering them chairs. Nin, with her good sense, chose one instead of her usual position on the floor, as Mrs. Wrigley had made it clear she thought it less than ladylike.

In spite of having dealt with Mrs. Wrigley's resistance to anything she considered improper to a wealthy school girl's education, Adele was nervous. Her fingers dampened inside her gloves but she dared not take them off for fear of encountering one of Mrs. Wrigley's lectures on etiquette. "We've come to offer you a gift, Mrs. Wrigley."

"You know how we like to do things for the girls," Nin added.

"Yes, I remember the party you gave us after poor Lucy Blackstone died." The last she said in a hushed tone as if she feared the girls were lurking outside.

"I understand you're not an enthusiastic supporter of the Barry Circus."

"Well, I can hardly be that, considering they're involved in a murder investigation." She said "murder" with a flinch as she poured the strong tea.

"That's not their fault," Nin objected.

"Still, such things don't happen among respectable people," Mrs. Wrigley said.

"The Marsh family were involved in a murder and they were respectable, weren't they?" Nin asked.

"That's hardly the same thing, Miss Branch," said the woman. "Oh, I've had a time keeping the papers away from the girls." She cast a worried eye to the ceiling where, on the second floor, her pupils were in the study rooms.

"They do keep to themselves, you know," Adele pointed out gently. "Mrs.

Henley told me so."

"Mrs. Henley?"

"The manager's wife," said Adele. "She's most concerned about the way people have behaved toward them." She felt Nin's incredulous eyes on her but she continued, "That's why she's offered to escort the girls through tomorrow's Saturday matinee so they can see the show."

"That's very kind of her, but I don't think I could allow it."

"They're anxious to go," Nin chimed in.

The woman gave her a fish eye. "How do you know, Miss Branch?"

As Nin stalled for an answer, Adele said quickly, "All children love the circus, Mrs. Wrigley, even the older girls. It's an event."

"True, true." The woman tapped her spoon on her saucer. "I may be honest with you, Miss Gossling?"

"Certainly."

"I'm not as much like Mrs. Faderman and the others as you think," she said. "I don't object to the circus's morals or lack thereof."

"Really?" This took Adele by surprise and Nin stared at her.

"No, you see, I was fond of it myself as a child." Here, the woman blushed. "My sister and I used to watch them rehearse. We had to creep out of the house, of course, since my mother didn't approve. But they were always kind to us and we never saw any wrongdoings." The last she said in a firm tone.

"We didn't see any either except murder," Nin said.

"Yes, well, that was rather unfortunate, and not something that happens every day, not even in the circus." The woman shrugged.

"But you still hesitate to accept Mrs. Henley's invitation?" Adele asked.

"Frankly, yes. It's not the morals, Miss Gossling, that worry me. It's the chaos."

"Oh, I see." Adele felt relieved.

"With people wandering about, I can't think how we would manage twenty-four girls," she said. "You do know I have twenty-four this year?"

"Yes, I do know." Adele smiled. "Your school has grown admirably."

The woman beamed with pride. "When one has the right foundation for a young woman's education, people recognize it."

"Indeed they do," Adele mumbled. "What if I promised you there would be proper ladies like Vanessa Faderman and Mary Lynn accompanying you and helping to keep order?"

The woman put her cup down. "Well, then, I could hardly object to that, could I?" She eyed her. "But I doubt Vanessa would agree to come with us, considering her mother's opinion of the circus."

"I happen to know Vanessa and her friends are anxious to see the circus as well and haven't had a chance to yet," Adele said firmly. "I hardly think even Mrs. Faderman could object much to her daughter coming along to keep an eye out for the morals of young girls on a Saturday afternoon."

"No, perhaps she would be more inclined to yield if you put it that way," Mrs. Wrigley agreed. She said in a decided tone, "If Vanessa and a few of her friends agree to accompany us, then I'll consent."

Adele smiled and rose. "Thank you, Mrs. Wrigley. The girls will enjoy it."

"I'm sure they will," said Mrs. Wrigley, shaking her hand.

"And so will she," Nin said in a snide tone as they left the office. "She'll enjoy it more than they will."

"That's to our advantage, dear," said Adele.

"You sound very certain you'll convince Vanessa and those young geese to come," Nin said slyly.

"I don't think we'll have much trouble," said Adele. "Vanessa is a married woman now. She's already shown signs of breaking away from her mother's influence and her friends follow her as much as their mothers follow her mother. I'm sure I can convince Vanessa and if she goes, they'll all go."

"You're very clever, Adele," her friend complimented.

Adele smiled and took her friend's arm warmly. "I just know the way young women think," she said. "Out of habit, not desire!"

"So now we go to hunt down Vanessa?" Nin asked.

Adele shook her head. "I can call on her later. Now we see the girls."

"Must we?" Nin groaned. The girls were often as blunt as she was and liked teasing her about being a witch.

Adele patted her hand. "We'll only see them for a moment. I need them to do a job for me."

"I didn't think you arranged this excursion out of the goodness of your heart," said her friend.

"I'm delighted the girls get to see the circus at last," Adele protested. "I just happen to need them for a job at the same time." She fluttered her eyes in innocence until both of them were laughing.

To make sure none of the teachers saw them and reported to Mrs. Wrigley, they went up the back stairs. They entered the third floor, knowing the older girls would be studying in the front parlor, unsupervised.

Beatrice was there along with her friends Mary and Rachel. Agnes, the new girl, was pounding on a piano in the corner to a ticking metronome, stopping every few notes to mark the music sheet with her pencil.

"Can't you stop that infernal beating, Ag?" Beatrice snarled.

"I'm already late getting this piece to Mrs. Rose," she said in an irritated tone.

"I can't think how anyone will ever stand one of your concerts," Mary remarked. "You don't even play delicately."

"I'm practicing!" Agnes snapped. "One needn't play delicately when one is practicing."

"I think you show a lot of promise, Agnes," Adele said.

The girls greeted her with smiles and handshakes.

"Have you seen the old powder-puff?" Beatrice rolled her eyes. "I can smell that tea of hers all over you."

Adele laughed. "Your powers of observation astound me, Bea."

"You have a job for us?" Mary asked eagerly, biting her pencil.

"Don't do that or you'll eat lead." Nin snatched it from her. "It's dangerous."

"I wasn't doing anything." Mary sniffed.

"We've come with good news," said Adele. "You're going to see the circus!"

"We've already seen it," said Rachel in a bored tone. "Twice."

"You're going to see it again," she said. "This time with Mrs. Wrigley's blessing."

"Which means she'll be on our tail all the time," Bea grumbled.

"There's a matinee tomorrow and you're all going," said Adele.

Rachel stared. "The entire school?"

"You say that as if there are millions of us," Agnes said. "We're only twenty-four."

"I find it hard to believe Mrs. Wrigley would let all twenty-four of us go," Mary said. "She ain't hardly one to let us play in the park all at once."

"Nevertheless, you're all going with Mrs. Faderman Cook and a few others tomorrow," Adele said firmly. "And Mrs. Henley, the circus manager's wife, is going to escort you."

"Bum it, it sounds tedious," Beatrice said.

"Don't say bum it anymore, Bea," Rachel chided. "It sounds disrespectful." She reached for her rosary beads.

"I'll stop saying 'bum it' when you stop carrying those beads around!" her friend challenged.

"What do you want us to do?" Mary asked with her wide-eyed stare. "Do you want us to handcuff someone?"

"We're not police women, Mary," Agnes said.

"There are women on the police force these days," Mary insisted.

"I'm going to have to ask you to be a little devious," Adele said.

"Like with Mr. Marsh last year?" Bea asked. "That was such a lark!"

"Hail the little criminal," Nin mumbled.

"Not quite as with Mr. Marsh's pen nibs, but similar," she said. "I need you to find something for me." She pulled out of her bag the scarf Abby had given her. "I want you to look for a scarf exactly like this."

"The scarf found near the dead man!" Mary gasped.

"The police have that one," Nin said.

"Now listen carefully." Adele took Bea by the shoulders. "I only want you to conduct a search and see if you can find it. Don't bring it to me. Don't even touch it. Just let me know if you find it and where you found it."

"Is that all?" Bea asked.

"No, that's not all," Adele said. "Every wagon has a double wall. There are panels over another layer of wood. I want you to pay attention to any panel that's loose or slides back. The scarf might be hidden behind one of them."

"Caroline could do it," Rachel volunteered. "Like she did with Mr. Marsh. She's like a snake, slithering from place to place without anybody seeing her."

"I hardly think your friend would appreciate that description," Nin observed.

"It should be easy enough," Beatrice said matter-of-factly.

"Don't let Mrs. Wrigley or any of the others see you breaking away from the group." Adele put the scarf back in her purse. "And for heaven's sake, don't let any of them follow you."

Beatrice was indignant. "What do you take us for, careless thieves?"

"No, dear," Adele said. "I know I can rely on all of you."

She and Nin were silent as they walked back to Bridge Street. As Adele said goodbye to her friend, Nin asked, "What are you up to, Adele?"

"I really don't know," she admitted. "It's a feeling I have about that scarf."

"Abby wasn't telling the truth when she said the third one was lost," Nin agreed. "That much was obvious. But why is it so important to find the third one?"

"I'm not sure yet," Adele said.

"But you'll find out," Nin said, smiling.

"I always do, don't I?" Adele winked at her and went to open her shop.

CHAPTER 30

*A*dele tried to keep her mind on her work for the rest of the day, but her thoughts wandered to the circus. People came in, many of them wanting to see the new pale orange and tan stationery she had just received to prepare for their fall correspondence. She had learned very quickly Arrojo citizens took their letter-writing very seriously and were willing to spend their pennies on seasonal paper and envelopes and even fancy seals. She was usually eager to sell them her latest, but today, she felt it was one more burden on her already burdened shoulders.

She was dismayed when ten minutes before closing time, Percy Faderman came in. He was a rather portly young man with a round face and head who resembled his father more than his strong-willed mother. He stumbled through the shop, first wanting to see one thing and then another. Adele stole glances at her lapel watch, feeling more agitated as the six o'clock hour neared.

"I'm keeping you from an appointment, Miss Gossling?" he asked in his high-pitched voice.

"Frankly, yes." She had little patience for politeness. "I'm meeting Nin and a friend for dinner."

"Oh, I see." He fingered a few stamps lying on the counter. "I rather thought — well, that is — ahem —" He made an attempt at a delicate cough but it came out more like a gasp.

"Perhaps you'll come by tomorrow, Mr. Faderman?" she asked. "I won't be in such a rush, and I'll be able to devote all my attention to you."

"Oh, that would be splendid!" The outburst made her flinch. "Miss Gossling," the man suddenly leaned toward her, "I know my mother can be — well, difficult sometimes —"

"Yes, well, mothers are like that," she said hurriedly as she put the cover on the cash register, hoping he would take the hint.

"But she has much admiration for you, really."

"She has a funny way of showing it," Adele remarked, thinking of all the arguments she had had with the woman.

"I realize you must have many young men, shall we say, chasing after you in this town."

She eyed him. "You make me sound like a wild turkey at Thanksgiving time."

"Oh, no indeed!" The man's high forehead turned red. "I only meant — well, if I may say so, you're a lovely woman —"

"You may not say so!"

The outburst came from the open doorway where Nin stood, dressed and hatted. Behind her, Adele could see Mr. Sipes lingering on the pavement.

"Oh, hello, Miss Branch." The young man coughed in the same way he had before. "We were just —"

"You mean you were just," Nin leaned against the door frame, "you were just making a damn fool of yourself!"

"Oh, I assure you —"

"I advise you to stop flirting with my friend, Mr. Faderman," she said, narrowing her eyes to their cat-like gaze. "You see, I don't like it."

"Oh, I wouldn't dream —" He cowered a little. "Miss Gossling, if I've offended you —"

"You haven't, Mr. Faderman," Adele said. The young man looked so frightened of Nin that she felt sorry for him. "I do have to close my shop now."

"Oh, yes, I'll come by tomorrow, just as you said," he breathed. "And maybe — well —"

"Yes?"

He glanced at Nin still standing in the doorway and lowered his voice to a whisper. "If you've no plans for Saturday —"

Adele was amused and touched at the same time, thinking of what courage the man must have mustered to make his offer. "We can talk about it tomorrow, Mr. Faderman."

"Yes, that would be splendid!" He put on his hat, its edge frayed from having bent it back and forth while he had gone around the shop. "You are kind."

"I try to be." She smiled as she locked the door. "You might remind your mother of that."

"Oh, yes, certainly."

"Your hat is crooked," Nin said.

As Adele stepped out to the pavement, Mr. Sipes grabbed her hand and kissed it with force. Mr. Faderman was all eyes. "Dear lady! How I look forward to this evening!"

"Good evening, Mr. Sipes," she said warily as she leaned her hat away from her face now that the sun was dimmer. "I'm glad to see you didn't bring Griselda to trample all over my shop."

"Ah, we will have our little jokes, won't we?" he said with a twinkle in his eye.

Mr. Faderman suddenly gasped and pointed an indelicate finger at the man. "Why, aren't you the man who terrorized this town on Labor Day?"

"Please, sir," Mr. Sipes said with dignity, "I'm with the circus. Known all over the world."

"Miss Gossling, I'm surprised at you." Mr. Faderman's hesitant manner disappeared and he suddenly resembled his mother. "Going with this man —"

Her temper rose. "Mr. Faderman, I go with whom I please when I please."

"I wasn't trying to tell you otherwise, but I would seriously reconsider going anywhere with this man." He leaned over and whispered, "You know what he is!"

"I assure you, sir, all that's behind me," Mr. Sipes said. He took Adele's arm. "Shall we, dear lady?"

Nin pushed Mr. Faderman aside and, to Adele's surprise, took hold of the other arm Mr. Sipes offered her. She glanced back as they went down the street. Mr. Faderman was still standing in front of her shop, his hat crooked and his eyes and mouth open.

"Rather a jellyfish, isn't he?" Mr. Sipes remarked.

"His mother is a tyrant," Nin supplied. "What the devil did he want in your shop, Adele?"

"I believe he was trying to gather courage to ask me to go rowing on Saturday," Adele said.

"How extraordinary!" Mr. Sipes said.

"Miss Naples left town yesterday, so I suppose that's why he's after you again," Nin said. "He always comes pawing after you when he gets his hopes up over someone else and she rejects him."

"I feel sorry for him," Adele admitted.

"I should think the prospect of Mrs. Faderman as a mother-in-law would be enough to erase any sympathy you might have," Nin said and Mr. Sipes laughed.

"I'm much more interested right now in seeing whether Abby will be at the Bright Light Saloon tonight," Adele said.

"I don't think so," said Mr. Sipes.

"How can you be sure?" asked Nin.

"I saw her with her sister in the dining tent," he said. "She was on the soup, so she won't be in."

"She might come for a drink later," Adele suggested.

"Ah, but the Barrys have strict rules about that too," he reminded her.

"Which neither she nor Miss Gerry Cowell have been following," she said. "Remember that, Mr. Sipes."

He stopped and turned to her. "Won't you call me Lionel, dear lady?"

"I won't," Nin said sharply.

"If you insist," Adele said. "You may call me Adele."

He took her hand and kissed it again. "You honor me with your friendship."

"I didn't say we were friends, Lionel," Adele said. "Don't get any ideas."

"I'm not like that impetuous young man," he promised.

Adele couldn't help but smile at that. "Was Miss Cowell in the dining tent too?"

"No indeed," he said. "I saw her leave so I'm sure she'll be having her dinner in the saloon." He sniffed. "It's as you said, dear lady. She thinks she's too good to dine with the rest of us."

"She did seem to have lofty ideas," Nin said.

"She has aspirations," Adele agreed. "The question is, how far will those aspirations go and does Abby have anything to do with them?"

"I don't follow you," said Lionel.

"You will," Nin assured him.

They crossed the bridge over the narrow river and passed the train station, emerging on Quarry Lane, the seedier side of town. It was more crowded than usual since it was a Friday but the noise did not disturb Adele. She had spent a few evenings on the Barbary Coast and had witnessed the raunchy goings-on there. Quarry Lane was tame in comparison.

They went into the Bright Lights Saloon through the ladies' entrance and found several women there, most dining with others. No one glanced at them. Roaring voices coming from the main saloon were muffled in the ladies' section, for which Adele was grateful. She had a vision of meeting Rex, the cowboy they had spoken with during their investigation into Lucy Blackstone's death and, unlike the last time with her watchdog brother present, he wouldn't take no for an answer if she declined his invitation to dinner again.

She caught sight of Gerry sitting in a corner booth. Her tall head towered above the back and the plates spread in front of her attested to her hearty appetite. She saw Lionel was right, as she was sitting alone and looked to stay that way, with a newspaper propped on her lap.

Lionel took the lead. He strolled over with Adele still on his arm and Nin trailing behind. "Why, Gerry! Fancy meeting you here."

"Hello, Lionel." The woman shook his hand. Adele was surprised by her friendly tone until she remembered they both worked in the animal tent. "The old grouse let you off tonight?"

"I told Verner I had a dinner engagement with two lovely ladies," he said with a bow. "He couldn't very well refuse me the night off."

"Courting the police now, are you?" She eyed Adele.

"We're not the police," Nin insisted.

"May we join you?" Lionel asked.

"Why not?" She moved over one place. "I know you won't say a word about seeing me here. Because I would have to say a word about seeing you here." She waved her hand to the waiter and they placed their order.

He laughed. "I'm surprised to see you alone. Where's your friend?"

She ripped a thick slice of bread in half. "I haven't male friends here as you have your women friends."

"I meant your friend Abby," he said.

"Oh, so you've seen her here too?" she asked. "Well, that was business."

"Business?" Adele asked. "What sort of business?"

"Or is it a secret?" Nin asked, almost as a challenge.

Gerry, whom Adele suspected had more courage than

common sense, rose to the bait. "I suppose it will be out when we get to San Francisco. I'm to be the new catcher for the Lightning Calls."

Adele caught her breath, as she had not expected this. Nin, though, was practical and forward. "What do you know about daredevil flying?"

"You mean because I shovel manure for a living?" the woman snarled. "I never intended to do *that* all my life. And I won't be a strong woman either." The last was said with her chin in the air. "There's no dignity in that."

"But there's dignity in risking your neck every night at forty feet in the air?" Lionel asked dryly.

"Twenty-five feet," Adele corrected, remembering what Abby had told them.

"Yes, as a matter of fact!" She put down her knife and fork. "I'm not afraid like her pigeon-livered sister!"

"That's unkind, don't you think?" Adele asked tightly. "Helen has been on the trapeze since she was fifteen."

"And hating every minute of it," Miss Cowell said. "That's clear to anyone with eyes."

"Maybe you ought to tell her sister that," Nin said.

"And ruin my chance for something better than manure?" The woman snorted. "She has a grand illusion about that sister of hers." She picked up her knife and fork and stabbed at the steak in her plate. "Frankly, I hope she runs off with that chicken-hearted young man of hers."

"There wouldn't be much of an act if she did," Adele pointed out.

"I know a woman who could take her place in a snap," Miss Cowell said slyly. "And she wouldn't be afraid to do the triple somersault like Julius was either!"

"Julius was afraid?"

"Abby says his knees were shaking every time he practiced,"

she said. "She never fell for his bravado, not even in the beginning. That's why she always intended for him to be out."

"His death was rather fortunate for her, then," Nin said in a caustic tone. "And for you."

"Oh, she never would have done anything," said Gerry. "Abby knows a good act when she sees it. She knew they needed Julius."

"But not anymore," Adele guessed.

"Well, things are changing, as you know, Miss Gossling," said the woman.

"Call me Adele," she said warmly.

"Back then, everyone wanted 'the daring young man on the flying trapeze,'" she continued. "Nowadays, people think it's more daring to see women flyers."

"Rather morbid of them," Lionel mumbled.

"No more morbid to see a woman fall than a man," Adele argued.

"As long as the net is there to catch her," Nin added.

"It didn't catch Julius, did it?" he pointed out.

"Abby was ready for her and Helen to leave him anyway," said Gerry. The waiter took away the plates and set a large piece of apple pie in front of her.

"But they renewed their contract with the circus," Adele pointed out.

"Abby only did that to stall for time," Gerry said. The beer she had drunk with her dinner had clearly loosened her tongue and she spoke rapidly. "She was sick to death of him."

"From what we heard about Julius, it's no wonder," Nin remarked.

"Confidentially," the woman leaned forward, her breath smelling of onion, "I think she was through with him before we even got here."

"How do you know?" Adele asked.

"Because she came to me," she said. "That night when the

elephant hurt his foot. Remember, Lionel?" The man nodded. "The beast was bellowing like a cow the entire night. She came around and watched with the rest of us as the veterinarian patched it up. She told me she might need a new catcher, as she wanted Helen to start flying and she thought I would make a good addition to their act." The woman's face shone with pride. "Never been up one of those things, but *she* knew I was no coward."

"She wants to make Helen the star," Adele said slowly. "She made a promise to her parents before they died."

"If she does, that's her business." The woman shrugged. "She knows I won't make any trouble. I just want something more than cleaning out muck." This last was said with a touch of despair.

Adele rose, placing the rather greasy linen napkin on the table and wiping her hands on her handkerchief. "I'm sure you'll get out of the muck, Gerry. Even if it isn't at the Barry Circus."

"What do you mean?" The woman suddenly looked alarmed. "You're not going to tell all this to the police?"

"Only if it's necessary," Nin said.

She wobbled to her feet. "Abby made me promise not to tell anyone!"

"Then you shouldn't have told these two ladies, should you?" Lionel asked with a little spite. "They work with the police, you know."

"But Abby has to tell Calvin first," the woman insisted. "He has to draw up a new contract. She was waiting until, well, the dust settled with this whole murder mess."

"I think you may have helped the dust settle on this whole murder mess, Gerry," Adele said as she took Lionel's arm.

They left the woman standing behind the booth, the napkin in her hand and her face as white as a sheet.

~~~~~

She persuaded Lionel to leave them in front of their shops even though he wanted to walk her all the way to Caliber Lane.

Adele noted he had broken circus rules and, although not drunk, he was a little too lively for her taste. She also feared Jackson would see him and, anticipating her brother's reprimands already, did not want to add to them.

She went through the front gate as quietly as she could, though the hinges didn't help with their squeaking. It was nearly nine o'clock and she saw from the lights that Jackson had told the Cordobas to retire. Only the parlor lamps were on and she flinched, knowing Jackson had waited up for her.

She tiptoed up the walk and when she reached the front door, took off her shoes. There was still a chance she might be able to sneak by the parlor door if it was closed or only half open, as it usually was when they retired for the evening. Then she could go to bed and wake up the next morning, teasing her brother about how she had come in from the back so as not to wake him and had been in bed by eight o'clock.

She managed to get the screen door and front doors open without a sound. She was in luck, as Jackson had chosen to sit in his new favorite chair, which faced the opposite wall so his back was to her. He was reading the evening paper, the smoke from his pipe rising above his head.

She crept to the stairs, keeping her eyes on the stoic figure in the chair. He didn't turn his head. She started up the stairs.

About halfway, she heard the roar. "Where the devil have you been?"

He was standing in the hallway, his hands on his hips, and his face all thunder.

A little anger rose in her at his watchdog expression. "I was working late, Jack."

"No, you weren't," he said. "I sent Tomas down to the shop at seven and the place was dark."

Now she was enraged. "How dare you send him to spy on me!"

"He wasn't spying," he insisted. "He was calling you to dinner."

"I'm not a dog that needs to be called for her dinner, Jack," she seethed.

"Percy Faderman stopped by." He chewed the edge of his pipe. "He said he saw you go off with 'that rather seedy-looking man from Labor Day.'"

"Did he indeed?" she sneered. "I'm sure he was only too happy to tell you all about it because I wasn't going off with him!"

This softened her brother's expression. "From the description he gave me —"

"I'm sure he gave you a very detailed one," she growled.

Here, he smiled. "He ought to be working for the police as a sketch artist." But as if remembering his purpose, his face grew thundering again. "I take it the 'seedy-looking man' was Lionel Sipes."

"Very good, Jack," she said as she came back down the stairs. "I see your powers of deduction haven't suffered because of your slippery work with the Anspaches."

"My slippery work, as you call it, ended fifteen years ago," he said. "I've forgotten their vigilante ways."

"Not to mention Hatfield successfully beat it out of you," Adele said. "Metaphorically speaking, that is."

"You're evading the question."

"Was there a question, dear brother?" She put her shoes back on.

"Was it Mr. Sipes who Percy saw you and Miss Branch going off with?"

"We weren't going off," Adele insisted. "I told you, we were working."

"What possible work could that blackguard have for a stationery store owner and an herbalist?"

"I meant police work." She stalked up the stairs.

He followed her. "Police work!"

"Yes, dear Jack." She felt almost smug as she took the scarf from her bag. "We've been on the wrong path all along. Do you know to whom this belongs?"

"If you took evidence out of the station again, Hatfield will tar and feather you."

"He's far too gentlemanly for that," she said. "As it happens, this is not the scarf we found at the scene of the crime."

He rubbed his chin. "Well, Miss Call did tell us she had one as well."

"She doesn't have one, Jack," she said. "She has two. There are three of these scarves. Or there were."

He sighed. "Del, it's too late for your circle talk."

"Abby said the third one was lost. I think she's lying."

"And why would she do that?"

"Because Estelle was telling the truth about her scarf being damaged," she said. "The scarf you and Hatfield found is the third scarf."

"Don't confuse the issue, Del," he snapped. "What 'police work' were you and Miss Branch doing tonight, and why was Mr. Sipes involved?"

"We couldn't very well go to the Bright Lights Saloon without a male escort, could we?" she asked in an innocent tone as she took off her shoes and put on her slippers.

There was a moment of silence, and Adele took the opportunity to rush up the stairs to her room. But her brother followed her and the thunder began again. "You and Miss Branch went to the saloon?"

"It's not as if we haven't been there before," she said quickly.

"What the devil possessed you to —"

"Don't swear, Jack. It isn't becoming to a gentleman," she said easily.

"Oh, bother that!" He sat her down on the bed. "I'm going to calmly ask you again. What were you and Miss Branch doing at the Bright Lights Saloon?"

"Talking to a woman who gave us a great deal of help."

"What woman?"

"Gerry Cowell," she said. "She may not have been much help to you and Hatfield, but beer seems to loosen her tongue."

"That's impossible," he insisted. "The Barrys said they were very strict about that."

"Not everyone follows the rules, Jack." She looked at him, amused. "Not even you, dear brother."

"So you believe the ravings of a drunken woman?"

"She was *not* drunk!" Adele snapped. "She has aspirations well beyond slinging manure for a living."

"Then she should be an admirable companion to your friend Elsie," he said dryly.

"She's not that sort of crusader," said Adele. "In fact, she's only interested in her own future, not the future of womankind."

"What about her aspirations?" He had calmed now.

"She's going to join Abby and Helen's act."

"I hardly think a woman of that size would be ideal for the flying trapeze," he said.

"But she's ideal for a catcher, with those strong arms," she said.

He considered this. "She did say they were going to make it an all-woman act."

"It's the timing, Jack," she said. "She told Gerry a few weeks before Julius was killed they would be in the market for a catcher."

"Did she?" His doubt was gone and he leaned forward with interest.

"As if she knew Julius wouldn't be around much longer." Adele eyed him as she leaned back on her stack of pillows.

"There was the rumor he was leaving with Estelle," he pointed out.

"A rumor no one really believed," said Adele. "Least of all Abby."

"So you think Abby got herself involved with Julius's death?" he asked. "Simply to bring in another catcher?"

Adele tilted her head back, feeling the coolness of the backboard. "I think it was more than that, Jack. Much more. Only I'm not sure of the details yet."

"And you want Hatfield and me to go storming into the Call wagon and accuse them of murder?" He sniffed. "You know our procedures by now, Del. We need more evidence than this." He waved the scarf at her.

She rose and patted his shoulder. "Nin and I will get it for you, then." She smiled. "We practically have a badge, remember."

"There's no word yet as to whether the mayor will agree to your being a consultant," he said, getting on his feet. "Don't count your chickens before they've hatched, dear sister."

"They'll hatch," she said, patting his cheek.

CHAPTER 31

*M*onday was brighter than the past several days and, looking at the way the zinnias in the backyard had bloomed, their petals like little fingers lifted toward the sun, Adele felt more hopeful than she had since the terrible tragedy of opening night at the Barry Circus. She had the conversation with Gerry on her mind as she strolled toward her shop.

Jackson left early to meet with a few deputies from Sacramento whom he was helping apprehend a suspect in a factory fire. The merchants of Bridge Street were unwrapping the shutters from their windows and pulling up shades on glass doors, making the day unfold in a leisurely summer manner.

Just as she unlocked her door, Beatrice, Rachel, Mary, and Agnes surrounded her. Peering over Beatrice's shoulder was Caroline. Adele marveled how the mousy-haired girl with the scrawny knees she had met only four years before had blossomed into a young woman of fifteen with chestnut hair that was so thick it could hardly stay in the rhinestone combs that swept it up and a figure as close to an hourglass as she had ever seen.

"Good morning, ladies," she said cheerfully. "I trust you had a good time at the matinee?"

"Oh, bum it, there wasn't anything without that handsome daredevil," Beatrice said.

"Such a shame he had to fall and get squashed like a bug," Mary said.

"That's hardly a delicate way of putting it." Adele led them into her shop and closed the door.

"There wasn't anything period," Agnes said. "I'm so glad I had a chance to see all the thrilling acts before the sheriff outlawed them." The resentment in her tone was genuine.

"He didn't outlaw anything," Adele defended. "He has an obligation to keep the town safe."

"Papa says he's the most responsible lawman he ever met, even if he is a giant," Rachel chimed in.

Adele bit back a smile, thinking of the expression on Hatfield's face if he were to hear her. "I hope you didn't cause any mischief."

"We're too old for that sort of thing, Adele," Beatrice insisted.

"Yes, I suppose you are." Adele pressed her shoulder. "A pity Mrs. Wrigley doesn't seem to realize it."

"Oh, she's all right," said Mary. "We had a time deciding how we were going to get away from her until Bea came up with the idea that we would drift away one by one while Mrs. Henley was walking us around."

"That was very clever of you, Beatrice," said Adele. "Did you find the scarf?"

Beatrice glanced at Caroline. The young woman reached into the sleeve of her jacket and, like a magician, pulled out the scarf.

"I told you not to take it!" Adele hissed.

"But why not if it's important evidence?" Beatrice argued.

"And if you were caught with it?" Adele put her hands on her hips.

"We would tell them the truth," said Rachel. "We're working for someone who is working with the police."

"And get yourselves kicked out of school and me kicked out of town!"

"No one would have caught Caroline," Mary said. "She got the evidence you needed from Mr. Marsh, didn't she?"

"No one ever suspects me," Caroline agreed. "Mama says I have the face of a cherub."

"We're almost through with school anyway," Beatrice said.

"Then we make our way out into the world," Mary said with a sigh.

"You mean we go back home and marry our sweethearts," Agnes said. "At least, that's what I intend to do. Once I have a sweetheart, that is."

"I don't!" Beatrice declared. "And I don't intend on going to Europe for the year either."

"Good for you." Adele smiled. She examined the scarf and found what she had expected to find.

"I'm glad you brought this to me after all," she said. "I apologize for my anger. I commend you, Caroline, for your discretion." She put her arm around the young woman's shoulders as she blushed with pride. "Where did you find it?"

"It was in the Call sisters' wagon all right," said Caroline. "Behind the double wall, just like you said."

"The double wall," Adele murmured.

"Shoved between two panels," said Mary with a sigh. "Such a shame to do that to a beautiful thing." The genuine distress on her face showed the interest she had acquired for fashionable things.

"I'm much obliged to you all." Adele opened the cash register and took out some bills. "Don't spend it all at Hyde's."

"Goodness, you don't think we waste our money on sweets anymore, do you?" Beatrice slipped the bill inside her glove. "I'm saving up for that butterfly brooch I saw in Moffitt's window."

"Books and magazines are a much better value than candy,"

Rachel said. "Candy is gone in a moment while you can keep the book or magazine forever."

"Who wants forever?" Beatrice shrugged. "How boring is that?"

"Yes," Adele said lightly. "How boring it is to stay the same year after year."

She immediately closed her shop and rushed into her friend's store. "I got what I wanted, Nin!"

"The murderer?" Nin put down the basket of herbs.

"Almost." She took her friend's arm. "A new direction, shall we say. Now all we need is a confession."

"We won't get one," Nin remarked as she closed her shop.

"Maybe we won't, but we're going to the man who will," Adele said.

The police station was half-empty since Hatfield had sent a few of the assistant deputies along with Jackson to Sacramento. The sheriff looked like an annoyed bull sitting behind his desk with files in front of him, tapping the edge of his fountain pen against his knee.

"Just the lady I wanted to see," he said when they walked in. "What's this I hear about you at the Bright Lights Saloon last night?"

"Your deputy couldn't shut his mouth," Nin snarled. "The man ought to wear petticoats and carry a rod!"

Hatfield's sullen mood broke, and he laughed. "I don't think Adele relishes the idea of seeing her brother as a schoolmarm." Then, more seriously, he said, "It was Percy Faderman who told me."

"I'm not surprised," Adele said.

"He mentioned you looked quite friendly with the seedy-looking man who caused us trouble on Labor Day," he continued.

"I don't think Lionel is seedy anymore, Sheriff."

"It's Lionel now, is it?" There was a strain in his voice.

"She's not sweet on him, if that's what you're worried about," Nin said in her shrewd way.

The sheriff put his hands in his lap. "I was worried about your safety, Miss Branch."

"I'm sure you were," she said warily.

"He was a perfect gentleman," Adele said. "He helped us get the information we needed from Gerry Cowell."

"Jackson told me about your 'information,' and I don't see it has much bearing on the murder," the sheriff said. "Miss Cowell didn't tell you anything we don't already know or could guess."

Adele moved the train on her skirt aside and sat down. "I think we've been approaching this case from the wrong perspective."

"Indeed?" He leaned forward.

"We've been looking at the concrete moves," she said. "Adultery, theft, betrayal."

"They all exist in this case, Adele," he pointed out.

"But they're too simple," she insisted. "We have to look deeper."

"I should think adultery, theft, and betrayal were excellent motives," he said.

"You know more than anyone, Sheriff, that murder often involves something deeper." She leaned back, holding her closed parasol like a baton. "Like obsession, sisterly devotion, and fear."

"Abby Call killed her partner?" He eyed her. "I thought that's what you were getting at."

Adele laid the scarf the Wrigley girls had given her on the desk. "You'll note the stains, Sheriff?"

He examined it with a jeweler's magnifying glass he bought earlier that year. "It looks like some kind of fuel."

"Kerosine," she said. "Can't you smell it?"

He took a sniff and nodded. "You're right, of course." Then, he looked alarmed. "It isn't ours, is it? I'll chop Edison to pieces if he let you get your hands on it again." He shot a savage glare across the room at the young man's empty desk.

"Your evidence is where you left it," Nin snapped.

"This scarf was found hidden in Abby's wagon."

"Should I ask how you got it?" He raised an eyebrow at her.

"I asked the girls I employ as my aid to look for it," she admitted. "They took it one step further and brought it to me."

Hatfield folded his hands on his desk. "It's a good thing your brother isn't here or he would give you a verbal whipping for encouraging them to commit a crime." But he seemed more amused than angry.

"She didn't encourage anything," said Nin. "That Beatrice has a keen criminal mind if I ever saw one. You ought to keep an eye on her, Sheriff."

"Perhaps I will, Miss Branch," he said. "It was hidden, you say?"

"I didn't say," said Adele. "*They* said. Or rather, Caroline said. She's the least fanciful of the bunch, Sheriff. She says it was hidden behind the second wall just like the knife."

"That is interesting," he said, looking at the scarf again.

"Estelle told us her scarf had stains," she reminded him. "These are in the exact places she described."

"I fail to see what you're getting at, Adele."

"There are three scarves," she said. "This one, which belongs to Estelle —"

"We don't know that for sure," Hatfield interrupted.

"We know enough to guess," Nin insisted.

"All right." He sighed. "Let's say we make an educated guess this scarf belongs to Mrs. Barry. Then what?"

"The second scarf is the one Nin and I saw inside the Call's suitcase. The one Helen showed us." She leaned forward. "I think the third scarf —"

"Which Abby insisted was lost," Nin chimed in.

"Which Abby insisted was lost," Adele acknowledged her friend's point, "was the one we found backstage."

"What are you getting at, Adele?" Hatfield asked.

"I think Abby cut the net so Julius would die when he fell," she said. "She was wearing the scarf and it slipped off her neck without her noticing."

"That's a little fantastic," he mumbled.

"Is it?" She eyed him. "Look at all she had to gain from his death, Sheriff."

"He was in the way," Nin said. "She wanted Helen to be the star."

"It's more than that, dear." Adele leaned back.

"The internal motive?" Hatfield asked.

"She loves the circus." Adele said. "It's her whole life. She made a promise to her parents she would see to it Helen was a success. She was going to fulfill that promise no matter what."

"This is all rather vague," the sheriff lamented.

"Why don't you question her then?" Nin demanded.

"Question who?" Jackson walked into the station, dressed in his travel suit, Edison and a few other assistant deputies trailing behind him. "Don't tell me Del has fill your head with her ideas, Sheriff."

"You know I'm always open to ideas, Deputy," said his superior, "as long as they make sense." He looked at Adele. "And this one is beginning to make sense." He motioned toward Edison, who quickly scurried to his desk and took away the files. "You forget one thing, Adele. In order for Miss Call to have cut the net she would have had to know what Mr. Rowe was planning on doing that night."

"You mean falsify an accident?" Adele asked. "That's exactly what I'm implying." She tapped the edge of the parasol on the floor. "I'm implying even more. She knew about the whole thing."

Jackson sat on the edge of the sheriff's desk. "You're not making sense, Del."

"Estelle admitted seeing the trapeze act's renewal contract on Calvin's desk," Adele said. "She claimed she didn't look beyond the first page but I think Abby did and saw the addendum she wasn't supposed to see."

"Good lord!" Hatfield was now all attention.

"I suppose it's possible," Jackson admitted.

"It's more than possible, Mr. Gossling," Nin insisted.

"She knew Julius intended to get her sister out of the act," said Adele. "And she knew Helen wouldn't fight it."

"She doesn't want to be there," Nin confirmed. "The messages I've had from the Generous Ones make that clear." Jackson could barely contain a snort, and she glared at him.

"So she decided to make sure it was Mr. Rowe who would be out of the act and not her sister," Hatfield concluded. "I don't see what the hidden scarf has to do with it."

"She may not have realized she dropped it until you found it," said Adele. "She had to account for it, you see. So she decided to kill two birds with one stone."

"Implicate Estelle by hiding her stained scarf so you would think the scarf at the scene of the crime was hers," Nin finished.

"Very good deduction, Miss Branch." Jackson smiled at her and she blushed.

Adele's eyes narrowed. "She expected you to blame Estelle, not Paul."

"Hence her rushing to tell us he was innocent after we arrested him." Jackson nodded. "I suppose it could be true."

"She was rather keen on having us believe Mrs. Barry could have been responsible for Mr. Rowe's death," Hatfield admitted. "But what on earth did Mrs. Barry do to warrant such a dastardly thing?"

"She refused to be her mother," Nin said.

"Really, Miss Branch," Jackson sniffed, "I hardly think Miss Call needs a mother at her age."

Adele exchanged a look with her friend. "Abby has very high

expectations of people, Jack. And when they disappoint her, she takes it hard."

"Meaning?"

"Meaning she cast Estelle in the role of the ideal mother, very different from the one she had."

"Her mother was more interested in creating new acts than she was taking care of her daughters," Nin said with a knowing look.

"When Estelle exposed her feet of clay, she turned away from her with a vengeance," Adele said. "She may even have had in the back of her mind getting even for not being the moral character she expected."

"And get even she did," the sheriff remarked. "She almost got her hanged for murder." He rose and plucked his hat from the rack. "I think it would be fitting for us to pay Miss Call a visit, Jackson."

"With the ladies?" Jackson eyed his sister.

"With the ladies, certainly," Hatfield said.

"Since we solved the case, we should have the privilege of seeing the murderer in handcuffs," Nin said.

Jackson flinched. "Must you sound like a bad detective novel, Miss Branch?"

"I only tell the truth, Mr. Gossling," she said, holding her head high.

~~~~~

Getting Abby Call to tell the truth proved easier than Adele had anticipated. She looked, in fact, as defeated as Estelle the day they found her packing her things. The Call wagon had a forlorn feeling to it. Helen was nowhere to be seen.

"She's gone away," Abby lamented, sitting on the bed with a vacant look in her eyes. "She just left in the middle of the night. It was all for nothing."

Adele sat down beside her. "You mean killing Julius was all for nothing."

The corners of Abby's eyes tightened. "So you know about that."

"Your misleading remarks about the scarf didn't fool us." Nin's human sympathy roused, she took the woman's hand.

"Perhaps you'd better tell us what happened, Miss Call," Hatfield said in his legal manner.

"I'm sure Adele already told you," she said. "I knew you were astute but the rumors didn't do you half justice."

"The police need to hear it from you, Abby," Adele said.

"I suppose it doesn't matter now," she said with a deep sigh. "She's gone off to marry that boy."

"Mr. Spears will be good to her," Adele promised.

"He'll keep her out of the circus!" she snarled.

"It's just what she wants," Nin assured her.

Abby looked at her with glassy eyes. "It was all for nothing."

"That's why you did it, isn't it?" Jackson asked quietly. "To keep your sister in the circus."

"I thought if she could be the star, she would forget about everything else," Abby said. "Just like Ma and Pa forgot everything."

"Including you," Adele said softly.

"I really thought —" She buried her face in her hands.

"You took a great risk, Miss Call," the sheriff said.

She uncovered her face, the lines set. "In our profession, Sheriff, we take risks or we don't succeed."

"You knew exactly what Julius was planning that night."

She nodded slowly. "I overheard him talking with Cal. I knew he was going to pretend the fall was an accident and blame Helen so he could get her taken off the trapeze."

"And she wouldn't fight it," Nin added.

"No, she wouldn't. And she would leave me if I fought it." She looked at Adele with vacant eyes. "But she left anyway, so it was all for nothing."

"You planned on making sure he didn't survive the fall," Jackson said.

"It was easy to slip backstage while the Delawares were doing their clown act," she said. "The crowds love the clowns and so do the performers." She blinked. "You didn't know that, did you, Adele? Clowns are rare in circuses like ours, and we're under so much pressure, their silly tricks calm us."

"While they were performing, you were doing some tricks of your own with Mr. Patton's serrated knife," Hatfield said.

"I studied Julius very carefully when he did the triple somersault so I would know just how to make the cuts," Abby said in a dreamy voice. "I wanted to make sure he hit the floor the moment he fell into the net."

"How gruesome." Nin shivered.

"It was necessary, Miss Branch," she said. "He had to die right away."

"You realize you almost caused an innocent woman's death with that knife, don't you?" the sheriff growled.

"Estelle deserved it!" she snarled. "Look at how she betrayed her husband."

"And she betrayed you," Adele said softly.

"She refused to be your mother," Nin said.

Abby stared at her with incredulous eyes. She collapsed on the bed. "I wasn't thinking," she lamented. "When I found out about that scarf, I thought if I could manage to hide hers and make you think the one you found was hers and not mine, I could — well, shift the tide, as they say."

"But you didn't anticipate it would shift to her husband," Adele guessed.

"Paul can be authoritative, but he's fair." Her voice gained defiance. "Like my own father." She gave a small laugh. "I thought Estelle was the perfect suspect! She's not only an adulteress. She's a thief too."

"We're aware of that, Miss Call," the sheriff said. "But how is it that you're aware of it?"

"I saw her coming away from Calvin's wagon one night with her hands full of bills."

"Not very smart of her," Nin observed.

Abby grimaced. "Estelle was never wily, Miss Branch." She played with the edge of the bedspread. "I followed her, of course. I saw her put the money in a small wooden box."

"The box with the key," Jackson murmured.

"It wasn't hard to guess what that key was for."

"Because *you* are wily." Hatfield eyed her.

"It's not a crime to possess feminine wiles, Sheriff," she said. "I never used mine to rob and cheat a husband."

"You knew what her plans were?" Jackson asked.

"Not at first," she said. "But later, when Julius complained she was suffocating him, I knew what she was planning."

"You knew she intended to entice him with money she was stealing from the circus," the sheriff concluded.

"He thought it was amusing," Abby said. "He kept saying she would never get away with it. Anyway, he was more interested in the contract we renewed than her." She blinked. "Everybody thought Julius wanted to live off women, but he was really biding his time until he could be rich on his own."

"You made sure he would never achieve that dream." Hatfield rose. "I think you'd better come with us, Miss Call."

The woman looked frightened. "I want Helen to know. I don't want her to find out about it in the papers."

"Nin and I will find her and tell her," Adele promised. "I have connections that know how to ferret out hiding women."

"I don't think Miss Call is hiding, Del," Jackson said.

"Then it won't be anything to find her, will it?" Nin glared at him.

Abby stared down at the handcuffs hanging from Jackson's

belt. "Must we — do we need to use those?" She looked at them as if they were razor blades.

Jackson glanced at his superior. "Sir?"

"I think we can dispense with the cuffs, Deputy," said the sheriff.

As they led the woman down the row of wagons, she suddenly broke into a run. Hatfield rushed after her with Jackson following. When she and Nin reached the gate, Adele saw Abby was waiting there. She also saw why. Standing in front of it was Lionel. He was holding on to a rope where, at the end of it, Griselda strained and growled, bouncing her small but powerful paws so hard on the ground they dug little holes.

"She hates Abby," Nin said in a low voice.

"She knows what sort of person she is," Adele murmured.

As Jackson snapped the handcuffs on her wrists, Abby lamented in a vacant way, "It was all for nothing."

Adele put her hand on her shoulder. "Not nothing, Abby. It was all for a young woman's life. Your sister's."

"Now she can live as she wants," Nin agreed.

The woman's eyes were still vacant when they led her away.

CHAPTER 32

*T*he Barry Circus left Arrojo later that same day with as much fanfare as when it had come in. The wagons and horses rode down Bridge Street as before and the band played loudly. Adele couldn't help but notice every breast seemed to heave with a sigh of relief as the last wagon rolled out of town.

They left a mass of papers, wrappers, and streamers in the park, much to Hatfield's annoyance. He recruited all the assistant deputies he had one Saturday to make the park immaculate again, mainly to silence the grumbling town council. But, in his usual generous way, he and his mother arranged a picnic dinner on the grass and even coaxed Jackson into gathering the men for a baseball game.

"You don't feel sorry for her, do you?" Nin glanced at her friend as they sat next to Lady Augusta and her companion Rowena watching the game.

"Who?"

"Abby, of course."

Adele shook her head, brushing the dandelion needles from her skirt. "She knew what she was doing and she knew she would have to pay for it eventually."

"Justice for the victim?" Nin peered at her.

"Justice for Helen," said Adele. "Abby trapped her, no matter what her intentions were. She's free now."

"Free to marry that poor wretch," Nin growled.

Adele laughed, putting her arm around her friend's shoulders. "That's justice too, Nin. A woman's right to choose her own life."

"What is this about choosing your own life?" Lady Augusta shielded her eyes from the sun.

"We were talking about Helen Call," Adele said. "She's going to marry Mr. Spears."

"Oh, yes, that rather bumbling young man," the woman lamented.

"The boy that waddles like a duck," Rowena said with her strange observation.

"Marriage isn't a bad end, my dear," said Lady Augusta. "There's no telling what might become of her with the safety of a wedding ring on her finger."

"It's true a wedding ring can be safe," Adele admitted.

"Even for progressive women such as yourself," Lady Augusta said with a poignant look. "Especially when they marry progressive men."

Adele blushed, knowing this was a reference to the insinuations the woman had made earlier that year. She knew how the sheriff felt about her, but the thought of letting go of her hard-won independence made her shrivel up inside.

"Well, well," Nin said under her breath, "we might not have gotten rid of all the circus people after all."

Estelle came trampling down the dirt lane toward them. The woman looked very different than the one they had seen at the Blue Springs jail. She was dressed more elegantly and her posture, with the puffed sleeves, looked determined. "Your servants said I would find you here."

"The Cordobas aren't our servants," Adele said quickly. "They're the caretakers of our house. And of us, I daresay."

"You've left your husband." Nin said. "It's a good thing."

"Yes, it's a good thing," she said. "It's always a good thing when you let go of someone you no longer love."

"He won't have an easy time of it," Lady Augusta remarked. "Losing his marriage and his star act at the same time."

"He's already found a replacement for the star act," said Estelle, her voice a little crusty. "He's signed on The Flying Ayers. Two brothers and a fiancée."

"They'll be fighting over her soon," Nin said with the authority of her gift.

"It wouldn't surprise me," Estelle said. "However, that's not my problem anymore." She looked down. "I don't mean to sound cold-blooded."

"If his passion is only for the circus, you're quite right," Lady Augusta assured her.

"Troubled hearts seek trouble," Rowena said.

"Yes, his will always be troubled, I suppose," Estelle said. "I wanted him to take back the money I took but he refused. He said it was a matter of pride."

"He was trying to hijack yours," Nin growled.

"Maybe so," the woman admitted. "Or maybe I hijacked my own by taking it."

"A woman needs money to start fresh," Adele said.

"It's more than that," she said. "I want to do the sort of work you do, but in my own way."

"I admire that." Adele smiled.

"This Vanya person you referred me to — can she help me set up a vaudeville house?"

"Vaudeville?" Adele stared.

The woman nodded. "I've been thinking about it ever since that day you found me packing. I don't want to run anymore. And performers, especially women, well, they run when they have nowhere else to go."

"Run to nowhere," Lady Augusta guessed.

"Exactly," she said. "Or into the arms of unscrupulous men. I want to build a place where they can come and find help, just as you've helped me." She gave a rueful smile. "Call it atonement for my sins."

"I'm sure Vanya can help, and if she can't, she'll find someone who can." Adele patted her arm.

"She's very resourceful that way," Nin said.

"You'll look me up when you're in San Francisco?" the woman asked.

"We'll be glad to," Adele said. "I've never seen a vaudeville show. Well, not a respectable one."

"Yours will be respectable, won't it?" Lady Augusta gave her a challenging look.

"As respectable as I can," the woman promised.

Estelle left just as Hatfield approached them. "Don't tell me she had more evidence for us."

"She'll tell all she knows at the trial," Nin said.

He laughed. "Miss Branch, we never make people 'spill' things. They give evidence in front of a judge and it goes on record."

"And convicts a murderer," Adele added.

He sat down beside her and, picking at the grass, he cleared his throat. "I finally heard from the mayor."

"About the case?"

"About *your* case," he said. "That is, my request to make you a police consultant."

She was silent for a moment.

"He turned it down." The man was plucking the blades, and Adele could see how annoyed he was. "Pigheaded idiot!"

"No," she said. "Only narrow-minded."

"It's a sign," Nin declared.

"From the Generous Ones?" Adele eyed her.

"From the common sense ones," said her friend.

Adele laughed. "Perhaps Nin is right, Sheriff. I'd better stay a stationery shop owner, at least for now."

"You know I will always welcome your help in any case," he said.

"And I'm not yet ready to give up, as Jack says, sticking my nose in where it doesn't belong." She winked at him.

Hi reader!

It's so awesome you've reached the end of the fifth book of the Adele Gossling Mysteries! I really hope you enjoyed the adventures of Adele and her friend Nin as they tackled murder and mayhem at the circus.

The circus as we knew it in the 19th and early 20th centuries doesn't really exist anymore. It was a big deal to people in the past for a number of reasons.

First, it was good, clean entertainment. It wasn't like more dubious forms of leisure in that era such as burlesque houses and saloon shows. Even vaudeville could get a little dicey. Circuses aimed to create a true family-oriented spectacle, which is why so many had animal acts, petting zoos, and clowns. The most people could see was women in leotards (which doesn't sound like a big deal today, but in the 19th century, showing a woman's legs, even under tights, was considered pretty risqué).

Second, it was one of the most democratic forms of entertainment. Anyone who had the price of a ticket could get in and see the show. Social standing, race, ethnicity, gender, and situation in life didn't matter.

Third, it was a place where people could see things they had never seen before and would likely never see anywhere else. Keep in mind there was no television or radio or internet to show us what life was like in other parts of the world (and film was in its infancy and didn't show much either). People could read about other people in books (if they had the money and the time, which many working class people didn't) but to actually *see* with their own eyes people and animals from other countries was a treat. Circuses knew this and capitalized on it by including exotic animals and people from other nations in their lineup. It might seem hard to believe but many people caught a glimpse of their first elephant or camel or giraffe at the circus. It was an early form of globalization.

So what's up next for Adele and her friend, brother, and the sheriff of Arrojo? How about a story that was inspired by a true unsolved crime? Read on for an excerpt!

Happy reading!
   Tam

BOOK 6 INFORMATION

A lady's maid was getting too big for her skirts. But does that justify murder?

Everyone agreed: Arabella Parnell thought far too much of herself. She worked her way up from scullery maid to lady's maid for one of Arrojo's finest families and the wife of a personal friend of the mayor's. She wrote letters to her former employer's daughter as if they were intimate friends. She flirted with some of the most prominent young men in the county. A young lady with high-and-mighty ideas indeed!

The Arrojo police are hardly surprised when they find her dead among the shrubbery in a wealthy bachelor's conservatory.

And yet, amateur sleuth and suffragist Adele Gossling can't help but wonder: Who was Arabella Parnell? Was she just a servant with arrogant manners and too much self-assurance? Or was she the victim of the pride and passions of powerful men, one of whom did her in? With only a hair comb, a broach, and a candlestick to go on, can Adele solve this case?

Read on for an excerpt from this book!

*M*issy Grace, the editor of the *Arrojo Courier*, hurried into her shop, her cotton hair flying as usual around her face. She pushed back her bangs with the edge of her pencil. "Adele, what can you tell me about that body found in Virgil Riddle's conservatory?"

Adele stared at her. "What the devil are you talking about?"

"Don't use such vulgar language, Adele," Beatrice chided.

"It's no worse than your 'bum it,' dear," Missy barked.

Beatrice's nose went up. "I stopped using 'bum it' last year."

"My congratulations." Missy turned her back to her. "I'm talking about the sheriff and your brother rushing out of the police station an hour ago, looking very official."

"They told you there was a body in Virgil Riddle's conservatory?" Adele asked.

"Certainly not," Missy said. "You know how hush-hush they are when they're being official."

"Then how do you know about it?"

"I caught Assistant Deputy Curd having his morning bun at the bakery and wheedled it out of him."

"It doesn't surprise me," Adele said dryly.

"Naturally, the boy was too dense to tell me anything of value," Missy continued. "He could only say Mr. Riddle had found a girl's body lying among the shrubbery in his conservatory, and she was most certainly dead."

"Golly!" Beatrice sighed. "Another murder."

"I wouldn't necessarily take Assistant Deputy Curd's word for it," Adele said. "He's not the brightest of men."

"That's why I'm coming to you," said her friend. "You remember our bargain, Adele?" She looked meaningfully at her.

"I tell you what I know if you tell me what you know." Adele nodded. "Only I honestly know nothing, Missy. This is the first I'm hearing of it."

"Well then," her friend took her arm, "it's our duty as star reporter and lady detective to find out, isn't it?"

"I'm not a lady detective, you know," Adele remarked, but she took off the apron she always wore when dealing with some of the dirtier aspects of her work.

"You're leaving me to mind the shop?" Beatrice's green eyes, which had become more almond-shaped as the years passed, widened. "Golly!"

"I see you've replaced your 'bum it' with another inelegant colloquialism," Missy remarked.

"A woman may speak as she needs to be heard," Beatrice said with meaning.

"You know how to handle the cash register, as I showed you?" Adele asked.

"No one will come in anyway," said the young woman. "It's too early."

"Nevertheless, we must always be ready to serve anyone." Adele put on her gloves. "We'll fetch Nin first."

"Has she appointed herself lady detective too?" Missy eyed her.

"You might consider her the unofficial medium for the

police," Adele said as they emerged from her shop. "She's helped them a great deal in the past, Missy."

"I don't object if she doesn't," she said.

What do Adele and her friends find among the shrubbery of a wealthy bachelor's conservatory and will it help solve a murder? Find out by picking up a copy here.

How about a little more of the Adele Gossling Mysteries, right here, right now? Read on for how to get hold of my free novella, _The Missing Ruby Necklace_.

When a jewel and a girl go missing on New Year's Eve...

Eleanor McCarthy, a lovely though somewhat flighty debutante, has graced the tiny town of Arrojo, California, with her presence. One of Arrojo's prominent ladies throws a New Year's Eve shindig to introduce her to Arrojo's high society — whatever little of it there is. Naturally, the daughter and son of one of San

Francisco's influential lawyers, Adele and Jackson Gossling, are invited.

But screams replace popping champagne corks when Eleanor's priceless ruby necklace is discovered missing. And soon, so is Eleanor!

In this historical cozy mystery set in the early 20th century, follow Adele Gossling, stationary store owner and amateur sleuth, and her clairvoyant sidekick Nin Branch as they search for a ruby necklace that may or may not have been stolen and a young woman who may or may not have run away.

Want to read an excerpt from this book? I got you covered! Turn the page.

"Coffee!" Miss McCarthy laughed. "Heavens, no! I haven't had my first taste of champagne yet." She flung her hand out to her brother. "Bring me a bottle of champagne, my good man."

"I don't mind," he said.

Before he could saunter out the door, Mrs. Abberton jumped up. "I'll get it."

"I really think we ought to get coffee," Mr. Abberton mumbled.

"She wants champagne," Mrs. Abberton was almost stern. "It's a celebration, after all!" She practically fled from the room.

Adele followed her and caught her arm. She spoke in a soft tone. "Mrs. Abberton, why did Miss McCarthy faint?"

"She just told you, didn't she?" The woman gave a shrill laugh. "Albert said we ought to open some windows, but it was such a windy night, I —"

"It wasn't the windows," said Adele. "Or the corset."

"Of course it was!" The woman examined some bottles on the floor. "I never could read these labels."

"You were staring at Miss McCarthy as if something that wasn't there."

"What an imagination you have, dear." The woman said.

"Miss McCarthy had her hands on her throat when she fell," Adele continued. "You kept looking at her throat."

"Nonsense," the woman hissed.

"Miss McCarthy wasn't wearing her ruby necklace," Adele declared.

Mrs. Abberton tore through a row of bottles lying on a table. One rolled onto the floor with a crack and the bubbly drink spilled across the marble. She sunk into one of the chairs. "You're too observant, Miss Gossling."

"You saw it too."

"Just before the lights went out," she said. "But Eleanor is one of those girls who gets easily flustered with her jewelry. She says it weighs her down."

"If that's true, why were you so alarmed just now?" Adele said.

"I wasn't," the woman insisted. "She locks that necklace in a box. Albert tried to persuade her to put it in our safe at the finance company, but she refused."

"That's rather unusual," Adele said.

"Eleanor's a lovely girl, but rather flighty," The woman said in a harsh tone. "I expect Celestine spoils her."

"If the necklace is missing, there might be a theft involved," Adele suggested.

Jewelry goes missing all the time. But does that mean theft? And why is Mrs. Abberton so nervous?

How can you get your hands on a copy of *The Missing Ruby Necklace*, not available in any bookstore? Simple. Go to this link: https://landing.mailerlite.com/webforms/landing/l2u0c3. What else will you get when you get this novella? How about fun facts about women in history and true crime classic mysteries, which are just as fascinating, if not more so, as contemporary true crimes?

ABOUT THE AUTHOR

Writing has been Tam May's voice since the age of fourteen. She writes stories about powerful women set in the past. Her fiction gives readers a sense of justice for women, both the living and the dead. Tam's stories are set mostly around the Bay Area because she adores sourdough bread, Ghirardelli chocolate, and San Francisco history.

Tam is the author of the Adele Gossling Mysteries which take place in the early 20th century and features sassy suffragist and epistolary expert Adele Gossling whose talent for solving crimes doesn't sit well with the ideas of some people around her about women's place. Tam has also written historical fiction about women defying the confinements of their era.

Although Tam left her heart in San Francisco, she lives in the Midwest because it's cheaper. When she's not writing, she's devouring everything classic (books, films, art, music) and concocting yummy vegan dishes.

Tam May can be reached at:

WEBSITE: http://tammayauthor.com/
EMAIL: tammay70@tammayauthor.com
FACEBOOK: https://www.facebook.com/tammayauthor
INSTAGRAM: https://www.instagram.com/tammayauthor/
PINTEREST: https://www.pinterest.com/tammayauthor/